RESURRECTION to RETRIBUTION

MINNOW SQUAD RETURNS

D.R. RICHARDS

Copyright © 2020 D.R. Richards
All rights reserved
First Edition

PAGE PUBLISHING, INC.
Conneaut Lake, PA

First originally published by Page Publishing 2020

ISBN 978-1-6624-2679-7 (pbk)
ISBN 978-1-6624-2680-3 (digital)

Printed in the United States of America

The sun began to crawl its way to the top of the jungle canopy, making us uneasy as transport had been delayed by foul weather moving in from off the coast. There was a smell of rot from the humidity slowly breaking down the vegetation that was chocked out by the ever-dense ground cover and canopy. It was an ongoing process of death and rebirth and a daily struggle to keep the land you have taken from being reclaimed. This country was as beautiful as it was dangerous. I started my tour with a rough idea of what to expect from those who had gone before me. They had taught us how to survive long enough to hopefully get back home. Dampness from the rains made life here a struggle to keep dry and protect our skin from breaking down. In time, you adjust to being wet from rain or just from sweat, twenty-four seven. This country brings back the words of my uncle back on his farm in upstate New York: "Mason, if you don't like the weather, just wait awhile. Maybe it will change to more of your liking." It was that way in the summer, especially as the sun would slowly form the needed ingredients for a sudden thunderstorm. Those thoughts made me drift off to those times that seemed like a lifetime ago. A million miles from that cold wet rice paddy I now found myself crouching in. So far from those hay fields and the family that formed the foundation of most, if not all, of my values. It was those thoughts that gave way to the nightmares that flowed back and forth before they repeated each day.

As the sun crept above the low hills, the smell of bacon on the stove below my room brought me to that middle place between awake and dreams. The register at the foot of the bed was meant to let heat up to the bedroom. It did nothing to keep the smells of a new day from forcing me awake. We all met at the table with little conversation as we dove into the plates of eggs and bacon and stacks of pancakes. It was this beginning of the cycle that made you feel ready to take on the day. Bellies full, we all ran out to the wagon to start another day of bailing hay. The long rows of cut hay lay in the fields, just waiting for our attention. The sun was up and drying the hay for our collection. No matter where you drove or walked, a cloud of dust from the drying hay rose up to meet you. It gave off a smell that only a true farmer could appreciate. Soon we were standing there on the hay wagon, waiting for a bale to come flying through the air, trying to dodge it while pushing each other into its path. The bailer that my uncle pulled behind the tractor would scoop up the row of cut hay and compact it into a long bail. Once it was a full bail, the machine would tie it off with two strands of twine. It then pushed the newly formed bale out and on to a long tray that would then launch it through the air, up and back into the wagon. Many farmers would just let the bales fly back into the wagon and land where they may. Then they'd take the wagon to the barn when it was full. My uncle was from the old school and wanted the bails to be neatly placed in the wagon. This would increase the number of bails on each load by threefold. This process meant less trips back to the barn and decreased the time needed to complete a field. Laughing, we would grab them and stack them as high as we dared while my uncle would just shake his head and slowly increase his pace. We were slow to notice that the bales were now coming at a quicker rate. The rate was increasing with each return and new run the tractor made. Soon the wagon was filling, and the area where we stood was getting smaller with each bale. The sweat started running off us, and our shirts were now nothing more than a second skin. This combination of hard work, great food, and family working together, along with strong family values, helped mold me into the man I was now.

RESURRECTION TO RETRIBUTION

    We always found a way to mix fun with work. My uncle was a quiet man with a sense of humor that at times bordered on sick, at least in my city view of things. Like the time we were feeding the milk cows in their stanchions. My cousin was cleaning manure from the pit that ran behind the cows to catch the processed hay that started out in the other end. A large piece flew off his shovel and hit my uncle in the back of his legs. He turned slowly with a strange smile on his face. "Guess it's time to show Mason what a true cow pie fight is like."

    I wasn't sure what he meant, but I knew should be prepared for the worse. He bent over and took a handful of fresh manure that the cows had just processed, from end to end. He made somewhat of a ball and threw it at my cousin, hitting him in the side. It left a large brown stain on his white T-shirt. Then I made a fatal mistake and broke down in uncontrollable laughter. The first one hit my chest, the second making a direct hit on the side of my head. I fought the sudden urge to be sick and reached for my own ball of crap. It lasted only a short time, but in that time, we managed to cover my uncle and all three of my cousins. They could not resist the chance to join in. I still remember my aunt standing on the back porch with a hose in her hand. "I hope you boys had fun!"

    "You're late."

    There was a devilish grin on her face. "Don't think about coming into this house till you have all that stuff off your bodies." My uncle was sneaking around the end of the porch toward the back door when she caught sight of him out of the corner of her eye. She turned the hose on high and hit him square in the back with its stream. "That includes you, Papa, as I know you must have started this."

    He laughed and danced around and around as if he was enjoying a nightly shower. Once hosed off, we stripped naked and headed to the mudroom door for fresh clothes my aunt had already put out for us. The smell of chicken and corn filled the house and drew us closer to the large table that would soon capture us.

    On the second day, as the wagon was filling, it was getting harder and harder to move the bales without getting hit. My cousin tripped over my foot and went down in a heap. Just then, I heard the familiar click as the bailer was about to throw the next projectile. It wouldn't have hurt him as we had bales bouncing off us all day. It was the look of panic and pain in his eyes that made me hesitate from laughing. When he had fallen, a sharp bale hook that had been hidden under the loose hay on the wagon floor had pierced his upper thigh. The blood was minimal, but the look in his eyes told it all. He looked to me to stop the pain and help him.

The visions of my cousin at family birthday parties, hunting trips, school, and church flashed through me. There is something that grows within you over time that causes a bond and develop as part of a family. In my time, families were everything, and being part of them was a natural progression of life. We laughed, cried, celebrated, and walked through life knowing we were never alone. With that came this auto response to protect them without question and without hesitation. The impending hit from the hay would not have killed him or most likely even hurt. We were both first string linebackers and shrugged of two-hundred-pound linemen with a smile. It was the pain he was in and the idea that the bale was going to compound it. That kicked in that auto response, and I stepped over him and faced the bale. I shrugged it off and turned to move him out of the way of any further bales. Having not turned and seen us, my uncle drove ahead. The next bale jumped from the throwing arm and was headed straight at my back and shoulders. The rough bale of hay touched my neck.

My head was forced down into the side of the rice paddy. Cold wet mud ran down the side of my face. Reflexes made me want to shout out in anger as I reached for my Ka-Bar knife. Training and the sudden return to the real deal made me remain quiet for what seemed like an eternity.

Austin slowly pulled my head up, a huge smile on his face. "You never saw that local boy running toward us? He came from the house on the far side of the fields."

I had to admit, I did not, but I felt I was low enough to be out of his line of sight.

Austin was one of the members of the extraction team and always the one that found good in any bad situation. Six-three and built for speed, he had an affliction for the TV and movies that we all missed so much. Lean and solid muscle, he would often be seen running up and down the runway back at the doghouse. More than once he was caught running head to head with a Huey chopper as it headed out on a mission. He was usually joking and always ready to put a positive spin on what was going on. He always found a way to bring in some reference to the TV shows or the movies he loved so. He named me Skipper because I was always calling him Gilligan from the *Gilligan's Island* show. It came from that stupid sailor's hat he wore when we were not working. It looked like it needed an oil change. He took exception to the less than cool nickname, so he decided we would call him Six. When we asked him why, he told us his given name was Austin, like Steve Austin.

We all looked at him and each other. "Yeah, so how does that end up as Six?"

"Steve Austin, the *Six Million Dollar Man*. I can run faster, jump higher, kick more ass than any of you, and I'm prettier than that guy that plays him on the tube."

"Skipper, if we don't get transport soon, we're here for another twenty-four, and I gotta tell you, my ass is soaked."

"I could run down to Arnolds and grab us some burgers while we wait. Maybe say hi to Richey's sister for you." I smiled and told him to hang in there because Mom would never leave us out there unless there was no other option.

It was now full daylight and still no word from Mom or the pickup chopper. We found ourselves in a nasty wet rice paddy in a country full of people we were leaving to fend for themselves. We all felt used as we walked away from the game we never really had our head in. After years of throwing bodies at the VC and filling the nightly news with new casualty figures, the US was now running out on these people. Our government saying the South Vietnam Army could take it from there was just so much bullshit. As we pulled out, the north gained more and more territory with their sights set on Saigon. There was no doubt the south would fall once we were gone or sooner. The locals now found themselves caught between a fleeing US and the now growing North Vietnamese Army. We had long since stopped bitching about Washington's lack of commitment to the South and looked at each mission as just payback for some politicians promise, as our focus went from military to civilian extractions. Every person we could spare from what was coming was a win for us.

I looked at Six and told him it was time to move back and get the packages ready. We had just received the call sign from our pickup, who also threw in "Get ready, boys and girl. Mom says get your butts home now."

A quick check of the area and it was clear we had not been seen, and there were no bad guys around. The old potholed road was empty as far back as we could see. Archie was settled in by a pile of dirt and rock at the point where the road turned and followed along the end of the fields.

"Wake up, Archie boy. It's getting close to time to go home, and you don't want to piss off Mom."

"Wake up your ass. I been a busy little boy."

Archie was our munitions expert and always had a surprise for us. He was from the school of overthink the problem and be ready for what you didn't think of. His name was given to him from Austin, and it took some time to grow on him. It stuck after the first time he was called Mr. Bunker from the show *All in the Family*. The name came from his uncensored comments on most things, solicited or not. Usually not. He loved to call all the green soldiers that came and left the base as meatheads. He was, as we all were, proficient in all forms of weapons and hand-to-hand combat. His specialty was explosives, and he loved his job. What made his nickname odd and was the reason for many fights was obvious. Archie was what he liked to call himself "the meanest, toughest nigger in Vietnam," which we all believed he was. Unlike the Archie Bunker of TV, who was less than fond of Afro-Americans, Archie's heritage was a matter of pride for him, and he got to like the idea of the name as he saw it as payback.

Austin and I pulled back to the edge of the first field from our cover spot on the side of the dike. Hours earlier, we had found our passengers in a small toolshed about four-foot square, at the end of the southernmost field. It was a man in his late twenties, skinny with sunbaked skin that came from long hours in the paddies. His hands were calloused from years of working his rice crop with no help from machinery. His skin was like leather. He had torn clothes and a large brimmed hat. Much the same as we saw on so many that worked each day, not knowing who they would bow to tomorrow. His wife was a plain-looking woman whose face was like tight leather as well from her hours in the sun. Dressed in a long top that covered her torn pants to the knees. Her hair was pulled back and showed a lack of any true attention in some time. Although afraid, she showed a strength that seemed to hold them all together. Their children, a young boy and girl that looked to be twins, were both in old worn cloths with the sandals that had seen many repairs. At first you could see the fear in them both as they clung to their mother. We quickly vetted them with a series of prearranged questions, several designed to only be known to the father. Austin made them smile when he gave them each a Hershey bar and sat down on the ground and slowly ate his.

A quick glance from each of us said what we had kept to ourselves. Why was Uncle Sam spending a ton of money and putting us all in harm's way for this worn-out family of farmers? Not that anyone's life didn't mean something. It was just odd we put together this extraction for a farmer and his wife and kids. The VC were executing many village elders and loyalists as they moved south, but what made these four special? It wasn't our place to question, just get the job done, but it still was an odd mission, especially after the one from just days ago. The shed was partially concealed in the thick growth that was slowly encroaching on the cleared fields. The jungle seemed to grow in front of your eyes and would relentlessly take back whatever piece of ground you tried to take from it. We picked this spot because it offered a clear field of fire in most directions and a clear view of the road back to the turn some half mile back. It was also a straight run down the dike separating the last two fields to the area we planned for our LZ. It allowed the inbound recovery bird the ability to clear much of the surrounding area before touching down.

The family looked like common farmers, much like the thousands that worked long days in this fertile valley of rice. The questions asked were answered, and it sure was not our place to make judgment calls, not as far as our packages value.

Archie made the comment about how it felt like déjà vu after our extraction from about forty-eight hours earlier.

The big difference was that we made the pickup in a large parking lot of an abandoned factory some one hundred miles away. We were fast dropped at 22:30, which was where the chopper came in a max speed at low altitude, then feathers like a Canadian goose came for a landing. The bird came to an almost complete stop, nose in the air, some four feet up. Just as quick as it slowed, the nose dropped, and it once again built speed and altitude. The secret was to dismount just before it appeared it would stop. Hit the ground on a slow run, keeping your balance when possible, tuck and roll when you can't. The pilot would not look to see if you're in or out. He just feathers, drops the nose, and goes. The thought here is that most shooters are going to wait for the bird to land or completely stop, so you don't do either. At 22:45, the LZ was set and covered. The big gun in his hands, Archie climbed the ladder to the catwalk on the top of the first building. The big gun was his favorite sniper rifle, an M21 slung across his shoulders with a full twenty-round clip in place. He also carried an M16 with an M203 grenade launcher attached. Extra clips for both and an assortment of rounds for the launcher were in their place on the belts that crisscrossed his chest. His backpack was stuffed to capacity with his extra special gifts, as he called them. Samantha (Sam) and Six secured the entrance near the north end of the lot, leaving just the southern entrance for our guests.

Austin gave her the nickname because she had this habit of making her nose twitch when she was excited. He said it was like *I Dream of Jeannie*, only usually nothing good happened when Sam got excited. She had beautiful blond hair which she always kept short to avoid any issues in combat. She kept as much in her baseball hat to avoid anyone seeing the yellow flag. Standing 5'6", her sleek body was well toned and hard from hours of working out. As the only woman in the entire outfit, she had to always prove herself. Not with us so much, but to the rest of the Green Berets that served with us. We all knew what she was capable of, and she had proven us right many times. She got cut off from us while moving two district governors to our LZ for pickup during one of her first missions. When we finally got the packages loaded in Mom's chopper, he just looked at us and said, "Go get your sister."

Arch, Six, and I, along with two other Special Forces grunts, headed back into the jungle, afraid we would just be recovering a body of a fallen comrade. About halfway back to where we lost sight of her, we found her walking down a game trail, gun slung over her shoulder and walking with an odd gate.

"What took you guys so long?" she said as she just passed by and kept walking toward the LZ.

We sent the two extra guys to form a rear cover while we went and secured a different landing zone. Later, the two Special Forces rear guard told us of the carnage they had found in Sam's wake. Five VC regulars in different throws of death, some shot and several cut down with her knife in close combat. Nothing was ever said, and she now had a new level of respect from all that knew of it.

Everyone clicked the three-click code on their mikes. That meant everyone was in place and settled in. I took up my position behind a stack of smaller crates near the center of the lot. Everything looked quiet, and not a single person could be seen in the area. I could just make out Archie's wave when he saw the incoming vehicle. At 01:00 a.m., the sound of squealing tires brought me to full alert. A large black sedan rolled through the gate, wasting no time. It pulled to the center of the lot and nosed up to the crates where I was waiting. Sam announced that our friendlies had been followed, and the trackers had stopped outside the gates. "A pickup and an old flatbed, with four in the pickup, two front and two back."

Austin said, "Seven, no, make that ten in and on the flatbed." Without pause, I asked if they were an escort party or a hunting party. After a few seconds of silence came "Looks like a fight, Skipper. They are raising a fifty cal on the pickup, and the flatbed headed around to the north, and everyone is dismounting. Should we invite them out to play with us?" Six always liked the straight-on approach.

"Negative. I repeat, negative. We have transport inbound, and I plan to use them to sweep the north to clean out the crap. You guys can get ready to get down here for the ride home." Archie was gauging the distance to the players to the north while Sam and Six were preparing to secure their ride.

I slowly stood and approached the car from my hiding place. Two men jumped from the car and ordered me to stay put. They were both big men and dressed in dark suits that needed a lot of letting out everywhere. Each carried M16s that were well polished and .45 colts in shoulder rigs. The one with a huge scar on his neck walked back and opened the rear door. A small framed man exited the car dressed in a tuxedo and walked right over to me.

"Little underdressed, aren't we, Skipper?" Archie whispered in my ear. The one with the scar took up position directly behind and to the right of the penguin. "If Scarface twitches, duck 'cause his head is taking a ride."

I slowly raised my hand to my ear so they all could see I was communicating with someone. "Roger that, but I need you to keep an eye on our friends in the north. If need be, keep them busy till Mom gets here, if any shit starts."

The man looked at me with a puzzled look. "Mr. Long, do you have everyone with you?" He turned and reached out his hand.

Archie cut in, "Damn, now that's a dress."

First came this long shapely leg with a hint of red material near the top, then another, and they both filled the slit in her dress almost to her waist. As she stood, the dress filled back in, and my eyes followed up to the plunging neckline that was filled with what I guessed to be diamonds and pearls. Her hair flowed down her back and reached her midback and the dress line. She was beautiful. There was no taking that away, but she also knew it and looked quite put out that she was in this dark damp place. On her tail were two children, both dressed in clothes that few in this godforsaken country could afford or for that matter want. Like little prince and princess, they took up a place next to their mother who pushed them back so as not to come in contact with her dress. They both had blank looks on their faces, so I assumed they were just another piece of jewelry to the parents, a matched set.

"Who is my favorite woman in the world?" I said to the overdressed man.

He got a shit-eating look on his face and said, "Ms. Jane Fonda."

My face like stone, I said, "And what is she the best for?"

He smiled again and said, "Target practice."

"Okay, you're golden."

"Did you know you were followed?" Both guards took up pre-arranged positions at the car, looking all around for signs of anyone. The family ducked down next to the car and huddled together. I stood my ground, not wanting those watching to think there was a problem or that we were on to them.

The one bodyguard with the scar looked uneasy. He slowly walked over to the other guard and, without a word, pulled his .45 and placed it on the back of his head and pulled the trigger. The woman and children screamed, and they all tried to huddle next to the car. The guard grabbed the little girl and pulled her to him.

"Tell your friends I now am in charge, and I will kill all of you if anyone approaches us." He pulled a grenade from his pocket and pulled the pin, throwing it over the car and out of sight. "Now if I die, you all die with me." He smiled with several teeth missing.

I raised my hands to show I understood and was no threat. He had me drop my weapons and move near the car so he could cover us all.

Archie whispered, "Want him gone, Skipper?"

I shook my head no ever so slightly, knowing Archie would be looking at me through his scope.

"The greeting party looks to be getting ready to join the fun," Sam added.

"Give us the girl," I said. "She is of no use to you, and we will do as you say."

The guard looked around smiled and said, "No, she will be my prize for bringing this pig to my general. I don't need these others." He pointed the gun at the boy. I dove in front of him and took the round in my chest, knocking the wind out of me, but the armor proved stronger. Luckily, he had old rounds, and they flattened quickly. I would have a bad bruise and pain for some time, but still ticking.

The guard stepped back, a small hole in his forehead and nothing from the ears back. The girl was now free ran to her mother. Archie had dropped the hammer on his sniper rifle the instant he saw me coil to make my dive. In slow motion, the guard opened his hand and dropped the grenade. I could not catch my breath, and the seconds counted down in my head. Then in a flash, the father picked up the grenade and rolled once then threw it over the car. More to this well-dressed man than I thought. He said something quickly to his wife and daughter, and they pulled me to them and tried to undo my jacket and vest.

Hearing the explosion, Sam and Austin went into action with no thought of what might have caused it. A storm blew across and through the pickup. In one window and out the other, across the bed and over the other side. Like a swarm of bees, only these bees were .9mm in size and didn't just sting but sliced and diced their way through. None of the four saw or heard it coming, the sound suppressors doing their job. With their backs to the north to conceal any muzzle flash from the others, Six and Sam let loose a full half clip each onto and into the truck. It was overkill, but they could not risk a lucky horn blow or scream. Sam opened the driver's door and pulled the driver out to the road. She jumped in and reached over to open the passenger door. Both feet on the passenger, she shoved him out and quickly closed the door. Not once did she hesitate, even though the front seat was now red instead of the worn gray it once was. Austin jumped into the back to find it cleared of everyone. The bees had taken their prey out and over the side of the truck with them. He was about to jump off and check their status, but with one glance it was obvious that was unnecessary. Both men lay there with their eyes wide open as if they were looking at the stars. He quickly checked the fifty cal. for damage. Old but looked operational. He pulled back the receiver slowly. Sam kept the motor idling and shifted into second gear, holding the clutch to the floor. She heard Archie chamber the first round and the click of the locking receiver. Sam popped the clutch and started across the parking lot. Austin almost fell over the tail gate but caught himself in time.

"Thanks for the warning, Sam!" Six smiled, putting his hands up like a surfer and started singing at the top of his lungs, "Surf city, here I come."

Archie later told us what a strange entrance they made, but admitted he laughed out loud. Sam headed to the prearranged point on the side of the lot so Six could let loose with the fifty cal, pinning the uninvited guests behind their cover. Archie was taking out some players, when and if they were dumb enough to look over the cover they were hunkered down behind. Out of the corner of his eye, he saw an attacker speaking to another man who had a radio to his head.

"Bet he is looking for help," Archie thought out loud. "Not tonight. Two for the price of one." He let the hammer drop. The bullet entered the back of the yelling man's head and entered just above the nose of the radioman. When he saw the inbound chopper, Archie started sending out flares from his launcher, lighting up the far side of the lot, hoping to partially blind the shooters. He also let go all of his fire and brimstone rounds he had for the launcher. Smoke rolled over the west side welcoming party, and a few high impact fragmentation rounds could be seen going off behind it. Most but not all of the party crashers were down.

My radio cracked with the harsh voice of Mom. "You guys start a party without me again? Man, oh, man."

Funny few can say their mother is a 6'3" full bird Special Forces colonel. His real name was Jack Fowley, and he was in charge of the Fast Action Recovery Unit. Fast Action Recovery Team as we were affectionately called by everyone else (FART). No one ever seemed to have the guts to call us that around Mom. He handpicked us all from different units and helped train us for this special kind of work. We all came from special ops or recon or some other down and hard unit. He was from the Midwest and had the same strong family ideals we all had or wanted in life. He truly looked after us like a stern all-seeing mother. He was quick to find fault but equally quick to praise. His favorite phrase "Man, oh, man" (MOM) is what gave him his handle. He had risen quickly through the ranks of the Special Forces and had made many, many friends on his way up. Taking over our unit had only added to his friends list, as he knew where many of the bodies were now buried. Also the special little favors the CIA and other agencies had offered up near at the end of the action.

Many of the local leaders that had helped the US during our time there were now in extreme danger as the north slowly took over and removed all the sympathizers permanently. We would pick up certain people or families and take them to a safe area for relocation, often to the US. On occasion, we would pick up a downed pilot, but that was seldom as flights were dropping off in numbers, and few were getting shot down. We had nothing to do with the CIA people as Mom preferred, "They need to play with their own species," which he said we were not. It was not uncommon for them to be around the doghouse or to ask for a pickup now and then. There were two teams of four that answered to Mom, and we had built a true connection between us all. We operated out of a small base far from the brass and their prying eyes. Our unit held a little more of connection with him as the firstborn always does. We had been operational for five months before unit 2 came with us. The number of operations was increasing as we got closer to pull-out time. We often picked up packages (people) in different areas throughout the south and north. Some US workers and businesspeople. Military was always a number one priority, especially if one of our people was down and needed evac. No one really knew much about Mom, but it appeared he was very well-connected and respected by most of the in-country units as well as back State side. He was there to see every operation, start and end. Often, he flew as the recovery pilot as he never let anyone do anything he wouldn't do, and he liked being close. He had a wife and daughter back home but spoke sparingly about them, and usually only after we had killed a bottle of scotch. Mom and I had hit it off right from the beginning.

We had a special connection which was handed down from my cousin who served with him at a forward base he commanded one year prior. He was a forward observer at the base and would often do recon for the base. He graduated Special Forces training high on the list and asked to be assigned to Mom when he landed in country.

He had heard a lot about Mom and his unit and their work so far north. Jake always looked for the most intense things and places to be. While at Fort Devens, Massachusetts, for his final training, he had heard stories of Fowley and his reputation. He heard how he held a forward command base for a week while outnumbered fifty to one and taking 80 percent causalities. He knew that was the man he wanted to serve under. He knew I was Special Forces, so that helped set his compass to where he was headed. I was doing recon for a unit of South Vietnamese regulars in the delta area when he made country. He worked directly for Mom, and they had a real bond, often both going out for two- to three-day recons. The two would live quietly in the jungle, collecting information on troop sizes and movements. Spending time like that will bring two men together and forge a bond that is unbreakable. I would later find out he talked about me all the time, and Mom often joked about getting us together as a team.

One afternoon, Mom was in the command bunker with a two star and some other brass discussing all the valuable jungle we owned and how long before it would be taken back. My cousin had just returned from a recon and was filling everyone in on enemy troop strength and equipment. A South Vietnamese officer who had unknown ties to the north was standing near the door and watching everyone carefully. Jake's hair stood up when he finished, and he walked over to the officer as he just felt something was wrong. The officer saw the look on his face and walked over and opened the door as if to leave.

Jake looked at Mom. "Does this guy belong in here with all this brass?" It was then Jake saw the grenade and watched as the soldier pulled the pin and threw it into the middle of the room. Jake watched as he ran through the door, letting it slam behind him. I can only image how time stood still and how Jake's mind must have raced through his options. Without thought for safety, he picked up the primed grenade and ran to the door and opened it. Mom told me later there was a second when he looked back. Their eyes met, and he saw that pained look of goodbye in his eyes as the door shut. Mom raced to help him but was forced back and on the ground by the explosion. When the smoke cleared, Jake was dead, the grenade destroying his once perfect body. Everyone's ears were ringing or ruptured from the blast. Mom crawled through the hole where the door once stood to Jake's side. He pulled him up, held him, and just prayed in his own way.

When he finished, he said, "You'll always ride at my side, son." Tears spilled from his eyes, and people who knew him said it was the first time anyone had seen that part of him. On uneasy legs, Mom got up and headed through the hole the blast had made in the ditch that led out of the bunker. Out through the trench and into the center of the camp, he searched. Standing near a tower was the officer he wanted, with his back to all the commotion, smoking a cigarette. He was trying to look unconcerned by the explosion that just occurred inside the camp. Mom walked up, grabbed his shoulders, and spun him around. He saw the shocked look when the officer realized his plan had failed. In one swift motion, Mom pulled his Ka-Bar out of its sheath on his shoulder rig and drove it home into the officer's chest so the point cut through the back of his shirt. He twisted it in a circle then pulled it out. He wiped it off on the officer's shirt. He pushed him to the ground then spit on him and said, "Die, you bastard, like the coward you are."

I had taken emergency leave to escort his body back home and to attend Jake's funeral. I only had bits and pieces of what happened, but it was clear he died a true hero in every sense of the word. I was shocked to find my travel orders waiting for me at HQ when I arrived. I was expecting a long delay as it was always hard to get anything done at headquarters. A lieutenant met me at the door and said there was no need for me to go in and handed me my orders. "Son, normally these orders are for thirty days out then back to country. Yours are open-ended. Rotate back if you want. Stay stateside if you wish. It's your call. Your ride will be here in just a few minutes."

My head was spinning. Who had the juice to issue open-ended orders and clear my way of red tape? I looked around at all the activity on the base and wondered, *All this and Jake's life for what?* A private with new to the area spit-shined boots took me to the airfield where a transport was sitting on the tarmac waiting. As I entered the rear of the aircraft, the pilot, an Air Force coronel, walked up. I saluted him, then he shook my hand.

He smiled. "I don't know who you are or who this soldier is, but I was ordered to stand by here for the last four hours waiting for you."

I said thanks and followed him into the belly of that huge bird, and that's when I saw the flag-draped coffin of my cousin Jake. The only cargo that day was him and me. I walked slowly up to the casket and placed my hand on that field of blue. A tingle went up and back down my spine when I first noticed the Honor Guard of Six Special Forces standing tall around me. My eyes were full of tears as I watched every man salute my cousin as they passed by and prepared to leave.

"Let's get wheels up and get you back to Schenectady Air National Guard Base."

I was impressed and became more so when he pointed to a Barcalounger that had been lashed to the side of the aircraft, complete with seatbelts. As those huge doors in the rear began to close for takeoff, I saw a Special Forces full bird colonel and what looked like an Indian with face paint and wearing master sergeant bars. They stood at the head of what must have been a hundred soldiers in full combat packs, all at full attention and saluting. I knew it was meant for Jake.

It was a lifetime away from that day on the hay wagon and the flying trip to the emergency room we made that day. I felt a huge hole and the bitter taste of guilt. I knew Jake had joined and accepted the appointment to Special Forces because of me. He always looked to me as a little brother would look to his big brother. He would never let anyone know, but he always wanted to be like me, or better if he could. I know our close family ties and the idea we had to always look after the other guy is what caused him to pick up that grenade and rush out without thinking of himself. My uncle and aunt were not much for the military and had fought to keep my cousin on the farm. Farming was a family business with little profit and not much opportunity for promotion. When I was unlucky enough to win that lottery, I didn't want to win. I knew I had to enlist so I controlled my future. No one was going to use me as cannon fodder. I was going to fight my way. I was finishing up basic training when I heard he had enlisted against his family's wishes. At the funeral home, they were adamant about no big deal from the military. They had allowed a flag-draped casket, I think, out of respect to me as well as him, but nothing more. My uncle had a bad taste for the war before it took his son. I guess when you watch the news each night and morning, it's hard to stay supportive when it all begins with the American body count. That made even more personal when you know your son was part of that count. They never blamed me, just telling me how much he loved me and respected me. I was in my dress uniform, my beret tight and in place. The service was nice and had mentioned his bravery that day so far away. Several of us spoke of times past and the fun things we would always remember and how our lives were better for him. I couldn't help but notice the contempt in the eyes of some of the people at the funeral. Maybe because I was in uniform or maybe because they just believed we were all baby killers over there. The news media just kept piling on the stories of civilian deaths, but never about the ones we saved.

As I and my other cousins carried the casket out of the church, the pastor must have sensed the tension, so he stopped and made this statement to the crowd: "Jake was part of us all. He died saving others. Rather we approve or disapprove of why he was there, he made the ultimate sacrifice for others. There is no greater love than to lay down one's life for others." To the hearse and then to the gravesite. it was hard to find any sense in this. The jungle was so far away now, it seemed like just a dream, a bad one.

My uncle didn't want an honor guard despite my aunt's wishes. She knew Jake would have wanted it, earned it, and deserved it. As the minister was finishing his graveside service, there was a low rumble from the north. At first, we all thought maybe an afternoon thunderstorm was headed our way. It grew louder and was constant, then it came into view. It was a F4 Phantom jet flying low with its gear down, so slow it looked like it would fall out of the sky. It was like a hawk headed down toward its prey. Everyone turned and looked as it approached the gravesite. People held each other, not knowing what was going to happen. The children pointed and giggled or cried, never seeing anything like it before. As it reached the cemetery edge, the gear folded up, and it went into a combat climb, which we could all feel in our chests. The pilot spun his aircraft as he took it almost straight up, flames pouring from its rear. We could see his helmeted head and the salute he gave. It climbed like what seemed forever then moved off to the south. As the sound went away, I heard what made tears well up in my eyes with an unexplained sense of pride and strange comfort. In the distance, a lone bagpiper was playing "Amazing Grace." As he played, it became obvious he was getting closer. We all looked behind us, and there was the bagpiper and a Special Forces Honor Guard marching directly to the grave, Colonel Jack Fowley in the lead. As they approached the grave, they split to each side of the casket and stood at attention. The master sergeant I had seen at the Saigon airfield stood at the head of the casket.

Mom walked up to my aunt and uncle who were sitting. He dropped to a knee, took my aunt's hand, and said, "Your son saved my life as well as that of five others that day. I could not live with that debt without showing my total respect for this man, soldier, son whom I consider part of my family. You can go from here proud and with the knowledge your son gave unselfishly. He gave all he had to give, and his sacrifice will never be forgotten." He looked at my uncle, a tear in his eye. "Sir, I never had a son, but yours was an example of what all men hope to see in theirs. Believe me when I say part of me died back in that godless country that day."

He stood, turned, saluted the casket, then placed a green beret on the casket. The master sergeant walked to him and handed him a small velvet box. He turned and once again knelt before Jake's parents.

"On behalf of the US government and the president of the United States, I would like you to accept this with our gratitude and that of our country." He opened the box and handed my uncle the Congressional Medal of Honor. He stood, spun around, and called out orders. He and the honor guard saluted one more time and walked off, never turning back in total silence.

My uncle's eyes filled with tears, and he held my aunt close and whispered, "He was someone very special. I can see now, and others knew it as well." It was at that point I knew where I was headed.

"Yup, Mom, things are fluid down here. We have Indians shooting from the west and a turncoat bodyguard down and out. Need you to clean up the west so the rest of the kids can catch the bus."

"You got it, Skipper. Just give me three to prep." The right-side gunner moved his fifty cal. to the pilot's side so both fifties would greet the unexpected and uninvited guests. "I will make a first pass and let them taste some rocket juice then set down with the twins playing a song for our friends."

"Rodger, Mom."

"Okay, kids, time to go home."

Sam and Six heard and headed for the building where Archie was. Sam slid to a stop, and Archie just rappelled down and into the back with Six, just as Mom let loose some rockets at the far side. The entire west side erupted in flames and explosions. Mom dropped the bird just thirty-five feet from the car with both fifties churning up the far side of the parking lot. The family wasted no time getting in, and the husband helped me. Sam stopped just short and let the other two get loaded. I yelled to her to mount up but saw that smile and nose twitch. She put the truck in gear, dumped the clutch, and threw an ammo box on the gas pedal and jumped out. The truck shot out toward the remaining attackers and the reinforcements that had just arrived.

As she jumped aboard, she smiled and said, "It's their truck, and Archie told me let them have it back."

Just as we started to rotate up and out, Mom let out a yell. "Damn!" He slapped Kevin. "Take over. I been hit."

Kevin took control, and we headed out and away from the lot just as the west side of the parking lot erupted into a huge fireball, scattering crates everywhere.

"Darn, I forgot my backpack." Archie smiled.

Mom had wrapped a combat compress on the wound and lit a cigar. "Guess I'll be babysitting our spooks for a few days."

It was an uneventful ride to the dog pound, and everyone kept an eye on our guest's dress as it fluttered in the wind. Sam saw all the eyes were focused on her slit, and she let out a loud "*Pigs*" and covered her with a blanket. Once we landed, the spook patrol ushered our packages away. It was the last time we saw them.

* * *

It was the sound we were waiting for, the unmistakable sound of the inbound bird. It came in low and fast for its clearing run. So close to the trees that it made what looked like waves running across the treetops. Over our heads and straight out into the fields and around the border of the clearing. Not wanting to give up our position, it stopped and hovered over a small outcropping of dirt on the opposite side from us. Not drawing any fire and seeing no bad guys, Kevin turned his nose to us. "Okay, people, let's do this like a Daytona pit stop."

Austin yelled, "Let's make Petty proud!"

I spoke. "Sam, it's green."

She got up on one knee, and now we could see her on the dike. She had hidden herself in the weeds so well, I only knew approximately where she was till then. She popped a green can of smoke and tossed it back toward us. It landed halfway between her and the shed. Kevin headed in, and we started running down the dike. The chopper flared and straddled the smoke. I pulled the two adults with me, and Six grabbed the kids behind me, one under each arm. We were about thirty feet from the door gunner when the father, mother, and I fell into a large washout. It was covered with the same tall grass we were running in, only this grass was three feet tall. It claimed us as we tumbled into a pile at the bottom. I turned back just in time to see Six flying over us and the hole, still carrying the kids. He was humming or making some kinda sound like you hear in those Batman shows. He reached the chopper and handed off the kids to the door gunner. He turned back toward us with a huge smile that seemed to drain out of his face, along with his color.

I turned and looked to see what had Six upset. At the turn of the road, a group of North Vietnamese regulars were just coming around the corner and were pointing at the chopper. The group started to run toward us, firing as they ran.

The door gunner yelled, "Get down!" He began firing his fifty at the incoming troops. Above our heads, the bullets passed harmlessly as we were in the hole. Firing from the door, the gunner kept the first group of soldiers pinned near an old truck on the side of the road.

I keyed my mike and said, "Archieeeee" in my best Edith Bunker impression. In that instant, my neck burned, and heat flowed over us like a superheated wind before the deafening concussion wave reached us.

The woman screamed as Archie jumped into the hole with us, not knowing what to expect from this large black man. We both looked up and back. There was a huge cloud of smoke and dust where the truck and the road once were. Archie had spent his free time placing plastic explosive (C-4) in strategic locations on the old junk truck that had been pushed off the road years ago. He was not known for being skimpy, so the charges had turned the truck into thousands of pieces of shrapnel. It totally incased the first deuce and half in a cloud of death and destruction. There was no escape for those souls in or around the vehicle when the old truck jumped up in the air as it detonated. We looked at the road, and we could now see another truck with men walking along side it.

"What now?" Archie had no equal in the knowledge of weapons or explosives.

When I asked what now, he smiled like that Cheshire cat and asked, "What do good soldiers do when their convoy gets hit?"

"I would get the hell out of the truck and into the ditch for cover."

"Exactly!" He reached under a flat rock and pulled out something, and it was then I saw the light gauge wire that ran out of our hole and into the road. He looked at the husband and wife huddled in the corner of the hole. "Sorry, I forgot to tell you about my hole here." And he pulled the detonator trigger. A large charge in the center of the road took the front end off the lead truck and destroyed it. Those troops left in the truck jumped to the road and dove into the ditches that ran along the road on both sides. Archie let them all get to the ditches and as well as all the stragglers. He just smiled and said, "Meatheads," and pulled the trigger again. One after another, the ditches along the road erupted in explosions. Both sides and the explosions that seemed to walk down the road like dominos falling for some three to four hundred yards. There was no escaping the death the C-4 and the claymores caused. "Shall we go now?" Archie yelled.

We grabbed the two and ran the last few yards to the chopper. The door gunner looked in shock. "Damn, I'm glad I'm on your side."

I looked him in the eyes and said, "When you're with us, your family."

The ride back was, for the most part, uneventful. Archie was making quarters disappear in his hands and reappearing in the kid's ears. Sam was helping the woman clean some of the mud from her face and hands. Austin was talking about the ride a few nights before when the wind blew that red skirt up and proved what he expected.

"I told you, she was naked under that thing. I could see the nipples in my scope, and the wind confirmed the rest."

I laughed and said, "She is so far out of your league, you couldn't get a job as her driver."

"Maybe, but worth a try."

"There are kids here, guys. Clean it up!" Sam yelled over the rotor noise.

Kevin leaned back and said, "Skipper, they want us to take a new heading." After, he had reported the unfriendly reception we just got. I was puzzled, but this was not out of the ordinary. Enemy concentrations or weather or a lot of issues caused us to change direction, so we weren't concerned.

I picked up a headset and called the mission leader for conformation. I expected Mom but got the head spook that had been assigned to the unit, along with his two idiot friends.

"Why the change control?" I asked.

"Listen, Skippy, if I think you need to know, I'll tell you. Got it? Now you and your little friends just shut up and enjoy the ride. *Out!*"

I tried to reach him through the mike and grab his throat. But oh well, it could wait. There was something going on as Mom would never give up the control seat to a spook. I felt very uneasy for the first time during the mission.

I was just about to doze off when it hit. The rocket must have hit in the engine compartment, which kept the majority of the explosion outside. Alarms were going off, and the chopper was spinning as it auto rotated down. All helicopters will auto rotate as long as the drive connection is disengaged. It is a slower descent than a crash, but not a whole lot. But if all goes as designed, most will survive. I looked at Kevin and could see pieces of shrapnel from above his head had ended his life and that of the copilot. I saw Sam in a heap on the floor and Six almost out the door. His combat harness had snagged on the door frame, and that's all that held him in. The gunner that was so glad to be with us now might have had second thoughts if he had not lost his head in the explosion that pulled him free of the bird ripping his harness off. The father stood up and reached for his son as we hit a tree, or so I assumed, and out the door they went, father clutching his son. The daughter was nowhere to be seen, and the mother was down next to Sam. Blood everywhere, I had no way of knowing whose it might be. Like a fool, I unbuckled to try and help. Just as we broke free of the tree, the chopper fell, and when we hit the ground, everything went black and cold.

* * *

The head agent was seated at the communication area with his headset on and feet up on the folding table in front of him. Leaning back in the chair, he was listening to someone with true interest while sipping on a fresh hot coffee. Since they arrived, it was clear they wanted nothing to do with us, and the feeling was mutual. Mom told us they were there with orders from outside the theater of operations, and he was not on the need-to-know list. They set up in their own little room off the main operations center and spoke little to any of us. Suddenly, his chair went out from under him, and he hit the floor flat on his back. As he fell, the headset was ripped from his head, and he was covered in scalding coffee. He started to yell but instead tasted the bitter taste of cold metal and cleaning solvent. His eyes flew wide as he looked up and saw Mom standing there with his stainless steel .45 pushed into his mouth.

"No need to talk. Just nod if you understand." The agent made a noticeable positive response. "What the hell is going on with my Minnow Unit? Is there a problem?" The head spook's eyes got much wider when he saw and heard the hammer being drawn back. The two other CIA agents entered the room and drew their weapons.

"Drop the gun, Colonel, or we'll take you out. You don't mean shit to us."

Without moving, Mom just smiled. There is nothing more distinct than the sound of a slide chambering a round in an M16.

Without looking, Mom said in his deep voice, "Do you boys know that these camp pigs the locals are raising will eat a man's flesh and bone in under twenty-four hours? Now drop those guns or disappear like the last spook that pissed me off." The two looked at each other and then handed the two Green Berets with the M16s their weapons. Pulling his .45 out of the agent's mouth, Mom started to speak, but the fool started first.

"You're in big shit, and I'll see you digging latrine ditches in—" *Wham.* Mom's pistol whipped him, cutting off his ranting.

"I told you I would ask the questions and you will nod to answer. Where is Minnow Unit?"

"None of your damn—" Blood flew from his mouth and nose that time. Both guards tried not to laugh.

"I know they have been diverted on your orders and without my knowledge, so watch my lips. Where is Minnow Unit?"

Spitting blood and thinking better of it, he looked at Mom and said he had orders from DC. "I was told to divert them to the new heading, and they would be contacted."

"I have tried all frequencies and even called in some friends that were rotating the area!" Mom yelled back. "No sign of them. Soooo, shithead, you want to tell me those headings? Or are you taking a ride with me and my bird while we go look for them?"

"You have no authority over me, and you can kiss my—" The agent covered his face to avoid the fist he was sure was coming. But he forgot to cover his nuts and protect them from Mom's size thirteens.

"Load this piece of shit in on my bird, and put his playmates in the old shipping container at the end of the runway."

The two guards gave a quick "Yes, sir" and pushed the two men toward the door.

Everybody moved out. The agent clutching his balls was dragged by his feet to the waiting command bird by two others. Behind Mom's Huey was another, all sporting fifties in the doors with two special forces commandos, heavily armed and seated.

As they reached the door, Mom said once again, "Where is my Minnow Unit?"

The agent smiled in some pain and made the mistake of saying, "Piss off."

Mom just smiled and shook his head. "Must have missed the roll call for brains along with common sense. Tie him to the struts. I'm not riding with him in my bird."

The agent looked around as the fear in him surfaced, and he realized he screwed up bad that time. Mom limped by him and stepped up into the pilot's seat using the agents head as a first step. No one spoke as he closed the door and started up the blades. Once up to rpms, Mom lifted off and put it into a nose down high-speed takeoff. He purposely brushed the treetops with his struts. Nobody could hear the agent's screams as he circled the field and made a pass over the small support village. The people on the ground pointed up and laughed as it looked like the guy on the outside would fall off at any moment.

The Special Forces master sergeant called Chief leaned out of the door and smiled. "Like the ride, jerk?" It looked as if the agent was crying, but it might just be the wind, or so he would claim later. "Mom says last chance before we leave without you."

A panicked look came over the agent, he screamed out the new flight plan he had given Minnow Unit. Chief went to Mom and told him, and they both looked at the map. They talked for a sec, and Mom said something to someone on the radio. Chief returned to the door and stepped out onto the skid. He reached down and grabbed the agent's hand, pulling him up so he was kneeling on top of the skid.

"Untie me," he demanded.

"You told us the truth about the new heading?" Chief asked.

"Hell, yes. It's too late for you to do anything anyways. They're toast by now."

Chief's face turned red, and he pulled out his razor-sharp Ka-bar knife that road on his left shoulder and sliced the ropes. Freeing the agent, he grabbed a handful of blond hair and pulled him to a standing position. Holding the agent up by his hair, he let him lean back and away from the bird.

"I always wanted to scalp one of you bastards." Chief was 100 percent Cherokee. His knife flew in a blur, slicing the hair clean where he held it, not touching the scalp but close enough to leave a burn. Chief stood there with a handful of the agent's hair and a smile on his face. He let out a loud war hoop so his ancestors would know what he had done. The agent's screams could be heard by the crew and all the villagers below. As he fell away, Chief passed on the new info.

Mom frowned and said, "Wish we were higher." Then he pushed the bird at full power toward his family.

The agent filled his pants as he approached certain death. He thought of his wife and girlfriend, not in that order. He was going places, and now some Indian just ended it. Why had he been such an ass to talk to the colonel like he did? Why had he cheated on his first two wives and stole that money during that drug bust? Only just then, *splat*. He hit the ground or what should have been ground. It was one-foot deep mud and pig crap. He lay there for a minute, wondering what could have just happened. The pigs ran for cover as he rolled over and covered himself with a smell only a pig farmer could appreciate. *Why am I alive?* he thought He could not get his feet under him and kept falling back into the crap. A laugh came from the fence. He looked up and saw the two MPs from earlier, laughing so hard they almost joined him.

"Let's go, asshole. Your friends are lonely."

He finally reached the fence, and the two MPs nudged him at rifle length toward the shipping container holding his friends. They opened the door and shoved him in. They slammed the door shut and locked it. His friends lost their interest in him shortly after the heat helped the smell reach every corner of the shed.

* * *

Approaching where they left the original flight plan, Mom keyed the mike. "Joe, you read me?"

"Yes, sir, I do."

"Have you found them yet?"

"That's a negative."

Mom keyed again and said, "I bet it will be hot when we get here."

"I've got you covered!"

"I'm about five mikes out and got some new toys I borrowed for this party. One of those Puff the Magic Dragon guys owed me some serious poker paper, and they did need a test flight after we fixed their radio gear for them."

"Do a recon and give us the numbers when you find them. These things can trim the jungle like my wife does the boys' hair."

Chief smiled when he heard the news. He had seen these Jolly Greens in action before. The VC had a healthy respect for these birds of prey as they showed no mercy in the rate of fire they rained down. Chief had seen one Jolly Green kill almost an entire company of VC that were about to overrun a forward base he was assigned to with Mom. It looked like a rainstorm that you see approaching where the wall just moves along the ground, those drops kicking up little geysers.

Chief was the toughest and hardest master sergeant in all the military, or as he told it and Mom swore to it. He was 100 percent Cherokee Indian and proud of it. Six-four and solid stone. He grew up on the reservation and joined the military when he was sixteen using his brother's ID. His brother was a drunk, and nobody could tell one Indian from another. They all looked alike. He rose quickly through the ranks and transferred to the Special Forces, where he continued to impress all his superiors with his fearless approach to all issues. An expert tracker, he would often find the enemy wherever they might hide. He had an unwavering respect for Colonel Fowley and would do anything for him, including laying down his life. He had not left his side for the past ten years.

"There! Mom, straight out toward that small hill to the left." Chief pointed. His eyes were sharper than any radar or binoculars. In the distance, a long thin line of smoke rose above the jungle canopy barely noticeable. Like two ballet dancers, the Hueys rolled left and went to nose down full power. As they approached the smoke, they could see the twisted wreckage of the minnow team chopper. "She went in hard, Mom," Chief said with no hint of what he was thinking. The two birds came to an abrupt stop and hovered above the twisted wreckage. "Berets away. I want the site secured and some intel. Now!" he yelled. As the birds hung there above the site, four commandos left and rappelled down in seconds. Chief left the colonel's bird before he had time to ask him to personally lead the recovery.

The first two ran for the jungle, and the others looked around the site. Mom told Captain Farmer, the number two pilot, to do a circle recon out five clicks. Mom made slow circle recons in close, waiting for the news he knew would be bad.

"Mom, this is recon 1." His tone did little to hide what news he had. "First off, all civilians DOA, and flight crew as well. Looks like they took a hit to the engine area, but no sign of the Minnow Unit. Expanding our search now. We'll find them, Mom. I can track a tick on a dawg." Chief was the best in the service when it came to tracking.

It might be good news if they were not with the wreckage, but not likely, Mom thought. He made short figure eights through the crash site.

Chief found drag marks, deep as if multiple things had been dragged away. He came across a male civilian on the ground with a single bullet hole in his forehead. He followed the drag marks to an area of brush, which was piled too neatly to be natural or caused from the crash. In front of the pile lay two bodies, which had little to distinguish them as to who or what they were. A quick search of their bodies found nothing to identify who they once were. He slowly approached the pile and pulled the top layer off.

"I got them, Mom. They're all in a pile hidden behind some fallen trees and cover." There was a long silence, one that made Mom's stomach twist. "They are all alive, but barely. They're beat up real bad, and I don't think we got much time."

"Mom, we got some company two clicks out," Farmer broke in. "They're coming in slow, but we are taking some ground fire and ducked one rocket."

"Get away and hold. I want you to drop red smoke right on them when I say. Joe, you hear that?"

"Yup!"

"Don't drop smoke. Repeat, do not drop smoke."

"On my mark, fire some rockets at an area three hundred yards south of their position."

"They will think you're just taking potshots and won't scatter. If you smoke them, they will expect a hit."

"I'll adjust and clean them up."

"What about an LZ, Mom? Clock's ticking down here," Chief said. "Fast."

Mom told them about a large flat rock about a hundred yards south of their position. He would clear the larger trees with his rockets and see if that would work. They started to send down stretchers. The gunners lowered the folding stretchers by lines to the Chief, and the medic that was with him. As they started preparing the wounded, Chief recalled the two scouts to help move them to the rock.

The medic was retightening the tourniquets on Six's legs when they heard Mom let loose with his rockets. All four had massive blood loss, and the medic had multiple IVs running on them all.

"Move them now!" Mom yelled. "I can hover over the rock, and you can push them in. I'll take the two worse and head direct to the carrier off the coast."

They had the best hospital afloat. Farmer was instructed to grab the other two after he gave Joe his targets. Joe called and told Farmer to mark the force below and drag it back to the kids. Farmer touched the fire selector and sent two tube rockets away from where the bad guys actually were and pulled out to make his pickup. The VC regulars below pointed up and laughed, thinking the helicopter pilot had no idea where they were and was running away.

Joe started whistling the "Battle Hymn of the Republic," and his whole crew joined in. As this massive prop powered Jolly Green came lumbering over the low hills, it looked like a fat bird trying to stay in the air. On each side, there seemed to be these large pipes filled with little ones. They started to rotate faster and faster, and then tracer rounds seemed to pour out like a long snake headed toward the ground where the twenty or so unfriendly regulars where standing. The AC-130 had six Vulcan sixty-one hydraulically driven Gatling guns (three on each side along with other weapons). With a fire rate of six thousand plus (.20) mm rounds per minute each, it looked like a giant fan had been lowered onto the jungle. The canopy of the jungle just melted as the fire storm walked its way toward the men on the ground. At a combined rate of thirty-six thousand plus rounds a minute, the Gatling guns just tore everything and everyone to pieces. Some died with one round. Some took a direct hit and had a large number of holes to show for it. The 130 made two quick passes then a slow circle over the area where the enemy had been, then slowly rose into the sky, having delivered its greeting.

"We will run high cover just in case anybody made it out of the blender."

"Roger that, Joe. We are loaded and outbound. Farmer will be loaded soon and outbound for the carrier group as well. I owe you more than I can say."

"Not likely, Mom. I would be long gone and kissing angels if not for you. Just get your kids taken care of and we'll kill a bottle some night."

* * *

When I think of that day, which only happens every day, I remember the look on the man's face and his sons. We had been hit in the engine compartment and auto rotated into the jungle. The daughter was gone, Six was halfway out the door, and Archie was in a heap between Sam and the rear bulkhead.

I knew the worse had happened. Sam was underneath the mother, and the daughter was nowhere to be seen. Then we hit the first tree, and it flipped us on our side. Six went the rest of the way out the door, and I just watched as I could not reach him as he hung below from is harness. The sound of the bird coming apart and falling out of the tree is something I will never forget. The ripping of metal and the breaking tree limbs was deafening. The chopper let go of its grip on the tree and fell to the jungle floor. When I started to focus again, it felt like my body had been cut in half, and I had no idea how long I had been out. The pain was intense, and it hurt to move, but at least I could still move. I looked around and couldn't see anyone. I pulled myself out and crawled away from the wreck.

I rolled onto my back, and there, looking at me, was the father I had seen go out the door. He had tears in his eyes, and I did not have to ask about his son. He was bloody, and his clothes were torn and soaked in blood. A small piece of branch was sticking out of his thigh, so I knew the canopy had slowed his fall and cushioned his landing to some degree. He quickly tried to stem the blood flow from my arms and back with whatever he could find. Once he felt he could do no more, he helped me to a sitting position. He pointed to the wrecked bird. I could just make out Six next to wreck with his legs under the right-side skid. With the farmer's help, I crawled to him, the pain so intense I had to will it away. His legs were mangled, but he was alive, so I set about getting tourniquets in place while the farmer returned with a large limb. With the farmer's help, we pried with a small log under the limb. I just lay on top of it, hoping my weight would help, and he pulled him out. He pointed to a thick area of undergrowth, and we carefully as possible dragged Six to the shallow hole where Sam and Archie were already deposited next to each other. They looked dead and unmoving. I knew Six was alive from the low moans that came each time we moved him. The farmer went about covering my friends with small branches and ferns, then turned to me. I had no idea how he managed to move my friends but sure was thankful and puzzled.

Why don't we just stay put till Mom comes and gets us? Why was he going to all this trouble to hide us? Then I heard the sound of someone using a machete to clear their way. Then I understood that the farmer had reasoned that whoever shot us out of the sky would come to make sure no one survived. He handed me a 16 he had found in the wreckage. He held his finger to his mouth, pointed, and started to cover me with branches. I wedged myself into a partial sitting position so I could see into the wreckage area.

He gave me a nod and said in fair English, "Thank you for trying. I'm sorry about your friends. You be safe here till help come. I watch for VC." He covered my head and headed toward the chopper where he knelt and looked like he was praying, but I could see the small arms of his daughter and a leg I was sure belonged to his wife coming out from under the wreckage. This man of no means and whose body had been racked by years of hard labor had no doubt saved our lives, and I regretted my doubting his worth. I knew I was going in and out and struggled to focus and stay awake.

A short time later, I heard voices, and two men walked out of the jungle and right up to the farmer. They talked, and it was English and some Vietnamese. I could only hear small bits of conversation, but it seemed to be about his family and the crew. He made it clear they were all dead. He looked at the men and asked them why they killed his family and the Americans.

The one laughed and said, "It's your fault for being who you are. The others are just what we call collateral damage." He was laughing again.

The farmer said something about being a good patriot, and then one of the men drew a sidearm and shot him in the head. My reflexes sent me to a position to fire on the men, but then I thought better, thinking they might not be alone, and apparently, they did not realize the size of the team. They systematically walked around, putting a bullet in the head of each victim. My anger was overwhelming but accepted that no one felt the shot. Then they saw the drag marks in the ground and began to follow them to where we were hidden. Circling to the back side, they talked and started to pull the cover off. Finally, I could avenge those they had helped kill. The selector on full auto, I pulled the trigger as they made the mistake of both looking into the covered area together. Their blackened faces became clear for just a brief moment, their Caucasian features clear but soon forgotten. Then a shooting pain and darkness.

* * *

"USS *Hancock*, this is Colonel Jack Fowley. I'm inbound with two critical. Get me Admiral Peterson on the line."

"Sir, the admiral is busy and does not want to be disturbed. I can assure you I can handle your situation. You are an unscheduled flight and need to be verified. What is today's call sign and your point of origin?" A Marine captain standing with his back to the radioman turned to warn him, but it was too late. A short silence ended abruptly, then it came.

"Get that son of a bitch Peterson on the line now and tell him Fowley is calling in his marker *now*."

"But, sir," the radioman began to say.

"Listen, son, I'll be there in fifteen minutes. If I have not spoken to Peterson before that, I will search you out, cut off your head, and shit in the empty hole."

The Marine laughed and said, "That's not just a threat."

Chief smiled at Mom. "Will they shoot us out of the air?"

"Nah, once that puke tells someone with some rank who just called, I damn well guarantee the next voice we will hear will be fat ass Peterson." Three minutes later, the radio cracked with the fat ass on the other end.

"What the hell is going on, Jack?"

"I'm inbound with two critical from my family. There is no doubt they need to be stabilized and then flown out ASAP."

"My med staff has been alerted and is standing by on the deck. What happened? I thought you guys were just playing taxi for all those special people?"

"We were, Gary, but some spooks from the DC hole set them and me up. Too early to know who or why, but you can be damn sure I will find out, and God help them."

"Don't blame you, Jack. I might have some good news, if it helps. Mark Johnson, the undersecretary of defense, is on board, and you know he is one of us old-school players."

"Good. Have him available for a sit-down after I unload. Our med flight left an hour ago, so I'm not sure how long." Then there was a silence.

"Never mind. Mark is here, and he has ordered his transport refitted for med care and fueled for immediate take off."

"Great! Tell him thanks, but I still enjoyed kissing his sister."

"Mark said something about your mother, but I know different. We'll be on the deck when you arrive."

The admiral cut off his line and turned to the captain standing near. "Make what I just promised happen. I want two ORs staffed and ready to receive the inbound. I want every stitcher you got on deck and ready to move them down to sick bay. Have Mr. Johnson's plane fitted to move our incoming guests as soon as they are ready. I would think only the two worse will be sent on now. Jacky Fowley does not ask for favors lightly, so these people mean a great deal to him, and now us, so drag your ass and make me look good."

* * *

I was in and out for most of the flight into the carrier. The constant movement of the chopper made my head spin. I remember I looked over and felt my stomach knot as I watched the commando cover Archie's body with a blanket, including his head. I was afraid he wouldn't make it when I saw his fatigues covered in blood and the huge gash in his stomach. I slipped back into that darkness that seemed to take the pain away. My last thought was for Sam and Six.

* * *

His bad leg stiff, Mom limped over to shake hands with Admiral Peterson and Undersecretary Mark Johnson. They all turned to the chopper as the med crew removed Six and Sam. The wind and flight deck noise made conversation little more than a shouting match.

"How bad, Jack?"

"I don't think Six's legs are too good, and he has lost a lot of blood. Sam has a depressed skull fracture and a lot of broken bones, possibly her back as well. Looks like Archie didn't make it, and the skipper is busted up inside and out. Maybe some back damage. They should be only about twenty behind us. Let's get inside and see just what we got, and start figuring who is going to pay."

"Okay, what the hell is going on here, Jack?" Johnson asked.

"No clue. It was a simple drop in, pick up a package, and go. Things got strange when the three CIA jerks showed up at my OP's center four days before this mess. They set up their own com center and kept my people out, or so they thought. Things started to go south the minute after they arrived. They supervised the pick of the Richie Rich family, two adults and two children from the old warehouse two days after they arrived. When the kids got back, they ushered them off before anyone really got to see them. Then today, we had scheduled the extraction of another family only not so well off from a working rice paddy. About half an hour from touchdown, the spooks locked my people out of their communication center and shut down ours. I was riding shotgun on a drop-and-go of rotating support personnel, so my people immediately contacted me and filled me in. The spooks refused my attempts to call in, so I knew there was something wrong. I beat feet home.

"Just as minnow was about to leave the pickup area, a large force of bad guys showed up. There was no intel to suggest these packages were anything special to justify such a force. It appeared they had driven straight to the LZ and set up their approach for combat, so it wasn't just dumb luck they were there. Thank God Archie was up to his old tricks of being ready for anything. That old Boy Scout is always prepared. He neutralized the entire force. After a further look, it showed them to be US trucks."

The undersecretary made a face. "A company party?"

"Looks like it. We could not reach my team, so Chief nicely asked the head spook. He told him we would be too late because they were already toast."

"He gave that up willingly?"

"He did, just before Chief scalped him and sent him out of my bird."

"Oh my god, Jack, you didn't do a CIA job on him, did you? You know how they hold enemy personnel outside a chopper and interrogate them, and after they're sure they got it all, they throw them out to shack up the next one?"

"Yes, I did, and he deserved much worse as it turned out."

"Jack, we can't help much if you let Chief kill a spook, no matter the reason."

Mom just smiled his big grin. "Well, instead of four hundred feet, it was just fifteen to twenty feet."

The admiral smiled. "I'd give a month's pay to see that. Where did he land?"

"In the village hog pen, with two of my people waiting for him. He was put in a tin can for safekeeping with his two friends. I have no words for how that must smell in this heat." Everyone smiled and turned to head to the admiral's cabin for a well-deserved drink.

"Now it gets worse." Mom downed a glass of scotch. "After they dusted off, the CIA boys rerouted them and told them they would be contacted. That's not unusual, as we sometimes pick up an extra passenger from time to time. But they were ambushed and hit with a surface to air." Mom looked at Chief and nodded as he also downed his drink.

Chief spoke. "On the ground, I found a lot of stuff. Each of the flight crew had been shot in the head at close range, a to-be-sure tap.

The main package had been shot execution style on his knees next to his wife's and daughter's bodies. Someone piled the Minnow Unit in a well-covered hideout. My best guess the farmer, although I don't know how. Then I find two bodies near where the unit's hideout was. Only know they were white, no papers, and thanks to the Skipper, no faces. This smells of a cleanup after the earlier surprise went bust."

"You can get some food and a beer, Chief. We need to have a private powwow. Thanks for your help. You have anything else?"

"Well, if I may speak my mind, two extractions in two days, both include one man, one woman, and twins, boy and girl. One rich and one dirt poor. I think we should look for a connection. The similarity is too striking for this part of the world." Mom nodded in total agreement. "Let's start there."

"Well, someone tried to use us for something. It stinks of CIA. I've lost a great flight crew and at least one of my minnow team, all for some secret spook shit. I have a scrambled call into Langley and the director who just happens to be my ex-wife's incumbent piggy bank. He hates her like I did but just can't sanction a black op in southern Virginia to make her go away." Everyone laughed.

"Let's grab some drinks and check on your people."

As they left the room, a sailor ran up to the undersecretary and whispered in his ear. "Excuse me, guys. That poor son of bitch my ex-wife lives with is on the horn."

The admiral looked at Mom. "What about the flight crew and the packages? We can't leave them."

"Nope, I ordered a full assault team in the air after we left. Should have everyone home by daybreak. Maybe we can get some answers from the bodies of the two that Skipper took out."

Once in sick bay, Mom went to the doc and asked about his people. He looked bad as he walked past and headed to the admiral's quarters, asking where he kept his scotch. It took a while and a few shots before Mom spoke. "Looks like Six will lose his legs at a minimum if he is lucky enough to live to get to a trauma hospital. Doc here doesn't want to chance a double amputation but doesn't think he has any choice. He thinks he can stabilize him to get him away. Sam has that depressed skull fracture and two broken legs and one arm. Also appears to have no feeling in her lower body. She is not responding well and is being put on life support. They hope to launch them in thirty minutes. It appears her back may be broken bad around the waist."

The undersecretary came in, took the bottle of scotch from Mom, and took a long draw and slammed it down. "This had presidential sanction but was never supposed to end up this way." Everyone just looked dazed. "This was and is a huge cover-up for some high-ranking people's asses, and the extraction of the big wig was a big-time payback. Everyone was supposed to be okay. Looks like the ground force at the farm was late or was given bad info. They were supposed to secure the family before our people arrived. Must be they didn't realize we dropped minnow team in early to make ready. I can only hope they were to take the family, not kill them. Someone in the program went rogue. They assume the South Vietnamese colonel whose entire unit got smashed by Archie."

"I don't think so," Mom said, "or how else would the CIA bastard know the chopper would be taken out?"

"The ambush and shooting down of the chopper must have been an attempt to save the mission, whatever it was. No one would have ever sanctioned all this blood, not our blood anyways. Now here is the stink. This was a high-profile and expensive shell game, but somebody changed the rules. That's all I was told and that he would investigate it, but I've heard that shit before. Richie Rich and his little show family was the one the higher-ups were looking to make safe. He has some big-time pull all the way up to the White House. No one knows or will admit what the farmer and his family had to do with it all, but we can assume the fact they were the same family makeup. Was no chance thing. Twins the same age and one boy and one girl are not very common in Vietnam.

"I also have some more bad news. While I was in the com-center, your strike force checked in. Inbound they found the wreckage area fully in flames. Apparently, somebody joined the game after everyone left and set the site ablaze with some serious stuff. When they were able to secure the area, they found the entire bird and bodies in a huge fiery pile. No dog tags to identify anything or anybody.

The heat was so intense, by the time it burned out, there was just a hole with a pile of melted gunship. Maybe they could recover parts of the bodies for possible identification, but the unit was called off and back to base. Headquarters claimed a large enemy force was in the area, and there was no air support available to cover the recovery."

"Gentleman, we need to get this circle jerk back under our control and need to do it now."

They started with redirecting the other chopper to the carrier where they would be able to protect them. As everyone made their way to the operation center, Mom headed for the flight deck and a quick shot of fresh air. When they reached ops, they all looked at the large outline of Vietnam and our location off the coast.

"Is that Fowley's other chopper there approaching the coast?"

"Yes, sir!" was yelled out. They were headed to the medical ship farther south from us. "We have redirected them here as ordered."

"What the hell are those three blips behind them?"

"Unknown, sir, but it appears they are gaining on your Mom's med flight." The radar operator immediately turned deep red and quickly looked away from the admiral.

The admiral spun back around, the veins in his neck sticking out and yelled, "Scramble ready 1 and 2 *now*! I want what and whoever they are intercepted and dealt with if need be."

Mom reached the deck just as ready 1 and 2 left the end of the carrier and clawed at the sky. Afterburners glowing, they headed to the coast at max speed. What was happening here? How had this all developed in only a few hours? Mom just shook his head and headed to the ops center and his friends.

"Ready 1, call sign Eagle 1 asking for instructions."

The admiral nodded, and the captain knew what he wanted and said, "Scare them off, Eagle 1. They are not approved to be in the med flight's air space." There was a slight pause as the captain looked up at the admiral, who just nodded. "If they do not break off their pursuit, you are green to engage." The tension in the room was growing with each minute. They all stood around and watched the small dots all heading for a single meeting.

"Contact Mom's boys," the admiral said. "Tell them do not go feet wet until our people are with them."

"Aye, sir!"

"What's up?" Mom asked, having just returned from the flight deck. He looked puzzled as he rejoined the others in Ops. After a quick look around, he understood what was developing in front of him on the screens. He knew if the pursuing dots meant to splash them, they will want them off the coast where the wreckage would never be recovered. The captain was directing them to give Eagle 1 some extra time to get there so he could play with them.

Just then, the speakers became active. "Eagle 1 to flight control. We have located three Cobra gunships hot on med flight's tail."

The captain never missed a beat. "Get them the hell out of there, Scott. Use whatever means you have to."

"Okay, boss. Here goes your version of thread the needle."

The admiral smiled. "Gotta love that guy."

"That's why he is my ready 1." The captain smiled.

Eagle 1 made a long high circle to end up on the gunships' rear. Still unseen by the bogeys, he dropped down like a rock where he came to a level position approaching from the rear, matching the choppers' altitude. Ready 2 remained high and ready to drop down like a bird of prey if the need arose. He knew he was there strictly as a backup because he respected no other pilot in the theater more than Colonel Scott and was just enjoying the show. The choppers were in attack position where they were at the same altitude as the med flight and about three hundred feet apart. Then they made the single most stupid move of their lives. They fired on Mom's bird with their forward guns. Happy with his approach, Eagle 1 pushed the throttles to the stops when he saw the tracers from the Cobra's guns.

"Hard bank right med flight and drop to the deck."

The Cobra pilots and their copilots never saw it coming or knew what happened until they felt the heat from the afterburners. Eagle 1 passed between two of them at approximately four hundred knots. The sudden air displacement caused the chopper on his right to go into uncontrollable spins and turns and began dropping. There was no doubt the pilots were very experienced and did well to recover without crashing. The one on his left was not so lucky. As ready 1 passed between them, he banked about 90 percent, and the heat and from his afterburner and wake melted and blew away the canopy covering the two Cobra pilots. Neither pilot suffered much as the Cobra exploded in midair.

"Oh, my bad," Colonel Scott said, but it was obvious he was smiling under his full mask as he climbed and pulled a victory roll. The other one was able to recover and was in the process of realigning itself with the third Cobra, and both maneuvered to form an attack position. Ready 2 approached from the south and laid down a stream of tracer rounds between them. They quickly pulled left and right, dropping down and heading back the way they had come from.

"Did you see the rear canopy on the starboard bird that spun out? It looked like it was covered with puke." Both ready 1 and 2 laughed. "Be advised, command. These were Cobras. Unmarked but Cobras nonetheless."

"Remaining two are bugging out. I guess they had not planned on us joining the party."

"Tell the med flight to resume max speed and course for your location."

"Eagle 1, keep our boys safe till they hit the deck."

"Yes, sir" was all the response needed. The room broke into wild laughter and cheers.

* * *

I barley remember the door opening and the face of Mom looking down at me on the flight deck.

"You're safe now, son, and I'll get you the best help available. You can count on it."

I dropped back off, the morphine doing its job well.

* * *

Back in the admiral's quarters, the three men sat quietly listening to the man on the other end of the speaker. The director of the

CIA was putting the spin on the whole issue. He could stop the hunt and look to try and clean up who went rogue. But nowadays, there was so much ass covering and spin going on with the war ending badly. There was just so much he could do. In a matter of speaking, it started way up the ladder, he explained, all the way to the president in some respects. The men listening just looked at each other with blank stares. Although he would never have agreed to the loss of American lives, he did start the ball rolling to get the package and his family out of Vietnam.

The three men looked at each other, not understanding why the president owed a dirt farmer and his family a favor. The director didn't know what they had on the president, but it was a presidential request. As best he could figure was someone got the idea that they needed to die and start over in the United States with new lives. That was where it all went off the reservation.

Mom sat back, his face growing redder with each moment. It now made sense to him. The Richie Rich and his show family were the prize. The farmer and his family were the body replacements to replace and fill the holes in the ground.

The director went on explaining how their deaths would make the president happy. Debt paid, and all the other players could breathe easier. The guy had strong connections in both the North and South Vietnam governments. The president had no knowledge of what went on there. He was under the impression the well-connected man and his family had been killed in a horrible chopper crash and explosion while being extracted.

"Somewhere, it all went terribly wrong. The farmer and his family must have been meant to die looking like they were the connected one and his family. I can only assume whoever is behind this thought, the farm family would be captured and dealt with before your people got involved. Your team was never supposed to make contact, only find an empty farmhouse and evidence of a family of four had been hiding there. Their mission was to just help confirm any story line that came up later. That's why we are on a scrambled line, and I will deny saying any of this." He said he would shut down the operation, both the official and the rogue one as he still had considerable power. But this all had to go away. If this did not go any further and no one looks into it or pushes for answers, he could hold the wolves at bay. Too many people with too much power were involved. "So it's in your court now, Fowley. I don't care how you do it, and I will help if I can, but this operation never happened, and those involved will never speak of it." The line went dead, and everyone finished their drinks in silence.

All Mom said was "Bastard" as he stood and left the room.

The next morning, the three met for breakfast, and Mom was the first to speak. "I know what we must do." He then began to lay out his plan. He knew the three of us were not the types to let anything go. None of us had any close family left, so new lives would be the best way. Separate from each other, we could never know the others survived.

"What the hell are you talking about, Fowley?' You still drunk from last night?"

"I wish," he said as he walked over to the ready board hung on the wall with a map of the United States. He explained how he planned to spread us all over the United States for recovery and new life training. He knew we would believe him and accept his word that the others were dead. We should be glad to start over if we survived and were in any condition to do so. He would have the bastard from Langley make our records show us as disabled veterans with maximum benefits and a special handling note in our files. We all knew the stuff we did was on the edge between sanctioned and not. We would just hunker down and let the past fade away. It's always less painful that way. He explained that if we talked together for even one minute about what happened, we just might want to push for answers, and that could get us all killed.

Just then, a young sailor came in and saluted. "Okay, son, what's up?"

"The doc says all four are now stable and ready for evac. Just need to know where to."

Mom questioned the fact that there were four, not just the three. The young medic got excited and explained how the big black guy woke up in the morgue about an hour ago.

"What?"

He looked scared and told Mom how he sat up in the body bag, and two seamen passed out right there. The doc heard the screams and came running. He ripped open the bag and went to work right away on him. All Doc kept saying was he wanted to know who pronounced the man dead so he could kill him."

Mom rushed out and headed to sick bay. Sure enough, there laid Archie with all types of bags hooked to him, and the doctor wrapping his head.

He turned to Mom. "Guess it wasn't his time."

"I don't know how or why, but this boy must have more to do here on earth."

"It's times like this I wish I was more of a churchgoer." He laughed. He explained how they would chopper Six to the med ship for the double amputation and then on home once stable. The others were stable enough to move to Saigon for evac to Germany and eventually home.

He explained to the doctor how we would need to be kept isolated from each other and not be allowed to meet or know the others survived. The doctor was confused but knew just enough about the day's events to know it was way out of his pay grade. Mom explained he needed to send our charts and status to Chris Roberts, a college friend of Mom who now was the head of Bethesda Veterans Hospital. He would oversee determining the best place for each to go.

"Let the shell game begin," Mom said under his breath.

* * *

I continued my physical therapy in my home state of New York, close to the Adirondack Mountains I had loved so as a kid. My rehab went well under the watchful eye of a student therapist I had met at the hospital in Albany, New York. Her name was Carol, and we took the patient/therapist thing to a whole new level. She had a unique way of stretching my back in ways even I could not have imagined. Don't get me wrong. The fact she was naked acted like a painkiller. My injuries were severe but not as bad as they could have been, and nowhere near what had killed my friends. I had a broken back, which did heal with some pins and screws and brace.

Carol and I moved in together once I could leave the hospital. Once cleared from hospital therapy, she helped me find my little piece of sanity in a place called Musgrave Harbor. This small close-knit village was located on the northern shore of Newfoundland. She was born there to a fishing family that worked the cod schools around the island. Overfishing and the involvement of the Canadian fisheries had caused serious damage to the once-lucrative industry.

I took some of the savings I had and bought a small charter boat that made daily trips out to the icebergs when in season and some short sightseeing trips as well. I enjoyed long days of fishing and settled into a somewhat retirement lifestyle. Carol helped me cut a deal on the purchase of a place with a rental business on the first floor to help offset the mortgage. I had a comfortable apartment upstairs, and Maggie, a local legion, operated her diner on the lower level. Life was good, and I still started each day as I had for all those years. I stretched the pain out of my back, slid out of bed, grabbed a coffee, and headed out on to the deck to check out the ocean view. The smell of Maggie's fresh bread and bacon always made me think of home, but this was my home now, and down I went for another rent collection. I ate almost every meal there, so rent was just something that passed back and forth. I had truly found peace there in this land of long ago. Carol had passed away five years prior from a heart defect that had gone undetected. Since then, it had become Maggie's self-imposed mission to find a woman for me. Her latest attempt was with a friend in St. John's, the capital of Newfoundland. She was involved in some sort of Iron Man event. The odds being three to one woman to men in some parts made me kind of like chum in the water. Maggie kept the sharks at bay and had her own ideas of what I needed and who was a match. So far, they had all been great, but none of them tripped that trigger that Carol had.

I asked Maggie what this Iron Man thing was all about because it was the first I heard of it. She told me that five years ago, Jane's father had started it to honor the memory of her brother, who had been injured some ten years ago. With deep depression, he had taken his own life a year later. Jane's father was an old-school outfitter who flew his own floatplane and ran a successful guide service during the caribou and moose season. He owned several cabins and rented several others from the fish and game department. The season was about nine weeks long and the only source of income for many of the locals.

Her brother, Joe, worked one of the many daily ferries that kept Newfoundland supplied. He worked for one of the larger companies that ran trips from Nova Scotia out of St. John's during the off-season. There was a storm which was not unusual for this part of the world but was more severe than usual. While working the auto deck, Joe was doing his rounds and letting his mind roam about the upcoming guide season, which was the best part of his year. Weeklong hunts where he could take these hunters out and walk them for miles till they begged for camp. Just to prove a point, and he would take them out the next day and sit them in some thick pines and go off to drive a keeper bull moose or big rack caribou to them for the kill. The backlands were like a tundra full of bogs and patches of pine so thick you almost had to crawl to get through. It was full of small pools of water that were often waist high or deeper. There was so much land to cover, you just climbed to the tallest hill and sat there looking for game through your binoculars. Once you spotted your trophy, you hiked the miles it would take to get close enough for the shot.

Those few short weeks were what made Joe feel blessed to be a Newfy. As his mind wandered, he started to cross from one side of the ship to the other. It was against policy to cross between vehicles, and cross ship travel was restricted to several marked crosswalks about six feet wide. Halfway across, he slipped, catching himself on the tire rack of a jeep. He looked down and saw the floor was covered with oil, which must have come from a major leak in the jeep's oil pan. At that second, he knew he had screwed up. None of the vehicles on the car deck were tied down, rather letting the parking brake do its job. The ship took a sudden forward nosedive as it ran down a huge wave toward the bottom. With the floor covered in oil, the rear tires had no traction to keep the jeep in place. The jeep slid forward, hitting the car in front of it, and before Joe could react, the ship ran nose height as it climbed the other side of the wave. The jeep slid back, the tires not turning, just sliding on the oil, pinning Joe between the jeep and the pickup behind it. The pain was intense, but he knew he had to get out or remain upright, or there was a chance of having his chest or head crushed. He hugged the spare tire, willing himself to keep from falling. His legs were broken. They would not support him.

He screamed for help, and the rocking of the ship intensified, as did the frequency the two vehicles slamming together. He was close to passing out and falling where the next collision might kill him. After what seemed like a lifetime, he felt a hand on his shoulder, and this time when the vehicles separated, he was pulled to the side of the deck. The storm was intense, and no chance of a rescue chopper from land, so the two and a half hours remaining in the runtime to port was the longest of his life. A doctor that was traveling on board was able to sedate him and stabilize his legs, which appeared crushed just above the knees. Once on shore, he was moved to the trauma center. After months of surgeries, his legs remained all but useless. The final determination was double amputation. He moved about well in his wheelchair, but mostly just to and from the liquor cabinet. His father and sister stayed by him and tried to push him toward prosthetics and a new life. But the weeks and months after saw Joe slip deeper into depression, which no matter the amount of encouragement could relieve the pain and loss within. He only dwelled on the fact that he would never again go to the camp and hunt the mountain flats which were full of those holes and sink spots. The thick pines and rugged environment made, for even a man with two good legs, intimidated at best.

Then one afternoon, he took his 30.06 rifle out to the shed and ended it. His father was committed to help people with handicaps get into the wilderness and enjoy it as his son had always done before that accident. It became all-consuming for him and led to the foundation that now sponsored the Iron Man competition. He now used his camps as places where people could go and challenge the rough land and their unique circumstances.

"That's the gist of it," Maggie explained. "Jane is very involved and is the organizer and CEO of the foundation." This was the first international invitational event with winners of other events around the world invited to compete in many age groups. It started today and winds up Friday with a big dinner. Maggie told her I would pick her up at her hotel at five, Friday. She let her know I could not book a room, so I would need to leave early to come home.

"So what did she say to that, Maggie?" I asked.

"Bring a toothbrush and at least one change of clothes," she informed me with that devilish smile she had.

I smiled and began looking forward to the trip because I knew Maggie would not hook me up with anything less than a nine. Jason—my breakfast, lunch, and dinner partner—looked up and tapped me on the shoulder.

"That means she wants you to sleep with her." He had a toothless smile on his face as he moved up to my ear and whispered, "I think she wants you to make love to her too."

Maggie reached out and slapped him on his bald head and called him an old horn dawg, which he was. But at eighty-three, good for him. He pushed back and laughed, explaining how he was just helping me out.

"These Newfy women can be a handful. They are all as horny as a fall moose."

She threw a towel at him, and everyone laughed.

Friday morning began as every day did for me. A painful start and a strong dose of Maggie's coffee. I finished my breakfast and was about to start the drive to St John's when Jason came in with a look of a child that just broke something. He looked to see if Maggie was looking and came up to me and sat down. He handed me a small foil package. "I can't keep these things on anymore, but you really should always take care with these Newfy women. There is a three to one ratio, so they do like their men, and lots of them."

Maggie turned bright red and stared at me and Jason. "Dad, you'll never change."

Jason laughed and said, "No, and your mom went to her grave with a smile on her face." The whole place broke out in laughter as Maggie came around the counter, cleaning rag in hand, and chased poor Jason out the door, still fast at his age.

Once on Rt. 1, you'd see beauty and different landscapes with every turn. The roads were outlined with those famous frost ditches, like most ditches along any country road, only these are five to six feet deep. Leaving the road to avoid a vehicle or the magically appearing moose is not an option along most of the highway. It is a land time forgot. On the way to the main highway, I passed through an area where on my right was a barren and desolate landscape with nothing growing and only rock and red dirt everywhere. This land of nothing stretched all the way to the top of the mountains that lined the way south. On my left was a lush landscape of trees and grass and small pools of water. A large bull moose was slowly walking toward the base of the green tree-covered mountains that lined that side. The road was a distinct boundary between heaven and hell.

It was nearing 2:30 p.m. as I pulled into St John's and made my way to George Street. O'Reilly's Pub was always my first stop when I found myself in town, and a drink of scotch was just what the doctor ordered. Finding a parking spot near the pub was great and a short walk to where I would meet Jane. I found this pub when I first came to Newfoundland and was lost in my thoughts of my new life or lack thereof. As it happened, a group called Shannock was playing, and I immediately fell under the spell of this group. They played old ballads and story-type tunes that were meant for this island in the North. Everyone in Newfoundland made you feel at home like nowhere I had been to in my life.

When I first moved to Musgrave Harbor, I met Maggie's mom, who was battling cancer. I asked her one day as she closed the dinner, "Why didn't you lock the door?"

She smiled and said, "If I have something my neighbors need, they are free to come in and take it. Replace it if they can. No harm if they can't." That's when I knew I had walked into another world, one I knew I could call home.

"Hey, Skipper!" the sexy bartender named Mary called out. The fact she used my old handle only showed how open and rambling my first weeks must have been, holding down the end barstool while waiting for Carol to decide if she would join me in my new home. She smiled and leaned across the bar to kiss me on the cheek. Still can't get above the boobs skip, her low-cut dresses never left much for the imagination, and she caught me checking those babies out.

I smiled back and said, "If you don't want me looking, stop leaving them out."

We both laughed and took up our well-rehearsed positions to check out the crowd. She explained how there were lots of non-Newfies around with this big race in town.

"Yeah, I see." I surveyed the crowd, counting not less than ten wheelchairs and a few with crutches. "Gotta give these people credit. Most of us find just everyday life challenge enough." She told me how the real tough ones left a few minutes ago. Twenty or so guys and one girl with those artificial legs and arms. Never knew it the way they partied and danced, and there was one American, older than most but the life of the party.

"Looked your age and looked tough and rugged like you." She smiled and made a real effort to bend way over for a bottle of beer from the bottom of the cooler.

"Just what do you think my age is?" I teased.

"Did you forget that weekend at my place already?"

She smiled when I said I could never forget those nights with her. I spent many weeks in St John's after the loss of Carol.

She smiled and turned her back to the bar. "And these missed you as well." She pulled up her shirt and let the girls run free, holding them up like I was going to enjoy them. I smiled and pulled her to me and kissed her long and deep.

"What time you off?"

"Around two," she said with that smile that meant "be here and be rested." I told her if my blind date went badly, I'd be there. She made a fake frown and said, "I'm your second choice?"

I downed the scotch and headed out to meet this blind date, turned, and said, "Not sure yet." I hoped Maggie was good to her word that I would not be disappointed. But if things went sour with Jane, I would be back to meet Mary at two.

I walked down the street thinking of all these exceptional men and women showing that they were still as good as anyone else. In fact, better than many. As I turned the corner and walked into the hotel, I saw this beautiful redhead standing there with this skintight green dress, talking and laughing with this man in a tux. Shit, Maggie never mentioned that it was a formal thing. I decided to duck out. I'd claim car trouble and head back to the bar and my late-night partner.

Just then, I heard this beautiful woman call out, "Hey there, Mason. Maggie lied about you." I turned, and she was walking to me with her hand out and a smile. "She said you were a handsome man, not a drop-dead handsome man." I know my face was red, and she did not push it, only bent over and kissed me on the cheek. "Come on, we got to get you into your monkey suit and catch our ride."

We shook hands, and she led me to the elevator, keeping are hands locked together. As we headed up, she kissed my cheek and said she was so happy I accepted the matchmaking of Maggie. They had been good friends for years as she often camped near our village and fished both streams and at sea. We entered her room, and there was my tux and shoes all laid out on the bed. Jane turned red with blush and told me, "Maggie said to surprise you with the tux so you could not say no."

I smiled and started to take my shirt off. "It's here. Might as well wear it," I said.

Still blushing, Jane turned around and headed to the door. I asked how long we had before the party. She told me we had a good hour or so.

"Why?" she asked and turned around.

I walked over and looked into her eyes and said, "That gives us time to get acquainted." I reached for her, spun her around, and enjoyed her neck and worked up to her ear. I enjoyed her soft moans for a second then unzipped that green dress and let it fall.

We pushed each other to the bed and fell in a heap on it. Seeing her naked except for her black stockings made me want this woman even more. Those rock-hard nipples made me wish we had more time. Her hand ran up my inner thigh, and I knew we didn't have enough time. This would need to be an all-nighter for sure.

She asked me to please zip her dress as she pulled it up and turned away. She told me that we just might need to make this a long, long weekend. I smiled and cupped those firm breasts, bit her ear, and told her those had been my plans since I first saw her. I pulled on my coat, checked my hair, and out the door we went.

Meeting her father was amazing as he was every bit a man of strength and character and no doubt where his daughter got her dose of it. Lots of small talk, but I was intent on learning all I could about this program and the people in it. We sat down and began dinner, which was moose and other game donated by the local guides. Many of these rough men and women worked hard guiding the hunters that flocked to Newfoundland during the short hunting season. With work in short supply, many lived on what they made from the outfitters and tip money from the hunting groups. Some hiked miles each day over the rough terrain, and some acted as camp cooks. I fell in love with this rugged land and its people when I first got there. Work hard, play hard, but just enough of both.

The hall was filled, and the noise was deafening at times. After a while, it came time for the awards. Jane and her father moved to the stage and began the speeches honoring the participants and the memory of a son and brother. The awards started with third place overall and worked through all the age groups filled with praise for their efforts and accomplishments. Then taking the mic, Jane coughed and began with a story of her brother and how he loved competition but never let it be all encompassing. How he had a heart that allowed him to care for others much more than people knew. She explained how he was entered in a shooting competition that he would have certainly won. But he went to a small town on the island and led a group that searched for two young boys lost in the mountains instead of competing. Two days of search was successful as they were found in good condition. It seemed they tried to follow a caribou they had wounded and got turned around. She laughed and told everyone how her brother made them track out the caribou and bring it back with them.

"As I look around, I see people who all live for those values and have overcome so much. But none display this inner strength and unselfish values as the man we now wish to recognize." She went on to tell how on the final day of the senior level competition, during the 5k cross-country event, a runner fell into a sinkhole and broke his arm. In intense pain, he struggled forward toward the finish line. Unable to keep his balance through the pain of his arm and a broken leg prosthesis, he sat back on a rock and waited for a spotter to see him. This man stopped and helped this injured man to complete the race and even pushed him ahead, so he finished next to last, not the one at the very end. She went on to tell that this selfless effort made this man deserving of their recognition. What made this more of a story of unselfish sacrifice was that by finishing last, he dropped from no. 1 to no. 4 in the US senior standings. "In my eyes and in the eyes of all here, you are and always will be number 1. Please stand up and be recognized for the true hero you are, Mr. Steve Austin."

The hall erupted into roaring applause and a standing ovation. All I could do was stare and fight a strange need to be sick. Standing there in the middle of the room, short hair and nice suit, was a man I owed my life to so many times over. A man that was as close to a brother anyone had ever been. A man I last saw being pulled off me and taken away to what I knew was a chopper, Mom's chopper, I was sure. A man that I knew was dead as Mom had told me so. Told how he was injured beyond the help of the doctors on the carrier. The man I cried for and now saw in my dreams and nightmares on a regular basis. The man whose death I felt blame for as his leader. I stood there as everyone else sat back down. In this huge hall, I stood all alone as Steve had. Steve stood back up and looked at me with no color in his face. There wasn't a sound to be heard as everyone could see the tears flowing from my eyes and Steve's as well. Jane stared at me, not understanding what was going on or what to say. The hall remained dead silent, and Jane just stood there until Steve broke the silence with "Skipper?"

Without thought, I responded with "Six?"

We met in the middle of the hall and embraced in a long bear hug. We looked at each other for a long minute and then said as one person, "We need to talk. Now."

We turned and headed out as the entire hall stood in a standing ovation. For what, they had no idea. Without a word, we walked through the hall out the door and to the safety of O'Reillys Pub. Mary saw me come in and who was with me and knew we needed privacy. She gave us a bottle of scotch and two glasses. She met us in the corner and pulled back the privacy curtain in front of the booth. She knew we had to know each other from our blank expressions. She could tell we were cut from the same cloth, so she kissed my cheek and walked out, closing the curtain.

I stared at Six, still unable to comprehend what was happening. "You're supposed to be dead." Six broke the ice.

My reply was "You don't look so bad for a dead man yourself." I went on to tell him how Mom had told me he had died en route to the trauma unit along with the others. Mom had told him I never made it out of the crash site. We both wondered out loud why he would have lied to us and keep on the story line going. I told Six how he visited me a lot while in the hospital and rehab and through the years. I heard from him through calls and an occasional visit. In fact, how I had just heard from him two months ago when he called and told me about his daughter's new job.

Six said he told him the same thing a few months ago when he called. We both felt this odd feeling of betrayal and confusion, along with relief to know our friend was alive. We speculated for an hour when Jane pulled back the curtain and stepped in.

"I think you two owe me an explanation." She was a cross between anger and confusion. We sat her between us, poured her a big hit of scotch. and gave her a brief rundown on our belief each was dead. She was soon red-eyed from tears and kissed me with intense passion, then got up and started to leave. "Call me when you get back from the states."

"What makes you think we are going state side?"

She smiled a big smile and just winked then turned and left. We looked at each other and agreed she was right. We needed to go see Mom and get some answers. As we stepped out to leave for my home, Mary stood there and smiled.

She said, "I would blow me off for her too." She was laughing as she left.

"We need to go see Mom and get this crap sorted out." Why the lies, why hide us from each other, and what about the others? Did he lie about them as well? Were Sam and Archie out there somewhere thinking we died? This was by far a need for face-to-face, not some phone call. We collected his things from his room and headed for my place to grab some clothes and cash.

As we lifted off from Halifax, I began filling Six in on my side of this *Twilight Zone* story we were now living. I told him how Chief had pulled me aboard the chopper with Archie and how I saw them cover him in a body bag. I passed out and didn't remember anything till I saw all the lights and equipment of the recovery room in the sick bay area. I saw a doctor and Mom talking with some guy in a suit at the far end of the room. When Mom saw I was awake, he came over and touched my shoulder and smiled. He told me I was going to be okay and that I had some broken bones but nothing that wouldn't heal. He introduced me to a guy named Ben. He said he was working with him to find out what happened earlier that day. I told him I could not remember much, but you guys might. That's when he told me I was the only one that made it. That was the beginning of my rehab for my body and soul as the guilt racked me every day including that day. Why did I make it and no one else? Why me? Through the process, Mom told me that they figured it was another fine example of poor intel from the spooks from Langley. Changed our return route based on bad intel, and we flew into an area where the VC had some hidden missile batteries. It sounded like one of the many screwups that often happened when the CIA was involved. But it left lots of questions in the background. Why had they killed the farmer? And who were they? Mom had told me they were most likely northern regulars that shot us down, and they felt the farmer must have been a US sympathizer. He believed they were right being we were extracting them for the CIA jerks.

I told Six how I finished my rehab at a place in Upstate New York and took a vacation with Carol up to Newfoundland. She thought I would enjoy the quiet yet rough life, which was an understatement. I told him about Carol and that short part of my life and how she had helped me both physically and mentally. I never left the island for two years until my aunt's funeral, which I felt obligated to attend being I missed my uncle's. It had been many years since that day our bird had fallen from the sky and changed our lives, but now it felt like yesterday. As we approached the airport for landing, we each downed our drinks and pulled again on our seat belts after a sickening feeling as the plane dipped down. Once on the ground, we headed to the US Air terminal to catch our flight to DC, where we would rent a car and head to Mom's place in Front Royal, Virginia.

The ride started out quiet and uncomfortable as we both wanted to talk about so many things that were unsaid. Why the lies? What possible reason was there for us to be made to think the others were dead? As we headed west, I could not wait any longer to ask what needed to be said.

"Six, what happened to you after you were pulled out of the wreckage? Where have you been?"

He explained how he now lived in a place called Clermont, Florida. How he now traveled a lot but called it his home. He had spent almost a year and a half in a rehab clinic and hospital in Tampa, Florida, that specialized in amputees and their rehab. When he woke up on that med flight to the States, he looked around and saw some other guys on bed stretchers and was kind of in and out. He tried to sit up but was belted in. A beautiful nurse came over and told him to be still and gave him a drink of water. She was sweet and had a great smile that just evaporated when he told her he needed to move because his feet were killing him. He said he saw the tears start to flow, and she turned and walked away quickly.

A doctor that was standing there walked over and put his hand on his shoulder. "Son, you are extremely lucky to be alive, but unfortunately, we were unable to save either of your legs."

"I yanked back the covers and saw the stumps and went nuts. There is no way they took my legs away from me. They held me down and shot me up with something. The next time I saw daylight, I was in a hospital room in Tampa. I refused to eat, speak, or have anything to do with anyone. Lots of physiological rehab as well as physical. I felt I was useless and no longer a man. Gone were my hopes to train others in the fine arts of battle. I felt sorry for myself but pushed ahead once the stubs I had for legs healed. I was getting pretty good at working the high-tech wheelchair they gave me. I could do wheelies and spin on a dime, but I still felt like I was useless.

Then one day, this gorgeous blond comes rolling into the dayroom in this fancy wheelchair. Her legs were gone, but, baby, everything else was still there. We both took a second to laugh and smile. She rolled over to me and said, 'So you're the one he calls Six?' I smiled as I hadn't heard that name in so long. I asked her who told her my old handle. She just smiled and told me a friend of hers who thinks I could be more than what I let myself believe. She leaned forward like she wanted a kiss. I reached out for her, excited to taste a woman's lips again. Just as I started to close my eyes, she grabbed me behind the neck and yanked me out of my chair and onto the floor. She spun around and moved away. he smiled at me and said, 'You like the floor, Six, or you gonna learn to walk like you once did, only better?'

"I looked up, puzzled and bewildered. This gorgeous woman just threw me on the floor and was taunting me. She just smiled. 'The man I was told was here thought he was the six-million-dollar man. You look like some self-pitying looser who wants no one's help.' That pissed me off, and I pulled myself toward her, but she kept moving just out of reach. She laughed, and that just made me madder. I asked her where her legs were. That's when she gave me that 'take me right now' look. 'Get your ass back in that chair and follow me.' She spun around and headed down the corridor. By the time I managed to get back up in the chair with no help, she was out of sight. I started down the hall, checking every room, when out of the far door came that blond, only this time nearly six feet tall. She walked right over and planted a kiss on my cheek.

"'Good start, soldier. Now let's see if you can go the distance.' She walked behind me and pushed me through the door and into a room that looked like a doll factory. Legs and arms were everywhere, hanging on the wall on the tables. She pushed me to a low table and told me to get on the fitting station then walked away. I sat there looking around when she walked up with a friend and strange measuring tape. They took twenty minutes and measured every part of my body, and I mean every part. She smiled and said, 'We can't have that getting damaged, as I have plans for it.' I then first noticed she had two prosthetic legs that were a match for her skin tone. She maneuvered as if they were real, and if she had on pants, I would never had known. My first legs were basic and took weeks to not only get fit and used to but to heal the blisters and raw spots they caused. Those were my fault because you know I tend to overdo when I want something. I went through four different legs, each a little better and flexible. I was getting around great and feeling good when she came up and asked me if I wanted to go jogging with her. I smiled and told her when pigs fly. She smiled and said, 'Oink, oink,' took my hand, and led me outside.

"We walked to a bench that had two sets of these metal legs that had on the end what looked like those scoops kids use to throw a ball back and forth. She strapped hers on and helped me into mine. She explained how they were experimental, 'but you got juice, so here are yours.' I stood up with her help and felt like I was on springs and needed her to steady me. They felt nothing like the standard type legs I was used to. Before she could warn me, I started out and flexed the legs like I was going to jump. I flew through the air a short ways before crashing, all the time hearing her laughing. It took days of me free falling to get the hang of a steady walk, then trot and a short run before crashing. Within a couple of months, I could outrun anyone I met at the track, including my angel Beth. These were experimental new legs that the government initially planned to strap on soldiers' feet so they could cover larger distances faster.

"That's how I found out Beth worked for the prosthetic company that designed such things with a government grant. They saw a new market in those people with double amputations as another option to the standard prothesis. That's how she got the cream job of testing the new designs and speaking for them at trade shows. Then one day, as I came around the track, there she stood with Mom. He smiled and grabbed my hand as I stopped.

"'I see my old copilot Beth has been successful.' I looked puzzled, so he went on to tell me how she had been his copilot for several months before a motorcycle accident had taken her legs while on leave. 'She is the most motivated and strong woman I know, and I knew you two would hit it off. That's why I asked her to check on you.' We all laughed and headed to dinner, never talking about the past. We talked about the unfortunate need for prosthetics keeping up with the growing need in the military for newer and better ones. How boots on the ground were bringing a whole new meaning to the injuries suffered on the battlefield. At the end of the night, we saw Mom off at the airport. Back at my place, I offered Beth a drink. As we entered the room, she pushed me back against the wall and kissed me like a woman on fire. When it broke off, she looked at me and said it was time for us to see what it's like for two legless people to screw each other's brains out. She was mostly naked under that dress as it fell. Now began my night of exploring a whole new world. Odd how it turned me on as I removed her legs and she helped me out of mine. I was awkward at first, but we were two people on a mission to try everything and anything possible for two adults. I'm telling you, it ain't as easy as you think, but great learning how again."

He told me they fell in love that night, and it was great for ten years. Then they kinda grew apart.

"I got a job like hers and spent more and more time with veteran's groups dealing with other amputees, showing them what the company had to offer. She followed her true desire for travel by starting a travel agency. She wanted to be with every group and go everywhere, but I needed to be grounded, or so I thought."

They are still good friends, but she has married and moved to Seattle.

"Me, still the poster child for fake body parts, but truly a six-million-dollar man."

I smiled and just sat there in silence. The picture of those two in bed together filled my head with pictures I didn't want to see. Then he said, "Come on, Skipper, your turn." The last he remembered of me was the look on my face when we got hit. I took a deep breath and started my story. For the next hour or so, I didn't remember the traffic or how we were traveling. I began with telling Six how I woke up on the ground with a pain that brought tears to my eyes. "My back, legs, sorry."

"No problem," he said. "I'm almost better than I was, a true six-million-dollar man."

I nodded and began.

"The hit and the crash was pretty much just a blur of screams and metal ripping apart, and then the sudden crash to the jungle floor. When my head cleared some, our package was dragging me away from the crash site, and his face was just white and expressionless. I could see some of the bodies and understood his loss. He had dragged Archie to a hole on the west side of the crash site. He needed me to help get Sam out of the wreckage and to the hole. Every step was intense pain, and I fell after a few steps. He finished putting Sam in the hole, and we went to work on you. He had a large limb under the skids, and I lay on it as he pushed down so we could get you out. I put tourniquets on both your legs, and we dragged you to the hole. He motioned for me to get in with you. and I did. He slipped in, checking to see how bad everyone was. He started covering us with branches and cover so we looked like part of the site. I never heard them, but he must have, as he pushed me all the way in and put an M16 in my hands.

"He went back to where his wife's body was just as the two guys in fatigues and cover paint entered the area. They put our friend on his knees and checked the crash site. The one came back and said something like 'Where are the others?' He hit him in the face with the butt of the gun when he said nothing. Again, he asked, and he just looked up and smiled, and my VC is not great, but I think he told him where to stick his head. With that, the guy walked away about ten feet, turned, and shot him in the head. I wanted to scream or start shooting, only I was starting to lose it from blood loss and pain. I remember the two guys standing together as they looked at the pile of cover over us. Together they bent down and looked in. I remember seeing those blue eyes and that smile as I let loose full auto inches from that smile. He screamed something when he saw me, but I was out before the slide locked back empty.

"From there, a stay in Albany, New York, at a rehab center that was attached to the medical center there. It was a good start because my aunt could visit me despite seeing me brought back memories of my cousin. My uncle had died of a heart attack while sitting in his favorite rocking chair on the front porch. Many said from a broken heart from losing his son. I met Carol, and we really connected. I could not shack the guilt despite all the head docs they sent in. Why did I survive and no one else? Why me and not you or Sam or Arch? I needed quiet and to be left alone to make my head right. So I jumped at the chance to move to a new Maine rehab unit in Portland. I spent almost a year there where my broken bones healed, and my back got fussed in a couple places. Carol and I stayed in touch, and she eventually took a job at the Portland rehab so we could be together. She was great and understood my need for seclusion and the struggle I had with my self-imposed guilt. She came from a fishing family of six that all died in a house fire that she blamed herself for back in Newfoundland. She truly understood the pain of being the only survivor. The Maine quiet life helped, but we needed more seclusion, so we hopped on the ferry and headed to Newfoundland. I bought a small boat and started an iceberg viewing business and did some fishing. To be honest, Six, I never got over the guilt of being the only one to make it."

Then I saw a tear and watched as he nodded, saying, "Me too."

Our exit came up fast as we pulled off and headed to a private road just short of Front Royal, Virginia. As we drove down the road, Six looked at me and said what we both wanted to but couldn't find the words.

"Maybe we aren't the only ones to make it back. I don't know why all his secrets, but maybe, just maybe."

We pulled up to the house and walked up to the large oak door where I slammed the huge knocker a few times. We opted not to tell Mom we were coming because we had heard enough lies. We needed to see his face. That decision might very well have saved his and our lives. The door opened, and there stood Mrs. Fowley, a beautiful woman for her age and with a full welcome smile that disappeared when she focused.

"Oh my god, oh my god, you boys are dead. I mean, I thought you were, and he said you were." She stared to get weak-kneed. Six grabbed her, and we helped her to a chair. We got to know her and became close when she made an unofficial thirty-day visit to see Mom at our base. He got her in as a missionary using her maiden name. It was him fulfilling a promise to always keep her close.

"Martha, who's at the door? I wasn't expecting guests." We heard Mom approach, and as he turned the corner, he about tripped over his feet when he saw us. Then his color left his face, and a frown appeared on that strong, weathered face. "Damn it, damn it, damn it. Oh, man, oh, man. How the hell did you two find each other? Man, oh, man, the shit will hit the fan now." He walked over to Martha first and bent down to ask her if she was all right. She drew back and let him have one clean to the chin that sent him backpedaling.

"You old bastard. You no good son of a bitch, and I knew your mother. What is going on here? What have you done?"

We all sat at the huge oak table and sipped some fine old scotch. Mom broke the ice. "I know you boys hate me, and I don't blame you. If I told you I did it to keep you alive, it would most likely not matter."

Mrs. Fowley said, "It wouldn't matter to me, you old bastard."

I looked at Mom, who was obviously very upset and just asked the obvious. "*Why?*" He sat there in silence for a few minutes. "Spooks. It was the damn spooks that had you shot down."

We looked at each other in disbelief. "What?"

He explained how those Langley bastards that were back at the doghouse not only knew about the ambush but led us right to it. We just sat there. Our mouths must have hung open.

"Why?"

His answer was the short answer, drugs and money. The long answer would take much longer.

"Drugs?"

He asked if we remembered the extraction a few nights before. The rich guy with that sexy red dress wife. Did anything about it ring a bell? Six and I looked at each other for a sec. They were similar packages, two adults and two kids. Some rich guy that bought a special ride to the US, we assumed. Mom got up and picked up this godawful looking vase. He twisted the bottom, and it came off. A thumb drive fell out.

"Gotta love this modern stuff. I got years and years of stuff on this thing." He walked over and plugged it into his laptop and keyed up something and spun it around. It was a press release showing a crash site in the jungle and a picture of the package we picked up that night in the warehouse parking lot along with his family. We both read it as our stomachs turned upside down. The vice president of the Republic of South Vietnam was killed today along with his family. A rescue mission of US special ops troops was moving him to safety from their country home when their helicopter had engine failure and crashed into the jungle. Their charred remains were recovered by ground forces that rushed to the crash site in an attempt to rescue them. The American air crew's bodies were also recovered as well. The pilot had radioed just moments before the crash that he was having engine problems. The vice president and his family will be laid to rest in an undisclosed location.

I slammed my fist down on the table. "Engine trouble my ass. That guy and his family were not the vice president. We moved him clean two nights before."

"I know," said Mom, telling us how we turned them over to our spook friends that ushered them away. "It appears our unlucky farmer and his family got a state funeral."

"I see," said Six. "They were fill-ins for the real things."

We all speculated on why all the cloak-and-dagger stuff. The vice president never would have been left behind. Mom told us how his research uncovered the rumor that the US knew of the vice president's involvement in the very lucrative drug trade.

"The VP was selling drugs?"

"Yes, tons of it under the watchful eye of CIA handlers. Nobody dared challenge the vice president and his connection to the South's army and black-market operators, so he was a good fit. He was a huge asset with not only contacts in the current administration but through strong family contacts in the North. Being the South was falling, he needed to change sides, but not as vice president. So they made it look like he died and brought him here under new identities and most likely set him up to keep the flow of drugs moving to friends of the CIA and others. It was originally set up to just get him and his family out of Vietnam safely. That part went all the way to the White House.

"Someone in the CIA came up with the new plan that satisfied everyone and gave everyone deniability. They tried to take you guys out all the way to the carrier once they found out you survived. Once we got you all on board, we let the people at Langley know what we knew and what we suspected. It was a standoff of sorts, and I had lots of people who now knew too much. So with the help of the director of the CIA, I made a deal with the devil. The deal was that I retire and stay out of it, and all my friends would just forget it happened. In return, as long as I kept quiet, you four could live. They knew they couldn't put us all down like an admiral and an assistant secretary of defense. Everyone agreed, and all records were destroyed. And as long as I kept you apart and no chance of you getting together, the whole issue would fade away. We were the wild cards, and they could not chance that if we got together, we wouldn't put two and two together. Guess that plan went to hell in a hand basket today."

"Four? What do you mean, Mom? Four of us?"

He looked down at the floor as Mrs. Fowley walked in and over to him, slapping the top of his bald head and leaving a red mark.

"Archie and Sam are still alive, aren't they? You…you—" She just turned and walked away, placing her hand on my shoulder as she passed by. We looked at each other, too confused to be mad. The explanation went on.

"It was important that we keep you separated and thinking the others were dead. My pain in the ass handler makes me aware of it every time I see him. Guess he won't ever forget being dropped into the pigpen or the thirty-six hours he spent in that locked box." Mom laughed and said, "That's a story for another time." And then he turned serious. "Guess we got to figure this out now being you two love birds found each other. This thing is still very alive in some people's eyes in the CIA. They have lived up to their part by helping set you all up and getting you the best care there was. But they knew where you guys were, and I have no doubt they know or will know that you two got together."

"I'm not sure about the skipper, but I want some payback for these plastic legs and my sucky life."

"I figured you would," said Mom, explaining that's why he agreed to separate us four and make like we were dead. Also why he kept visiting us and kept an eye on us.

"Ohhh, so all those business trips were just so much bullshit," Mrs. Fowley spit the words out.

"So now I guess the old plan B is activated."

"Bet the idea of getting away from political problems was a bit of a lie as well."

"Let's not split hairs, dear. Go get things ready." He told us he didn't blame us for being mad or hating him, but we may be in over our heads now.

"We?"

"You plan to help us in our quest for the payback?"

"Of course, I plan to help you." Our meeting would put in motion forces that would stop at nothing to eliminate the problem (us). At his age, the physical part was not what it was, but he had been secretly keeping his finger on what was going on the best he could. "I may be old, but I'm not dead yet."

"The key word is *yet*," Mrs. Fowley growled from the kitchen door. She asked us to come in and have something to eat. "Your old man can wait for leftovers, maybe."

We looked at Mom, and he motioned us away to the kitchen. He said he was too busy anyways, and besides, he needed to put his plans for this day into motion. We looked at Mom and could tell he was getting emotional. He commented that they would not take this well. They would come for him and in turn anyone close to him. He needed to make his family safe and put up the shield he had made ready for this day. It took Mom all the next day to get Mrs. Fowley to understand what was happening and what she needed to do. It didn't help that she hit Mom every time she got an opening. She left to collect their daughter around four o'clock with a real tough-looking thirty-year-old driver.

"Friend of yours, Mom?"

"Yes, his dad served with me. He got dropped from Rangers when he blew his knee out and has been plying his trade to anyone who needed it and could pay. He kinda owed me after I got him in with some Merks I know. And he also likes me, so he agreed to put his life on the line for my family."

His eyes were red, and you could see the strain was getting to him. Things were in motion or would be soon that we needed to get ahead of. Our lives and the lives of his family counted on it. We knew we needed to take the heat off us and end this damn thing now. We told him he could go protect his family and we would do the dirty work. He smiled and told us he never let us kids get too far away on a mission. He knew he needed to be there when Archie and Sam saw were alive and explain why he did what he did. He had lots of the information in his head, but those drives had it all as well.

The next day, all three of us grabbed a flight to Spokane, Washington, to look up Sam. We figured we had time to slip through Homeland Security before the CIA put us on a watch list. Apparently, we weren't on the list yet as we cleared Canadian customs together. By flying, we would most likely trigger a standard search and report order, and our friends would soon see we were together, if they didn't already know. We did not have time to drive because we feared for Sam's life if they already knew about the reunion between Six and myself. I know she can handle herself, but she also has no idea what might be coming.

After clearing the security check point while holding our breaths, we boarded our plane and breathed a sigh of relief. Once in Spokane, we rented a van and headed out to find Sam. On the way, Mom filled us in on Sam's life over the years. She had been broken in half by the impact and was paralyzed from the waist down. She had been moved from Bethesda to this little rehab center in the mountains of Washington State. There she mastered her wheelchair and new talent of computer programming and new pastime of super hacker. She had a severe skull fracture, and the doctors weren't sure how much she might lose in function, other than the paralysis. It was some kinda of miracle of sorts, they said. The brain was not damaged. Instead, it was somehow stimulated. She had taken to it like it was built into her soul. She spent hours upon hours, days, months studying her trade and mastering it. So much so the new Department of Homeland Security had put her on retainer, working antiterrorist stuff. The agency did not like it, but to pull her out or cause a scene and would only draw attention to them and their secrets, so she works to help keep the homeland safe. Like all of us, she had limited family, and after a period of remorse and guilt and therapy over being the lone survivor, she had moved on to some degree. Now the cat was out of the bag, so to speak, so everyone should know what was going on and any plans we might have, along with the option to bow out or jump in. We really didn't know how the agency would react but sure it won't be nice.

As we drove out of town, we found the small lake and the cabin right on its shore. No neighbors and lots of quiet. A minivan was parked in the driveway and a pickup closer to the house. Mom told us the minivan was Sam's, and he no idea about the pickup. As we walked up to the door, it appeared ajar. That would be very odd for Sam, Mom explained in a whisper. He motioned us to take different sides of entrance. On the trip into the mountains, he told us how she had become very private and security conscious being her line of work and her situation. He pointed out the cameras mounted around the cabin. Two were in old birdhouses that hung from the corners of the roof. Then the weathervane on the roof. It looked like a horse jumping over a small fence. If you looked closely, the fence had a round hole in the center and was in no way pointing in the direction of the wind. Mom pulled out his old faithful .45 silver plated sidearm.

"How did you get that here?" I asked.

He smiled. "It's not what you know but who." He slowly entered the living room in a practiced combat stance. There in the center of the room lay two men in jeans and wool shirts, facedown and not moving. Wires came from under them and ran over to a place near the desk. Nothing looked out of place, and then we heard that familiar sound of a shotgun being primed.

"Who the hell are you guys?" The voice came from across the room and to our rear. "You come to see why your friends were late? If you move, I'll kill you like them."

"We are the guys that always had to carry your ass home. Damn it, girl, we are looking for that special woman in our life."

She screamed, "Skipper!" We heard the gun hit the floor and the quiet hum of her electric wheelchair. She drove straight into my knees and buckled me over into her lap. She hugged me so hard then pushed me back and slapped me for all she was worth. "What are you doing alive?" Then she saw Six and she just lost it. The woman I knew that would and had cut the throats of men and killed without hesitation was a complete basket case, crying and whimpering so bad there was no understanding her. Mom tried to hug her, but she pushed him away and spun off toward the porch that overlooked the lake. "Take care of that spook mess I made over there before they wake up, and then get the hell out of my house."

She moved out on to the porch and to the rail, looking at the lake as the fog seemed to be rolling across the opposite bank. We tied and gagged the two men just as they were waking up and pulled the wires out the stun gun had left. Dragging them to their truck, we looked at each other, trying to decide our next move when she made it for us. On the back porch, she sat staring at the lake and yelled out, "You people owe me some serious answers! Get your asses in here and start talking." About an hour later, she had the basic story of that day in the jungle and where we had been and why Mom kept it a secret. "Well, I guess that dog don't swim anymore being I had these two visitors."

"What happened to those guys?" I asked.

She told us how they knocked on her door and asked if they could come in and use the phone. Cell service here sucked, and they said their friend's jeep had gotten stuck and they couldn't pull it out. She had asked why they were up here, and they told her hunting white tail, which would have made them poachers as the season ended a week ago. She told them no and offered to call someone for them, but they just pushed their way in. They told her it wasn't personal and it was just company business as they approached her, standing side by side. She told them she understood, but that it was personal to her, patting the arms of her wheelchair. Each one had a hole in the end of the arm rest, and she told us they were hit with her own designed stun guns. At the different level of a standing man and a wheelchair, it meant they took a direct crotch hit. She smiled and said only these had settings from turned on, to knocked out, to wasted.

"I used a low setting because I wanted to have a talk with them." She patted the keypad mounted to her chair. "I had to disconnect from them when I saw you drive up." She pointed to an array of displays showing views around the property and house. "Girl living alone needs to be careful."

Mom smiled and explained we needed to beat feet out of here. Those guys would have backup, and they would be here soon if they didn't check in. We helped Sam get what she needed and packed in our van. "I need to have a discussion with our friends." I opened the truck door and pulled one out by his hair. His head hit the sidestep as he came out, unable to catch himself. He made comment about my real mother, and I took exception. I placed my foot on his tender crotch and stepped down. My questions were direct and short. Who sent them? Why the hit on Sam? And how many of them were there?

He squirmed and screamed as I placed more pressure on him. He yelled out, "It was a sanctioned hit from the company, and there were no others!" I knew it was a lie because they always used redundant teams in case of a problem. I was interested now in knowing more, so we got down to business. Having heard enough, I left him on the ground and returned to the others near our van.

"They know your minivan, so we gotta get rid of it quick." We needed to secure clean wheels, but they would be watching all our credit cards. I was sure they must have picked us up on security cameras at the airport. I used my credit card for the van because I never expected them to be that quick. Sam raised her hand, holding several credit cards. She told us they were clean as she made them herself. The payments were made direct from several government agencies.

"I've kinda been doing my part for payback because I never really liked this whole deal."

Mom opened the van side door and looked back. "So it's time to go find Archie and get this payback train on track?"

Sam smiled from ear to ear. We looked at each other and said in unison, "Archie is still alive too."

We loaded up what electronic stuff Sam needed in the van and the minivan. We pulled the spooks over to a large tree and bound the agents to it in the front yard. Mom explained to them what it would be like if he saw them again. They both looked truly afraid, and one was wet where he must have peed himself.

"Is there anything else you need inside or we need to destroy?"

Sam looked up and smiled. "I'm a woman who knows how to clean up." Sam typed into one of her laptops. "You will see a real show soon."

We would need to get a different vehicle and drive to Mexico as the airports would be watched after today. We headed into town to make our arrangements to go get our last member. We pulled over when Sam asked, and we all huddled around her and her laptop. We could see the two men struggling to get free. Soon one was free, and he helped both of them out of the ropes. "Awww, I hoped they would just sit still and enjoy the show." The camera in the abandoned bird's nest in the large pine near the cabin gave us a clear view of the cabin and men. "No, no, stay away from the house." Sam spoke like they could hear her. "Who are those guys, Skipper? Did they say?"

I told them they were private contractors and thought they were real tough guys. They came to kill Sam and collect all her hardware. Just some private dirt team that knew we weren't going to kill them, so they got chatty. They were playing macho until the one said they got the good draw being they got the sexy cripple.

"Shut up," the other one said, but the guy just kept talking. He told me how the other guys got some old broad and her kid. "Shut up, you fool. Over there is the colonel." I kind got mad and shoved his own .9mm down his throat till he couldn't breathe. Lost a couple teeth and wet his pants like the other, which brought a short chuckle from everyone. It appeared that all bets were off, and they are coming for us and Mom's family.

The two men were free now and slowly approached the house, hoping they could find important information inside and salvage this humiliation. One had his cell phone out and was talking to someone as they crossed the doorway and entered the cabin. It was a good bet they were discussing what they were going to do to us when they next found us.

"Nothing personal guys. Just business." We looked at Sam and then the screen. A white mist or fog surrounded the cabin and encased it in a cloud as it came from vents underneath the cabin. The cloud enveloped the cabin, turned from pure white to a darkening black, then a flash of bright red and a huge fireball. "There. Clean as a whistle." And she closed the laptop. "Should we get back to your family and protect them?" Sam asked.

"No need. They are safe by now, and I have no idea where they are. We have a system when it comes time. Can't torture out of me what I don't know."

I asked Mom if we should call and warn Archie that the company hunters were looking for us. He said no and it would be fine because the last anyone knew, Archie was in Nevada, a pastor for a small church.

"Church. Pastor?" I almost fell over, and Sam and Six just looked on in a daze. Archie was a good man but had no issue blowing up or shooting a man while looking into his eyes through a scope. He specialized in helping people meet their maker, not talk to them. Mom went on to tell us that after a very long rehab, the guilt had broken this huge black man. His body healed fast and left no lasting problems. He had found his way to Canada to a private center for spiritual healing once he was up and about. He believed he was spared for a reason, and his father had been a Baptist minister, so that seemed to be a draw him to a higher being for comfort.

"When I told him the story of how he woke up in the morgue on board the ship, he saw it as another sign he could not overlook." He had no memory of that happening or anything before he woke up in the hospital. The fact he had been pronounced dead and would have been prepared for a flag-draped casket was an even stronger sign to him. A sign he was kept here on earth for a higher purpose. The kicker that sent him down the path of the ministry was when he slipped into a coma shortly after reaching the hospital in Nevada. Mom had just left him after filling him in on his rebirth. They told him that he was just sitting there and slumped over. It was four long years before he woke again. The doctors were stumped as to what caused the coma or why he just woke up again. There was some memory loss, and the doctors said to let things just progress at their own pace.

"The last we spoke, he did not remember anything from the war or how he got to where he was that day. I filled him in on some stuff, but no real details. He had a little church near Reno, but I know he was headed to Mexico. Seems this little Mexican girl had been dropped off at his church by her mother. He later found out she was killed in Mexico in a small town, San Elizario, and the little girl still had grandparents there." On Mom's last visit, he said if he called him in Nevada and there was no answer, then that's where he would be. No one knew of it but Mom.

First Sam and Mom rented a stretch van with Sam's card and used a local assisted care facility as the renter to help cover their change of vehicles. Six and I took Sam's car and our rental van to a less than high rent area of Spokane and parked them in a lot near several noisy bars. We left the keys in the ignition so the drunks wouldn't have to look too hard. Sam double-checked with her super laptop to make sure the LoJack was working well. It just stood to reason that these guys had the ability to track her car. Letting it get stolen would give them some false hits for a while to slow them down. We walked several blocks and caught a cab back to an area near where the other two were waiting. After getting the van, they returned to the midlevel motel where we had unloaded all Sam's gear. Once Six and I had walked the mile back to the motel we loaded up our stuff and headed for Interstate 5. The ride was long, and we took turns driving while all the time going over the past and what turn our lives had taken getting there. After twenty-four hours of old girlfriends and boyfriends and relationships, it was clear we were all scared from that day in the jungle. It was also clear we were healing, now that all the guilt was gone and now nothing but questions remained.

Sam started her story of the past years with the last thing she remembered that day in the jungle. Everything was like in a fog and slow motion. She remembered the trees spinning around us then the hard stop. Funny, as she had very little pain except in her head. It was like someone was cutting the top of her head off. "Those damn berets never did do much to protect us." She laughed. Then being dragged, and the next was the smell of the hospital. She could not understand what people were saying, but they did keep pushing her to open her eyes. Then one day, she did. The first thing she saw was the sky outside her room. She could never remember seeing such a beautiful blue. A nurse came in and called for a doctor, and several of them came running in. It seemed she was some kind of special case for them. She laughed again.

"Later that day, they told me I had been in a coma of sorts for five months, fading in and out from time to time. Once fully awake, they began test after test on my motor skills and my mental cognition. They said my brain was not only good but seemed to be better. I don't know how that could be." She chuckled. "Everyone was shocked because my type of depressed skull fracture often caused serious brain damage. Guess they didn't know how great I was before." She had taken the news about her back not so good. She told us she wouldn't talk with anyone and started her own pity party for one. Then one day, she was in the dayroom sitting alone, and this little boy of about twelve came rolling in. He was in the corner and deep in thought as he read his book. He would laugh and then turned to her one day.

"Hey, you want some ice cream?" he yelled. She didn't know what to say, as she had shut down. He just laughed and said, "Chocolate it is." He looked around and pushed himself over to the nurse's station, which was always empty. Around to the desk side, he went and reached up and typed something into the computer. Then he rolled back to his corner and went back to his game. In about fifteen minutes, an orderly showed up with two cups of chocolate ice cream. After he left, she built up the nerve to ask the little boy how he did that. He rolled over and handed her a cup and spoon and smiled. His dad was a computer programmer and built his own computers. He would teach him things, and he would watch and learn and read all he could. He saw the nurse order his lunch one day on that terminal, so he just played around and found the patient food service page. "The rest is pure chocolate." He laughed.

"He told me the secret to computers was to not be afraid of them. They were still very new, and most programmers make lots of mistakes. Mistakes were the future breakthroughs, his father always told him." For the next few weeks, he and Sam would fool around and race up and down the halls and eat ice cream. Afternoons and nights, he would let Sam work on his computer, a present from his father.

"I bet you knuckle draggers still use floppy discs like the ones I learned on."

Mom laughed and replied. "*Watch it, little lady. I got lots of those thumb drive thingies.*"

We all broke into laughter, which was great to break the mood. Sam went on with her story. One day she asked him where his dad was so she could thank him and how she wanted to meet him. That was not a good move. His smile disappeared, and he pushed away.

"I let it go, and he didn't talk to me for a long time, days. I took his advice and read about programming and coding computers as it sounded like it might be a good fit for me. It appears that the head injury I have must have woken up a part of my brain I didn't know I had. I could remember things like it just happened or it was just said, almost a photographic memory."

At first it was a curse that kept her up at night, then a challenge to turn it on and off as the subject deemed. Then one day, the little boy rolled into her room.

"He smiled and said he was sorry he didn't talk to me. He was leaving to go live with his aunt and uncle in North Carolina in a few weeks. He wanted to thank me for being his friend. He started to leave then stopped and turned to me. 'My dad was in the same car crash that put me in here. He was killed along with my mom and sister.' After the tears stopped for both of us, he went on to explain. Some guy that was all messed up on drugs hit them head on. He had woken up in the hospital, his back broken and all alone for the first time in his life. I could see the tears in his eyes and felt mine coming back. I rolled over to him and hugged him for a long time." They spent the next two weeks talking, playing, learning on the computer, and eating chocolate ice cream. "Then one day he gave me a paper with a phone number on it, which was where he was staying. He kissed my cheek and rolled away."

Well, from there it was like she had mission in life. She went to college, thanks to Uncle Sam, and took a ton of other courses. She graduated the head of her class and got a free ride for her master's and then PhD. She went to work for a programing company right out of the gate and spent all her time becoming the best.

Six covered his mouth and tried to sound like an intercom. "Calling Dr. Sam. Calling Dr. Sam. You're needed at the bar." Without thinking how close he sat to Sam, he took an open hand to the side of his face. I laughed so hard my stomach hurt. When we all calmed down, we let her finish her story.

It was like the crash set her on a new course. Before she fell from the sky, she had over seventy confirmed kills. She was respected as well as feared as most Special Forces members were and should have been. "Of course, it took lots of getting used to having a chair attached my ass twenty-four seven." She hit Six on the shoulder. "Just like it must have been for you, stubby."

He turned like he was mad but just smiled and said, "Glad you're back too."

I turned to Mom and asked the question everyone wanted to hear. Why the whole thing with the company, and why didn't they just kill us off and be done with it? They knew Mom was involved along with some other big players.

"I also told them I had a copy of all the communications and statements that would be automatically released to the *news media* if anything happened to you guys." Nobody wanted any more bad press than what they were already getting. Too many people in that big White House, and those alphabet agencies had skin in the game. He had no idea who changed the deal and started this. He had been quietly looking for answers but had to be very careful. There were others looking into it for him, but he couldn't say just then. He had no idea where the fancy-pants vice president ended up but was sure someone did, and he wanted to know.

The worst thing for Mom was they that put that puke from the pigpen in place as his handler. As far as the rest of the story, he had not been able to learn all that much more. He was sure they used those poor farmers' bodies to fill the caskets of that drug lord bastard and his family. He had asked some questions of his friends, and that flying pig showed up at midnight at his house and warned him to stop looking. He made it crystal clear his family would suffer along with him if he kept looking into the whole mess. "He also made it abundantly clear they knew where you four were, and he personally would enjoy putting you away." He told Chief what had happened and that he should not look into anything further. He was pretty sure he broke the rules and started looking into it as the flying pig made the comment, "Indians can be scalped as well." Chief did say he found some good intel, but he never passed it on.

"We might want to make a stop in Oklahoma someday and ask him. He went off the grid as soon as I gave him the news of my visit from the spook."

We stopped in San Antonio to recharge our bodies and get some supplies. Sam's cards got us some rooms where we could stretch out and sleep. To avoid bringing any attention to the four of us, we got separate hotels and only those with a four-star rating. When people are running, they always look for quiet out-of-the-way dives. Big mistake, as they were the first one's checked if someone was looking, not those four-star hotels with all their services and perks. We all met at Mom and my hotel and headed to the pool and hot tub.

As we approached the spa, we could see Sam and Six sitting at a table next to the hot tub. Six lifted Sam out of her chair and on to the edge of the tub, then took off his prosthesis and slipped in with her. Even at her age, her body was perfect and toned to a point that would make any woman envious.

"Come on in, guys," she said. "Lots of room for you two."

I smiled and started to take off my shirt to get in. Mom said he had some things to do that he hoped would make our run into Mexico easier. He was going to reach out to a friend or two to see what they might be able to do to help. Once he was gone, Sam asked about his wife, Martha, and daughter. Jamie. "Won't they try and grab them up to hurt Mom?"

We told her that before we left, he made a call, and a nasty-looking ex-Ranger showed up and took them away. All Mom had told us was that they would be taken to a super safe house that Mom had set up in case this ever happened. The Ranger would stay with them and protect them with his life until he was relieved at some point. They would be okay, and the rest of us had no close family members to worry about. We hoped that at some point, we could sort all this out. With any luck, we could find a solution and hopefully end the bullshit.

"Did they know this day might come?" Sam asked, still not sure how to take all this.

We said that we thought so from Mrs. Fowley's reaction to being whisked off. She knew they might have to go underground one day, but honestly did not know it involved us still being alive. She was just like Mom, and I think so was Jamie, although none of us had ever met her. Mom explained to them that if they were taken, it would mean Mom's death and ultimately theirs because he would never let them be hurt. The plan must have been put in place years ago, and Mom had told us he had no idea where they were going. There was a complicated procedure for him to contact them and verify his being alive and another to set up the hopeful reuniting of them all. We all agreed we would do whatever it took to end this show and get all our lives back to some level of normalcy.

The next morning, we were up and moving by 6:00 a.m. We called Sam and Six to let them know we were coming to pick them up. Six told us to take our time as Sam was on her laptop talking with someone and typing like her fingers were on fire. She didn't know when she would have solid internet service again, so she needed to get some things going. When he asked who she was talking to, Six said she would only say she was following the Yellow Brick Road.

We stopped at a McDonald's that was on our way to the border. After the last fast-food meal we would have for a while, we moved out. As we headed down Interstate 35 toward Laredo, everyone was quiet and deep in thought. Then Six broke the ice. "How are we getting into Mexico?" We had grabbed our passports being Six and I were in Newfoundland and the other two had theirs, but they were in our real names. If the company had put our names out, the borders would be the first place.

"I know," said Mom. "That's why we get in line at nine p.m. sharp and stay in row 3." He went on to tell us how after he left us last night, he went to see a friend. This friend had an uncle who still worked for the Border Patrol on the Nueva Laredo side. A great guy he had served with and told him many times to stop by. He told stories of how his uncle was building his nest egg with a six-figure income that sure didn't come from the Mexican government. Not many people trying to smuggle things into or get into Mexico, so everyone can be bought, no questions. If the US was looking for someone leaving the States, they let the Mexicans make the stop at their checkpoint and hold for a US border agent arrest. The new immigration policies were all designed on keeping people out and not so much on keeping them in. He had made the call and were expected, pro-bono so to speak. "I'm not lying. Getting back out of Mexico could be an issue," Mom announced.

We left the parking lot of Walmart and headed straight to the border crossing. We stopped at one of those self-storage places and unloaded most of the equipment from Sam's house. We also left the weapons we had secured from the hit team and those Mom had brought. We did not want any problems if things went wrong, as we could always claim to be a bunch of missionaries headed across to preach to the people. We had found a sign maker the day before that made us two vinyl signs that read "Phoenix Baptist Church." We had placed them on the side of the van on a side road we found. At this point, we didn't think Mom's babysitter knew of Archie's home in Mexico, but they would start at the borders in case we were looking to get out of the USA. That would bring its own issues as the company might have us on a hold as a persons of interest list. As we approached the US side of the border, it was obvious that people leaving for Mexico were not scrutinized anywhere near as much as those coming in. On the US side, each car in front of us stopped or was motioned ahead or just sent through. If they were stopped, the guard would take their passport and ask them to answer the few standard questions. Where you from? Where are you going in Mexico and why? The US Customs Agency started interviewing people that were leaving the US more thoroughly right after 911. Basically, just to check IDs and collect data and look for fleeing fugitives as they did not trust our friends south of the border to be too thorough.

When it was our turn, everyone held their breaths. The guard looked angry, and he stared at us all, walked around the van, and looked like he was going to make us get out. He took the passports over to the scanner and passed each one through as if he were checking them. When he came back, he handed them to Mom and, for the first time, smiled. "There is a stop and hold issued for three men and a woman. Damn it, Mom, who did you piss off now?"

"You know me never start the fight," Mom said and laughed.

He stepped back and waved us through. "Good luck."

"Who was that, Mom?" I asked.

"He was one of the first FART unit leaders I had before you guys. I called him before we left my house on a burner phone. He is as brave and loyal American as there ever was. He never asked why or anything other than if I need his help for anything else. I told him I would let him know. His help had already put him in some danger. No need compounding it."

As we made our way closer to the Mexican checkpoint inspectors, we all started to sweat, not used to this type of pressure for some time. As we pulled into the little booth, a Mexican Border Guard walked up and reached out for our passports. We all became tense and were afraid he would see it in our faces. Mom handed them over and watched as the guard started to open the first one.

Just then, another guard stepped over and said, "Oh, thank you, my friend, for holding down things for me." He handed him a brown bag with the neck of a bottle peeking out. The guard smiled and turned away as he tasted his prize. "Well, Senor Fowley, glad to see you made it. I told our friend there I needed to piss so he covered for me. The bottle will make him forget you ever were here." When he laughed, he showed perfect teeth, a bonus from his extra income. He took our passports and went into the little shed where the electronic readers were kept. If we got flagged there, it not only meant our arrest, it would go to bite Mom's friend on the US side. Mom instantly became on edge and felt we had been betrayed. From the back, Sam could see through the window and told Mom to relax. The guy had a smut magazine over the reader. He came back and handed them to Mom. He explained he had to make it look like he checked them because of the bosses. They had told them that morning there was a stop and hold on three men and a woman who might want to go to Mexico. "Take care, my friend. My nephew says he owes you his life, so I also owe you a debt as well. When you return, I can get you past the Mexican side, but those gringos will not be so easy. They rotate them at random times and pairs. Guess they figure our exporters might bribe them. Good luck, my friend, and good hunting." He backed off and waved us through.

As we departed the border checkpoint, Mom cleared his throat and said, "There is one thing you guys should know about Archie. When he woke and met his long-term caregiver, he promised her he would go back with her to San Elizario in Mexico. He would do whatever he could to help her brother and the rest of her family come to the States. Her brother was the priest of a little church just outside San Elizario where her parents were from and she lived till they sent her to live with friends in Reno. It is a dirt-poor area with lots of crime and controlled by the local cartels. Maria had been his caregiver for the whole time and the first person he saw when he finally opened his eyes. Guess that's why he latched on to her, and the rest was history." Mom had visited him on and off, but not in some time as the doctors wanted him to regain what memory he could on his own. He did remember him, but not really from where or how, which Mom felt worked well as he started his new life. "So don't be shocked if he does not remember any of you or what happened or is the least bit interested in vengeance." He told us he had not really been in contact with Archie for over six years until the two calls he had made to him last year.

The streets were dirty, and many of its residents seemed to just be walking around without purpose or interest in these four gringos in the dusty van. It was a shame that this dusty hole of a city was so near one of the main crossings with the United States to the north. Everywhere you looked, there was an old school bus parked or rattling down the road, leaving an oil-smoked cloud. I looked around and laughed. I had always wondered where old school buses went when they died back home. Guess that was the elephant graveyard of all yellow school busses. We saw many cops and a few troops driving around or walking in pairs. They gave us little attention as if a van load of US Baptists was no big deal here. Many churches from the United States and other countries wandered around Mexico. We soon left the downtown area and headed south toward San Elizario and whatever we would find there. It was hot, and the air-conditioner barely kept the inside cool. The road was straight and potholed with some dirt fit in here and there. Along the way, we saw old abandoned vehicles of all shape and sizes. As we approached this little village, we saw an old mission on a small hill. It looked like those you would see in the old Italian westerns that we all used to love. In the courtyard were several kids playing soccer with a semi flat ball. They were dirty and looked like they could use a good meal. A taller and older boy was talking to them and started to push some of them around as we got closer. We saw this tall black man in brown robes approach the boy and give him a swift kick in the ass.

"That's gotta be Archie!" Six yelled.

As we pulled in and exited the van, we must have been a something to see. Three men in wrinkled cloths and a wheelchair-bound woman strolling across the hard-packed dirt courtyard. Sam grabbed an old basketball as it rolled near her and started toward the basket, a barrel ring nailed to the side of a shed. The bully from before approached Sam, telling her in broken English that it was his ball and to give it back.

She smiled and said, "Block my shot and it's yours. If not, you will have to clean up the garbage around this courtyard."

He smiled and lunged at her just as she spun the chair right, then left, and then made a one-handed shot with her left hand, moving the chair with her right. The ball went up and through the ring without ever touching the wall. The bully looked puzzled and smiled an evil grin. He walked over and stood there in Sam's face.

He said, "Too bad you can't make me do the cleanup." Suddenly, he was on his knees. Sam twisted his wrist back and forced him to his knees.

Archie walked up, looked down on the boy, and told him to mind his manners and pay his bet. He reached to shake Sam's hand and then pulled it back. A pained look in his face made his confusion evident. "You look so familiar. So familiar." Then Six walked up and put his hand on Sam's shoulder. Archie's face was getting red out of confusion and anger as he struggled to put a name to the faces before him. He wanted, needed to put a name to these people he must know. It was ripping him apart, knowing he should recognize these new strangers. Then it was my turn on Sam's opposite side. He looked at each of us, puzzled but calm now. His eyes showed that we had touched something in his memory.

Next, Mom walked up directly behind Sam with his hands on her shoulders. "Minnow team report."

Without hesitation, we yelled, "Skipper go!"

"Sam go!"

"Six go!"

And without hesitation, we all heard him say, "Go" in a low hushed voice. Then he smiled and yelled, "Archie go, go, go!" He smiled then grabbed his head with both hands as if someone had just hit him, turned, and ran for the mission.

I started to chase after him, but Mom yelled, "Stand down, everyone! This has to be a real shock to his system. Let's give him some space."

We all knew he was right, so we headed to the van to grab some water and kill some time. The courtyard bully was picking up papers and other pieces of trash. He worked his way over to us by the van and, in his toughest voice, called us out. "Who are you to come here and make my padre cry?" He caught us off guard, but Sam recovered first.

"He is our friend. No, part of our family. He cried because we all thought that the others were dead."

We all sat around the large table on benches that had been repaired beyond their usefulness. Archie held his head in his hands and just kept saying, "Why, why, why? I pray every day asking for what reason am I here. There was a huge hole in my life and my heart, but now..." He did not remember till just then, and it was coming back in wave upon wave. He didn't know what was real or if his mind was just playing tricks on him again. He said the last true memory he had of us was being in the chopper and the loud explosion. Then nothing till Maria was washing his face and that smile, that wonderful smile. Mom told him a surface to air missile had caused that explosion that he remembered so vividly. We explained how the spooks back at the headquarters had set us up. After the story of the head spook falling out of Mom's chopper and into the pigpen. Then after Mom told how Chief stood on the struts holding a crop of his hair, Archie laughed for the first time. His laugh brought back so many good memories, and we all joined in. After a bit of fun, Mom told him of the two company men at Sam's. He went on to tell him how they told me they were sent there to kill her. Also, how another team was after his wife and daughter. Archie took it all in and just sat there. Mom went on to give him the short version of a drug dealing politician that had made a deal with someone to disappear. Archie accepted the information without any questions or change in expression.

He took his hand and pointed outside. "See that beautiful little girl on that tire swing? Her mother and uncle were killed by the drug traffickers in this crap hole of a country. It's the same here as in Vietnam. They suck the life out of everyone to feed their selfish fat bellies and fancy homes."

"What happened?" Six asked, his head down and in a low caring voice.

Archie explained how Maria was one of his faithful parishioners back in the States. He had looked her up when I returned from Canada and opened his own small church. She had cared for him those many years and was a faithful part of my new life. She became pregnant and gave birth to a beautiful little girl which Archie dedicated his time to when he could. He never asked about the father or any details. Then one day, she just disappeared. She left him a note to look after her baby till she returned, which for him was a no-brainer.

He found out in time she had returned to San Elizario. She hoped she could talk her grandparents and her brother into coming back to the United States with her. She had often talked about going back to Mexico where her brother was a priest in her hometown and where her grandparents still lived. She felt she needed to go there and make her case to them and convince her brother he could find a perish in the Reno area. She knew the drug trafficking was going on and that they ran the whole area. She was afraid for her grandparents but more so for her brother, who she knew would not bow down to the cartels. She saved up her money and headed down on her mission.

Her body was found some three3weeks later in a ditch outside of the town. The local police, cartel owned, said she had been beaten and sexually abused before the bullet that killed her. Kidnapping was not uncommon here, and especially women. They were not taken for ransom, as these people had nothing to pay. They were just taken for the thugs' pleasure. Those that fought too hard ended up dead; the others ended up working in the local whorehouses. As for her, she was forced to work as a drug mule, taking drugs to the border to be moved across to the US. In order to keep US politicians happy, the local military and the DEA made raids now and then to show how they were working together to stem the flow. Arch laughed. So ten locals died that night in a firefight. Odd, because only two of the ten had guns, and they were empty. None of those that died were involved in the drug trade, at least not willingly. Those poor souls were nothing more than a photo op for the politicians in Washington and Mexico City. Maria's body was found several days after that raid but was just added to the total of those bad drug runners the DEA took out. He had mourned the first woman he saw when he woke, which had made her much more than a friend.

"She was so much more to me than a nurse or caregiver." She had talked to him for hours while he lay there in a coma, and he was sure she was what made him come back to life. As far as the padre goes, her brother, he did not show for services about five months prior to Archie's arrival. Everyone's best guess was that one of the drug lords had taken care of him. He was constantly asking for answers to his sister's death, and that alone was enough for him to disappear.

The fact he was the local padre just made it worse as the only person people listened to after the drug lords was their padre. From there, it was a short walk for Archie to the pulpit of that rundown church we could see around us. Archie felt he should take Maria's daughter back to her mother and what family she had there. When he arrived and her parents told him what had happened, he wanted to turn around and go back to the US. But Maria's daughter clung to her grandparents as they did her. Not sure if he could have changed things if he had gotten there sooner, and that would always haunt him. The small church without a padre was another sign to him that he should stay and look after the rest of the small village. He made himself at home and went to great lengths to avoid any contact or issues with the cartels. Constant guilt ate at him as he saw and heard so much yet did nothing to change it.

We then heard a horn in the distance. Archie got up and told us all to please stay inside and away from the windows. There was trouble coming. It would be okay. He would deal with it. He got up and went to the edge of the town with a group of women and old men and children. The clean new Chevy pickup drove up and stopped in a cloud of dust and dirt. The passenger got out, and two men in the back jumped down and reached back in for something. They pulled on this old tarp and let it fall out of the truck to the ground. A woman dropped to her knees and screamed. It was her husband. We could see from our place on the roof walkway that it was a man bloodied and covered in mud. Archie walked over to one of the men and said something and received a rifle butt to the stomach for his trouble. The other two each took turns hitting Archie and kicking him down as the driver laughed. The bully from earlier in the basketball court tried to pull them off Archie and was hit in the head with a rifle butt and fell back.

He got up despite the blood covering his face and screamed at the boss, "You killed my father and took my mother! Now you beat my friend, the padre. What gives you the right?"

The leader smiled with his missing teeth and walked over to the side of the truck where everyone could see him. He said, "This does."

And he drew his pistol and shot Jesus, still laughing. Jesus fell to the ground and was motionless. We were sure he was dead.

It was then, out of the corner of our eyes, we saw Six walking across the road to where they had Archie. Just behind him was Sam in her chair, making for the group. They had been downstairs, and we never saw them leave. Two of them had pulled Archie to his knees when they saw the new players coming toward them. They let Archie fall back and went to meet these new nosy people. Mom and I ran to get better positions to help our friends when the shit started, which no doubt was coming.

"Stop there, gringos. This is not your business."

Sam piped up, "Yes, it is. That monk is a good friend of mine."

"Oh really? Listen to the crippled bitch telling us what to do."

Six started toward them, talking about their mother's poor choice in men when one of them shot Six in the right leg. He spun around and went down in a heap. Sam yelled to him, and Archie lifted his head to see his old friend go down. He later told us a sense of rage had come over him to a point he didn't even think what he was doing. Their backs to Archie, the two of them never saw him struggle to stand. As he did catch his balance, he pulled their machetes from the sheaths on their belts. Feeling the tug on their belts, they spun in time to see the razor-sharp machetes coming across at neck level. He raised them between them and swung them right and left. Their bodies and heads fell in different directions. As he finished, he was in a crouched stance. He stood, spun, and threw the machetes at the remaining two men. One hit dead center in the passenger from the truck, as it was meant to. The other just grazed the driver as he spun away in time. He reached for his gun when suddenly a single sharpened stick came pushing through his chest from behind. It was the wife of the man that lay dead in the street where they had thrown him. She kept pushing and screaming till the driver fell forward, dead, held up by the stick in his chest. By then, we had come off the roof and met up with everyone at the truck. We helped steady Archie, and Mom started him back. I carried Jesus back to the church. Sam was helping Six limp back as he used her chair to steady himself. Arch told us we needed to clean up the square and hide the truck and bodies. I went back out, and with some help from the locals, we loaded the bodies in the back of the truck. After we located all the parts from the players, we parked in an old shed behind a rundown house. The woman went about cleaning the blood with buckets of water and sweeping away the tracks that led to the shed. These people worked without a sound but with the passion of knowing it had to be done. Several older men had brought a wheelbarrow and were taking the body of the woman's husband to their house. Soon to be another wooden cross in the church cemetery, which was filling quickly.

When Archie saw Six walking back with a slight limp and no blood, he looked puzzled till Six smiled and dropped his pants. His shiny skin-colored "walk-around legs" that he called them looked wet in the sun. There was hole in the left one from the shot he took. "Glad it didn't hit anything too important. A little Bondo and she'll be good as new."

Archie just shook his head, knowing there was a story coming as Six never told him of his injuries. Jesus had taken a bullet in the shoulder, but it was in and out and appeared not to have hit anything of importance. We put him in a bed in Archie's room and let him rest. The local doctor would come and do what he could, but not till way after dark. The cartels made it clear to him their needs would always come before the peasants. After some bread and water and dried chicken, Archie broke the silence.

"I'm afraid I have started a fire that will burn this town down. When those men do not return to their boss, they will send many more looking for them. When they find out what I have done, they will kill many of who are here."

"Bullshit," I said. "You have turned the other cheek for too long, Archie. You would have let them kick you till you were dead."

"You don't need to be part of this, but when they come back it will be their last ride, I will make sure of that." Everyone shook their heads and added their thoughts. We asked him who the hell were they and what was with the dead local guy. Archie took a deep breath. "They work for Sanchez, a local drug lord who moves tons of drugs each month."

The farmer was most likely taken to work in the drug labs or shops and fields. He must have broken a rule or tried to escape and was beaten to death in front of the others to set an example. They promised to smuggle men and boys to the States and then just take them to work the trade. No one misses them as they think they are either in the US or detention. We asked how many would be back and what if we hid the bodies and truck.

"They will send a few to look for the first four but will grow suspicious after a few days for sure. We could tell them they dropped the body off in the road and then headed out to drink. That will cover a day or so, but they would return with fifteen to twenty guns as they cannot tolerate people challenging their control. They know the men were headed here, so they will start looking for them here. So we need a plan. Leaving these poor people to suffer for our actions is not an option."

We talked and threw out some ideas as we felt time was not with us. We all felt guilty we could not intervene in what happened to Archie or Jesus. It was not like us to sit on our hands. Six and Sam didn't hesitate, which made me feel worse. Mom sat on me, reminding me we were outnumbered and had no weapons to play with. Just then, Archie came in and told us Jesus was resting well and would be fine in time. The doctor said it was a clean in and out, and there appeared to be no real damage.

Mom looked up and asked Arch, "What is our next move? When will more of those assholes be back?"

Archie made it clear he didn't expect the four of us to get into his fight. He killed those men, and he'd face the consequences in order to protect the people that made him their padre.

As if we practiced it, we all said at once, "Like hell you will."

He explained that we had other issues with the CIA looking for us and hunting the four of us down. Mom laughed and told Archie he meant the five of us. He was now in the same boat as the rest of us, a loose end. We explained that the company had no idea we were in Mexico, let alone all reunited, or so we hoped. Besides, Mom was working on a way to kill a whole bunch of birds with one big stone.

We all had no idea what he was talking about, but like always, we trusted him completely.

First things first, we needed lots of firepower and transport. Mom smiled and said, "We need to find a way that makes this all seem like something else." That just confused us, but we knew more was coming. Archie said we needed to make this look like a war between the two cartels to avoid any payback on the villagers. Mom nodded in agreement, and we now understood a little of what they had planned. It was time to collect what intel we had and formulate a plan. We all sat around the table as Archie filled us in on the everyday life in San Elizario. He explained how the people were under the thumbs of two cartels. There had been an uneasy peace between the two, but each kept to their own business and territories. The other major cartel would be the Chavez cartel. We decided it was time for that peace between the Chavez and Sanchez cartels to end. If we could make them fight each other, we could then wait and just clean up whatever was left. First, we decided to have the truck moved to an area that was controlled by the Chavez cartel. We could have the bodies laid out in a way that looked like they had been ambushed. We needed an out-of-the-way place because the bodies were showing signs of age. A young woman, very unattractive woman, which was why the drug people left her alone, knew of a perfect place. It was in the Chavez area but was not traveled often, and there was an old barn where they could set the scene. That was a good start and would take the heat off the village for now, but we needed to do more. We needed to make more waves on both sides so the gears of war would start to grind. There was no way we could do this without enlisting some help at some point. Mom suggested there was no one better than the ones hunting us from back home.

We were all puzzled, but Mom just kept smiling and said, "In time, you'll see."

We also had to admit that most of us were a bit out of shape and practice, so not a real match for a hundred plus gun toting drug smugglers. Then there was the small issue of no cash to buy guns and supplies, let alone a place to do so. The credit cards we had were useless when buying guns, as most gun dealers were cash only for obvious reasons. Sam had a smile on her face that made it glow. "Let's let the bad guys finance their own funeral. These jerks must have lots of cash around for the taking, so let's take it."

We all smiled, and Mom said, "I like it." Then on cue, "Man, oh, man, let's find the bank and make a withdrawal."

The next day, as we were putting the final touches on our plans, we heard another pickup come into the center of town with the head of the Sanchez's dirty little drug army. They stopped in the center of the square and blew the horn. Odd that he would come with just a one guard for protection. His arrogance would be his undoing. He jumped out and yelled to the people, "Come out! I mean you no harm. I look for information on the murder of my men by those Chavez dogs. I know they were here and brought you the body of the coward that tried to flee our generosity." It had not taken long for the bodies of the men to be found near a barn which was used by Chavez's men for a party place. We had placed them there the night before and made it look like an execution had occurred. Archie saw him and went into his office and came then came out into the street and walked to the truck. He had his hands tucked into his sleeves of his robe, hood over his head, and his head down as he walked. A crowd of mostly older women and older men had gathered. All the young ones were hidden in their homes. Archie stopped short of the boss whose men had changed his life once again.

"What do you want here today? Did your men not have enough fun the other day?"

The boss laughed and said, "I come here for your head, padre. We sent you a present yesterday, and I am here to find out why my men did not come back to the hacienda. It appears someone has murdered my men, and I want to know who. Do you know anything, padre?" He told the boss how the vultures he sent did return the body of their brother to them. While they were there, they made sport of shooting a young boy who tried to protect the padre. They then took the two young girls they had with them and headed away. The boss laughed. "Those stupid bastards." He picked up a radio from the truck and spoke to someone we were sure was the head of this group of jackals. He was explaining how the men had left for some fun and must have been hit by Chavez after they left.

"Now what do you want here?" Archie asked again.

His patron had decided he had lived too long, filling the empty heads of the people with untruths and giving them hope where there was none. "He thinks like the last padre. You don't understand his power over these people. He owns this land and the people on it, and his power unchallenged." The patron no longer wanted him stirring up the people, so he was going to help him meet up with the old padre, who he had sent to his maker. "I expect you to be a man and not beg. The young padre did not, even as I slowly cut his throat."

We could see Archie's body stiffen. We all looked at each other and cursed the fact we were unarmed. We started to get up to make our charge when Mom said, "Stand down. Arch has got this."

"Make your peace with your maker, black man. You have one minute!" the boss yelled so everyone could hear. He laughed and looked around the crowd that had gathered. His driver just leaned back on the hood of the truck, with his automatic weapon just hanging from its strap. About six feet in front of the boss, Archie started to kneel. We all rushed for the door, not caring about what would happen. Then like time stood still, Archie rolled forward, pulling two short fighting swords from inside the sleeves of his robe. He made one upper motion with a blade that took the boss square between the legs and then stood, opening him to his belly button. In a smooth motion, he's spun on his heels and threw the swords in a crossed arm motion. The remaining guard looked down as if not believing there were two handles sticking out of his chest. He collapsed dead, and the woman screamed, not in fear but sheer pleasure to see their abusers finally challenged.

Arch turned and looked down at the first guard. "You came here with death in your heart. The same mistake the first bunch made. I warned you many times you would pay and feel the wrath of your misdeeds." He then turned to the woman and just walked away. He stopped just long enough to retrieve his short fighting swords.

For a minute, the woman just stared at the guards on the ground. "This is for all the husbands and sons and daughters these dogs have hurt or taken from us." One of the women rushed the boss and began kicking him as the last bit of life left him. Others picked up rocks and sticks because, for once in their lives, they felt the power that had been stripped from them so long ago. Sam smiled and told Archie she liked his new style but wondered where a padre learned the sword thing.

"I said I was a man of peace. Never said I could not protect myself. I spent some time with an old shaman priest that had been turned away from his order." He had taught Archie to control his inner anger and focus it for the right time it would be needed to be released. Just sitting around got old for Archie without some exercise. The priest spent hours working with him, which helped fill both needs. When they parted, the priest gave Archie the two swords he had just used so well. "I'll show you some time." Archie smiled and told Sam.

The first part of our plan was to keep the two cartels looking at each other and not talking. We found one of the Sanchez cartel men in a local bar enjoying some time off. I walked up to him and shoved the .9mm pistol we recovered from the dead guard with the boss into his side. "Step outside. We have a message for your padrone." When we reached the old pickup parked in the alley, I pulled back the tarp, and our new friend lost his last three tequilas. His old boss looked like he had been run through a chipper and put back together. Next to him was the guard he traveled with. "Take these pieces of meat to your padrone and tell him he may leave now." I explained if he did, these would be the last of his dead. Stay and they would be but the first of many. "Like the first four the other night. Tell him Tiger, the head of the Chavez cartel, left them for him. And tell him a new boss runs this part of Mexico, the Tiger. Tell him also that we are but a few of the Americans working for him. We work for a real man, and all this is part of the plan to remove the stench of Sanchez from Mexico."

Next, we would need the Chavez cartel to think Sanchez was trying to take over the whole area just as we had just done with Sanchez's man. Archie felt a good place to start was with Miguel, the brother of the man called Tiger.

We also were having bad feelings about the boys back home catching up with us. Mom had decided to help them out a bit, but not just yet. He felt you can never know when you might need an unwilling friend. As far as weapons go, we needed cash, lots of cash. War is expensive, and we needed some seed money. We set a plan in play to build our war chest on the backs of the drug lords. Intel on the cartel and their movement wasn't hard to come by when the peasants know you, and a few bucks means life or death for some. We felt another poke at Sanchez was needed to keep him on edge. Sanchez had a plane come in once a month with his profits. He used some of this money for bribes and payoffs and other incidentals and living expenses. The system was flawless as no drugs or anything to flag suspicion was ever allowed on board. Bribes on the US side made sure the plane was never held up for random checks and always asked for the drug dogs to check it out. Being no drugs were ever allowed in the plane, the dogs always gave it a clean bill of health. Prescreened and searched by corrupt US customs officers got it a free ride into Mexico with a destination of a private strip twenty miles from the cartel headquarters. The luggage in the back was always filled with personal clothing and easily passed any inspection. The plane had been modified to carry the large sums of cash hidden within. A section of each fuel tank in the wings had been sealed off and made into a storage area for the cash. Sections of the wings would be removed, and the hidden cargo retrieved once in Mexico. This intel was collected from an old man that cleaned up and kept the refrigerators full of bottled water. It appeared the heat was building for Sanchez, so he had moved the flight up so he could have extra money for hired guns if he needed them. That was perfect for us as we planned to start collecting funds to fill our war chest. Sanchez knew that spineless Chavez would not act until he had made a lot more noise. We heard the flight was coming early from a young boy that worked at the old airstrip. He hated the cartels because they had taken his mother two years before and was more than glad to tell Archie anything he wanted to know. He was to work that night for the incoming flight and asked how he could help.

It would be a combined mission that night with three different agendas. I would go with Sam, and we would secure Miguel for future use. Archie would get the money with Mom's help. They would be armed with the two assault rifles we had secured from the last visitors to the village. There also would be whatever surprises Arch might bring. Six was on his own and armed only with a nine-mil taken from one of the dead guards. He stood in the dark as the few cars that passed by looked for that special pickup. There was a new Ford pickup headed his way, and he knew it was the one. Loaded with supplies, it was one of the many supply runs that went to the Chavez compound on a regular basis. As it passed, Six let it get a lead then started running after it, his shorts on along with his flex steel legs. They looked like two curved barrel staves hooked to his legs. As his pace picked up, his stride went from somewhat normal to almost twice that of a normal person. He quickly reached the rear, and with a jump, he was able to pull himself up and in with ease. The bed was loaded high, so the rear window was blocked and gave him all the time he needed. When the truck started into a right-hand turn, it slowed, and Six was able to easily step off and match the speed. He turned back for town at a leisurely pace, wondering if everyone was having such an easy time. For the first time in many years, he felt alive and useful.

I entered the bar and scouted around. There were lots of Americans drinking and at different levels of drunkenness. In the back corner, I spied Miguel and his two bodyguards. He had two young women, like fourteen-year-olds, at his sides. His addiction for sex and need to explore was well-known in the towns around there. The younger the better, the prettier. He had an insatiable appetite as well as an uncontrollable temper. I walked up to his table and was stopped by his guards.

"What do you want, gringo?"

I held my hands up and said, "To speak with Miguel about something he might enjoy. Something I bet he has never had."

Miguel waved the guard back. "You have my attention. Go on, gringo."

I told him how my friend sitting there in her wheelchair thought he was sexy looking and would like to enjoy his company.

"Who?" he asked, looking around the bar. I pointed to the blond in the wheelchair in the corner. "Mmmmm, she has sexy legs. Unfortunate she cannot use them. How would this be good for me?"

I told him she said she would make up for her shortcomings with other efforts.

"What is in this for you, gringo?"

I told him that we knew who he was a very important man around there. We figured he could offer us some great recreational drugs, and we didn't have a lot of money.

Miguel smiled and said, "You have a deal. Bring her here and let me get to know her."

I waved to Sam and motioned for her to come over and join us. She had picked a midthigh dress that did show her best assets. She rolled over and smiled as Miguel stood and bowed.

"Nice to meet you, senorita. May I buy you a drink, or maybe you would prefer champagne in my private room?" His hand went to Sam's legs that were exposed in her short dress.

"I do like those bubbles. They make me crazy." And she bent over so he could see those tits that still made men do a second take. He turned and spoke to one of the guards and then other. He told me to follow him out to their car to get our reward.

Mom and Arch had made their way around the pitiful excuse for security, two padlocked gates. With all this money being brought in, you would have thought the security would be massive. But in Mexico, large groups of men just made for lots of stories and talk. Besides, only a total fool would mess with the cartels business. The area around there was filled with the bodies of those that had made that mistake. The low-keyed process didn't raise any interest and was never on the same day or time, but always at night. What they did not think of was the young boy they always hired to run the old gas-powered sweeper on the runway, always on the afternoon of the day the flight arrived. He was all too willing to share his information with Archie. He knew him as the man that set his brother's arm when he broke it months ago. It was pure luck that this month's flight was due that evening. We had hoped Sanchez would call for more spending money and were excited when it happened so soon. Once inside the only hangar at the airfield, they found the ground crew asleep with an empty bottle of tequila on the floor next to them. Must be Archie's friend was able to deliver the booze with the sleeping stuff in it. He had never failed to get anything Arch had ever needed for the mission. One of the oldest men left in the village, he had seen five padres come and go or disappear. The ground crew had old coveralls on, as there was no uniform policy being very few planes ever come there. They heard the plane on final, so they knew it was showtime.

A lone SUV pulled to the end of the taxiway, which ran parallel to the runway. They quickly dragged the unconscious men to a small equipment room and put on their coveralls. Archie and Mom jumped into the old pickup that they used for towing and luggage when needed. They pulled onto the taxiway near the waiting SUV and turned away from it so they could not see in the windows. The twin-engine plane settled on approach and lowered its landing gear. The SUV started down the taxiway toward the other end of the runway to accompany the plane when it ended its rollout. As they passed the flight line truck, they both waved without showing their faces. Once passed, they fell into line behind them, keeping a safe distance. As the plane touched down and approached the waiting SUV, a loud wave of automatic gunfire erupted from the rocks near the end of the pavement. The men in the SUV returned fire but really had no target. Little did they know it was mostly fireworks with one gun stitching the runway and occasionally the SUV. The women who hid behind the rocks giggled at the thought they had scared these not so tough men. Right on schedule, the plane came to a hard stop and spun around and headed back in the other direction for a quick takeoff. It did not have enough runway left to just take off, and that would have put him directly over the guns. He didn't think much of that idea. His thoughts were to just turn and take off the way he had just landed. Archie and Mom made it look like they were scared workers scrambling to get into the truck and get away. They jumped into the truck and took off running up to and then in front of the plane. The pilot cursed as he had to slow below takeoff speed to keep from hitting the stupid jerks in the pickup. The four men in the SUV fired one last time into the hills around the end of the runway. They all jumped into the SUV and made a run for the other end and the plane. When they reached the area where the flight truck had been parked. all four tires blew out at once. The driver jumped out and saw hundreds of roofing nails and X-shaped nails that Archie had made laying there where they had done their job.

The gunmen quickly took cover behind their vehicle and searched the perimeter for those shooting. They all knew what their future held if these people took what belonged to their padrone. They turned and smiled when they saw the line truck pulling up to the side and the plane as it was reaching the other end of the runway. The plane spun around when it reached the other end and was ready to take off, as were the instructions if there was any trouble. Archie pulled in front of the plane, and Mom pointed the assault rifle at the pilot. He held his hands up, and Archie opened the side door, calling the pilot out. They duct-taped him and put him on the ground, telling him, "Tiger says thanks."

Arch moved the truck while Mom jumped in the cockpit and pushed the throttles to the boards and headed down the runway. The whole process took only a few minutes, and to the SUV driver and gunmen, they were sure the pilot was doing just as he should. Getting the cargo that was on board out of there and safe would be his only priority. They smiled with the thought they had done well, and their patron would be appreciative and maybe reward them. Later, when the night's true outcome was known, they were all led into the courtyard of the main house. In a fit of rage, Sanchez shot the pilot in the head and sent the other four to the barn for a severe beating as he could little afford losing any gun hands right then. "This looks like war," he muttered under his breath.

* * *

When we reached the car, the guard opened it and reached into the trunk and pulled out a small box. He growled for me to enjoy myself then grabbed my arm. "What kind of man sells his crippled friend for drugs?" He shook his head and bent down to close the trunk. I slammed my fists into his kidneys and kicked his leg nearest me just below the knee. He started to scream out in pain. I quickly pushed him forward and slammed the trunk hood on his head several times till he went silent and limp. I took his .357 and the retractable nightstick he carried on his belt. I duct-taped him and gagged him. I knew he would come to and make lots of noise, but I knew few would want to touch the car of the Tiger. I was sure hearing someone in the trunk was not out of the norm. I walked inside and hung out in the bar for a while as we had agreed it might take her fifteen to twenty minutes to subdue Miguel. Sam had planned to use her stun guns in the chair handles, just like she had on the hit squad at her home. She was using her power chair that she had brought with us but had to limit its use due to power issues. Not a lot of places to recharge.

When they reached the room, Sam rolled over to the bed and smiled at Miguel who was already getting undressed. He walked over and reached between her breasts and ripped open her blouse. She took a deep breath and then smiled.

"You don't waste any time."

"You said you had champagne." He put one hand on each armrest of the chair. Too close for a good hit from the electrodes. "I will break both your arms if you disappoint me, bitch. You do well and maybe you live to have another man." She was about to light him up when he stepped aside and out of the line of fire. She looked to swivel to get a good hit but didn't have the room. He pulled out a knife and let it run down her leg. He let the point push against her thigh, then pushed it into her leg about a half inch. "Guess you don't have any feeling in your legs." The blood started to soak through her dress. "I'm going to mark you up to show everyone you were with Miguel." He stuck his hand up under her dress. "No feeling here either. Guess I'll cut you here as well so I will be the last you ever enjoy."

"Really?" she said, and he smiled.

"Yes, I have carved my name into the faces of many whores that could not preform. I have killed others just to watch them beg. You think you're special, but what good is a woman that cannot feel me inside her?" She asked him if he could get it hard enough to get inside. He slapped her face and pulled her to him. "Tell me what special talents does this half a woman possess?"

"Well, you are going to love this." He had moved back in front of her and in perfect position. Sam pulled the hidden trigger on the armrest. The homemade taser found its mark in his groin. He shook uncontrollably and fell to his knees. She grabbed a handful of hair and brought his head down hard on the corner of the armrest. She let him fall and dialed down the power to the taser. He lay there unconscious but breathing. "Gee, did I disappoint you?" She let a smile cross those lips as she covered her breasts. She applied pressure to the knife wound on her leg to stop the bleeding. Suddenly, Miguel jumped up and pulled another knife from his boot. He pulled the electrodes from his groin and threw them aside.

"Now, you piece of crap." He smiled and rubbed his balls. "I'm going to enjoy slicing you up." He lunged at her and she tried to spin out of the way, but he got her in a neck hold from behind. He brought the knife around to let the sharp edge run over her breast to the nipple that was exposed. He left just a drop of blood there and then raised the blade to drive it into her chest. Unfortunately for Miguel, he had both of the handles of the chair wedged into his stomach to hold Sam in place. He loosened his grip just enough so she could speak. "Wanna beg, bitch? Beg for your worthless life."

"Nope. What about you?" She laughed.

In a rage, he raised the knife to drive it home when she triggered the ten-gage double 00 buckshot shells in the handles of the chair. It blew Miguel across the room and nearly cut him in half. It sent Sam in the other direction for a short distance. I heard the shot from where I leaned up against the wall down the hall from Miguel's room. I bolted for the room, the others in the bar ignoring the sound of gunfire as it was not unusual. The guard outside the room kicked in the door and rushed in, ready for anything except seeing his boss almost cut in half on the floor. He raised his gun to take out Sam but never heard me or the .357 round I put in the back of his head. She was a basket case at first. Her breasts had found their way out again in the commotion, and she made no effort to cover up. I threw a small blanket over her and led the way to the other end of the hall and the street. We went directly to the van, and she motored up the homemade ramp we had made back when we got the van. As I reached the driver's door, we heard lots of screams and yelling. I pulled out onto the narrow street and headed to meet up with the others. Through her sobs, Sam moved up behind me and put her hand on my shoulder.

"Thanks, Skipper. I need to tell you something. I always had a crush on you and wanted you to see these in better times." She wiped the drops of blood from under her nipple. We both laughed, and she covered up with the blanket. The sounds of police cars approaching was clear, and we watched as they flew by.

* * *

Once airborne, Arch went about cutting the seats open and pulling out the cellophane-wrapped bundles of money. After the third seat, he just whistled and sat back. "Gotta be at least a million, if not more. This can do a lot of good for us and my friends."

Mom explained that the money in the seats was just seed money and might even have been the pilot's. The real money would be in those hidden compartments in the wing fuel tanks. "It will make that pile look like pocket change," Mom said. "Now we gotta land this thing."

There was an old mine where the Tiger cartel used to package and hide their drugs before it was raided by DEA and the locals some two years ago. The mine had been sealed with explosives, and no one ever came there. It was easy to set down, and they had the cash from the seats loaded in the canvas bags they found in the storage compartment. By the time Sam and I arrived for transport, they had both sides of the wing tanks opened. Lots of screws to undo in order to pull the metal skin back. The money was all wrapped in bundles and neatly packed in the compartment. I backed the van over and opened the rear doors. We had brought two fifty-five-gallon drums with tops to carry the money. We formed a money chain, like a bucket brigade, and moved the bundles into the drums. We had both drums about three-fourths full as we did not take time to neatly stack it. I closed up the van, and everyone got in except Arch, who returned to the plane. He punched holes in one fuel tank with his fighting sword. He walked back and opened the door and told me to get out there fast. As I put it in gear, he lit the truck flare in his hand and threw it toward the growing puddle of fuel coming from the plane. It caught fire instantly, and before we could get too far, we heard and felt the explosion of the plane going up.

"Everything go well with you guys?" Mom asked.

"Not so much," Sam said. "You owe me a shirt, and we didn't get Miguel alive as we had hoped."

Mom noticed the field dressing on her thigh and just rubbed her shoulder. "Shit happens."

She gave the hard points of the night's activities, and it was never mentioned again. We all agreed the death of Miguel would serve the same purpose and maybe even ignite the war sooner.

Back at the mission, we went about counting the money like kids playing with bricks. Six built a tower with the packages of money while Archie set some on end like dominos and let them fall in sequence. There were millions of dollars in used bills and in dominations of twenties, fifties, and one hundreds. I had to admit I liked the idea of using the blood money for good, but I felt guilty. A lot of people suffered and died to get this money, but now we would use it to return the favor.

"Now let's go shopping," Mom said. "We have ten plus million to play with." We all laughed. There were no Walmart's here or shops that sold what we needed. Mom smiled and looked at Arch. He explained how we had received an invitation from an old man that stopped by the mission that morning. He said he knew of a man who ran an off-the-grid one-stop shop with anything we just might need. He gave us an arm patch of the Special Forces so we would know he was a friend. We were still on guard, but we didn't think he was connected to any cartel people. "I have a number to call later tonight with our answer." Mom went on to explain that he had heard of an ex-Special Forces gun runner down in Mexico that was better armed than the Mexican Army.

When we left the hotel and the body of Miguel, we left a message for Tiger. A small doll made of straw made by one of the little girls at the mission. We threw away the original note and added a new one that said, "This is what happens to fat pigs who want more than what belongs to them. It is you who now must leave this land or die like your piece of crap brother." Sam then ripped it almost in half for effect.

Tiger arrived at the hotel around 6:00 a.m. and went directly to the room. There the local police had covered the bodies and were standing around, waiting to be told what to do. The captain of the local police stood in the corner with sweat running down his face, wondering what the Tiger would do. When he entered the room, he walked over and pulled back the sheet. A tear formed just before his face turned as red as those peppers his brother had loved so. He raised a hand, and his bodyguards dragged the captain to him.

"I have no idea what happened her padrone. They tell me an American sold your brother this blond woman in a wheelchair and they came up here. We knew nothing till some people in the hall saw the open room and the bodies. We searched for them but only found Martinez, your brother's guard, in the trunk of your brother's car."

"Nothing else?" the Tiger roared.

"No, padrone," the captain managed to say through his fear. The guard from the car was escorted into the room, dried blood covering his face and limping. He needed to be held up due to the injured leg. Tiger walked over to him. He put his arm around him and walked him to his brother's body with the help of the guards. "This is what happened when you failed my brother. This is what happens when you fail me." Tiger grabbed the back of the guard's belt and his collar, pulled him quickly to the window, and threw him out. There was a scream followed by a car horn and more screams. He turned to the captain, who was now standing there his shirt wet with sweat and the look of a dead man. "Anything else to tell me?"

The man squirmed and pulled the doll from his shirt. "This was in your brother's hand."

"Why did you not show me this when I first got here? Is it because you work now for both me and Sanchez, or were you hoping to see who paid more?" The captain was now shaking in pure terror as he had witnessed the Tiger's anger before and had just watch him throw a man to his death. "Stand over there by the window." The captain was now noticeably shaking. "Now!" As he moved to the window, he knew is life was over. "Look down. See what happens when you fail me." Below, a crowd had formed around the new sedan with the legs of the guard protruding out of the driver's side of the windshield. "Now you will find me a way into the Sanchez compound very soon or you will also prove that pigs don't fly."

* * *

Archie sat at the table and was just finishing giving the young boy some twenty dollars when we came in and joined him. Sam rolled up next to him and up to the table. The final count came to 9.6 million dollars.

"This guy has some big expenses." Sam whistled and laughed. "That will be plenty for us for now anyways." We needed to travel about 150 miles to meet up with the supplier, which we hoped would be worth the effort. This guy was an ex-Combat Marine and was excited with the chance to do business with Americans again. Mom had given the old man who had approached him the number for his burner phone. They had a long discussion that included a lot of laughter and old combat stories.

When the conversation ended, Mom smiled. "We'll head out in the a.m."

Everyone hit the rack except me, as I was still wound up over the day's activities. I wondered what the hell we were doing. Just a few weeks ago, I was in Newfoundland dreaming of having that beautiful redhead again. Now I was in some crappy Mexican town trying to start a war between two ruthless drug lords. My life went from one of guilt and remorse to one of confession and betrayal.

I heard her roll up in her self-propelled chair. She touched my shoulder and whispered, "Want some company? You know I owe you my life for yesterday. That bastard was going to punch my card."

"Just helping a friend," I said. "You would and have done it for me."

I saw the tears in her eyes. "It's not the same, and I'm just part of the woman I once was." She told me how he never would have stood a chance with her in the old days. "I can be so helpless at times."

I tried to comfort her. "Sam, you're different, sure, but never helpless. Still tough, smart, and gorgeous."

She blushed just a bit and said she never thought I noticed. I don't know why, maybe all the stress of finding out my friends were alive, or maybe just true lust for this woman that was like family. I reached for her and pulled her to me and kissed her long and wanting. She slipped just the tip of her tongue into my mouth and then plunged in and explored every inch. Our hands roamed without thought till I reached her thighs, where I must have hesitated for a second.

She pushed back a bit and smiled. "I'm still all woman, and every part still works. And I do want you." She reached out and moved her hand up my thigh, smiling. "I need you to kiss my cuts and make them better." She had a look I had never seen in her before. I smiled, and for the first time, I wanted her like I had never before. I picked her up and placed her on my bed.

The next morning, I woke in her arms. I kissed her, and we both got dressed and prepared for our shopping trip. It was a long dusty five-hour trip. The roads were dirt and potholed all the way. Our destination was an old farmhouse with a huge barn. The house and the barn both looked like they would fall down soon. We were met at the gate at the end of the driveway by the old man, now in a tall straw hat. When he smiled, you could see he had few teeth left, which was the way most older people looked down here. Good dental practices were not on the weekly budget for most. He moved slow and looked like he was a hundred years old. He pointed to the porch on the house where a man in fatigues sat with a Mexican woman pouring him a drink.

"Welcome, welcome, my friends. And what can a poor farmer do for you today?"

Archie reached out for his hand. He wanted him to know up front we were taking on both the Chavez and Sanchez cartels. He let him know we understood if he would rather not become part of that war.

He rocked back and forth a couple times then said, "I hate those drug pushing bastards." He went on to explain how they were the scum of the earth. He had principles and never sold to anyone that brought death and pain to the innocent. "If you're a soldier, you get what you get and know what to expect. These poor people were just used up and spit out, murdered, raped, abused. Hell, they got more money than god, and they just go direct," he said, laughing. "What can I get you guys and lady?" He gave Sam a friendly nod.

Mom handed him a list of basics, wants, and wishes. Sam had some special needs of her own and wanted to discuss them with him. Sam's needs and wants were more technical than the bulk of our list. She doubted he could supply much of what she really wanted as it was hard to find a good supplier stateside. He waved to the old man, and he came forward.

"Take my new friends here to our special display area." As we all started to walk away, the arms dealer touched Archie's shoulder. "My wife is from San Elizario. You are a new legend in Mexico. The black padre with his swords." He told us that was why we were getting such special treatment. He appreciated what we had done for her people. "Doesn't get you a discount, but I appreciate your efforts." Laughing, he walked away. The old man led us to the old half-collapsed barn. He told Sam he was sorry, but she needed to ride the equipment lift as the stairs were long and not made for her chair. He showed her into the stall with a pair of goats and a floor two inches deep in hay. It looked like any other stall in any working barn, and the goats seemed unaffected by our being there.

"Come on in, guys. Room for us all." We all stepped in. He pulled twice on a leather strap that hung on the wall. The floor slowly began to drop into the ground. We descended about twenty-five feet. The outer walls were smooth concrete, and then we slowed to a stop. It was completely dark, and we could not see each other. Then we were blinded by strong floodlights. "All is well, my lovely," the dealer said to someone beyond the lights. The floodlights mounted on both sides of the elevator went dark, and we could start to see where we were as our eyes adjusted. In front of us was a vast area with stacks of wooden crates and gunracks mounted to some walls. Directly in front of us was a sand-colored Humvee with a fifty cal. mounted at the excess port with a beautiful dark-haired woman at the ready. "I would like to introduce my wife, Maria Smith, and my name is Rodger Smith." He laughed.

We started by just walking around the Humvee and throughout the cavern of weapons and equipment. An hour later, like kids in a candy store, we began loading the supplies onto the elevator to be taken up. Mom was on the porch enjoying an iced tea with the old man that had delivered the invitation. Sam was being led to the end of the display area to a door set back in the wall. Mr. Smith reached for the door handle and opened it so Sam could move through. He switched on the lights, and she took a long deep breath.

"What is this, a RadioShack in the desert?" Mr. Smith laughed and told Sam that electronics were his main interest now. He had sold almost every weapon ever built or used. He now spent his free time on his true passion, not counting Maria. The walls were covered with monitors, servers big and small. Laptops and routers were in their original packages. The workbench was immaculate, and it appeared it was as close to a clean room someone could have in such a location. He explained he now spent his free time learning computers and programming. He also enjoyed designing new things that might come in handy to his customers. "I'm no match for you, my dear, but you only need to ask. If I have it, it's yours. And if I don't, I'll find it."

Sam whistled. "Where do I start?"

Two hours later, we had the elevator loaded with our purchases and stepped on for the ride up. Sam had told us she would be on the next trip as she was still shopping. I smiled at her as we started up.

"Some things never change. Looks like we are a go, Arch," I said as Six was backing the trailer into the barn for loading.

He looked sad. "Death is never the preferred action. But these scum understand nothing else." When the trailer was across from the stall, we started to load the crates onto it. The goats wandered around, not the least bit interested in us.

Mr. Smith joined Mom on the porch and grabbed a glass of tea. "Here," Smith said, pulling out a bottle of single malt scotch. "Let's drink to our new friendship and business relationship."

Mom looked puzzled. "No offense, but I hope this is the last time we need to do business."

Smith smiled and just sat back. "If you really think this will end here in Mexico for you and your people, you're fooling yourself."

Mom was afraid he was right but preferred to worry about now and let later catch up. "Yes, it's time to settle up." Mom reached down and pulled a large military style duffel bag. The dealer scratched his head and made faces like he was adding up in his head. "Well, the cash and carry price today is $650,000." Archie pulled bundles of cash out and placed them on the table in front of him.

"Done!" Smith smiled and offered, "I do have someone you can do business with when you're back home. If the need should arise, my home base is in the US. This is kind of a summer home for me. I have several residences in the US." He offered Mom a blind e-mail drop. He told him to leave him a message and he would get back to us. He had been in this business for thirty years and inherited much of it from his uncle. He had a varied range of clients but found it easier to do business with his international friends from Mexico with less problems in shipping and storage. Many years ago, this was an underground storage facility that the Mexican government built to store weapons. He got it for a song from a retiring general that used to do business with his uncle. That's why he was so well stocked here. Back stateside, his inventory was spread out so as not to have all the eggs in one basket, so to speak. He turned and winked at Sam. "If you need my services, that sexy young lady over there knows how to reach me. I'm sure she knows what I mean, and from the tech stuff she bought."

Sam waved and said, "Gotcha covered, boss."

Archie closed the bag. "Here, put this on our account in case we are short of funds later."

Maria smiled and walked over and gave Archie a huge hug and kiss on the cheek. "Your credit is always good with us." She pointed to the old man. "My father." She told us how they held him as they raped her mother and then shot her for slapping one of them. The leader of the enforcers that had done it was a young gun who later became a boss. "You split him in half the other day." She looked at Archie. "You are God's Gabriel, and these are your army of angels." She pointed to us in the van. She told Arch they were headed stateside in a week or so. They would wait to hear the war had ended and be ready in case we needed their assistance.

Mr. Smith smiled and said, "You have brought out the young man in me, as Maria does. I will begin work on a special gift for you when you return home. By gift, I mean purchase. Nothing in this life is free." He chuckled and started to walk away. He stopped and turned around. "Good luck, my friend. These are dangerous people, and you are few in number."

Mom just looked at him. "We are few in number, but we prefer the challenge, and what's right is always right."

All the way back, Sam worked on her new laptop, downloading some of the many thumb drives she had brought from home. Six and Mom were field stripping some Berettas and Desert Eagles that were part of our purchase. Arch was filling clips with ammo of all calibers. I kept the road in my sights as this was still like the old West in many ways. As we went around a small hill, the road was blocked by an old school bus. I skidded to a stop, which brought everyone alive. From around the front of the bus, a young boy of maybe sixteen walked out, holding an old long rifle. It looked to be a very old and rusted .30-30 Winchester.

"Looks like a holdup partners." He tried to sound like John Wayne, but Six wasn't even close. The boy motioned me to get out, so I did, along with Arch. As we approached him, the boy turned sheepish and dropped the end of his gun.

"I'm sorry, so sorry, Padre. We had no idea." Arch raised his hand to silence the boy. He told him to come forward, and I took the old gun from him. It was so old and rusted, I wouldn't have fired it because I would be afraid it would blow up. Arch put his arm around the boy's shoulder, and they walked back to the old bus and disappeared around the front. I returned to the van to find both Sam and Six with automatic weapons primed and ready. After fifteen minutes, we became concerned when around the bus came Archie, followed by a group of children from ten to fifteen years old. There were nine of them, both girls and boys. They all walked toward us, looking like they had just received a scolding from their mother. When they got to the van, they all stood around and looked at us.

"Let me introduce the Lopez gang, the most feared gang in all of Mexico." We smiled and nodded to the small group of desperadoes.

Arch went on to explain how they came from a small village south of there. The village was poor, and their dug well had gone dry. Everyone was trying to get enough money to get a real well drilled to supply their families. Mr. Lopez, the leader of the gang, came up with the idea of sticking up any travelers they might catch on the open road. We were their first target, and they were shocked it happened to be a padre and his friends. They apologized over and over, and the two girls even broke into tears. They had all been so afraid, but their thirst and dedication to their families had won out. Arch explained they all could have been killed if they had picked the wrong vehicle, and thank God they had not picked a drug shipment or lord.

"Now if God and I buy you a new well, will you promise to never do this again? You promise to work hard, go to school, and serve the Lord and your families unquestionably?" They all said yes quietly. "Well, *do you?*" Arch bellowed.

"*Yes!*" they all screamed with huge smiles, dancing in small circles. Arch walked over to the window, and Sam handed him a small bag with over $100,000 in it.

As he pulled back, she grabbed his arm. "You're the man we all remember, missed, and love so much."

He smiled. "Just glad to be back and able to change things for the better." He walked back to the head outlaw and handed him the bag. "Give this to the padre in your village or the elder one."

"I will, Padre, and God bless you." He turned to the bus as all the others followed and waved goodbye to us. As they got on the bus and pulled it out of the way and headed home, we all looked around at each other.

"This is what it feels like to make a difference. I think I like our new lives." We all agreed with Arch and headed out for what we knew was not going to be easy or fun. But it was going to make a difference.

Archie just sat there, rigged and eyes shut, breathing long and paced like a sleeping man, yet I know he was wide awake. As we approached the outskirts of town, we saw some smoke coming from the square. The church was on fire, or rather anything inside the adobe structure that was wood was burning. Archie's eyes flew open, and the rage was overtaking his face. Before I could come to a complete stop, he was out and running. There was no saving the contents of the church. An old woman came to him crying and spoke to him in rushed chopped sentences. He turned and walked back to us and the van.

"Chavez the Tiger sent his men for me, and when they could not find me, they burned the church."

"Were any of the people hurt?" Mom asked.

"No. The men that were there had told this old woman they must turn the padre over to them or they will be back. He knows I have some new friends, and I figure he knows we were involved in his brother's untimely death. They believe we are working for Sanchez, so the splitting of the cartels into warring groups is working." He laughed. "They each think we are working for the other."

Time to crank up the war. We made our plans and decided on a two-prong attack. If we did it right, each would think the other was responsible. First, we hit the Tiger where it hurt, his supply line. Sam spent the night packing her gear for the next day. Her motorized chair had been in the church, so it was toast, but she had no issues using her lightweight manual one. That morning, Mom and Sam headed toward the Tiger's stronghold to the north of the city. Archie had found them an old rundown shack on the side of a hill that looked down on the compound. With their new high-resolution binoculars and long-distance lens cameras, they were setting up for forward support from a safe distance.

Tiger's supply network in that area was based at an old Mexican Army outpost that had been rebuilt and fortified. His drugs were brought in and made ready for transport to the US. He used all varieties of transport from planes, boats, to tunnels. Human mules were a big part of the transportation arm of his trade, using legal visitors to Mexico that traveled back and forth. It was imperative that we kept any noncombatants safe as well.

Over the past few days, the cartels had exchanged multiple attacks on each other, and the death toll was now at fifty plus. It was a sure thing that the reprisals had begun in earnest between the two drug kingpins. Drive-by shootings and attacks on each other's business had become a daily occurrence. The local police and military were unable to stop or even reduce the violence. The thought process was to let them fight it out and congratulate the winner.

Sam and Mom headed to the forward base we had agreed on. It was far enough away that it posed no danger to the compound and had been abandoned for years. They unloaded their gear at midnight on the far side of the hill so as to not be seen. Archie took the truck back so there was nothing to get the cartel guards' attention. Sam had been able to excess the Tiger's Wi-Fi and wireless network with little trouble. They used a satellite Wi-Fi connection because there was next to no service for much of Mexico. There was little concern inside the compound as it was well fortified, so the perimeter guards made their security sweeps only a few hundred yards from the walls. The two guard towers had an unlimited view in almost every direction. She was able to hack into a secure file that had all of the cartels' cell phone numbers and assigned users. Once she had that, it was a simple thing to set up listening and recording software. She had set everything up to transmit a copy back to the old barn near the church where we had set up a makeshift HQ. It appeared they were preparing for an all-out assault on the Sanchez compound. It was set for the morning in two days as they were waiting for more guns to come in from around Mexico. Tiger had actually left for a meeting with some small, less powerful dealers that he was trying to enlist in his private war. Sam was talking with Archie and giving him an update on two of the burner phones we got from the Smiths.

Mom had just started to open an MRE for lunch when there was a knock at the door. Mom grabbed his Desert Eagle and Sam her Beretta. Mom opened the door slowly, and a young boy of about eight or nine stood there. He was white in fear, and Mom knew they were compromised. The boy looked up and asked them to please come out or they would kill his mother. Pulling the door back a little more, he saw the young woman in the grasp of a man with a gun to her head. "Come out please. They said they will not hurt you."

Sam quickly gave Archie a sit-rep and forwarded what intel she had to another server we had set up in the burned-out mission. With the stroke of several keys, the computers went into self-destruct sequence. All data was deleted, and a small acid charge attached to the hard drive started leaking acid, the final destruction of all data. Then both her and Mom left their guns on the table and went outside. It was a good move as there were ten to twelve guns pointed at them, and any resistance would have been futile. The kid ran back to his mother that was locked in a kiss with the man that held her, her husband. The boy turned and smiled. "You should have asked before you took over my special place." Apparently, the boy used the shack as his go-to safe place. When he was coming up to spend some time that morning, he saw someone pass by one of the many holes in the walls. He went directly to his father and told him of his discovery. The rest was history. It was just bad luck that he and his mother were visiting his father. They left that day for home as the compound was going to lock down in preparation for the Sanchez attack.

Archie came bursting into the room where Six and I sat checking some of our arsenal. "They have Mom and Sam."

"Who?"

"The Tiger crew at the compound."

We all felt our stomachs knot up and looked around for someone to have something to say. Everyone took off in different directions to collect the items we needed.

We all sat around the table with the maps in front of us of the compound, which Sam had forwarded to us first thing after getting set up. A full-out attack was a joke as the defenses were such. We would need fifty well-armed and trained men. We were not convinced we could make it in time before they execute them if we did not act fast. We needed to formulate a rescue from within. The trick was to get in quietly so we could get them and get back out. Every truck was checked, and nothing went in or out without guards checking every inch of the vehicles. In frustration, we all got up and walked around. Six went out and took a short run. I walked over to my area and sat on the bed thinking I never should have made love to Sam. Now all I can think about is her and getting her back alive. Archie walked in to check on Jesus. When he saw Archie, he smiled and pushed up.

"Hey, Padre, I'll be in fighting shape soon."

"Hopefully you will not need to fight again. Here, have some water." Archie went to pour the water. He noticed the pitcher was empty, so he got up to go fill it.

"Don't bother, Padre. The well outside is mud as it often gets this time of year."

"They will bring some from the well in the square soon." Archie smiled and left the room. When we got back, he was going over the reports Mom and Sam had sent earlier. We knew Chavez was not there but would be soon as he had new prisoners to torture and kill. He turned to us and a big smile formed.

"How long can you hold your breaths?" We all thought for a second and then smiled. "We go with a different tiger in the tank." Originally, we planned for a huge explosion that would draw their attention and we would slip in, but now.

* * *

They took Mom and Sam back to the compound and placed them in a shed near the center of the compound. They were treated surprisingly well and wondered why. A guard came in that was obviously a boss of some sort.

"My padrone has said to keep you alive and well till he returns so he may enjoy your deaths at his own hand. You, old man, are of little consequence, so he will kill you quickly in front of the American whore. She, however, must answer for the death of his brother. I would not want to be you." He smiled and spat at Sam. He did want to know who they were working with and how many of them there were. "Ask Sanchez when you see him before he kills you." Sam tried to duck before he backhanded her but still felt the hit. He raised his rifle to hit her with the butt when he must have had thought better of it. He smiled and said, "Good thing my patron wants you healthy." He turned and left.

Once gone, Mom approached Sam on the cot. "Now what do we do. kid?" He was in rough shape from some fierce punching and kicking from his captors. They had a guard posted at each corner of the shed, and they appeared to be very diligent in their duty for fear of their own lives no doubt. Mom called out for some water. The guard opened the door and smiled. "Not enough for you two, and we won't get another delivered till tomorrow." Then he slammed the door.

* * *

Archie had some bread and water for us as we talked and worked on the MREs. Big improvement from the c-rations we had before with the small cans or food and cigarettes and candy in sealed wrapper. It was the only way to get in quickly and before Tiger got due back in a day or so. We went over the list of equipment we needed and headed out for the short ride to town. When we arrived at the common well in town, we met with some locals and then sat to wait just inside a small cantina across from the well. After an hour or so, the old oil delivery truck, which had been retired from somewhere in the US, arrived at the well. On the side, you could still make out the faded name Able Oil.

The driver went about setting up the small portable pump and hoses he would use to fill the tanker. The shotgun rider was just that. He had a sawed-off shotgun and walked around sending the locals away. The pump came alive after several pulls on the cord, and the process began. The driver walked across the street to the cantina on the other side of the square and sat down at an outside table and ordered some tequila. He yelled for the guard to join him and accused him of being a little girl if he refused. The guard reluctantly joined his friend, and they enjoyed their drinks and chips the young waitress had brought them. Three young boys joined us and were there to help hump the equipment for us. Once we were ready, Archie flashed his flashlight, and a group of young women arrived with several older ones. They approached the two water boys and formed a wall between them and the truck. The older ones went up and rubbed the men, asking them for a drink for which they would return a kiss. In no time, the two men forgot the water truck and gave all their attention to the women.

We quickly made our way to the truck and up on to the narrow catwalk that ran the length of the tank. I opened the top hatch which was about two and a half feet across. The boys handed us the bags of equipment which we dropped into the tank. Then we each quickly dropped into the cold water ourselves. We hoped our homemade waterproof bags worked. We all were in combat dress for the sandy landscape around us. Arch looked odd as we were used to him being in those brown robes. Each of us had lengths of rubber hose we cut out of some old abandoned cars. Now the plan should work as long as they did not fill the truck to capacity and left us an air space on top of the water. Archie had thought of that and told us we just had to wait and see. Normally they just kept filling it till it overflowed, not the least concerned about wasting the water that was so precious for the villagers. As the water level started to rise, we all thought of the things that could go wrong, but always back to how we were going to rescue our family.

The water was now almost to our chests, and the airspace was dwindling. Archie took a small white flag and raised it up just over the tank lip. In a few seconds, there was a huge explosion that lifted two abandoned trucks five feet in the air. The driver and guard pushed the girls off their laps and onto the floor. The women were now all screaming in fear and ran to hide inside the cantina. The driver ran over and just pulled the hose out of the top of the truck and jumped up and closed the hatch. With everything going on with the Sanchez attacks they had no intentions of being another body for the vultures. Not sure what was happening, the two figured they had enough water for that run and quickly headed out of town as fast as the old truck would go. For the next hour, we were washed around the tank and often got mouthfuls of water. Waves ran from one end to the other and side to side. Now I know what it's like in a washing machine. Soon the ride smoothed, and we stopped. The waves kept coming but started to subside. It was a good guess we were at the guard shack and they were checking the truck for explosives or unwanted hitchhikers. We all submerged and moved to the sides of the tank using our hoses to breathe. The truck rocked, and we saw the hatch open then close. The guard was very happy to see just water sloshing around, so he closed the hatch. The truck started up again and headed across the compound to the underground water storage tank. They backed up to the water tank connection and hooked up another flexible hose that hung nearby. The gate valve was opened, and the water started to run out. The truck shook again as the driver climbed up to open the hatch to allow the water to flow quickly by eliminating any suction buildup. As the water receded, we could begin to see each other's faces and spoke in a whisper.

"My legs are cold," Archie said.

"Mine too." Six smiled. It was near dark, but still the sun gave off a slight glow. Archie raised his head up. Looking back, he smiled. "I don't need black face paint." Everything seemed to be okay so far. Few men walked about the compound, and the driver was nowhere in sight. Then the truck shook as someone was climbing up the ladder. Archie pulled his head back and stepped out of the light from the opening. The water was almost completely out, and we had to act to keep the hatch from being closed and latched. As the guard got to the opening, he stuck his head down inside the tank to see how much remained. Without a second thought, I brought my Ka-Bar knife across his throat just below the jawline. Razor sharp, it made the end short and quick. As my knife made short work of him, Archie grabbed his shoulders and pulled him down into the tank. The water turned red from the blood.

Six smiled and said, "I sure ain't drinking that stuff." The water was now gone, so we opened one of our dry sacks and pulled out our weapons. We primed our handguns and waited to hear if anyone noticed. After a few long minutes, Archie once again moved his head slowly above the lip of the tank. Thumbs up as he pulled himself up and out of the tank. He slid down the side of the tank and jumped to the ground. We handed down the equipment bags and then joined him on the ground. We had decided in advance to use the small shed left of the center of the compound for our starting point. As we rounded the corner of the watershed, we stopped and decided that plan wouldn't work. There were four guards on the shed, one on each corner, each with automatic rifles.

Six looked at us and said, "I bet I know where Mom and Sam are."

We moved back to the water truck. Well, now we needed a quick plan. First, we needed a way out. Our first plan of using one of the pickup trucks we liberated didn't seem so solid now. No matter how we worked it, we were going to take some serious fire. But getting to the shed and freeing them seemed to be an issue as it was in the middle of the compound, and those guys didn't look like some peasants. They had guns. We all looked around. The one place with a commanding view of the shed was the old guard tower on the west wall. Problem was there was a guard in it. Also, he had a large search light that would come on soon as dark closed in.

"Two birds, one big rock," I said. The other tower was directly next to what seemed to be the barracks or mess hall. We decided to move the tanker to what we assumed was the motor pool, or in this case, repair shop, and make some modifications on it. Once dark set in fully, I got into the tanker and drove it to the motor pool area, backing it in. The old steel tanker probably spent most of its time there being fixed and kept running so no one noticed or paid any attention in that moonless night. The garage was empty except for a pickup with benches in the back. Most likely a transport for multiple soldiers, and that seemed to get Archie's attention. We quickly rolled over the set of torches from their place in the back.

"I think this little modification is going to work." I went about cutting along the back end of the tank. I had it almost cut completely around, resembling a large door. Once I had cut the top and two sides of the door, I cut straight across leaving a twenty-four-inch uncut piece across the bottom. That held the cut-away door in place and would act as a hinge when we pulled it down. Six was moving some of his surprises into place and checking them for operation. It took less than an hour, but we were now ready. I jumped into the driver's seat and fired the old beast up. Six got down inside the tank and pushed on the back to be sure it flexed with his weight. I handed him our remaining supplies and equipment, which he pulled down with him in the back. Archie had left earlier to make his way around the compound to the guard tower we saw earlier. When he reached the base of the tower, he moved slowly until he could see the guard. When he lit a cigarette, Arch let him have a three-tap silenced .9mm greeting.

None of the guards were very interested in what was going on inside the camp. The work on the old water truck was nothing new as holes needed to be patched often. None of the guards expected any problems from within. They expected any trouble to come from the outside.

Quickly, he moved up into the tower and put the American baseball hat on that the guard was wearing. To those on the ground, it looked like the guard had just moved out of sight for a few seconds to take a leak. Once he had his silenced sniper rifle put together and set on the folding tripod which rested on the small table, he found in the tower. He swung around and looked through his scope at the guard in the other tower and kissed him once as a test for his weapon. He made the three-click signal we were waiting for on his com. I pulled out of the shop and headed across the compound, which was for the most part empty. What few men were walking about were more interested in their conversations than the old water truck. As we passed the shed where they were keeping Sam and Mom, we did a quick look around. I drove past and then stopped and started to back up toward the front door. The truck was loud to start, and I had cut a few extra holes in the muffler to add to it. The guards in the rear looked around and moved around to the front to see what was up, and that started our play.

Archie put the guard from the rear on the left away first with a shot to the head. Then the other rear guard felt Archie's rage from behind the scope on his rifle. The ones in front never heard a thing or saw the men fall. They both stood there waving at me to stop, which I did when I was ten feet from the door. Six knew it was his time and pushed hard on the back of the tank which folded out and down, hitting the ground and making an odd-looking ramp. The two guards looked at each other and froze at what they were seeing. That was the biggest mistake of their now ending lives. As the back hit the ground, there stood Six with his silenced Uzi pointed at them. It was unfair as they had nowhere near the experience of Six. Two short bursts and each was stitched from groin to neck. Unfortunately, one of them did have time to wrap his finger on the trigger and let out a short burst as he went down. The sound echoed through the camp, which was dead silent before that and we were sure would bring a deadly response. Archie put the spotlight directly on the front door of the camp barracks so the men running to the alarm were blinded where they stood. He picked off three guards running from the door in so many seconds, forcing the rest back inside. I joined Six, and we opened the door to the shed to find our two friends.

I scooped up Sam, and Six helped Mom to his feet and mostly carried him to the truck. The truck blocked us from most of the camp, and they had yet to figure out what was going on or where the shots were coming from. Once we had our passengers inside the tank, I helped lift the door while Six pulled on the rope we had attached to the top of the door cutout I had made. The door closed, and he tied it off inside while I ran for the driver's seat. Slowly, they were getting the idea what was happening, and we started to take hits. The tank was more than enough to fend off the attack, and Six popped the hatch and pulled his compact fifty cal up and through the opening. He swung from side to side if for nothing more than to make them drop and hide. As he sprayed the compound with rounds, I saw the flash and tail fire of a LAW rocket as it left the tower where Arch was and struck the barracks. Made of cheap plywood and metal, it just jumped up in the air and flattened when it came down.

"God help you poor sinners that were in there," Archie spoke to no one in particular. A second LAW hit the generator building, throwing the entire compound in darkness. We pulled up next to the tower, and Archie was part way down his rappel line when they noticed him and opened up. Six did what he could to keep them pinned down, but one managed to hit Arch in the middle of his back. His hands fell away from the rope, and he hit the ground flat on his back. I was out of the door and at his side before he bounced the second time. Six was firing in all directions, and he yelled he was running low. Sam, from her chair, untied the rope and Mom, and she pushed the best they could till the back fell open.

This was all that little piece of metal could take. Being old and rusted, the piece I left uncut to act as a hinge broke away, and the ramp just fell to the ground. I pulled Arch to a sitting position and then up and across my shoulder. I let him roll over the short wall we had left on the rear of the tank and headed back to the cab. Sam dropped to the floor and rolled Arch over, and Mom took up a firing position at the door opening in the rear. All hell had broken out as the cartel guards were running around the compound, and we were the center of their attention. It started to look like we were doing our impression of Custer's Last Stand when it was like someone had turned up the heat and turned up the lights. In the back, Arch was awake and sitting with that stupid smile on his face.

"Guess you need my help again." He smiled, flinching from the pain as he had several broken ribs. The lightweight body armor had done its job, but you still always paid a small price. He reached in his vest pocket and pulled out a small radio detonator and pushed it. In unison, every garbage pail or pile of crates in the compound erupted in a massive fireball. On his way to the tower, Arch had been busy tossing blocks of C-4 in and around the camp. Being the compound is an explosive, it needed some extra punch to help it be more destructive. Arch had Jesus put hundreds of screws in the blocks as a form of therapy for him, and so he also felt a part of the mission. It also added to the deadly outcome from their detonation. Many in the immediate vicinity of Arch's little gifts lost their lives in an explosive hail of heat and screws. As I drove toward the gate, I smiled to myself and thought about Arch, the deadliest Boy Scout that ever lived. As I approached the gate, I saw the tail of fire pass the cab of the truck and hit directly in the middle of the gate. It became a cloud of smoke and flame. And as we reached that part of the wall, it was gone just as Six had hoped when he fired the LAW.

They brought me up-to-date on the comm link that everyone was good. Archie had taken the hit in his new Kevlar vest, a gift he found when we unpacked. Maria had wrapped it in colorful paper and left it in the trailer with our purchases of that day. It had a special tag on it that said, "For my black angel." The old tanker was doing the best it could, but it was a slow run to town with the outer duel tires shredded or flat. We were running on the inside set. On the way to town. we passed a small motorcade of four SUVs headed to the compound at maximum speed. As I pulled to the right, I lowered my head and pulled down my hat so I could see them as they passed. As they slowed some to go by on the narrow dirt road, I saw in the rear of the third vehicle the head of the Tiger cartel. Chavez was screaming at the driver and everyone else. He gave no notice to the water truck, and the last car even waved to me thinking I was part of the usual crew. I swerved back and forth so the tires would create a dust blanket to hide the gaping hole in the back of the truck. I didn't want them to see the fresh pot marks made by the hail of bullets in case they gave us a second look back. We were back on the road to town and started to feel relaxed, at least for a while.

As the group of SUVs approached the compound, Chavez pulled out his .45 pistol, and everyone in the vehicle thought they were about to die. His car stopped at the hole in the wall where the gate once stood. He got out, kicked the vehicle till it was dented, then fired his entire clip into the air. All around him was destruction. Most of the buildings were either destroyed or on fire. He felt anger at the loss of millions in drugs but little compassion for the many men lying dead or seriously injured. The pickup that was in the shop now pulled up alongside him, and the boss in the front seat got out to meet his destiny.

"Who did this?" he screamed.

"The Americans came in and the freed the old man and the crippled woman. She told me they worked for Tiger."

"The drug!" he screamed. "What about the drugs?" He had no concern for the thirty men dead around him; his only concern was the drugs.

"There, padrone." The boss explained that the majority of the drugs were in the main warehouse and safe. "We had many men die protecting it."

The bastard smiled. "That is good. The drugs mean money, and that is our power." But just then, the warehouse was engulfed in a massive fireball that shot far into the night sky and turned night to day in a flash. The termite explosives Archie had placed under the warehouse had done their job. He had set them on a timer to give us that one last big play if we had needed it, not to mention destroying the drugs. From where we were on the old dirt road, we could see the huge fireball as it filled the sky behind us. Millions of dollars of his product were gone.

"You pitiful excuse of a whore's droppings!" He grabbed the boss and shoved the gun under his chin.

He begged for his life and kept saying, "The water truck, padrone. The water truck."

Chavez pulled the gun back and screamed at the man. "What about the water truck?"

He told him how we were in it, and that's what we used to get away. "We were just now going for them."

He pushed the man away. "Then get to it. I want those Americans. Go. I will come watch them die." The boss jumped back in the truck, and they sped off at the best speed they could manage, knowing they must catch that truck before their padrone did.

The ten men in the back had all they could do to hang on as they pulled away. One poor soul made the mistake of trying to stand and move up when they hit a huge hole in the road. He bounced up about three feet in the air and then back down, falling backward. Several tried to grab him as he landed on the tailgate with a face of pure terror. But then he was gone. The group with Chavez was almost up with pickup when the SUV took a violent jump.

"What the hell did you just hit?" Chavez screamed.

The driver turned to him, white and looking like he would be sick. "It was Martin!"

We managed to get close to town when I saw the headlight bearing down on us. I spoke with the others, and we only knew we did not want to drag this war into the village. Arch came on comm and asked where we were.

I laughed and told him Mexico. "How the hell do I know where we are?"

"Have we crossed the bridge over the old wash?"

"No," I told him, but I could see it coming up fast.

"Slow down then!" I yelled.

"*What!*"

"Slow down and let them catch up. When you cross the bridge stop about five hundred yards on the other side."

I figured he wanted to take a stand at the bridge, but I didn't know how many LAWS we had left or how the ammo was holding up. It was his show, so I did as he asked, stopping in the middle of the road after we crossed. I stopped about five hundred yards from the bridge with the rear door in position to see what was coming. I got out and went back to find Sam propped up in her chair and along with Mom and Archie smoking large fat cigars. Six was just getting there, and as he did, Arch handed him a cigar and smiled.

"Thanks" was all Arch said.

In the distance, I could see the convoy of death approaching.

"How much ammo we got and LAWS?" I asked.

"Not enough," Mom said. "But we got Arch."

The cars slowed when they saw us and stopped short of the bridge. "Well, I did not see this coming," Arch said in a matter-of-fact way.

The men piled out of the pickup and took up firing positions, as did all the men in Chavez's detail. "Do they think I am stupid?" he spoke to anyone listening. "They have put explosives on the bridge. You." He spoke to the boss he had threatened earlier. "Drive the pickup across the bridge and park on the other side. The rest of you go through the wash on foot and check for explosives on the bridge."

We watched as the truck came across and parked on our side. The men in the wash checked the bridge and then came up on our side and got back in the truck.

"It's safe, padrone!" the boss yelled. The rest got back in their vehicles.

"We better get out of here!" I yelled, and everyone piled into the back. I fired up the tanker and was just about to start out.

Sam yelled on the com, "Stop! Archie is just standing there in the road."

The cartel soldiers saw us start to run, so they started after us. The first SUV stared across the bridge with the second one on its tail. When they saw Archie just standing there, they all stopped. The pickup stopped, and they were all pretty much bumper to bumper.

Chavez screamed, "Get me out of here now! Hurry or we will all be dead."

The driver slammed it in reverse, running into the last SUV and pushing it back. The drivers were well trained and did a 180, spinning the SUVs around and down the road.

Archie raised his arms in front of him and screamed, "Feel the wrath of Gabriel!" And the pickup disappeared in a flash of flame and torn metal. The force of the explosion engulfed the first SUV and shattered every window in the second, killing one and injuring the rest. Chavez was well out of range, and so was the fourth SUV as it sped away as fast as it would go. I got out and walked back. Archie was walking back with this blank look. "I have condemned myself to hell, but I will not go alone. It is my place to end evil where I can." And he walked by and down the road. Six had placed a large block of C-4 in the road on our side of the bridge where Archie had asked him. It was painted a reddish color like the other rocks along all the road.

We regrouped at a small abandoned farm outside of town. We left the water truck on the road after we got to the van where we had hidden it. Arch had not spoken since the previous day at the bridge. Jesus came in the backdoor and hugged everyone after he placed a box of what fresh food he could find on the table. Sad, but the MREs we had purchased were many times better than what these poor people lived on. He walked over to Sam, who sat in her chair near the table.

"Bet I can beat you in basketball now." He smiled, and Sam did in response. We all needed to rest and let our sore muscles recharge as all of us hadn't been in combat in a long time. The next morning, Mom walked in and joined us for some breakfast and just made the statement.

"It is time we bring this war to an end."

After his brush with death, Chavez had retreated to his fortified hacienda with as many guards he could muster throughout his network. Sanchez had pretty much done the same, only his protection included some police and military he owned. Sam had set up her laptop equipment to start the wheels rolling. First, she had the data she had recovered when she hacked into Chavez's network and phone network. Next, we rode in an old school bus past the Sanchez hacienda several times. Archie had made a small charge for the front wheel that would blow out a well-worn part of the tire. On the last pass, we blew the tire when we were far enough away to not look suspicious. His was a little more secure so it would take her a little longer, so that's why we had to stay in one place for a while. Two locals showed up to jack up the bus and replace the old tire. Our driver was another local who everyone knew, so there was nothing suspicious. Sam and I were in the small cargo compartment under the bus. We made the best of our time as her laptop sucked all the data we needed from the Sanchez servers. By the time the whole process was finished, she had all she needed, and so did we.

Once she had the two Cartels wired for sound, she started the process of heating them up. She called Chavez on his private cell phone and left the message, "We who are taking over your business will call before eight p.m." Then she made the same call and left the same message for Sanchez. The calls were short, so there was no way to track even if they might have a system in place which she was sure they did not. She knew they both would have plenty of time to set up a trace on the cell call when it came at eight. So she left with me at around five o'clock and drove to a small a café near the border crossing. The handicap accessible laws did not filter down to Mexico, so

I went into the men's room that was actually just a door into an alley where most just used the walls. I waited till I was alone and placed Sam's package on the back side of a dumpster that was surrounded by vomit, so not well used. I returned, and we set about making ourselves seen by as many of the people in the café as possible. I reached over, pulled Sam's face to mine, and gave her a long tongue-filled kiss.

When we broke, she slapped me as hard as she could, yelling, "You pig. Think you can just push a crippled woman around? You kiss like a little boy." And many in the bar laughed. We exchanged some more insults, and I stood up.

"Bitch, let's go." We finished our drinks and headed back to our new HQ.

The ride was long and slow and dusty. We both needed to discuss that night we spent in each other's arms, not to mention the kiss a few minutes ago or those we shared while collecting Sanchez's data. Neither wanted to start the conversation, but she finally broke the ice when she leaned over, kissed my neck, and said, "Let's not let what happened make things stressed between us."

I agreed and told her I had never really seen her that way till then, and now I can't see her any other way. She agreed and moved next to me.

"What do we do?" she asked.

I told her we needed to concentrate on what we had going. We needed to finish what we started here and then back to the US to put an end to our being targets. Then we could relax and decide where this could go. She smiled and squeezed my leg, kissed my cheek, and move back. "I did enjoy how you threw me under the bus." We both laughed hard at that then finished the ride in silence. We both knew it would not be long before it surfaced again. As we pulled into the front yard, the others were loading equipment in the old pickup Arch had procured.

"Hey, did you miss us?"

They all looked up, and Six told me, "Did you leave?"

Jesus perked up. "I missed you, Samantha." She turned a little red knowing she had a very young new admirer. She smiled at Jesus and told him she loved hearing her given name.

Eight o'clock came, and it was time to start our plan.

Sam went about setting up her laptop and worked her magic on the keys. First, she secured connection with the package I placed behind the dumpster earlier. We were on the outskirts of town, parked alongside a small manufacturing building. We had to be a limited distance away for a good connection to the repeater at the bar. Unfortunately, we had to remain relatively close for the time being. It only took a few seconds for her to hack into the server and begin using their IP address and internet. We had removed the center seats from the van, leaving the front two and the far rear bench. A small table was there for Sam to work from and the rest of us to huddle around. Once that connection to the bar repeater was made, she proceeded to get Sanchez's phone ringing. He let it ring four times, like he thought we would think he was not concerned with the call. He was waiting for his IT tech to complete the first phase of the trace and was stalling for time. When he picked up, he just said, "Sanchez."

Mom started right in with "You mother of a dog, your time here is over. I want you and those pieces of crap you call your men to get out of this part of Mexico. I'll give you one week. Don't make any plans to return, or I will kill you like the useless snake you are." He told him that his business was now his, and there was no need not stay around. Mom told him not to take very long to resettle under some other rock. We all looked at each other, holding back our laughter. We knew he was at the boiling point.

He started to speak again. "I know you work for Chavez."

Mom cut him off. "One week to get out. And don't test me, or I will kill you and all your family." We could hear Sanchez stuttering and trying to put words to his anger.

He raged, "I'll find you!" Then we broke the connection before he could finish his rant.

"That went well." Mom laughed, and we all joined in, looking forward to the next call.

Next it was Chavez's turn. This time the phone barely rang once before Chavez came on with a blistering barrage about Mom's mother and her tastes in men and such. Mom never said a word and just hung up. When he paused for effect and got no response, he went off on another rant until he was out of breath.

"Speak, you bastard. Who is this?" Again, silence. Then he realized the connection was dead. The new IT guy sat there in silence till Chavez yelled, "That bastard hung up on me!"

"Sir, you must keep him on the line long enough for me to trace the call."

Chavez threw a book from his desk at this young computer person. "I know that, you jerk. He hung up on me."

Sheepishly, the young man said, "Maybe less insults and a little more patience would help."

Chavez pulled his gold plated .45 from his shoulder holster and shot the vase, shattering it on the shelf behind the smirking men that stood there.

"You guys think this is funny? I will kill the next man that looks like he does."

We waited exactly five minutes then called again. This time, the phone rang six times before it was answered with a stern "*Yes.*"

Mom handed Sam the phone. She spoke in a soft and low tone. "Your brother told me he was going to cut me and did. Then he died like the dickless man he was. Does it run in the family?" She smiled and handed Mom back the phone.

Chavez was stuttering. "You…you legless whore. I'll—"

And Mom cut him off. "One week, Chavez. You have one week to get yourself and what men you have left out of this part of Mexico." Mom made it clear we now ran the business around there and he would be just a bad memory. Along with his remaining men, they would die like those men at the bridge. He started to speak, and Mom cut in, "All your men will die, and then you will be last."

Chavez screamed and started to run off at the mouth before he realized the line was dead again. He threw the phone across the room, where it shattered on the wall. He looked around. "That bastard hung up on me again." One young guard did not hide his amusement very well, so Chavez shot him in the foot. "Laugh now."

Two young computer technicians miles apart were both desperately trying to locate the people that had just called their new benefactor. Surprisingly enough, behind each of them the drug dealers paced back and forth.

Sanchez's man was the first to exclaim, "Got 'em!" The call had come from the Border Town Cantina. "Get every man you can!" he yelled to the boss. "Get them loaded, and go find these people that think they can just come here and take what is mine."

Meanwhile, Chavez had shot two vases and several pictures as he paced. The IT tech was so nervous his hands kept having to be dried. Chavez kept yelling at him, "Well, you better hurry!" Then he ejected the empty clip from his gun and let it fall to the floor next to the young hacker.

As he slammed the fresh clip in and let the slide run forward, the young man exclaimed, "Border Town Cantina! The call came from the Border Town."

Chavez slapped the young man on the shoulder and walked to his head of security. "I want these people dead, but not the crippled woman. She must be brought to me still alive. I want her to see my eyes as I cut her throat." The man nodded and left to collect what the padrone had ordered him to.

Now phase 3 needed to be put in motion. Sitting in the passenger seat, Jesus was watching and listening to everything going on. He had begged to be allowed to come with us, and he not only deserved it but became part of the plan. This time, Jesus held the phone and waited for it to be answered by some half-asleep police sergeant at the headquarters for the local district.

"I need to talk to the captain. Please, it is an emergency," he blurted out. The sergeant tried to blow him off with the story that the captain was too busy for some stray dog with what he called an emergency. He said he would take the report and take care of it. Jesus looked around and smiled. "Sanchez is planning to kill Chavez in town tonight."

The sergeant almost fell over backward in his chair. "Hold on, son. Here comes the captain." He motioned wildly to the captain that sat across from him. The phone went dead, and suddenly the captain was on with a definite tone of concern.

"What do you want?"

Jesus explained how he was working at the Sanchez compound that had been mostly destroyed, moving garbage and trying to pick up around the place.

"*Yes, yes.* What is this about Sanchez killing Chavez in town?"

He told the captain he heard the men talking about a payback in town tonight. Heard they were going to kill Chavez when he is at the Border Town Cantina for a wake for his brother. Sanchez knew that it was Chavez that had stolen his money and had hired the Americans that had destroyed his compound while rescuing their friends. The captain covered the mouthpiece of the phone and told the sergeant to get every man they had loaded up to go. He already knew the details of the money plane being taken and the violent destruction of the compound. Many men had been killed, and a large amount of Sanchez's drugs had been destroyed. He just assumed that Chavez had something to do with it and knew a day of reckoning was coming. He desperately hoped he had picked the winning side. His life depended on it. After hanging up with the caller, he joined the men that had been assembled to head to town and hopefully stop the war that he knew was coming.

Without a warning knock, the door flew open and Ted came bursting inside, obviously excited. "We have them!" he half yelled.

Russ motioned for him to shut up and motioned for Kevin to close the door. "This is a private party. Let's keep it that way. Now what have you found?"

Ted explained they got the first hit on the old bastard's cell about a week ago and had tracked it as long as it was hot. Apparently, they had let it run down on power or just destroyed it. During the time they could track it, the phone had made several trips into town and back to the home compound of the drug dealer Chavez (the Tiger) near San Elizario.

"The last hit we got was yesterday at the compound. The odd thing is they never used the phone for calls or texts after the first one when we tagged it." The three looked around and smiled. These amateurs must have forgotten to remove the battery.

"What I don't understand," Kevin asked, "was why they were mixed up with a drug lord." No one could understand why those

Girl Scouts always looking to be the good guys were in bed with drug dealers. "We need lots more intel."

"Kevin, get me the satellite photos of this compound." He told Russ to find out who they had on the ground near there and their loyalties? "Let's get some real-time intel from the village and see if we can pin them down to a certain place and time."

"Ted, get me the current files on Chavez and his business. We just might have a real win-win-win scenario in front of us, so I will talk with our friend and let them know we have found the problem." Just then, a knock on the door and a beautiful woman of maybe twenty-six walked in.

"Sorry to bother you, Assistant Director, but your transport to the capital is here."

"Thanks, I'll be right with you. Would you be so kind as to grab my copies for the briefing, and you know how the president always wants hard copies. Paper will be the death of him one day." They all laughed.

* * *

It was a clear night, and the cantina was full of drunk locals who washed everything down with cheap tequila. More and more men were filling the room, and it was clear they were not drunk or there to drink. Two large men grabbed the bartender and pulled him to the end of the old bar. They asked him if there had been any strangers there tonight, and if so, where were they? The man was truly frightened for his life as he knew the two Chavez men were known for their brutality. Suddenly two more men arrived at the end of the bar and pushed their .45s into the backs of the Chavez soldiers.

"Our patron wants these strangers delivered to him."

"So does ours," the Chavez men stated, now confused over the competition. He explained they had twenty men with them, the one Chavez boss bragged. He spoke with an air of confidence coming over him and his speech.

The Sanchez man shoved his gun deeper into his fat bartender's side and said, "We have thirty, so it will be a true battle to see."

The blood leaving his face, the Sanchez boss stated the obvious. "How is it we are both here to retrieve the same package?" All four of the men relaxed a bit then brought their attention back to the bartender.

"Where the hell are they?" all four yelled at once. Someone unplugged the old jukebox, and the room became deadly silent as everyone turned to the end of the bar and the loud discussion. Suddenly it was like everyone in the room had a gun and held it up at once. Any customers not involved dove for cover under the overturned tables. Both bosses raised their hands and yelled for everyone to be calm, that there was no problem.

"We need to call our patrons and clear this up!" the one boss yelled, placing his gun on the bar so everyone could see. Outside, the rumble of heavy trucks and screeching breaks got everyone's attention. The doors burst open, and in came both police and military personal, all heavily armed and in protective gear. After everyone had lowered their guns, in strutted a police captain in full dress uniform.

"You drug trash are going to kill each other tonight?" He walked over to the bar and the bosses. "So where are your patrons? I do not see them, and I was told they would be here and looking to kill each other."

Chavez's man told the captain they were there to pick up some old friends of the Tiger. Sanchez's man quickly added that it appeared they were there for the same friends. The captain looked puzzled and wondered who these men were that were so popular. No one spoke until the bartender sheepishly handed the captain an envelope. He opened it, read it, and crumbled it into a ball and threw it back at the bartender.

"It appears we have all been tricked," the captain remarked, his face growing redder. "Someone wanted to send a message to all of us and maybe hoped we would all kill each other in the process." He went on to turn and address the entire room. He spoke loud enough for everyone to hear. He told everyone how the patrons had wakened a sleeping giant. It looked like they were going to try and clear this land of the drug people. "As of this minute"—he looked around—"tell your patrons they can no longer expect any help from the police or local military. If they kill you all or you kill each other is no longer my problem" The captain planned to wait till the dust settled and then establish a connection with whomever remained standing.

When the two drug lords heard what their men had to say, they were both angry and confused. Again, an American man and a crippled woman had set them up. They both thought the other was trying to take over their business when it now appeared they had a common enemy. The note had been recovered from the bartender and shared with both bosses. It made clear the police and military involvement in the drug trade was not only well-known but well-documented. Times and names and actions were going to be released to the US drug enforcement people as well as the press in the US and Mexico.

Both drug lords were having the same thoughts. How should they move against this threat to both of them? Could they join forces to solve both their problems? Together they would have enough power to squash anyone that challenged them, even the police and military that had abandoned them both. Maybe together they could expand their US business, which they had both been making inroads. It was Chavez that blinked first.

"Get me Sanchez on the phone. Now." When Chavez picked up the phone, the hair on his neck raised. He was about to offer a truce and possibly a merger with the man he grew up to hate. The man that had killed his men, stole his workers, and business at times. He hesitated when he heard Sanchez's voice.

"Why do you call me, you piece of shit? I have enough problems without wasting my time with you."

Chavez bit his tongue and said, "It appears we have the same problem. These gringos think they can just come here and take what is mine." He paused. "What is ours." He went on to say how they both had lost many men and product to these people. It needed to end now, was Sanchez's remark. "Big talk from a man who had them once and let them get away." Chavez knew he shouldn't have said that.

"True." That made Chavez sit back as he never thought he would hear him agree.

"Alone it will be difficult, but together we can solve both our problems. We should join together." There was a few minutes of silence, then Chavez made the offer. "When we eliminate these jackals, we can then talk about the future of both our businesses. Maybe work together to increase our US customers." Chavez knew that would get his attention as he had an insatiable appetite for new markets and the money they brought. "Think on this. We can talk more about a mutually beneficial alliance tomorrow."

* * *

Jesus came into the small work area in the barn. "Padre, there is a man in the town looking for you. He is American, and my friends say he is with the drug people that work with the government."

Archie told him to find him and bring him to the old church. Archie sat down with us all, and we discussed the now fast-moving dance we were in. Now it appeared a new player has entered the scene. Someone from the DEA could have a connection with the CIA. I went to the church first to take up a defensive position in case it was a trap. I was in the burned-out church bell tower where I had a commanding view of all roads into town. Both Mom and Six had set up firing positions where they could cover Archie at the meet. We all had multiple weapons and plenty of spare ammo. We each had taken three LAW launchers from our munitions stockpile. Sam worked on the taps she had on the drug lord's phones. They both used new age scrambling devises, which just slowed Sam down but didn't stop her. She monitored all the phones she had logged in. Also looked for satellite phone communications from the area. There had been a lot of activity and several cryptic discussions about an upcoming summit.

The DEA agent got out of his car and walked up to the old church and sat down on one of the few wooden pews that had been moved outside, which looked out of place with all the burnt wood. He looked around as if to check out the scene but was not the least bit worried. Arch walked toward the agent from the corner of the church. His hood pulled over his head with his hands hidden inside the long sleeves. We were sure those fighting swords were hidden the sleeves. He walked right to him and stood in front of him.

"I understand you are looking for me."

"Yes, I am, Padre. My name is James Pritcher, and I am with the DEA here in Mexico. Your name has come up recently in talk about the two local cartels and the problems that seem to plague them both." He went on to state that they both seemed to have suffered something interesting problems with a superior force.

Archie agreed he had heard of their misfortune. "How is that my business, or how could I be involved?"

"I'm not sure, but let me first say I have no issues with these drug pushing bastards killing each other off." If someone was helping to rid every one of them, so much the better. He told Arch they had chased their tails for years over the two local cartels. This was the first time they had seen their business suffer to such a degree.

"I must agree. It's good to see them suffer so," Archie said, but he wondered how a padre from such a small burned-out church could help him.

The agent asked him to help gather intel from his flock. He told him he appeared to be an American. "And from the way you carry yourself, I'll bet a veteran." He didn't know much more about this padre from a small burned-out church, or so he said. "I don't even know your name."

Archie smiled at the DEA man and said, "Gabriel. I hear the two cartels are thinking of banding together to fight their mutual enemy."

"If you hear anything or can think of anything, I would appreciate you calling."

"And I will do the same."

James got up and started to walk away. He turned. "More than just one three-letter agency is looking for you and your friends. Believe me when I say I'm truly your friend and will help if I can." He turned again and walked back to his car.

James was a dedicated man that was driven by the death of his little sister from an overdose given to her by a Mexican dealer in Los Angeles. The dealer had been arrested and returned to Mexico four times previously for being in the US illegally. They never got him for his drug dealing or his constant abuse of minor girls. He just kept coming back, and the authorities didn't seem to care. "Come here, have your fun, and worst case you get a free bus ride back to Mexico." He had raped his sister and then gave her the hotshot to keep her from testifying. After her death, he felt a need to make a difference in the drug enforcement. He joined the DEA to help stem the flow of drugs to the US and maybe keep someone's sister from ending up the same way. Eventually he was assigned to a satellite office in Mexico. It was fate, or so he thought, that put him in a small Mexican police station. The police there had a prisoner that had offered up information for his freedom. He knew this was the normal cycle for people in the drug trade. Get caught, give up someone else, and walk. Imagine his surprise when the prisoner turned out to be none other than the lowlife that had killed his sister years before. They could never prove the murder, so they once again deported him. James never forgot, and the man's face was burned into his brain where each day he prayed he would find him. He gladly took the prisoner from the locals and gave the local chief his expected payoff. He could hardly control his anger and extreme excitement he felt. As he drove with the dealer in the back seat, he asked him if he was ever in the US. He laughed and said he goes there often for vacation. It was not hard getting in if you knew the right people. James fought the thoughts running through his head the best he could. He couldn't stoop to his level. But then the fool made his last mistake. He told James how much he loved little girls in America. How they were so easy and dumb when it came to drugs and sex. He was looking forward to getting a little once he was released in the US. James slammed on the breaks and lifted his elbow to meet the face of the mouthy dealer. He shot forward, unable to stop himself because of the cuffs which held his hands behind him.

"What the hell you doing?" he screamed through broken teeth and nose. James jumped out, opened the rear door, and pulled the bloodied man out. He slammed him against the side of the car and then spun him around. The drug dealer's nose was broken, and he kept spitting blood at James. "I'm not telling you or your bosses nothing."

"I can't wait to tell the cops what happened here." James looked around. There was no one to be seen for miles in any direction. "Remember a girl named Sara in Los Angeles? The one you raped and murdered, and they just let you go?"

He smiled and said, "Yeah, she was a sweet young piece. A little bit of a fight. But well worth the effort. She was—"

He never got to say *worth it* because James blew the back of his head out with one shot between the eyes. Removing the cuffs, he left the body behind some rocks far off the road, just another pile of coyote bait. He headed back, putting together his story of how he jumped him and escaped. He would lose his gun when he got back, telling how his prisoner got it away from him.

That was the day the CIA recruited him.

Someone in a computer room in Langley made the connection between the well-documented drug dealer and the young DEA agent. It was a constant fishing tournament to land new operatives or find ones that could be compromised. When the small-town cop arrested him and entered his name and fingerprints into the system, the compromise was in motion. He was requested from headquarters to transport the dealer back to the DEA holding area. He had no idea who he would be picking up for transport. It was a fifty-fifty chance as to rather he would seek his vengeance for his sister or not. No matter, the dealer was going to die, and the CIA would hold his death over James from that point on. So many innocent men were used by the company in this way. Using him to keep the CIA up-to-date on the activities of the DEA in Mexico. Another less than willing asset of the CIA that could be used in any way they wanted. James wondered why there were no questions about his prisoner when he returned. Apparently, no one knew he went to pick him up or cared, let alone returned empty-handed. His life changed forever when that CIA agent walked in his office and closed the door.

"Guess you're wondering why I'm here." He went on tell James the story of a lowlife drug dealer who seemed to have disappeared. About a young DEA agent that had lost his beautiful teenage sister some years back to the very same missing dealer. "See where I'm going with this? My name is Kevin, and I'm from Langley." James squirmed a bit, waiting to hear more. "We own you now." There it was. His life was now in the hands of the spooks he hated so.

We all asked what the useless drug agent wanted. "I think he knows I am involved but doesn't seem to have a problem with it. He actually came across as trying to warn me or us." Arch went on to explain how he told him about the cartels getting together to fight someone. He also made the comment about other three-letter agencies looking for the same people. We knew he must mean our friends from the CIA.

"I'm sure," Mom said. He was hoping they might be of some help. He was surprised it took them so long to connect the cell phone we planted to us. We assumed they would do anything to get ahold of us or kill us. "We had better step it up." He asked what the latest was on our cartel friends and if they had kissed and made friends yet.

Sam spun around. "It looks like it. They are arguing as to where and when."

It seemed that being Chavez had come up with the plan, Sanchez wanted to meet at his place. Which made sense as we did not leave much for them to use back at the Sanchez compound. The Sanchez home was beautiful but lacked the security needed for such a monumental meeting. Chavez, however, had a large hacienda. It was remote as well and very well protected, more so now for sure. They were hashing out the numbers of men each could have with them. It sounded like maybe sixty to eighty bad guys could be waiting for us.

"Wow, we can't do that by ourselves." Six whistled. "Even with me here."

We all got a good laugh despite the fact we were wondering if we had bit off more than we could chew. That's when Mom began to fill us in on his plan.

He felt if we could get the boys from the pigpen involved, we could make it look like we were dead and gone. Everyone laughed when I said, "Again?"

Mom thought if we let them think we were killed trying to hit the big meeting, they might have the military and DEA show up and arrest all the bad guys. It would be a huge feather in their hats, and doing that everyone wins. DEA would get two drug lords and whatever else they could salvage; CIA would make sure we were dead and no longer a threat. They would whisk off the old drug lords for disposal, and the cartel boys would reopen with new bosses. He bet the CIA would help them get back operational before the end of the next day.

"This helps us how?" Sam asked. "I don't like the dead and gone part too much."

I smiled and squeezed her shoulder. We would pull the old switcheroo just like Mom had pulled on us in the beginning. We would make them think we died trying to take the compound. It would take some planning, but it was worth a try. We all agreed and began making preparations for our deaths.

First, we bought an old New York State school bus for $2,000 from a used car dealer in town. He only wanted $1,200 but the $800 tip would seal his lips, at least till we were done. There were hundreds of these old yellow beasts running around, most spewing dark black smoke. No one would give ours a second look as there were so many running around. Second, Archie went about installing enough C-4 to make a show and in turn ignite the phosphorus and homemade napalm. We needed a controlled burn that would not leave much but some DNA in some hidden areas. There was no doubt the CIA boys would want samples for DNA testing and verification. We each had two units of blood removed over the twenty-four-hour period. We then froze the blood to make for easier handling and placement. We found Sam's old powered wheelchair and placed it in the bus. It had been destroyed in the fire that gutted the church. They would be able to cross-check the serial numbers back to her. Six donated his fancy running legs that looked like stainless steel barrel staves that also had serial numbers stamped in them. The chair we placed next to the side emergency door in such a way as it would be blown out. We used old shoes that were our sizes and some of our clothing to add to the deception. We trimmed from our heads, except for Arch. Mom suggested pubic hair as well if we could because no one would guess we salted with that. We all just smirked when Six told us he didn't have much of that to offer. Archie took all of that and extra clothing and prepared it by taping it to the windows so it would be blown clear and not destroyed by the extreme heat from inside of the bus. Mom told us that the CIA cleanup crews were always in a hurry to get in and out. They wanted DNA samples from hair, blood, anything easily found. They'd see a metal leg, that's great. A tore-up wheelchair would be a find that would excite them. Clothes with blood or blood residue anywhere gets them excited as well, so that's why we played vampire. Sam had added some old laptops that she had scrubbed and preheated the hard drives. Six took some weapons with extras clips and added them. We all added our driver's licenses and wallets, along with other IDs and credit cards that we knew we would need to replace later. We took about $60,000 in the bills we had liberated and spread them through the bus.

Archie walked out with fatigues on and his robe in his hands. "I'll replace this when we get home."

When the time came, we would take the frozen blood and put it in pockets along with the hair to match the person it was meant for. Some on Six's legs and on Sam's wheelchair to help sell the scam we hoped would work.

Sam left the room for a few minutes and returned with a smile. "They set the meeting for tomorrow night."

We all headed to get some sleep because tomorrow we would die in the eyes of the people that were hunting us. We all found our cots and let sleep take us. What seemed like hours was only minutes when I felt a soft hand find my groin.

As I opened my eyes, Sam covered my mouth. "I'm not going to die without having you again." She let the blanket drop from her shoulders, and I pulled her naked body from the chair to me.

* * *

Russ sat in his chair, feet up and tilted back which was his trademark position. He listened to the caller for a while and then hung up. "It appears the two warring cartels are becoming friendlier. Our DEA asset says they are planning a big meeting at Chavez's compound tomorrow night. He met with the black monk and is sure he knows something but not sure how much. No one else was around, and he claimed not to know about our problems. The DEA agent has no idea what is going on and thinks we are looking at the monk as a future asset."

The agents believed there was no doubt he was one of the five they wanted. It made sense the others weren't too far away. All they needed now was to put the cartels and their prey together and just go in and get them. Everything was set with the locals. They were the easy part. A few bucks spread around here and there and they were ready for anything. Justifying the operation from their side would be a bit trickier as no one ever wanted to step on Mexico's toes or make them look bad. Russ said he had mentioned in a passing conversation to the president that the drug trafficking was getting much worse. They seemed to have no fear of the US ever doing anything to them. As the past governor of Texas, he knew that would light him up. Russ wanted the president to think about taking some sort of action. They wanted him to stew and get angrier.

"Sir, I may be able to take two drug lords out in one raid by the DEA and locals."

The president was excited. "Make it happen, Russ. We will deal with the fallout later."

"It's time to make these pains in our asses go away for good!" Russ exclaimed. "We have the operations center to ourselves tomorrow tonight. Kevin, you bring the beer. Ted, you bring the food. It will be a real show, I promise."

Kevin wondered out loud if the locals could be trusted to hold the five in body bags or jail for them.

"I'm sure." Russ waved the question aside. "Everyone will be well taken care of, the cartels and the five pains in the asses." He spun in his chair and picked up his phone and asked if they had contacted the gentleman he had asked them to find. Then he hung up. He smiled and looked at the other two. "Don't you guys have anything better to do?"

* * *

Sanchez's convoy was made up of three SUVs and two trucks, each loaded to the max with men and guns. Sanchez sat in the front of the second SUV with a double playing him in the third. Not trusting anyone, let alone his rival Chavez, he took lots of precautions, including another twenty-five armed men just minutes away from the compound. Once through the main gate, they pulled up to the front door and began an exit that was well rehearsed. The men in the truck first formed a lane for Sanchez to walk through to the house, and the men would move forward, taking the line of protection in with them. All the SUVs emptied at once and headed inside. The body double remained in the vehicle he came in. Once inside, each of Sanchez's men matched up with one of Chavez's men, already at their assigned positions in the great hall.

Chavez came from a door on the right and walked right up to his old school friend. Sanchez move in and reached for Chavez's hand. There was a pause, and then both men had a quick shack. Chavez motioned for everyone invited to enter the room for the meeting. It was pre-agreed that only four bodyguards would accompany their patron. Once inside, the men formed a semicircle around the two drug Lords as they sat in two overstuffed chairs with a small table between them. Chavez began by offering Sanchez a cigar and a glass of tequila.

"So how do we put an end to these people?" Sanchez asked.

"With our combined strength, we can take on anyone. The Mexican government, if we wish," bragged Chavez. They both laughed, and the tension began to reduce.

"This is what we know," Sanchez began. He explained that the meddling padre from town was involved with four of his friends. One was a crippled woman in a wheelchair. Sanchez looked to see if he struck a nerve with Chavez.

Chavez just smiled and said, "She is to be brought to me alive. I have no interest in seeing the others, but she owes me."

"I truly understand," Sanchez said. "You have my sympathy. I know how much Miguel meant to you. It shall be done, my friend, if we can."

"I see your family is in Mexico City, shopping," Chavez stated as matter of fact rather than a question.

Sanchez became stiff and turned bright red. "How do you know where my family is?"

"The same as you know where mine is."

Sanchez relaxed and smiled. "Maria and Sophia planned this, didn't they?"

He did not wait for an answer. "I've known of their little shopping trips together for years."

"You cannot stand between sisters. Believe me, I have tried." Both men laughed and sipped their drinks.

"Maybe we would do better to listen to our wives and make this a more permanent venture. To the death of the Americans and the beginning of a new era."

They were both excited and almost giddy with the thought of a new cartel, both picturing themselves as the heads. They puffed on their cigars and talked about plans to rid themselves of this gringo plague that come. Chavez felt they should hold the villagers as hostages until they surrendered. Sanchez told of his run-in with them at his compound. They did not seem to be the type to just give up. Besides, those people meant nothing to them. The padre maybe would come, but he doubted the rest would follow. The first bottle of tequila was gone, and another came to replace it. Like old hunting friends, they talked about traps and ways to kill their prey.

Chavez sat back. "I would offer you some food, but I sent everyone away earlier."

* * *

Sam had made sure our communications were able to be picked up by anyone with real-time listening equipment. It only stood to reason that if the pigpen boys knew we were there, they would be listening to try and find us. All our communications were run through a repeater in the bus, so anyone listening would triangulate the bus as the source. We began our night by taking the pickup to a location far enough away yet where we could see the compound in the distance.

I took the now prepared bus to a place about one mile from the compound and waited for the time to set our deaths in motion. Our frozen blood was placed in different locations in the bus. The clothing had some in the pockets or rolled up in them. Some of Sam's hair was wedged in the chair and Six's wedged in the old leg along with some blood. I had a new dirt bike, compliments of the Smith's one-stop military shopping center. The plan was to get close to the action and set the bus on a collision course with the compound gate, where it would draw attention and gunfire. I would detonate the explosives which would start the show, then escape to the others with the bike. When the police and army arrived, it would look like we had tried to breech the main gate but were cut down by the superior firepower. We had no doubt the drug lords and their men would be taken to the police station. Their pockets ran deep, so they would most likely spend less than an hour at the station before being slipped out the back. The CIA people would let it be known they wanted to find us or whatever was left. They would let the police take what drugs were there and make many token arrests. It seemed like a solid plan and only hinged on rather our friends in the CIA were listening and were willing to take the bait.

Sam and Mom talked on the comm link as if they were preparing for our assault. Mom told her how he was almost in position and would meet her back at the bus for the assault. Back in town, Jesus was sitting across from the army barracks, which they shared with the regional police. We kept checking with him as he would tell us when the cavalry was on their way. We had timed it to take them approximately thirty minutes at full speed to get there.

Mom looked at everyone and shrugged. "Maybe they don't hear us so they don't know what were up to."

"If they are listening, they hear us, I'm sure," Sam said.

It all seemed wrong. We made lots of chatter like we were prepared to hit the hacienda.

"Okay," Mom said. "Let's make it a go, a quick hit and run. Regroup at the bus for our departure at the front gate."

We all gave the go signal as if we were headed into the compound to begin our attack. We made it clear we were all in the bus and on our way. I removed the bike from the homemade rack on the bus and hid it in some brush. It was overcast enough that we hoped it would hide us from any satellite the boys in Washington might have access to. Just in case, I had set up several scarecrow-type figures around the bus. I walked around several times and didn't hide my moving the bike around. Now that it was time, I took the scarecrows and led them to the bus as if we were talking with them. Mom had warned us they might have a satellite repositioned to look for us. Once they intercepted our communications, they would know where to look if they weren't already.

Jesus came online. "There is something happening." A truck had pulled up, and they brought a body in the front door of the police station. It had been about forty-five minutes, and it didn't appear to be anything unusual as that happened all the time. He could see inside the parking lot, and all the trucks were empty. They are washing them. It looked like a siesta for everyone. "I guess the police will not be coming your way, Senor Gilligan." He went on to describe how there were lots of people coming and going. The local commander had come and left again. There were men that looked like Americans standing around talking on their phones. It appeared they were upset, but he could not get close enough to hear.

It sounded strange hearing that call sign again. I had told Jesus he could use it to make him feel more a part of what was happening.

"Something's wrong, very wrong," I said to myself. Then to the rest, "It looks like the locals either don't know or don't care about our party."

Mom checked back. "Send the bus. I don't know what's going on, but we should go for it."

I got in and drove the bus lights off, a short distance to the crest of a slight hill that ran straight down to the main gates. I got as close as I could, and when I saw the men pointing and aiming at me, I got up tied off the knot in the rope that held the steering wheel in place. I pulled the throttle part out, and the bus began its run for the gate. I ran down the aisle and pushed open the rear door and jumped, tucking into a rolling. I found some cover behind a rock and turned to watch. The bus was on its death run. It built speed as it went down the hill and started to take a few hits from the gate guards. By the time it reached the gate, it was taking a massive number of hits, and all the tires were now flat, the bus rocking. The windows were all blacked out with paint, so the guards had no idea who or how many were in the bus. It came to a stop only a few yards from the gate. The guards actually cheered as they slowly surrounded their prize.

I pressed the detonator. The explosion was a true credit to Archie's talents. The bus literally blew apart, killing anyone that was within fifty yards of it, protected or not. A fireball at first, and then a fire that was so intense I could feel it at the top of the rise. The windows in the main hacienda blew inward, and everyone was partially or totally deaf from the explosion. The two drug lords were thrown behind desks and sofas for protection by their personal bodyguards. The doors burst open, and the two groups of guards came in, taking up defensive positions and looking to their individual patrons for orders. Chavez screamed for answers, as did Sanchez. Was it an attack? There were no more guns firing outside as they were before. A bit of calm came over the cartel leaders. A guard ran in and reported that there was an attempt to breach the main gate, but it had been stopped. Unfortunately, it destroyed the gate and part of the wall, as well as killing many of the guards. There appeared to be no second wave of attack. The two leaders stood and walked cautiously to the shattered windows and surveyed the destruction. At the gate was a huge ball of fire that was so intense it hurt to look directly at it for too long. With no real fire equipment to use, the fire would just need to run its course. What available water there was would be preserved to protect the main house.

They faced each other, and Sanchez said, "We need to kill these American bastards now."

A combat dressed guard entered the room, out of breath. "Padrone, we found a mangled wheelchair with scraps of bloody clothes embedded in the wall, along with some weapons."

Chavez smiled. "Well, at least we got the wheeled bitch and hopefully the rest as well. Let's drink to their deaths and that of anyone else that tries to challenge us. The Mexican government nor the spineless American from Texas that sits in his big office in Washington will dare to oppose us."

I watched the compound for a while to see how things shook out. The whole area was in chaos when I was shaken by a sudden gust of wind and sandstorm. Seconds later, I heard the loud scream that I knew could only come from a jet engine. I looked back toward the compound just in time to see a long stubby winged missile. It was the body of a cruise missile, and I watched as it entered the hacienda. Like an arrow, it went right through the wall just above the front door. The explosion was something I had never seen in all my combat experience. The entire house just blew apart and became a large pile of burning rubble. The beautiful home of the Chavez family was no more. Then the second cruise missile flew over me, and another huge explosion. The second was almost directly where the bus had once been. There was nothing left of the compound or home. Everywhere there were secondary explosions from cars and trucks and ammo. *This is what hell on earth looks like,* I thought. A deafening silence came over the area. It seemed like no one remained alive. The bus explosion was pale in comparison to what I had just witnessed.

* * *

The satellite view cleared and showed bodies strewn around the area and a few men running or crawling about what was left. The entire wall screen showed nothing but death and destruction.

"Damn, that's what I'm talking about!" Russ yelled, taking a big hit from his beer and pointing at the screen. Ted and Kevin had that deer in the headlights look.

"What the hell just happened?" Ted asked, almost in shock.

"I just put an end to drug traffic from two big hitters. The two that have been making inroads into our friend's turf. The whip cream is, I killed off five people that could have been pains in our asses." The screen showed a massive ball of fire at the main gate. He got up and pointed to the screen. "That, my friends, was the last bus ride our five friends will ever take. I just wish we had the satellite feed in time to see the whole thing. Now let's wrap this up and go get laid."

"How did you get permission to make two cruise missile hits on a Mexican citizen's home?" the other two men said in unison.

"I told you that I let the president know they had no respect for him. They shouldn't have pissed him off like they did."

"How did they do that?" Kevin asked.

Russ dropped the empty bottle in the trash and pulled another from the cooler. He took a chicken wing and ate the meat from it, throwing the wing after the empty bottle. He told them the murder of an American DEA agent was a line you don't cross with the big man.

"He had told the president that Agent James Pritcher had been taken several days ago, and we feared for his life. The president said that was the last straw. He had warned the president of Mexico he was thinking of taking a major step. He directed us to find the agent and let him know of his condition. He also wanted potential targets if anything happened to him. He was prepared to set the new bar in his war on drugs. Too bad about old Jimmy." He motioned to the operator seated at the console. "Tell bravo team they can make their way to ground zero, and get me the proof I want. Well, gentlemen, we should know if we were successful in a few days or so. Let's get out of here. I suddenly feel like a steak."

* * *

I just stood there in complete disbelief. I heard the missiles go overhead but never had time to register what they were till it was over.

"What the hell?" Mom asked to anyone in general. There were a few men staggering around, but no one that had any fight in them. The road was covered with bodies and body parts. I took one last look and ran for the dirt bike. When I reached the rest of them at the pickup, I walked over, shaking my head.

"What was that crap?" I asked. "Looks like they used extreme prejudice to get the five of us. It makes no sense to me to kill sixty or seventy people to get us."

The ones that ordered this strike could not have known if there were and innocent civilians in there. I wondered if any of the Chavez family, women or children, had been in the house.

"Who could have that kinda juice?" Sam asked, the fear now obvious in her face.

"Only the president could authorize a strike of this magnitude in a friendly country."

"So he is in on this and looking to kill us as well or is being played."

Sam's concern was now reaching a new level. Mom walked over to her and put his arm around her. "If it makes you feel better, I don't think the president thought he was killing us tonight." Two heads of local drug cartels and their men along with sending a message to the others was more like it.

"Why would the president take such defined action on just a couple drug dealers?" Archie questioned.

"I guess it's time to tell you guys who is after us."

We all looked at each other and said in unison, "You think?"

"We know the three pigpen jerks from the war were involved."

Then Mom dropped the bomb. "I might have failed to mention that the head spook that set all this in motion so many years ago doesn't just work for the CIA but is the assistant director now. So he could have set up the president to help him clear up a personal issue without his even knowing it." Everyone walked away in different directions to digest the new information.

After about twenty minutes, Mom called us all back to the truck. "We know now how they got the president to do it." He went on tell us that the body dumped in front of the police station was that of the DEA agent. The one Archie had spoken to yesterday. His throat was cut, the warning of "Go home Gringos" cut clearly in his chest. The Internet had been all about it. They showed the covered body and kept showing photos of the young agent. The US president was telling everyone he ordered the strike against the killers of an

American DEA agent. How he was fed up with the Mexican cartels filling the streets of America with their poison and killing our people.

"How the hell could the president have known about it and ordered the strike so fast? Just minutes after the DEA body showed up?"

"He couldn't," Mom said. "These things can take hours to prepare, and someone must have told him about the agent before the body even turned up. Someone that knew it all ahead of time. Most likely the ones that ordered it and set things in motion." It seemed like these guys would stop at nothing to get us. They were even willing to kill one of their own, the DEA guy.

"What now?" Sam asked. "It sure seems like they will do anything to kill us."

"Oh, but remember, we all died in that old bus tonight, or at least they will think we did. For a while."

We needed to go home and find out just what they think we knew and why it scared them so much as to kill without remorse. We underestimated them and their unlimited abilities and apparent true need to silence us. We needed to get out of that hole and start data collection. We needed to know and understand what the game was before we started to join in and kick their asses. They all piled into the truck, and I followed, keeping to the side and shoulder to avoid their dust storm. My mind flashed back to that rice paddy so many years ago and the dirt-covered family we were supposed to save. How had that day brought us here and cost so many lives?

Our departure from the hill and back to town had gone unnoticed as all attention was being paid to the violent end of the two cartels. We saw a steady line of lights from vehicles headed to devastation. We pulled off the road, and everyone ducked down and covered themselves with the tarp we had. Sam laid down, her head in my lap so it appeared I was alone. No one gave the old pickup with the man driving any notice because they were all busy looking at the huge glow in the sky ahead. Several large trucks full of soldiers passed by, along with police vehicles and private trucks. Once they passed and there was a break in the line, I pulled back on the road and headed out. We headed directly to the old mine we had used before and where we had stored our extra items. We had moved all our remaining supplies and weapons into the dilapidated and abandoned mine. When I pulled up, I parked the truck behind a large pile of discarded dirt and rocks. We all went inside where we found the table and some kerosene lamps we had left. Six pulled down the tarp we had placed across the entrance to keep any light in the mine from being noticed from outside.

There was doubt that none of the cartel leaders or bosses had survived the total destruction of that night. We had only planned to fake our deaths and hopefully get the CIA off our backs till we could formulate our next move. We never dreamed that the pigpen boys wielded that kind of power or would use it. We sat and discussed our next big problem—getting back home or at least back into the States. The Smiths had set up a trust in the only international bank in the area for us. They used some seed money we had liberated from the cartel. They were able to discreetly open it with a deposit of 1.5 million dollars. It was for the people of San Elizario and would be distributed anonymously for the needs of the village and its people. It would assure that enough food would be available and rebuild the church in the process. There would be health care for everyone, and the school that closed years ago would be reopened. We all agreed that we owed them all of that and much more. Mrs. Smith's father would administer the trust and make sure it never ran out. He had made it clear to everyone that the village was protected by the black padre's friends. If anything bad happened to anyone, they would come and rain vengeance on them in the name of the dead padre. It was hard to leave Jesus and the others as we had become very attached to them all. Jesus would be in charge, or so he thought, along with the woman that had lost her son and husband to the drug dealers. It was hard not going back to say goodbye, and worse letting Jesus and the rest think we all had died in the battle. It was the only way because there would be people looking for any sign of us being alive. No one would be safe if there were any rumors of our survival. It might be a cruel way to leave, but one that we knew was right for everyone. We had hidden what remained of our arsenal in the mine for Mr. Smith to recover later and most likely sell again. We could not get the weapons or other hardware into the US. It was going to be interesting enough getting ourselves back as it was.

At that point, we did not really know what our next move would be, nor what equipment might be needed. Besides, we had Smith's number, and he seemed to have an endless supply of anything we needed. We also formed a bond with him and had no misgivings of leaving the remaining drug money with him to get across the border for us. Taking just a few thousand each for the road back would be reasonable to anyone that found us with it. Americans entering the US with several millions of dollars would certainly cause undue scrutiny. We dared not do anything to slow the process of getting through Customs. Sam took a laptop with her, having wiped the others clean and encrypting what remained on the one she had. She left the others where Jesus would find them hidden in the old church. He had a favorite hiding place he told Sam about one night. She never said anything, but we know she missed her old chair. The power chair was like her throne where she felt safe and in control. She had spent hours designing her hidden toys and making it a control center for her hacking. We had all agreed it would be a priority for us the replace it when we got back and settled. Everything else stayed, and we wanted it taken cared of so the locals didn't get their hands on it and use it to get themselves killed. That's why we had given the Smiths the location of the mine so they could take care of things for us. We knew it would only be days before a new cartel was formed. What had happened would slow them down, but ultimately all the money involved in the drug trade would help bring the serpent back to life. Mrs. Smith's father's warnings of the black padre and Gabriel's army should keep the village safe.

We took the van and headed to Northern Mexico to make our crossing at El Paso. The bad roads and our choice to use the side roads on and off made the journey take some three days. We only went into a small town when we needed to get gasoline or water. Stopping at night, we would find a secluded spot to make camp. It was a way for us to decompress and clear our heads for what was in store for us. On the second night, we decided to clear the air. We sat around a small campfire and began to let out our thoughts and find words.

Archie was first. He was upset to have to leave his small group of followers and especially Jesus. We knew we could never get him across the border and feared for his life through association with us. "Don't get me wrong, guys, but I wish you had all just left me alone." Then after thinking, he said, "No, I was just existing, hiding from my past that I did not even remember." That was a blessing for him, even though deep down he still remembered and hid from the guilt. We all looked at each other and agreed that we lived, but it was just an existence for us. Each in our own way, we had dealt with that survivor guilt that had haunted us.

Six put all his effort into helping others learn to live with their disabilities and making them a positive part of their lives. He filled the emptiness with a purpose that drove him to stay strong. Me, I just hid in the middle of nowhere and lived day by day. I convinced myself I was happy, and the vastness of the land made me feel small yet part of it. I woke each day thinking of them and my small family I lost that day in the jungle. I looked at Sam. A tear in her eye showed the woman that lay in hiding behind the warrior.

"I worked hard to get over the loss of you guys." Her eyes met mine. "It was hard, and I never stopped thinking of that day and that little girl and her smile. Losing you guys was the start, but getting over the loss of my mobility was an equally hard struggle." We were all back together, and all she could think of was how the president, whose office we all swore to protect, tried to kill us. We all knew or at least prayed that he had no idea we were the true targets. Now her tears were flowing. "We don't have a home to go back to. Who are we? What are we? Where do we go from here?" The silence was deafening. We all just sat there in quiet and thought. I pulled Sam to me, and she buried her face in my shoulder.

After some time sitting there in silence, Mom rose and stood in front of us. His voice had a quiver to it that none of us had ever heard before. "This is all on me." He had made the decision that day back on the carrier. He could see just how intent those guys were to cover up whatever crap they had done. He saw the power they could muster when those Cobras chased us to the coast. He needed to keep us alive, and this was the best way he could come up with. "My friends helped me make the CIA director at the time understand that we had taken steps. Ones that would blow the whole operation out of the water if he did not agree. They knew he felt pressure from many directions, but he agreed. The primary agreement was that you four never get your heads together and start questioning what happened."

"We would have kept quiet if it was a sanctioned operation for our country's good," I spoke out. But never if it meant the death of those poor farmers and their kids, which everyone agreed. Mom knew that, but this operation was so far off the books and had fingers going way up the chain. There was no way anyone could have trusted anyone's word.

Mom went on to tell how when he returned home, he set about making sure we all got the best we could get in care and rehab. It seemed we were becoming as well-adjusted as possible. We all laughed. We just help killed fifty plus people, bad guys, but we killed them. Looks like we were all back close to 100 percent. He wanted us to understand he had no idea the hate and need to silence us was so strong. Shortly after he got us all settled, he had a visit from Mr. Russel Gordon at his home. That was the name of the bastard that started all this, the head of the pigpen group. He made it clear that Mom better keep the deal alive or he would not like the consequences. He mentioned the name of his wife as well as that of his daughter. Told him his family was in play as far as the deal, and if it fell apart, they would suffer as well. He then took a small container and poured pig shit on his boots. "How's that smell, old man?" He laughed, walked away, and got in his car and drove away.

After that, he had put together a secure network for Martha and Jane to use and become part of if this ever happened. They were safe now, but for how long he had no idea. He worked with some cyber people that he had served with to dig into Russ and anyone else that might be involved. He did find out the director of the CIA was involved. Russ was still just a low-level department head but had juice with the director. He later rose to the position of assistant director when one of his predecessors moved up the ladder. He visited him at least once a year for ten years or so but stopped and changed to just pointed e-mails and calls several times a year. He liked to call on his birthday or anniversary to keep that control fresh in his mind.

Chief remained his strongest and most dedicated friend. They stayed in contact using payphones and later those disposable cell phones. He had been doing his own research through some Native American sources that were deep under anyone's radar. They had set up a network to communicate through different medias in the event of this day. Mom had placed an ad in the *New York Times* looking for office space in DC before we left for Mexico. The ad had a call back number that was the code for him to go underground until he heard from Mom or could confirm his death.

We all listened in silence until Sam boke it. "None of us blame you for anything. In fact, we are still alive to have this campfire dance because of your efforts. You have suffered and sacrificed right along with us, and so has your family. Now how the hell do we get our lives back?"

We knew that the dead farm family was used to fill the vice president's and his family's graves. We also knew the CIA helped put it together and most likely were still deeply involved. We were sure drugs were once again the driving force and source of all the money. Money had to be the end game for everyone involved. First we needed to know who, where, and how it all came together. First, we needed to find that fancy dressing son of a bitch vice president that we unknowingly rescued that night at the warehouse. Then we needed to take him apart and get some answers. If we could understand the flow of the money to those people in Washington, we could maybe make it less profitable for them to protect him and possibly end this hunt.

"We could try and go to the press and let them expose the assistant director," Archie spoke out.

"Yes." But Mom was sure they had put in place lots of cover stories for the operation after all those years. For example, the vault that held the bodies that poor farm family was completely destroyed by rioters and the bodies taken and disposed of. A well-orchestrated move by the pigpen crew, I'm sure. The new government condemned the desecration by the rioters but wrote it off as reprisals on the past administration. The president was relocated to the US but was killed along with his family by a bomb placed in their home. A mentally ill man who claimed he had murdered his son set the bomb. We were willing to bet that was too convenient as well. The vice president and his family would have blended in with the other immigrants, especially being no one was looking for them. We needed to find him and his family to find out why the US government was still working so hard to keep their secret.

We had agreed to meet in El Paso on the US side at a Dunkin Donuts at 5:45 p.m. the following day. Sam and I were in the van we had started with. She had hacked the Mexican DMV so the van's plates that we stole seemed good to the look. As we approached the border, I felt the hair go up on my neck, and it started to tingle. Sam reached over and squeezed my hand and smiled.

"Those passports will pass any sort of scrutiny. That was some of my best work." Besides, we were sure the spooks thought we were all dead. She had gotten into the federal passport verification network and had just clicked off the Hold for Questioning tab on our real passports. When they scan them, they would get no flags.

I whispered to her, "This most wanted crap is all new for me and not the way I saw my life going."

She smiled and said, "Yeah, I was enjoying my cushy government job as well until we took on those drug dealing bastards. I won't lie to you, it felt good to be back doing some good and this time seeing the results of our work."

I agreed with her as she pulled up and stopped at the guard post. We had fashioned the steering column with a push for gas and pull for break contraption that Sam had designed. She truly missed driving and the freedom and sense of control it gave her. We felt it looked less menacing for a woman driver, and it also gave me some freedom if something went wrong. The guard would never realize she was paralyzed unless he asked her to step out, which we gambled he wouldn't. Even if they thought we were dead, the old boys in DC might still have a watch list for a woman in a wheelchair. Just in case she had survived and tried to come home. She gave him her best sexy smile and explained we had come down a month ago for a long overdue vacation. We had and entered Mexico through a seaport in the south from a cruise ship. That would explain why the computer database did not show our entry into the country. The ports were notorious for poor record keeping, and few people leaving a ship didn't get right back on. The fake entry stamp Sam had placed on the back of our passports should be acceptable to show our story was good. He looked in the van, which was now empty except for three suitcases. We had left the makeshift ramps back at the mine along with the wheelchair. Two people traveling together would be just the norm, but if she had a wheelchair, it might cause them to rethink their inspection and check more for alerts. He turned to his partner that handed him back the passports with a look of okay.

He handed them back and smiled and said, "Come back again and be prepared. The US side is running very slow."

She smiled at me and told me she had told me so. I explained to her that the tough inspection was coming up. She pulled the short blanket over her controls on the column so if someone looked in, they wouldn't see anything. She had a short dress on so their eyes would go to her legs first. When we reached the US side, we were directed to an inspection pit which we drove over and stopped so two inspectors could look to see if anything looked disturbed or was hidden underneath. Once over the pit, they pulled us over and opened the back and let a dog jump in and sniff around. They asked if they could look in the bags, and we both said, "Sure." Sam explained that there were some dirty clothes in there being we hadn't taken time to clean them. As they searched our bags, a woman guard walked over and asked where we were coming from. Sam told her the same story of how we entered Mexico. We had been in the hills taking photos and just enjoying the time off together.

"Where are you headed?" she asked me, and I told her Jacksonville, Florida, and back to work, which matched our passports.

"I guess all good things come to end," I said, squeezing Sam's leg. She smiled and waved us on, and we headed out for the meeting, letting our nerves relax some.

Mom's crossing was uneventful as he was just another member of a tour group from a senior citizens group from Dallas. He had met with the tour guide in a cantina and discussed the glory days of Vietnam over some local tequila. He explained how his now ex-girlfriend had left him in a cheap motel and went home to the US, taking his wallet and credit cards.

"She at least left me my passport," he said, patting his breast pocket. He explained the young local woman she found in the bathtub might have been part of her issue. After some laughs and more tequila, he convinced him that he would appreciate it if he could help him get back to the USA. He offered him $500, which was all he had left in cash, he said. The tour guide just smiled and told him to keep it. He had been in a similar position while on R&R in Seoul, South Korea. They enjoyed a good laugh and finished their drinks and headed off to the tour bus. He handed the tour guide his passport as he got on and found a seat in the middle of the bus. An older woman sat in the seat next to the window and made no attempt to hide her pleasure of having someone to ride with. He struck up a conversation with him and kept it up as the border guard walked the length of the bus and back. Neither side of the border gave anyone on the bus a second look and were satisfied with the passports and the quick inspection of the compartments underneath. Once again, Sam's magic with the passport worked its charm.

Archie and Six were not so lucky. The Mexican side was painless as they saw Archie's robes that he had secured before we left. They gave him the respect a man of the cloth should get. Rather they were good or bad, no one wanted to take any chances with their final entry to the hereafter. Once at the US side, it changed quickly. The old pickup they were using could barely run, let alone pass any kind of safety inspection. They were pulled to the side and told to get out of the truck. A large boarder guard who appeared to have some authority came over to them. It was apparent he was not having a good day from his stride and look on his face.

"Where are you headed, father?" he asked with a tone of sarcasm in his voice.

Archie told him Waco to see some old friends and try and raise some money for his church. The one he headed up had been destroyed by the feuding drug lords.

"Ahh, yes, I've heard that happens a lot down there. So who is this with you?"

"A parishioner to help carry the money."

He laughed and looked over at his men. "You two smell of drugs," he stated in a matter-of-fact way. A black pastor and his white friend in a truck that looked like it needed to be pushed or hooked to two oxen. Another laugh for his troops, then he grabbed Archie and spun him around and pushed him against the truck bed. "Spread them, father." And he began to roughly search Archie for contraband or weapons. He pulled his robes up and over his head. Under the robes, he had on a pair of old torn jeans and white T-shirt. With a dissatisfied look, the border guard turned to the men and told them he was clean. "Now you," he said to Six, who turned and spread his legs.

As he started to tell the guard about his legs, he was pushed hard against the truck, and the frisking began. Again, before Six could say anything, the guard reached his legs. When he got down the legs and felt his walk-around legs, he kidney punched Six and slammed his head against the truck. Archie spun around, ready to defend his friend when the other guards rushed him and punched him to the ground. They had their guns out and pointed at Arch. The head guard punched Six in the stomach and pushed him to the ground on his back. He reached down and cut his belt off. "What are you hiding here, Mr. Churchgoer?" He grabbed the cuffs of Six's pants and ripped them off in one motion. Once his pants were off, his prosthesis shined from the overhead lights. The head guard stood there with his mouth open. "What the hell, you don't have any legs."

"No shit, Einstein. When you're done sucking air, I want your supervisor out here. And I want him to bring legal with him cause you're going to need them." It was a dangerous bluff but worked well.

The head guard yelled for his men to get off Archie and help them both to their feet. One of them handed Six his pants, and another walked over to the head man and talked into his ear. Then he turned, and the head guard walked back to the offices and the other back to Six.

"I can't even begin to apologize for our boss or what happened here. I will call the shift supervisor and the incident response team, but you gotta know it will be long into tomorrow before everyone has finished covering their ass and making up the story that will be written. Your ex-military, I can see that, so you know I'm telling the truth. I know it sucks, but if you two get in your truck and leave right now, this will end here."

Six looked at the guard. "I've had my share of watching things get changed to fit the right story. And you're right, I'm ex-military. It's been a real pleasure. *Not*. Now show us how to get the hell out of here."

It was 5:30 p.m. when Sam and I pulled into the donut shop. We parked and saw Mom sitting at one of those metal picnic tables out in the back of the store. He had one of those boxes of coffee on the table with cups and all the fixings. Archie and Six were there, and Six pushed a new wheelchair over and positioned it so Sam could jump over into it.

"It's not anything like your old armored tank, but best we could do on short notice."

She had a big smile and said, "I've already begun my plans for the replacement of my new grocery getter."

We all shook hands and had coffee. We all told our stories of the crossing and told Sam what a great job she did on the passports. She gathered them all up and lit one on fire, then added them all to a pile on the ground.

"Those IDs will self-delete from the mainframes of all that share that type of information in about twenty minutes, so they are useless. Back here in the States, we don't need them, so I'll go to work on new driver's licenses and IDs as soon as we land somewhere for a few days. I'll need some special equipment to reproduce them, so I'll start looking for a supplier. A quick trip to OZ will make it all happen."

We all just looked at her and decided to leave it alone.

First thing we needed to do was get some better transport and some carry-around weapons just in case. Mom went off to get some new throw-away cell phones while we checked into a local Motel 6 and one other discounted motel. We then took the van and pickup to a local Walmart. That's where we ditched the truck and took off in the van. While there, we all headed in to get some new clothes and personal stuff before heading back to the two motels. The two motels were located across the street from each other, which we liked. We agreed to catch some shuteye and meet at the twenty-four-hour IHOP down the street at 21:00.

I stayed at the Motel 6 while Sam stayed at the other, as we both agreed to not let our feelings escalate for the time being. She had her own room, and it came with internet service. Mom and Archie bunked together, and Six and I did likewise. He and I sat out by the pool and discussed where we thought our future was headed. I explained to him how Sam felt recharged after the whole drug cartel thing. He laughed and agreed he felt more alive than ever having used his skills for good.

"I know it sounds lame, but we are good at what we do. Knowing what we did made things better, even if only for a little while made me proud."

I shook my head and agreed. Glad someone else had said what I was thinking. We killed men, but they truly deserved it, and we could see why. Back in Vietnam, we killed many men and mostly young boys who were doing nothing more than following orders. Some had to be forced into the situations that ultimately meant their deaths.

Six laughed and started making that noise or music that was supposed to be the Batman theme. "Come, Robin, we need to get some bat sleep."

We all got there on time after long showers and slipping into new crisp clean clothes we got from Walmart. It had been a long time since we felt and smelled as good as we did. The personal hygiene supplies made a huge difference, believe me. Mom was on the phone when we arrived, and from the smile on his face, it looked like he had found our friend. As we approached the table, it was clear everyone was enjoying their Walmart resupply. Sam smiled at me, and I made a point of brushing her shoulder with my hand as I passed.

Arch sat next to her and Six said, "Mmmmm, you smell good enough to kiss." Sam turned her head to accept the kiss, and Six bent down between them and gave Arch his kiss on the cheek.

"You need a shave, you nasty black boy." We all broke into uncontrollable laughter. Even Mom, who was still on the phone. Arch charged after him, but he tipped several chairs in front of him as he ran.

The waitress, a beautiful black woman, said, "You boys better calm down or I'll throw you all out." She smiled and topped our coffees off.

"I think you look great the way you are."

When Mom finished his call, he told us Mr. and Mrs. Smith were glad we all made it back to the USA. "He told me he had a surprise for us." He said he drove by what was left of the compound on his way to retrieve the stash of weapons. "I hope I never piss you guys off like them poor bastards did." He told him there were lots of people going through what was left. "But I gotta tell you, there wasn't much left." Mom had explained to him that we didn't even scratch the surface there. It had been two delta wing cruise missiles that joined the party without being asked. Mr. Smith had been very surprised the US government would have made such a move in Mexico but had to admit it had quieted things down a bit. They had stopped at the village, and the new water well was in the process of being drilled. The first thing his father-in-law had ordered done. They had already started clearing the burned timbers from the church. We could see Archie was moved, and we all felt a sense of pride that we hadn't in some time.

We were to go to this atlas point in New Mexico. He said Mrs. Smith wanted us to come for dinner and see the surprise they had for us. They would be thrilled if we would stay a few days, as there was no safer place for us in the States. "It was her idea to invite you after she saw what we had done to those drug lords. They will drive to us once we get there and show us the way to their home. He told me he thinks we are beginning a great relationship. He never had a customer that just rented his merchandise." He thought we would head out after breakfast and see just what they had in store for us. We all laughed and dove into the eggs and pancakes and coffee.

"So what do we do now?" Archie said in his low tone with his head still down. He sat in the back of the van with Mom. "We are all being hunted for something we had nothing to do with." The four of us had all suffered great pain and loss over the years and never knew we had been part of such a sinister plot. A plot that none of us truly understood.

Mom patted his shoulder and just said, "At least you're alive." It was his idea to spread us out and help see that we built new lives. The CIA guys, especially the three spooks from the command base, just wanted everyone to go away quietly and permanently. They were the only faces that we could be put to the whole thing. "They wanted all of us dead, along with everyone else that knew of their operation that went south. Luckily, Mark Johnson, the Defense Undersecretary, and Admiral Gary Johnson knew all about their little switch. They both sent the director a message stating as much. With so many high-ranking people with the knowledge of what happened, he shut down Russel Gordon and his band of merry men. He made it clear it was with the understanding you four never got together to discuss that day or look into what happened. I guaranteed them I would make it happen and keep an eye on the four of us. Of course, I did not stay out of it, and they caught me checking on the vice president and his family."

He had been looking to see if they appeared anywhere in the US. He got a call one day and a prerecorded message that simply said, "You were told to stand down. The next time it will be your wife I visit." He wasn't sure what it meant till he went out to get his old hunting dog, Rex, and brought him in for the night. Rex was lying next to his kennel like he often did, so he thought he was asleep. But when he got closer, he could see that Rex's throat was cut.

"Mrs. Fowley thinks he ran after a dog in heat or something." Just one of many lies he had told her over the years. Mom's investigation pretty much ended there. Leaving just what he had on those thumb drives, which wasn't much to work with. He had a few names and background stuff on the vice president and his family.

"None of us blame you one bit, Mom," Archie said. "Your efforts kept us alive. We have all changed, but somehow better. Now we are a team again." We all agreed so the two of them knew we had been listening in on their conversation. This was now our fight, and we agreed we would make sure Mom and his family were safe until we all got clear of this crap.

"I have a part in this still," Mom said, and no one disagreed. "However, the Chief I could not control." He felt we were all just thrown away to the government. The government he had fought so hard for and watched so many friends die for. He had broken off all communications with Mom, and they only met a few times in prearranged places. The last time, he never showed, but a young girl came to his table and said, "Chief knows it all," then left. That meeting was for last Thanksgiving at a truck stop on US 1. He had been debating about going to look for him, but things were good with the four of us, and he feared for his family if they found out.

"That ship has sailed when you two lovebirds got together in the farthest point of land you could find. It defied all reasonable odds. Newfoundland." It was very clear they were still monitoring us, and we didn't know to cover our tracks. We figured Homeland put the two of us together through flight information. Now the question was, where did we go, and what we do when we get there?

Sam asked, "What will happen if they find out we are still alive?" It was clear the spooks would have to deal with us themselves through the agency. They wouldn't dare have locals look for us or find us because we might give them an earful. They knew we couldn't just go to the press as we all had people we cared about that they could hurt. Not just family but friends and acquaintances they could get to. My thoughts drifted back to Maggie and her dad. We might not have close family, but we all had people that were special to us.

"These bastards have no sympathy or compassion," Mom spit out. They were perfectly fine with us, the flight crew, and that poor farm family being killed just to further a political and personal agenda. What we really needed was intel, and lots of it. We knew we had to make the next move and get in front of them. We all turned and looked at Sam. "You up for this?"

She nodded and said, "I'm good, very good." She smiled, but not her best one. Seems she hadn't wasted her new brainpower and had worked on perfecting her computer talents. "I belong to a super-secret hacker group." When they were working together, they were unstoppable. They all had a true distain for the government, both federal and local and their power. They helped dig up dirt on the Big Brothers, and exposing their secrets was a full-time job for them. They each had our own little *specialty*, but together there was no system or server that was safe from them. "We are the wizards of cyberspace." We all laughed, and Six asked if she was Dorothy or Toto. "You can laugh, but last year they hacked the IRS mainframe and sent every person that paid taxes a $250 refund."

"Seriously?" I said. "That was you?"

"Yes. The president and congress had an emergency meeting and authorized the refund calling, it a one-time stimulus payment. They didn't dare let the people know someone had hacked the IRS and gave them an April Christmas present."

"I remember that," Six said. "I was in Vegas and stimulated their economy. Lasted almost ten minutes."

By the time the government realized what had happened, the checks were in the mail, and some were getting cashed. We all looked at each other with a newfound respect for our team member.

"I'll start the list of what I will need, but I gotta be honest, it's going to cost a lot." Money would be no problem, and we always knew where to get more. None of us had any issue with taking from the drug dealers or anyone else that profited off hurting people.

We pulled into an abandoned 7-11 and waited to be contacted. Mom had called about two hours earlier and set the time and was given the location. Soon a red Mercedes convertible pulled up alongside the van. As we watched, the top started to go down and fold into the rear. The passenger who had been hidden from view turned and smiled.

He looked up at us, saying, "What take you gringos so long?"

We all shouted at once, "Jesus! What are you doing here?"

He laughed and said, "I'll tell you when we get back to the rock. Follow us." And they pulled out and drove ahead.

We all just looked at each other and wondered out loud why our favorite Mexican boy was here. We drove for over an hour into the barren land on one back road after another. We reached an outcropping of a rock about five hundred feet high at the end of a mile-long dirt road. As we pulled closer to the rock formation, a huge steel door appeared. It was set back into the rock and had what looked like a huge curtain pulled back on each side. It opened as we approached, and we just drove in. As we stopped in a large parking area, the door closed behind us, and as it did, we could see the curtain was closing as well.

"Nice digs," Six said. "Reminds me of the Batcave. Come here, Robin." He motioned to me as he got out of the car.

Arch almost knocked us all down rushing to the boy and lifting him high in the air. "What are you doing here? We left you to run the church."

He started to speak when Mr. Smith walked up and said he would fill us all in at dinner. We were late, and Mrs. Smith would not be happy. He led us down and into a hallway on the right side of the door. He pointed to the small elevator built into the wall. "We'll meet you upstairs." He smiled at Sam. The stairs opened into a magnificent living room with stone from the rock making up the walls. A fireplace taking up the center of the room offered a 360 view of the burning logs. A large bookshelf built into the stone wall swung inward, and there was Sam exiting the elevator. Squealing like a little girl, Mrs. Smith came running over and hugged Archie with all her strength. She held him tight for a long time.

"Welcome! Welcome to our home!" she yelled. "Come sit on the deck and enjoy the setting sun and the meal I have prepared. I just hope it's still hot." She glared at Mr. Smith.

We followed her out onto a large porch area where a long table had been set for us. Looking around and over the side of what looked like a broken and dilapidated railing, it suddenly made sense. The outside deck was part of an old rundown rustic cabin set on a ledge near the top of the hill. From below, it would look like an abandoned old cabin that was ready to fall off the side of the hill at any moment. Wallboards missing or falling off, roof shingles missing, nothing to give away the beauty and warmth of the real home contained in the hill behind. From our seats at the table, we were treated to a spectacular sunset over the mountains far away. The table was covered with a beautiful tablecloth that made the fine china and crystal stand out. The center had a collection of wildflowers in a handmade Mexican vase. We sat and enjoyed a wonderful meal and conversation till we were stuffed. Mrs. Smith had prepared chicken breast and steak you could cut with a fork. Each of us had a fajita set up so we could cut up the meat and make them if we wanted. All the fixings were at hand, and we all ate like we hadn't in a long time. As the sun began to set over the horizon. Smith offered up some fine Cuban cigars and some Russian cognac.

"Compliments of some of my many customers," he stated.

"Okay." Arch finally spoke. "Why did you bring Jesus here?"

Mrs. Smith spoke first. "You remember my father?" She told us how he went to the church and town the afternoon after we left. He had been talking with some of the elders about how he could and would help them. Her father was born in that town and was excited to be able to make it better for those still there. While he was there, two men came into the square, dragging a boy by the legs behind them. It was Jesus. They called everyone to come watch what happened when they helped strangers. Jesus looked up in fear as he now recognized the drug boss that had worked for Sanchez.

"It appears that while I was away, this dog of a boy helped strangers kill my boss and friends. Now you see what it gets you when you help strangers." He raised a large machete above his head in preparation of beheading Jesus. Two shots sounded as one, and both of the old cartel gunmen folded with small holes in each of their foreheads. The women screamed, and everyone scattered.

"My father was in a ball as if hiding behind an overturned table. He wanted everyone to think he was cowering in fear of the men. When the square cleared, he went to Jesus and helped him up and untied his hands." He brought him back to their home for safekeeping. Those should have been the last of the old guard, and the ones looking to take over would give the village a wide berth. They felt it was better in case others knew of his helping them and might want to question him. They decided to bring him to the United States with them. "He kinda grows on you," Mr. Smith said with a broad smile.

Archie put his arm around Jesus and told him how sorry he was to have gotten him involved in all this. I smiled then thought for a second. "Hey, who shot the two jerks?" Jesus smiled and looked at the old man sitting at the table lighting a cigar.

"My father was bored when he first came to live with us in our home," Mrs. Smith offered. Her husband had given him a new .9mm Beretta and told him to learn to shoot. He wanted my father to know the business from the bottom up. After thousands of rounds of ammo, he had become pretty good/ "Don't you think? He had been able to draw, fire two rounds, and fall behind the table looking like some scared old man. My father is a scared old man, not so much."

We all laughed, and Sam told Mrs. Smith, "We want to keep him on our side." She opened her arms to hug the old man. It made him blush for the first time in many years. His smile showed beautiful teeth, where the missing and broken ones were when we first met. We figured he had several sets of dentures depending on what and who he was with.

After our meal and cognac, we sat down by the fire to discuss our next move. Sam sat at the table with our host, and they discussed her shopping list of computer hardware. Mr. Smith obviously enjoyed having a computer person to spend time with. The rest of us were talking about the whole issue of how we got where we were and what could we do next. Six, Archie, and I were taking turns hashing over the years we had spent not knowing the others were still alive. Talking about what we could do to get our lives back and just what we wanted our lives to be. We all agreed that we were combat breed and had always felt empty for the adrenaline rush and the satisfaction of helping and making a difference. Not bloodthirsty but willing to do whatever it took to gain the result.

Six motioned toward Mom and spoke just loud enough for us to hear. "He has got some age on him."

"We aren't spring chickens by any means," I commented.

We all felt Mom needed to be more careful. He had taken a beating when he was captured that we could still see the effects of.

He was still the best one to lead us, but not necessarily on the front lines. We hoped the combat shit was behind us now and we could find a solution with less guns. We all looked at each other and knew it wasn't going to happen that easy. The destruction of the cartels made it clear they were looking to kill us and anyone that got in the way. The longer we were dead, the more time we had to formulate a plan. It would be nice to make it happen without more shooting or death. That was totally up to those jerks in Washington. None of us believed it would.

Mom came back over and joined us by the fire, a six-pack of Bud Light in his hands. "Smith says we can stay here as long as we want. He has more than enough room for us all. He also made it clear his wife was so excited to have house guests. It would make her very happy." They didn't get many friends that came to their home. In fact, we were the first her husband had ever invited home. This was their sanctuary, and he never trusted anyone enough to share it with. "He still says he has another surprise, but it won't be ready for a week or so." It would be a good thing to have Sam have full use of his computer room. He had offered look into what intel his contacts could provide worldwide, but we asked him not to. We had no idea where the CIA could go, and they had many informants. Smith must have made enemies and had competitors all too willing to help put him out of the business. We preferred he remain a clean resource for us going forward. Last thing we or he needed was for our friends to know he was working with us. It appeared that he and his wife had adopted us, along with her father. He not only appreciated what we did in Mexico but had some payback he would love to see rain down on the CIA. The company had used him from time to time, but they outed him to a competitor years ago. It caused a price war that evolved into an actual shooting war. He won the war and eliminated his competition. Unfortunately, he paid a huge price. His son and daughter were killed in an attack on a shipment he was receiving. It was no big deal, so his two children wanted to be involved. He was sure the company found out about the delivery and told his competition. Of course, they denied it especially after he killed off all the others. They now know nothing of his operation other than a shell office and staff they must deal with to get information to him.

This home, as he called it, was built many years before his involvement with them and could not be traced back to him or anyone he was connected with. A close friend had started this fortress to suit his reclusive nature and house his private auto collection. He was a multimillionaire, and his company had mined this big rock for some kind of precious oar. It set on 950 acres of nothing but sand and small outcrops of rocks and brush. He had made some real modifications since taking over as we could see all around us. He kept very little of his vast inventory of weapons there so it would not draw any attention. That's not to say it wasn't fully protected and prepared for a real fight if it happened. Walking around, I noticed the slots in the ceiling that I bet were for blast doors. Parked on the ground floor were several heavily armed Humvees. I was sure I was only seeing a very small part of the site's protection and security. We realized that Mr. and Mrs. Smith were not people you would cross or mess with unless you had a death wish. We were all shown private guest rooms off a common corridor and settled in for the night. I couldn't unwind enough to fall asleep, so I headed out to the deck to see if the night air helped. It appeared Mom had beat me to it and was seated with a glass of scotch about half drained. I sat down next to him and waited for him to speak.

"Skipper, I need to get to my family as soon as I can, but not till we have a plan and I can see what's coming." He told me he was still good, but not as good as he once was.

"None of us are, Mom. You need to let us take point on this thing."

He nodded but explained we still needed him for backup and support. "Your all fresh recruits to this deal." I agreed and told him his direction would be critical for us to clean this up in a reasonable length of time.

"What is our first move?" I asked.

He was clear. We needed to find Chief and get his intel so we knew what we were up against. He had sent him to ground in case the pigpen boys went looking for him as a loose end. Finding him was going to be a real job. He came from the southern section of the reservation in Oklahoma, somewhere between the I-40 and I-44. Mom had a contact in Broken Arrow, where we could make our presence known. From there, we would have to wait to hear from Chief. The nation was very tight-lipped about its people, and you only got what they were willing to give.

"I'm leaving for there in the a.m. I was just sitting here collecting my thoughts."

"Sounds good, Mom, but you aren't going alone." I felt that some of us needed to be there with him for backup and support if the need arose. I told him Six and I would be his shot guns. Sam was working on her laptops and getting back in touch with her friends in the Land of Oz. Arch needed some downtime as he had undergone the most transition of any of us. From super soldier to the peaceful padre back to the angel of death had to wear on him. He could spend time with Jesus and put his life back together and in sync. I also knew that he and Mr. Smith had the same interest in weapons of destruction, both old and yet to be built. The two of them could play in the weapons lab that held secrets I wasn't sure I wanted to know. Mom didn't argue and just smiled as I got up to go tell Six. It felt good to be a family again even under the circumstances. On my way, I passed Sam's room and heard those talented fingers pounding away on a laptop. I knocked and waited for her to answer. I told her briefly what we were doing and that we would be leaving in the morning.

She told me about her friends and how they all were excited to have a problem to solve that actually might make a difference. They had all been worried since they hadn't heard from her since the day she left her home. This was a close group of people that shared everything, not just their hacking skills. She personally knew each one as they only worked with people they knew in real life and trusted and felt a bond. There were five of them, counting Sam. They were the real control center, but each had networks of their own that would put hundreds of the very brightest hackers in the world at their disposal. They lovingly called them the munchkins. As I started to leave, she grabbed my arm. "You can stay the night if you want."

"Oh, I want to, but things are just getting started. Hold that thought till I get back."

I gave her a long kiss. "You got it, Skipper."

We all met in the large garage after a huge breakfast with Mrs. Smith, filling our plates over and over. John, as he asked us to call him, met us by a new Chevy Tahoe with the rear hatch up. He was pushing a cart covered with a black blanket.

"You boys can use my car here, and I thought you might feel better with these." He pulled the blanket off, and there was an assortment of handguns and clips. I took my old favorite, a stainless Beretta. Black would be better for night action, but I didn't think we would have any of those issues. This was a soft probe for information that Chief had, so we hoped to avoid any firefights. John handed me a box and told me there were extra magazines and boxes of ammo along with holster. Six smiled when he saw the .357 magnum and picked it up along with his accompanying box of supplies. "I have been in love with these little babies since I saw my first *Dirty Harry* movie." Mom picked up a .45 and played with the action, making sure it was ready for action. John had a big smile on his face when he handed Mom a box. He had some friends break into the storage area we had rented before crossing into Mexico. Mom opened it, and there was his silver-plated .45.

"How did you know about this?"

"You told me you had to store all your extra equipment before you crossed the border." It was easy finding out which place as a group like ours did stick out and cause people to remember. Mom grabbed John in a bear hug and thanked him for all he had done. On another wheeled table were Sam's computers that we had brought from her cabin and stored as well. Sam was excited as those extra laptops had stuff on them she wanted but didn't think she would ever get back. They shook hands and embraced each other again like newfound brothers. As we got in the SUV to leave, John reached into the back and patted the spare tire compartment. I filled this special compartment with some extras you might need.

As we pulled out, Arch, Sam, and Jesus were by the door as we passed, waving and wishing us luck. The Smith home was near

Roswell, New Mexico. As we started out, we all joked about the Area 51 deal and wondered if Smith was involved with those people.

"No, but I bet he would sell them whatever they wanted," Mom joked.

We all had a good laugh and settled in for the ride. We traveled on several different roads and non-interstates till we reached Interstate 40 where we headed east. From there on to Oklahoma City. where we would head northeast toward Tulsa. Mom said we would cut off and head to Broken Arrow and spend the night. We needed to hear from Chief before reaching our final stop. Late that night, we pulled into a bed-and-breakfast called the Stone Creek Inn. The lights were still on as Mom had called ahead and they expected us. We checked in, and after the paperwork was done, the woman at the desk told us she had some sandwiches for us in the dining room. She was an older woman and carried the wrinkles that a long hard life must have given her. As we were finishing up our meal, she walked back in and asked, "Which of you three is called Mom?" with a slight blush.

Mom spoke up. "I am. We can talk about why another time."

She smiled and said, "I bet that is a great story, but I have one of my own." She pulled out a chair and sat at the table with us. She began her own story. "A great warrior left our lands many years ago. He fought hard and with honor in a place far away. When he returned, he took his rightful place as a chief of one of the many tribes. He has now gone to the back country to find peace and find his new path. He has spoken of this man they call Mom many times and asked if I were to meet him to send him on to meet with him. In the morning, another great young warrior will arrive to take you to him. Sleep well. The path will be long and on horseback." She smiled, patting her butt as she got up. With that, she turned and left us.

When we woke in the morning, the smell of bacon and sausage filled the air as well as the aroma of fresh brewed coffee. We all dressed for the ride ahead of us and met at the large table for coffee. It was no doubt one of the best breakfasts I've ever had. Midway through my second pile of pancakes, a man in his late thirties walked into the dining room and sat at the far end of the long table. We looked him over and figured he was just another guest. He didn't speak to anyone but did look us all over as he drank some coffee. Just as we finished up, he pushed his chair back and spoke.

"Why do you wish to talk to Chief Sky Rider?"

Mom looked him in the eyes and spoke. "We have information for his ears only." Mom pushed back his chair and reached under his vest. From nowhere and in an instant, a bone-handled knife appeared in the table in front of Mom. We all pushed off from the table, but none of us had come to breakfast armed. Mom looked down at the knife and then at the warrior dressed in hunter's plaid and jeans. He laughed and said, "Your father said you could be a bit of a hothead. He also told me you were the best with a knife he's ever seen."

The Indian just barely broke a smile and said, "The chief told me you were a man of strength, and he loved you like a brother. Let's get going. We have a long ride ahead of us." I looked at Six in a way he understood as *what the hell was that?*

We drove to an old farm outside of town where there were four horses saddled and waiting near the barn. We collected our gear and secured it to our saddles and headed into the low mountains on a trail that none of us could make out, but our guide seemed to know it without looking. It snaked its way around the brush and dried up streams, around rock formations and small stands of trees. As we reached a small bluff, we all got down and stretched and walked around, no one daring to rub their ass. Our guide had not said more than a few words since back at the table.

We saw them in the distance but never heard them. It was a pair of dark-colored helicopters, and they were headed toward Broken Arrow. They stopped for a few minutes and just hovered. The man leading us had pulled out some high-definition binoculars and watched the two birds without speaking. After a few minutes, they started out again, heading for town. The warrior just ran to his horse and pulled himself up into the saddle with one hand.

He turned to Mom. "You will be able to follow my path from here." And before we could say anything, he kicked his horse and disappeared in a cloud of dust. We looked at each other with no idea what had just happened.

Mom just yelled, "Mount up! Something is very wrong."

None of us had the skill to ride at the speed that Chief's son or had any idea where we were going. We started out slowly at first but did pick up the pace as we got some comfort level and idea of our direction.

"This is very odd," Mom said as we turned and came around a large rock outcropping. In the distance, we could see our new friend, and he appeared to be standing with his hands outstretched toward the sky. Mom just kicked his horse hard and headed toward our guide at a full gallop. Six and I followed suit and closed the distance to Mom, who was already leaving his saddle. As we got closer, we could see what had their attention. On the ground was an older man dressed in buckskin and no shirt. He looked like he had taken a fierce beating. The brave that had led us was still reaching for the sky and yelling chants. Once we were alongside Mom, we could see the broken body of the man. Distinctively, we knew he was the man that worked so hard to save us. Chief lay there, broken and dead with that stern frown on his face he always seemed to have. The hair above his forehead was missing, and it was obvious someone had scalped him. No one had to say it. We all knew who had done this and what needed to be done in retribution. It was no longer just stopping those men from our old days. It now was finding them and making them pay, permanently. We stood in silence until Chief's son had finished his ritual for the dead. He reached down and took some blood from Chiefs head and placed several lines on each his cheeks and then his own.

We went about loading Chief on his son's horse and followed him deeper into the scrub brush to a small hill about two miles from where we found Chief's body. On the hill was a platform standing some six feet above the ground. We rolled and secured the body in the thick leather skins that hung there. Placing it up on the platform, we helped secure it and then stood back as Chief's son said some prayers over him. Then Mom stepped up and spoke low so we never did hear what he had to say. The two men turned and looked at each other.

"His death is a debt that must be collected. I shall collect it," the son said.

"*No*," Mom said. "He was my brother, and the honor shall be mine. Yours if I should fail."

The man known to the tribe as Snake bowed his head and agreed. As we prepared to leave, Chief's son walked over to one of the posts that supported the platform. He kicked away some rocks that looked like they were supporting the pole and dug down a bit, pulling out a green beret. There was no doubt it had belonged to Chief. Inside was a key and number wrapped in plastic. He handed it to Mom. "My father told me if he ever passed, this was where he wanted to rest." He told us that Chief had built this burial platform weeks before, as he had seen his death coming. He had also told him where this was and to be sure Mom got it. Mom took the key and note, then the beret. He climbed on his horse and rode up to the platform and stood as best he could and placed the beret under Chief's head.

"Rest well, my friend."

The ride back to the farm and our SUV was silent and full of reflection. Chief's son just rode with no expression on his face or word from his mouth. Once we arrived back at the farm, we all piled in and set out for the bed-and-breakfast and the discussions that had to happen. Tears in the eyes of the woman at the B&B flowed hard as she sat and held her head in her hands. "He was truly the greatest man I have ever known." The young brave walked over and held her head in his hands. "You must find and kill the man that has taken your father from us." She sobbed, looking at the man who had just lost his father.

Mom placed his hand on her shoulder. "That honor shall be mine as Chief was as a brother to me. But why had he never mentioned you to me?" Mom asked.

"It was our way, as I belonged to another man. He was abusive and a drunk." They had become friends and then much more, which was not right, but was the way it happened. "Our love gave us Mark here. Strike of the Snake, as his father had named him." He always looked after them even after her husband drank himself to death. He had spoken of Mom often yet was very secretive as well. Mom showed her the key and asked her if she knew what it meant or went to. "Yes, it belongs to a strong box that is displayed in the museum of dead in town." It had belonged to her father, and she had given it to the museum for display. She knew from the number that was on the key that it was the number inscribed on the inside of the box lid. It was the number of braves killed by the white man at Broken Arrow. "I have no idea how he got this key." We asked if we could get into the museum right away as it seemed the bad guys were around. "Yes, but be assured, if you hold the key, then Chief did not tell them of it."

Mom shook his head and said, "Yes, I'm sure he never would have given any information up."

* * *

The sun had been up for some time, and the man known as Chief sat crossed-legged on a bluff that let him look out over the land below. He sensed rather than heard the helicopter that came up behind him at full attack speed. He rose in a fluid motion and ran to the edge and simply leaped into the air. Below his pony of many years stood where he had been left. Chief hit the blanketed back of the horse known just as Paint. He kicked him in the ribs and headed for a stand of small trees and rock formations to the north. As he cut around a large rock, he felt his friend of many years stiffen, then heard the shot. Paint went down in a heap, dead before he finished sliding across the hard sand of the wash. Chief instinctively tried to roll and continue his retreat on foot. Unfortunately, Paint had landed in a way that pinned Chief's leg under his body. He looked back to see two men out of each chopper rappelling down to the ground in full battle dress and heavily armed. There was no place to go. After they beat Chief with their rifle butts and kicked him bloody, they pried Paint's body up enough to free him. They dragged him to one of the choppers that had landed by then. They stood him up, and he was face-to-face with that bastard that had caused all his problems over the years. Still as tough and hard as he once was, he tried to break free and kill the man that had Paint.

"I guess my friends are coming for you. That must be why you're here."

He smiled and said, "No. All the others are dead, and now I'm just cleaning up the leftover crap."

Chief struggled again to reach for the man he had hated for so long. He received a punch in his stomach and a hard backhand for his trouble. "So, my red-skinned friend, what is it you managed to find out about me and my partners?" He knew someone was digging into the past, and he figured it had to be Chief.

Chief smiled and spit out a tooth that had broken off, hitting Russ between the eyes. "I have no interest in the dogshit that spoils our land." Another punch and then a Ka-Bar knife at his throat, Russ told him it was his last chance. "Kill me and my braves will hunt you down and your friends like the wild pigs you are." Chief smiled, remembering his screams as he fell into the pigpen back in Vietnam. "Only cowards scream at their inevitable death, like you did."

"Put him in my chopper and let's get out of this hellhole." Once they were airborne and at 2,000–2,500 feet, they dragged Chief to the open door and held him there. "Well, you little squaw, do you remember when you gave me this?" He pointed to the thin scar that ran along forehead and his hairline.

Chief smiled and said, "Yes, I guess you were lucky as I was in too much of a hurry to go find my friends." With that, the knife ran across Chief's forehead, taking the front part of his scalp almost to the bone. The pain was intense for sure, but Chief's face never changed from its expression and never flinched. The man that he wanted so much to kill stood there laughing, holding the scalp piece in one hand and the Ka-Bar in the other. In a flash, Chief twisted and hit the one holding him on the bridge of the nose hard enough to drive the splintering bones back into his brain. He died before he had any idea what was happening. In a fluid motion, he brought his tied hands up and cut them free on the knife that had just cut him. Russ stood there, still holding the knife and not believing what just happened. Chief grabbed the knife and twisted it free and held it up in front of him.

Everyone was struggling to bring their guns to bear, and the pilot struggled to keep the bird steady. It was the last minute of his life before they cut him to ribbons with their assault rifles. Chief stood tall, smiled at the men in the chopper, and just let himself fall backward out of the open door. Just before he fell completely out the door, he threw Russ's knife back at his prey. In a flash, the man from the CIA pulled the man next to him in front of him and let him take the blade dead center of his neck. Everyone looked out the doors of the two birds and watched as Chief fell and raised a cloud of dust when he hit. One of the two men in the door of the second chopper looked at each other.

The one said, "Not a sound. He just fell and died without a sound."

* * *

We arrived at the museum around midnight, and the three of us did a diligent recon of the surrounding area and any place where someone could be watching the museum. We had no doubt Chief had taken his secrets to his death, but we needed to be careful. Thanks to Mr. Smith's extra tools he hid in the spare tire rack, we were well prepared for company if we did run into any. Six took the breakdown sniper rifle and a few grenades of different types and set up on the roof of the local gas station. We had each taken an Israeli-made Uzi and spare clips as well as our handguns. We had ear comms in and heard him when he said the place was clear and quiet. Everything was go, so we walked right up to the front door and found it unlocked. We opened it and walked in.

We found Chief's son standing next to a large strongbox on a table in front of a display of a stagecoach with the occupants in different poses of death killed from arrows. The sign above read "The Whiteman's Wagon" and showed how the people from the east were welcomed. We put the key in, turned it, and opened to box. Inside was a stack of folders and a note. Chief had never really moved into the electronic age, so no discs or flash drives were there. There was a note on top of the pile of papers. "If you're reading this, then I have moved on. Take care. This is bigger than we ever dreamed. I will wait for you, my friend, but be in no hurry to join me."

We collected the folders and made sure we had everything. Before he closed the box, Mark took out a marker and scratched two lines through the faded numbers on the inside of the top. He then wrote another number, adding one more than what had been before. We quickly left the building and grabbed the SUV and drove over to pick up Six. Back at the bed-and-breakfast, we packed up and decided to head out for the Dream House, as we had nicknamed the Smith's home and business. We all ate some sandwiches and grabbed some thermoses of coffee for the nine- to ten-hour run. As we were about to get in to leave, Mark came out with a bedroll and threw it in.

We looked at Mom, and he just said, "He's one of us now."

No question from us. We just got in and headed out. I drove the first shift so Mom could look over the files and see what Chief had found. Once back at the house, we all headed off to bed as none of us had slept in many hours. Mom told us and planned to meet for a powwow that night. Sam was in her room, so I went in and filled her in on the past couple days. She took Chief's death hard but only made one statement.

"It sounds like payback from the guy that Chief did that to." I thought the same thing. It just didn't make sense why these people were being so bloodthirsty. Whatever they were hiding must be big, real big. I kissed her cheek and headed off to bed, her hand running the length of my thigh as I left.

I woke to a soft kiss on my lips and the smell of coffee. Sam smiled and said, "Mom has called for a sit-down at nine, and it's eight now. Gives you time to shower and get yourself together. You need a shave and some soap." She turned and rolled out the door. Forty-five minutes later, I walked into the formal dining room and found everyone there sitting at the table. Smith pushed a remote, and a video screen the size of my bed came dropping from the ceiling. It came on showing a photo of Chief in full uniform being decorated by the president of the United States.

I sat down, and a plate of roast beef and mashed potatoes appeared in front of me. Everyone was eating and involved in conversations. Sam rolled up next to me with a plate. "I helped Mrs. Smith make this meal," she bragged.

"Getting real domestic, are we?" I asked.

Just then, Mark came in the room. Mom got up and walked over, putting his arm around him. "For any of you that have not had a formal introduction, this is Mark, Chief's son. He is well versed in most hand-to-hand combat styles and trained by one of the best I've ever known." He motioned to the screen. He went around the room, giving each person's name and nickname as well. "I think his father would agree that Mark's nickname, Snake, fits him well."

Sam nudged me. "Where does that come from?"

I told her he could strike like a snake, fast and as deadly. He handled a knife like no one I've ever met. After we finished and the cigars and brandy were given out, Mom stood and raised his glass to the photo that covered a large part of the wall. We all joined him. "To one of the best men I have ever had the privilege to know or serve with. To the man that helped make it possible that we are all here tonight." His voice broke only slightly, but we all heard it. "Chief protected the information we will look at tonight to his death. I know this because it was still there when we went to recover it." We all raised our glasses and emptied them.

The screen went dark and came back on with the photo of the vice president and his family that we had secured those many years ago. These were the people that started it all and made our lives what they were today. The screen blinked, and it was a list of refugees that were flown out to the United States the day after we had made the recovery. Chief had friends in the admin office back in country, and he hit them up for some information. He said he was looking for a family that had saved his life during a recon when he was wounded. He just wanted to thank them as part of his bucket list. His friends were able to get the refugee lists from the now Department of Homeland Security. They ended up with tons of paper on refugees from all over the world. He had been collecting information over a long period so as not to look like what it was. He found several families of four around that period and actually checked them out. In time, he got it down to one family. His resources were limited. So when he went to put eyes on them at their listed new address, he found an empty lot. He believes they changed names after reaching the US in order to start their new lives. He felt the trail had gone cold there until he saw a picture of the father. It was from a meeting of the Indian nations ten or more years ago. He was involved in a negotiation with the nations to take over operations of all casinos that were on Indian lands. He was looking to add more casinos to his existing holdings. He came across it when he was looking into the history of casinos and the Indian nations. There was a new effort to put up a new one there in Oklahoma. He went on a hunt for whatever he could find out. It just happened an older chief he met at a gathering in North Carolina was involved in those negotiations. He remembered the man and the company he was involved with. "The House of the Dragon," or something like that, he said. He did not trust him or his family. He couldn't get past the fact there were more Orientals working in the casinos than there were Native Americans. The old man had talked for hours about the time when the tribes were strong and did not need these places of drink and cards. His patience listening payed off as he found out that the little girl and boy were now part of the company. They stood in the background and were very attentive to what was going on. A photo came up of the two children helping cut a ribbon, and that was about all he got. He did, however, come up with the name of the father. Chung was the last name, and that's were his information ends.

That night, my need for her overcame my better judgement, and I went to Sam's room. I walked in as quiet as I could and moved to the bed. It was empty and actually didn't look like it had even been touched. I looked around and saw her laptop was gone, and she always had it with her. She had a mount on her chair, and it snapped into it so she always could work. I headed to the computer room at the end of the hall. As I approached, I saw that the light from the side of the door which she had left cracked. I opened it and stepped in where I was greeted with a huge smile on the face of what looked like an exhausted woman.

"I've got 'em. I've found the Chungs. Good news. We now have a starting point. The bad news is the parents are dead. They were killed in an auto accident about ten years ago."

It happened right after Chief's friend dealt with them on the casino deal. She had a printout of an accident report in front of her. Their car went over a cliff, killing both of them and their driver. Police reports were thin and inconclusive. No real reason found for the vehicle leaving the road except equipment failure, which could not be confirmed from the wreckage.

She went on. The son took control of the company, and he appointed his sister as VP of Dragon Enterprise. This company was huge and covered a vast amount of interests from imports to casinos to properties, and real estate. It was all based here in the US with their headquarters in Washington, DC. Of course, they owned the building they were in, the DE Towers on the river. So far, everything looked on the up and up, but it would take forever to get through all the different companies and sub-ownerships and such.

"I will need to call in the wizards for help." She laughed.

"Time for you to get some rest." I pulled her away from the keyboard and pushed her toward the door.

"Hey, Skipper, I'm way too wound up to sleep right now."

I kept pushing and then slid my hand down the front of her shirt, cupping that thinly covered breast. She never resisted. "Who said anything about sleeping?"

"Hey, you said we should cool things for a while." I pulled her head back and kissed her deeply.

"I lied," I said as I pushed her through my door and kicked it shut.

The next day, we woke to a knock on the door, and Mrs. Smith came walking in with a tray with two cups and a pot of coffee. "I started at Sam's room and then knew where I should look." She had a slight blush to her face and smiled as Sam tried to cover our naked bodies. "Oh, sweetie, you two are so cute trying to hide what everyone already knows. Now you two get some coffee and get dressed. The boss"—she forced a cough—"has a surprise for you, my dear. So don't take all day." She chuckled as she closed the door behind her.

As we came into the room, everyone was at the table enjoying breakfast. No one looked up, but everyone looked like they were about to explode.

"See," John Smith said. "I knew my little bird dog would sniff out the lovebirds."

Everyone lost it then and laughed and made fake coughing noises. I sat down, giving them all my best mad face as Sam just blushed and rolled up to the table.

Six laughed out loud. "You can blush?" Her face was now red, but not from embarrassment.

"Now, now," Mom piped in. "Let's get this day underway."

As we drank our coffee, Mr. Smith walked in and stood at the head of the table. "Samantha," he said.

"Yes, Mr. Smith."

"John," he said. He stepped back. "We are way beyond the Mr. crap. It's Smith to everyone or John from now on."

We all agreed when there was the voice of Mrs. Smith. "Get on with it, Smith. Papa is going to blow a gasket."

"Okay!" he yelled. "Samantha, I know you lost your power chair in Mexico, and you did share with me some of your drawings and thoughts for the next generation. Well, here it is, everyone, the Sam Mobile no. 2." With that, the old man came shooting around the corner, spinning in circles and moving back and forth. It was a beautiful black polished finish with black spoked wheels. Sam's mouth just dropped open, and she watched as he ran across the room and around at what seemed like an unusually fast speed for a wheelchair. He did a quick 360 and parked next to Sam.

"Get in. Take her for a spin," the old man said with chuckle.

Sam looked around and moved over to transfer herself from the table to the new chair. The old man stood next to Sam and put his hand on her shoulder and told her to take her time to get used to it. "She is fast and nasty when she needs to be." First, he told her to take it for a spin to get used to its balance and speed. He explained how they had used gel batteries and made some modifications to the transmission for speed. The controls were in that full pistol grip handle on the right armrest. They had installed a backup on the left armrest. It was just a small rollerball mounted to the underside of the armrest. It was engaged by just pushing it in like a button to activate. The transmission control was under the right armrest, just under the pistol grip. It had three speeds in both directions. Dead slow for traction on bad hills or off road. Midspeed was like a normal power chair for getting around at a good pace, but nothing like the third speed. The third speed was geared to give her maximum speed for a limited time, as it sucked battery power. It could reach twenty-five miles per hour on a flat hard surface, maybe a little more. We all laughed and whistled.

Six started singing "Little Old Lady from Pasadena," which made everyone laugh that much harder. Sam flicked it to third gear and slammed the grip forward. It spun out on the polished floor and tilted back like a dragster doing a wheel stand. Lucky there were two wheelie bars in the rear that kept her from going over backward. She quickly pulled back, and the chair slammed back to the floor.

"See, little lady, I told you to get used to it first."

She dropped back to second gear and flew around the room and furniture like a pro. Mom looked at Smith and winked. "Thanks for this. She deserves to feel back to normal as much as possible."

As she flew by the table, she yelled out, "What is this little digital screen behind the grip?"

The old man just jumped up and down in place, rubbing his hands together. As Sam went by. she grabbed Jesus and pulled him on her lap and took him around the room. Mrs. Smith's father couldn't hold it any longer. He yelled, "It's your weapons systems, my dear!" Sam came to an abrupt halt, which caused Jesus to tumble forward from her lap.

We all looked at Smith, and he just shook his head and said, "Can't have the lady go out into the world unprotected."

Archie and Snake had developed a bond through their love for blades and their proficiency in their use. They were in the section of the small armory the Smiths had hidden well below the parking structure. Archie had taken to Chief's son and was passing on his specialties in explosives and firearms. It was Archie's request that Jesus be kept away from all the implements of death and destruction in an effort to protect him. He did not want him to be any more of a part in this quest than need be. It was Snake that made Archie rethink that position when he explained that Jesus would be exposed to things and situations that might require him to protect himself. Chief had taught him at a very young age that a strong and knowledgeable brave would always be in a better place. Arch had to agree so the two of them were giving basic lessons in weapons and their use and care. Jesus was a very good and quick learner and soon made his instructors proud of their new student. Field stripping and reassembly came first. They explained a weapon was no good if it failed from neglect. It seemed Jesus had a natural talent for knives. He learned about their balance and the different throwing styles. Throwing so the blade flew end over end for long distance throws. In close, the flat underhand straight throw was preferred. The blade never turned. It just flew straight and level to its target. After several days, Mark gave Jesus his first knife. It was a six-inch double-edged blade with a bone handle.

"Chief made this knife. Respect it and take good care of it."

Six was finetuning his new legs that Smith had procured from a friend in the prosthetic business near Dallas. He had secured a new pair of the curved steel legs that Six liked to call his run-around shoes. There were also two pairs of the standard flesh-colored legs that matched his skin color so well you really had to look twice to tell they weren't real. Those were his walk-about legs, he called them, and liked how they made him look as normal as possible. He still had an odd gate when he walked, but nowhere near as others in the same situation. He had spent countless hours perfecting his walking style to make it hard, if not impossible, to tell. The one from the box he was trying on for the first time. They seemed to be slightly heavier than what he expected them to be. He held them up for closer inspection. There were two very small recessed tabs on the inside of each leg. He held one up and pushed them one at a time, and the side of the leg just popped open. Once he opened it, he could see a .338 semiauto pistol in a cut-out section of foam along with two spare clips. It was a compact semiauto pistol with multiple laser sight settings. It had a steady constant red sighting laser or an intermittent one that flashed like a strobe light. On the lower section of the leg, there was a compartment with two razor-sharp throwing knives and a coiled wire garrote. Six smiled and said to himself, "Now I have a real kickass pair of walk-arounds." He opened the other leg to find multiple foam compartments that could be cut to accommodate most anything he wanted. Two compartments contained sand-filled containers to match the weight of the one carrying the weapons. Six lifted them together and could not feel a weight difference, which was good for balance. He slipped them on and started to stroll around the room. It didn't take him but a few minutes to adjust to the new legs. He walked back to the bench where he was fitting the legs. He took off the ones he had on and opened the compartments on the second one. These were both just full of foam that could be cut to accommodate whatever Six wanted to fit into them. He smiled. "I can put snacks or a few cans of beer in here."

Mom was off talking with Mr. Smith, and I was reading through Chief's files for the fourth time, hoping to find something new. I didn't know how the CIA boys were involved or what could be so special to need us silenced. What intel Chief had been able to secure only added to the mystery. The best way to get answers was to first find out who the Chungs really were and what the Dragon Enterprise was. I was just going to go find Sam and ask for her help when she came rolling in, operating the new chair like a pro.

"Hey," she said, rolling up and giving me a bear hug and kissing me on the cheek. "This thing is fantastic. I'm so thankful to the Smiths for giving me back my independence. What are you working on?" she asked.

I threw the stack of papers on the table and looked at her. "I think it's time you get your wizards of Oz on the job." She pushed back with a sour look on her face. I knew that given enough time, she could get all the information we were looking for and more. I told her I knew she could, but time was not a luxury we had right then. The longer we waited to start our operation, whatever that was going to be, the better the odds the three little pigs might catch on to us being alive. That could begin a shooting war that we might not be able to win. She agreed, and we headed down the hall to the computer lab. She rolled up to her station and began to type.

"This could take hours or even days to get the information we want from these guys," she explained. "They are wanted cyber criminals, and making contact and getting the intel will require many checks and reroutes of data to be sure they remain safe." Luckily, she had already made contact with them, letting them know she was okay and would be contacting them. She typed again, and the screen came alive with the video game Grand Theft Auto. As she played and worked her way deeper into the violent cyberworld of Grand Theft Auto, she would smile and laugh during different parts of her game. This was the first door she needed to go through to get to her friends.

"You know I love you, Sam," I said with a laugh.

She paused and looked at me. "Really, Skipper?"

I blew off the comment and told her, "We do have a clock ticking down on us."

She told me that the first step to reaching them was through the game. They played till someone recognized the other, and then they would chat online. Their chat would be cryptic and would bounce all over the world, changing at random times.

"I'll call you when I make first contact and we are on our way." I kissed the back of her neck and headed out the door. "Skipper," she said, which made me turn. "I love you too." She never looked at me, and I just turned and left.

At around six, we met on the deck for dinner and some discussion on where we thought we should go next. Sam joined us and rolled up next to me. As we passed the plates of pulled pork and other fixings, we made small talk about our day's activities. Arch began the discussion by asking if we had any idea what we would do next. We all just looked to Mom for a response. He wiped his face and pushed back in his chair.

"We know this all has to do with the Chungs and their children, who now have assumed control of the company." It had all started with our extraction of the vice president and his family from the warehouse. Then the decoy family from the farm. From there, it took on a life of its own. When we all managed to survive, it left some serious loose ends. Other than that, we could assume that drugs made up a big part of the story. The drug trade was like owning a printing press. The money just kept rolling of and piling up. But he felt there had to be much more to it. Drug dealers were like ticks on a dog. Remove one and another just moves in right away. For those boys from the pigpen to use such extreme prejudice, it had to be more. Those bastards managed to get presidential approval for that cruise missile strike on a drug dealer's stronghold. The follow-up cover story was it was in retaliation for the brutal murder of a DEA agent. The president had reached his final straw with the Mexican drug traffickers. All wrapped up nice and neat, but we all knew it was a direct attempt to eliminate us. It was obvious from what our friends back in Mexico confirmed. They tracked the company cleanup squad as they collected samples only from where the bus ended its run.

We needed to find out and get just what made so many powerful people willing to do anything to keep it private. It was obvious the three stooges from the pigpen were not the brains of the operation. They were being managed by someone with a lot of clout and the willingness to kill whoever got in the way. It got really dirty when we all lived. Mom had put in place the cover that he would spill his guts if they didn't back off. Way too many other players for them to kill them all to shut them up back then. But now many of those people were gone and we were all that needed to be cleaned up. For now they thought they had it handled for the most part, as we all died again in Mexico. That was our saving grace for now, so we knew we had to protect that at all costs. No outside contact with anyone. The only exception was Sam. We trusted her, and I believed those guys were used to keeping secrets.

She smiled. "I trust these guys with my life. No worries."

As far as that went, Six asked, "Where are we on intel from those guys?"

"Not a lot so far, but they're digging deep."

The basic stuff was all out for public consumption and was squeaky clean. Which, for a company that size, did look suspicious. The parents were both dead in what seemed like an everyday auto accident. But it also happened at the perfect time for the kids. Their deaths put the son, Long, in the CEO seat for the company. That in turn allowed him to put his sister, Bian, in as senior vice president. The company was just about to get into international banking. Long stands for "the dragon," and his sister, Bian, is "woman of secrets." He appeared to be very well-connected with the Washington muckety-mucks, and she was the good little girl, supporting the arts and other charities. It looked like the kids were expanding the company and were much more aggressive than daddy was. They both lived on a huge complex just outside Ashland, Virginia. She had a family just like the parents did, one boy and one girl. Both their spouses seemed to just exist in obscurity, no real footprint electronically or publicly. Long had a wife but no kids and appeared to like a smorgasbord of women. The company offices of record were near the capital in DC. The rest was just the usual corporate crap. They owned the building through a holding company. It made for a true maze for any IRS audit, although we doubted that was a concern.

"How do we begin?" Snake asked, his impatience showing.

Mom said as a matter of fact, "We need to get inside the company and anywhere else we can dig for intel. Any thoughts on how or who we use to that end?" Mom asked. We all thought for a while.

Sam started it off with "I can get a job in IT with the company, maybe dig through the computers."

Six raised his hand. "We should look at the sister's interest in charity work. I might have a way in through there. The Iron Man thing might give me a way to gain access to her." I mentioned I could get Jane to help set that up. Arch and I thought we could look into the security company they used and see if we couldn't get jobs working at the company office or the family compound. We all agreed that Mom would coordinate us all and act as our overwatch from headquarters. We would be running blind as we had no idea what we were would looking for or what to expect. The discussion went on for two hours, and finally we all agreed on the next step.

Sam went about creating our back lives with IDs and the paperwork we needed, driver's licenses, and social security cards. Archie and I sat and worked on a plan that might fast-track us into better security positions with the company. We would have to first get hired by the security company they contracted with. The Chungs owned it, but we needed to go slowly. It was owned by them but supplied security to many other customers. Our being assigned to the Dragon industry would be a crapshoot at best. We came up with several scenarios where we could make ourselves look good to the Chungs. In time, we would have to make a move to stand out.

We all gathered around 1800 in the parking garage as the Smiths had requested. We moved around and asked each other if anyone knew what was up. Suddenly, the louder than normal bellow of a set of train horns spun us all in the direction of the entrance. Through the large overhead doors came this huge motor home. The RV was a combination of brown with gold highlights. Then two large panels on each side changed in color and had the message "Your home away from home" flashing across the side. John Smith was at the wheel, and the Mrs. Smith was waving out the passenger window. He pulled up in front of us, and the door opened, exposing John sitting at the wheel. The stairs came down automatically when we opened the door.

"Come on. We need to go for a ride," he said, laughing like a young boy. We all stared and started for the stairs when he yelled, "Where are your manners? Ladies first." He hit a switch somewhere on the dash, and the bottom step moved straight out and down to the ground. It extended some four feet out from the coach and just settled to the ground with a small ramp moving out from the step kickplate. "Going up." He laughed as Sam rolled onto the platform and stopped. It lifted her quickly to the floor level of the coach, where she moved ahead and turned left into the motor home. The passenger seat had been folded up against the wall to give Sam better access to the back of the coach. The lift quickly returned to the step configuration, and we all piled in and found seats on the fold-down plush seats and coach that ran along the walls. The interior was beautiful but tight with us all inside. The door closed, and we headed out of the garage and down the dirt road that was maintained better than most interstates. The engine was in the rear and seemed so quiet we weren't sure it was running. The coach seemed to fly down the road at a speed a large vehicle should not be doing. The ride was smooth, and we barely noticed any sway when we went around a corner.

"This thing can fly and corner like a sports car," Mr. Smith said to Mom. "Well, the engine is a turbo-boosted diesel, and we are riding on not less than twelve oversized airbags. They allow the coach to change level and tilt instantly based on the road it's traveling on." We came to a small clearing, and we pulled over and came to a stop.

"This is the surprise I was waiting to show you," John said with a huge smile. "Took a bit longer to complete than I thought it would. The basic stuff was already done as I started this project two years ago. Thought I might need a portable office one day." He knew our story was yet to be written, and he knew we might need some special help. He had made a few more modifications after it was clear we were headed home. Home to the beginning of a crusade to find our old lives. He stood up and reached up to some switches on the wall. He pushed two buttons, and both sides of the coach just pushed out away from the main body. Soon the room was three times the size it had been while we were driving. "The back does the same," he said. It was sleeping quarters and bathroom facilities. To save space, the kitchen was just a small sink but with a full-size refrigerator and microwave/convection oven. "Mrs. Smith says you can cook anything in a microwave." He chuckled. Storage for food and other supplies was built in everywhere to maximize the use of all available space. We looked around and were amazed at the size and efficiency this house on wheels had. There was no doubt we could live very comfortably in this RV for as long as we chose. John stood in the middle of the room and did a bow like you would see an actor do. "Now the hidden surprises of my little prize." He pulled a small panel open and hit some switches. "You guys must stand for a second," he said. As we got up, the walls on the side of the coach folded down in sections, forming several shelves and a wider work area the length of one side. When the work area folded down, it exposed multiple flat screens. A small shelf under the screens held compact wireless keypads. The seats could now be turned around for us to sit at the work counter. The windows all became tinted and would allow full view from inside. From the outside, they were blacked out so no one could see in. All the screens came alive with different programs and even some in foreign languages. Sam just kept spinning in circles.

"I have died and gone to my idea of auto heaven," she said. The driver's side seat could be removed so she could drive as well. She smiled. "Can I play with it?" she said as she reached for a keyboard.

"*No*," he said with a frown. She pulled her hand back quickly. Then his frown changed to a huge smile. "Your touchpad you have mounted to your chair has been wirelessly matched to the network. You can control everything on this baby from your chair." It was possible for her to control everything from far away through a secure internet connection. "You can control everything from computer and security systems and to the weapons systems."

"Weapon systems?" we all spoke as one.

"Yes, this little girl can pack quite a punch." His friend and himself were like kids in a candy store when they designed the weapons systems. He laughed. "Let me give you a demonstration of her bite." He sat down and took up a keyboard. The screens blinked, and there was an entire 360-degree view around the RV displayed. He made some keystrokes, and a sighting circle appeared on one of the screens. He slowly moved a joystick he had. A large dead tree appeared some hundred yards away but was small in the view we had. John made the view bring the tree in closer and much clearer. Then we could hear a slight hum. It looked like the tree was being attacked by hundreds of insects.

Arch whistled. "A Gatling gun." The tree was being torn apart by an onslaught of bullets. We knew what was happening from the tracer rounds that were mixed into the ammo, which made it look like a long red snake. "The roof has two Gatling guns of my own design, .9mm rounds in canister clips that hold a thousand rounds." He stood and reached up and pulled on the ceiling light. It dropped down, and there was the loading compartment with two spare canisters of ammo. The light in the back acted as the same loading area. They were great and covered 100 percent of the perimeter. The only drawback would be up close. The downward angle would make us vulnerable up close. "I thought of that and took care of it." The screens changed again to show the perimeter of the coach right up to the sides. "All those fancy running lights you see that do look great at night, they are miniature claymore anti-personnel units."

Archie coughed. "You said I was helping design those for a customer of yours." He turned to us. "Those are very nasty little babies there. Trust me."

You could tell Smith was getting more excited by the way his voice cracked. "These were an afterthought, my friend, but they are so much fun to play with." He laughed. The main screen came on and focused on a clearing and something at the very far end of it. We could not make out what it was we were looking at because of the distance. As the screen zoomed in, the object became clearer. We could see an old pickup, and standing next to it was Mrs. Smith's father, waving a flag. Mr. Smith spoke into the microphone built into the system. "Come back, Papa." He dropped the flag and got on a four-wheeler and headed our way. That truck was over half of a mile from where we were. "You can reach out up to two miles if you have the targeting information. These are both ground to ground as well as ground to air defenses. They each have multiple programs." We all had the deer in the headlights look as we turned to each other.

"Say what?" Six stuttered. We heard the hum on the roof as the targeting was sent from the keyboard. The coach did shake slightly as the missile took off. Smith had turned off the window masking so we could look out. We saw the fins and the exhaust from the missile as it left. The smoke dissipated around the opposite side of the coach. Before it could really register, the pickup erupted in a huge ball of fire and explosion.

"What the hell?" Mom yelled. "What is that thing?"

"I call it the HK, Hellfire Kiss." He laughed. The oversized central air-conditioning unit on the roof did not put out any cold air. It covered a four-unit pod launcher. "These little babies are French made and can be programed from the launch control or set to lock on and intercept a target. They don't have a huge explosive impact, but more than enough to take out most threats."

We named our new mobile home the War Wagon. After another hour of show and tell, our heads were spinning. It was the ultimate headquarters for the collection of intel. It was more than capable of both offense and defensive operations. It also came with a little tow behind package. Mrs. Smith drove it up and parked next to us. It was in the form of a Humvee made to look like your standard road use only model. "It may look like a yuppie grocery getter, but it's well armored and equal to the off-road version of its military brother."

As we drove down the road back to the Smiths' home, we asked him why this special gift. He just looked ahead as he drove and explained, "I knew just the very basics of what happened back in Mexico and that you would be returning to the United States." He knew we were being hunted and we would need to do some recon. After the big bang we made back there, it was safe to assume we would need to be well armed for phase two. "Besides, I been wanting to build something like this forever. I started it before I knew you but decided you needed it more than I. Now for just over my cost, this baby can be yours. Fully equipped and a full tank of fuel for just one million."

"The War Wagon must have cost twice that or more," I said.

He just waved me off. "You can owe me the balance." We all laughed and asked how good our credit was. He smiled and said, "I know you will be able to afford it. You can pay me when you get it. Your generosity in Mexico is well-known. I'll hold the paper for now, and you can pay when you can. I bet you'll come into a lot of cash when you take it from the people you're after." We knew he was right. War was expensive, and it only made sense they paid for their own destruction.

When we got back to the house, such as it was, we were met in the garage by Mrs. Smith and Papa. They both looked mad, real mad. "I'm in some deep shit now. Not sure why, but I can see it coming." John got out of the RV after we were all out. He took a slap upside of the head from the Mrs. Smith. "You almost blew up Papa with your new toy."

"I forgot my new hat in the truck where I left it when I unloaded the four-wheeler. I turned around to go get it, just as you blew it up."

John tried to hide his laughter. "I saw you stop. I would have self-destructed the missile if you were too close." He stormed off, mumbling in Spanish while Mrs. Smith dragged John off by the ear. Out of respect, we didn't laugh too much.

At dinner, we discussed the War Wagon and all the things it could do and wondered what other surprises it had in store for us. Sam had checked with her friends' Dropbox account to see if they had anything. The only message was "These people are like flying monkeys. Still headed down the Yellow Brick Road. She translated for us that it meant they were bad people and they were still looking, doing a deep dive. Mom seemed out of sorts, and after some time, I found him out on the deck of the run cabin on the side of the rock.

"What's up, Mom? You don't look so good."

"I need to get to Martha and Susan. I think they're safe, but I need to make sure. They look good, different hairstyles and color but happy." I asked him how he knew they had changed their hair and how he could see that they were happy. Apparently, they were in a community for retired or soon-to-be retired people. Where they were, there was a town square where they had live entertainment 364 days a year. A lot of the people there went there every night to meet friends and listen to the music. There was an active video feed from the square where you could watch online. Martha and Susan would go down every two days and stand where the camera would pick them up so he would know they were okay. He looked at me, and I saw his concern. "They have missed the last two check-ins, and I know there is something wrong."

I put my arm around him and told him to go get some sleep. "Don't worry, Mom. We got this." I watched as he went back to his room without speaking to the rest. They were all sitting around the fireplace in the center of the room, talking and laughing. Papa was there, and it was obvious he had forgiven John as they were both talking about the War Wagon's demonstration that day. Mrs. Smith must have calmed down as well as she sat on the arm of John's seat, stroking his shoulder.

I walked over to the edge of the circle of my friends and stood behind Sam. "John, is the RV good to go on a shakedown cruise?"

He looked puzzled. "Yes, of course. Just need to rearm from today's show." Everyone looked at me for an explanation.

"Mom's family may be in trouble. We need to make a road trip to Florida." Six asked what the problem was, and I explained to everyone about the video check-in.

"When?" John asked.

"I would like to leave ASAP, even if we need to rearm when we get back."

John nodded. "You have three missiles in the rack, and the Gatling gun can be reloaded in two minutes." He looked concerned and then explained to us that we had not yet been cleared for the weapons system operation. He also told us there were still some aspects of that system we have yet to be told about. There were also things with the operation of the War Wagon that he needed to show us. He looked at Mrs. Smith at his side and placed his hand on her leg. She bent down and kissed him. "I'll have your clothes ready and the galley stocked in thirty minutes."

"Guess we are having a real shakedown trip," he said, looking at each of us. No one argued as we knew the operations of the War Wagon would need lots of training. Everyone got up and looked at me. "Wheels rolling in two2 hours."

Papa had already left to reload and prep everything for our departure. Everyone headed for their rooms, and I went to tell Mom about our plans. I knew he wouldn't be sleeping.

I opened the door, and I could see his laptop was open and displayed a view of an area with a large gazebo in the center. There were hundreds of people walking around. Some were dancing, and others just sat there watching.

"Any sign of them, Mom?"

"No, and this will now make the third missed check-in over a weeks' time."

"No problems, Mom. We will be there before the next scheduled check-in." I went on to explain that we were leaving in two hours for Florida. It would take us twenty-six hours for the trip but put us there in plenty of time. He started to object about Mr. Smith accompanying us but realized we really didn't know how to operate our new RV. I went on to explain we would split up the driving so everyone would be fresh when we arrived.

He put his hands on my shoulders. "Thank you, son. I hope we aren't jumping back into a firestorm. I'm not sure I dare do this alone and possibly put Martha and Susan in a crossfire."

"You're not alone. None of us are." I gave him a bear hug and headed to my room to grab some clothes.

In one and a half hours, we all stood in the garage, eager to get on our way and secure Mom's family. Mr. Smith was in the driver's seat with Papa at his side. They were going through the final checklist together. Archie and Jesus were just finishing up connecting the Humvee to the rear hitch on the RV.

Six was helping by handing up boxes of food and supplies to Mrs. Smith to stock the refrigerator. She stuck her head out when she saw me standing there. "Almost done. Hand me up your stuff and I'll put it away with the others." Six reached for my bag, and I let him hand it up to her. After a few more minutes, Mrs. Smith gave her husband a big kiss and came on out. Sam was already inside getting a hand on moving around. Her motorized chair was in the lower section of her closet where there was a charging port that kept the batteries at 100 percent. She was using her standard chair as it was narrower and easier to move around inside, especially when the RV was closed up. We all said our goodbyes to Jesus and Papa, along with Mrs. Smith. As we boarded our new operations center, we all had a sense that things were going to get interesting for sure. I pulled down the shotgun seat and made myself home. Archie and Six took the workstation chairs, and Mark laid down on the couch. Mom had retreated to his bunk in the back to try and get some rest. Sam had also transferred to her lower bunk as her long hours had caught up to her. The train horns sounded loud and long as we pulled out into the night. The War Wagon was headed on its first run, we hoped not a combat one.

The ride was so smooth it was hard to stay awake with the oncoming lights helping to relax me. Everyone except our chauffeur had got some sleep through the night. In the morning, everyone slowly came out to the main area and enjoyed the coffee Mark had made fresh. He handed each of us a breakfast burrito that he had heated in the microwave. They were delicious, and Mrs. Smith had outdone herself. I asked John to pull over at the next rest area where I would take the wheel and we could all stretch our legs.

"Sorry, Sam. You too, Six." They both laughed. We walked around the War Wagon like we were getting the lowdown from a sales agent. First, he told us the tires were puncture resistant but had an auto inflate to seal and inflate if needed. He also pointed a slide opening above each set of tires. When deployed, a bullet resistant shield would drop down to protect the majority of the exposed tires. As we moved down the side, he pointed out the running lights that were actually small claymores that Archie had helped design.

"These things are small but deadly at close range," Archie bragged. Each side had many compartments for storage and access to the fresh water and sewage holding tanks. There was also a long spool of electrical cable to attach the RV to power sources in campsites or where we could arrange or it. He pointed to the side of the coach, saying the best way to hide something this big was in plain sight. He showed us how using a small iPad he had brought. He changed the colors, the graphics, even displayed a sign for an advertising company. Around back, he pointed to a door at the top of the coach. He used his iPad again, and the door opened and a five-pod launcher slid out.

"These are similar to those you had in Vietnam on your choppers. The big difference is these can be targeted through the fire control system, not just fixed like the old ones." There was another one on the front of the coach as well.

Mom whistled. "Damn, this thing is deadly." We all climbed back in, and I pulled back out onto Interstate 40. I asked if we needed to run the generator all the time for power. Smith told me the engine heavy duty charging system was all we needed to keep the batteries charged up. A large inverter supplied the 110 volts to anything that needed it. He was very proud of the solar panels that covered most of the roof, but more so of the awning system. When parked and the awning was put out, it became a large flexible solar panel that could supply all we needed.

We planned to take forty top Memphis and then cut across to Florida. As we went down the road, Sam and Smith enjoyed hours of her playing and him showing her the computer and surveillance equipment and capabilities. Mom and I discussed the best way to check in when we got there.

We pulled into the parking lot of the Walmart and found an empty and secluded area in the back. I pulled in so there was room to open up the wagon and deploy the solar collector awning. Mark and Archie went about unhooking the Humvee and pulled it around to the front. With all four slides pushed out, we lost that cramped feeling he had to deal with coming down. Smith walked down to Burger King to get us some food while we discussed the plan to locate Mom's family. Mark was an unknown, so we opted for him to make first contact in case someone was watching. Mom and I, along with Six, drove Mark to a street that was opposite Mom's place. There was a golf course that separated the homes from where we were parked and the homes that lined the other side. Mom's was toward the end of those on the west side of the course. Mark had a rake he bought at Walmart and wore a gray work shirt and started to walk across the fairway. To any golfers or people sitting outside their homes, he looked to be a groundskeeper. He circled a small pond and started raking along the short wall that lifted and separated the homes from the golf course. When he got in front of Mom's home, he stopped and rested on his rake, wiping his head. He pulled out his cell and started to act like he was talking to his wife or girlfriend. He sat on the wall and carefully scoped out what he could see of the house. The curtains were pulled back some, and he could see no lights or activities. He jumped up on the wall and walked up to the side door. It was a sliding glass door, and he could not see any activity or hear any radio or TV. He asked us what we wanted him to do next. Mom directed him to go to one of the neighbors and ask if they knew where the women were. Mark walked down between the two homes and across the street to a house with the garage door open. He was met by an older man who looked to be planting flowers in his front yard.

"Can I help you?" he questioned Mark. Mark explained that the people across the street had scheduled him to do some yard work, but they didn't seem to be home. "I'm afraid I can't help you."

Just as Mark was about to walk away, the man's wife came out of the garage. "They haven't been home all week. Not sure where they have gone to. They are lovely people." She explained that there seemed to a have been lot of people looking for them all week. The first of the week there were several plumbers that worked in the house all day. There had been another plumbing guy there every day the rest of the week, sometimes twice a day. He had been awful noisy looking all around the house and in the windows each day. "Now this guy doesn't care about any of this. You're just way to nosy."

Mark thanked them and walked down the street. Minutes later, we picked him up and headed back to the wagon.

We sat around and discussed what Mark had found out so far. It was obvious someone was looking for them and that they had been gone for a week.

"Where or what would they do if they had to go to ground?" I asked.

"They would have made their way to a friend." They had always discussed as a last-ditch option to call him. His name was Jerry and ran an airboat ride company about twenty miles from there. He apparently was a good man that had a very hard time adjusting to civilian life. He and Mom used to hunt gators whenever they got together. His wife died of cancer shortly after he got out, so he passed his time drinking and running his airboat. He owed Mom big time from their time in Vietnam. His unit had been ambushed, and he was the only one that had got out alive. The brass called off the search and rescue because the patrol wasn't supposed to be where they ended up, and there had been no contact. Mom knew him and knew if he survived, he would make it to the original evacuation point. His copilot was Chief, and they agreed to stay on that evac location till they ran out of gas. Just before that happened, Chief saw him running through the corner of the field. He was being chased by some VC, and they were closing. Mom told the door gunners to lay down cover fire as he let go with his last two rockets. He put the bird down, and Chief jumped out and ran to meet Jerry and help him into the chopper. They cleared the field and took a few rounds, including one that hit Jerry. Chief patched him up the best he could as they beat feet for the airbase. Mom laughed. "As I feathered out to set down, the engine stalled, and we hit so hard it bent the struts flat. *Out of gas.*"

We headed out the next morning for the airboat ride location. There were signs all over so it wasn't hard to find. Sam and I went alone to make first contact as a couple looking for a fun ride. When we got there, I rolled her chair around and helped her transfer to it. Once at the office, we purchased our tickets and headed to the dock. The group in front of us was just coming off the dock, and everyone seemed to have had a good time. The pilot was Jerry, and he walked over and welcomed us.

"Ready for a good time?"

We both said yes, and I grabbed his arm. "A good friend of yours, Mom, told me about your boat. Chief says you're the best there is, despite the hole in your leg."

He just smiled and turned to walk away. "Not too many Indians around here anymore." We got on the boat, placing Sam's chair in the back by the raised driver's seat. Jerry jumped into the seat and started the engine that drove the propeller in the rear. Another couple was hurrying down the ramp to the dock when Jerry yelled, "Sorry, folk! I have to leave. The next boat will be here in about ten minutes."

He swung the boat around and headed down the narrow path in the water. He swung way out and around an outcropping of land and into a little bay. He shut the engine off and glided up to the shore, where a small gator about six feet long dove back into the water.

"Okay, you two, who are you and what do you want? Think carefully before you talk, or you two will end up gator food." The .45 on his hip was at the ready with the safety strap unhooked.

I raised my hands and stared right at him. "Martha. we need to know if she and Susan are okay. It appears someone is after them, and we're here with Mom to make sure they don't get them."

Jerry scratched his head. "Mom is here? Chief too?"

I thought for a second. "No, I'm afraid Chief is dead, killed by the same guys looking to hurt the ladies, we think."

Jerry sat back, buckled his seat belt, and started up the engine again. We pulled out of the little bay and then flew down the swamp, making our eyes water. We pulled into a dense area of high grass and old oak trees. Ahead, we could see a small cabin with a porch and a dock built right off the porch. He let the boat glide right up to the dock and jumped off and tied it securely. He pulled his gun.

"Better hope you told me the truth," he grunted.

"Skipper!" came the excited voice of Martha. She ran down the porch and threw her arms around me, crying. "Put that damn thing away, Jerry." She looked in the boat. "Oh my lord, Samantha?"

"Yes, Mrs. Fowley."

She turned to the house. "Come down here, Susan, and meet some of your father's bastard children. No offense, you two."

Sam and I both replied, "None taken."

Susan Fowley came down the steps of the house with what appeared to be an AR-15 dangling from a strap. "So you two are part of the group that has destroyed my and my mother's lives."

"Susan!"

"What? You know it's true. Look at us hiding in a swamp with one of Dad's drunken buddies. Larry is dead, along with the two men that tried to kill us."

I looked at Sam and could tell she was hurt but never fired back. I never responded. I just dialed the encrypted phone and handed it to Martha. She walked away, and from the sounds of it, she was excited to hear Mom's voice. Susan was a different story. She sat there on the steps just staring at me and Sam. Jerry had wandered off around the back of the cabin. Sam finally broke the silence.

"We don't know what you two have been through, but I'll tell you this. Your father moved heaven and earth to get us all here to check on you and your mother." She started to comment, and Sam stopped her. "I'm here, alive today because of your father. He saved me and him and the other two back at our home base, and countless others. Your beef with him is yours, but badmouth Mom in front of me again and I'll jump out of my wheelchair and kick your ass."

Susan looked truly sorry and shocked to be talked too that way, but she just got up and walked away. A few minutes later, Mrs. Fowley came bouncing down the walkway carrying a bag. "Let's go, people. I got my man waiting for me."

The ride to the pickup point was uneventful, and Susan just stared at the shore as it passed by. Sam felt bad about jumping Mom's daughter back at the cabin. She felt bad but did not regret it. As we came around a point of land, we could see a house set back from the water with a dock. Parked in the middle of the yard was our Humvee, Black Beauty. The sunroof hatch had been opened, and we could make out Six standing up through it with a fifty cal. setting on the roof. No one else was visible, but we were sure the others were there somewhere. As we approached the dock, Six pointed to his ear, which was a sign for Sam and I to place our ear comms in.

"Welcome home, gator hunters. You'll find weapons under that tarp on shore. Everything looks cool. We'll wait till you are all at Black Beauty." Everyone got out and headed off the dock. Sam, back in her chair, reached down and pulled the tarp away as I pushed her up the short ramp. She handed me a short Uzi and a bag of clips. She took a sawed of twelve-gage that had extra rounds attached to the butt.

"Where's mine?" Martha asked. I told Martha and Susan to stay behind Jerry, who was already checking his weapon. As we approached the Humvee, Mom stepped out from behind it, his arms outstretched. Martha ran to him and put him in a bear hug and kissed him over and over. When they broke apart, he raised his hand to offer it to Susan. She walked very slowly toward her parents then stopped.

"They said you were dead." Her tears were now flowing, and she ran the rest of the way. "Daddy, what the hell is going on?" Sobbing uncontrollably, she locked her arms around him.

As we all got in Black Beauty, Jerry and Mom were having a short conversation. "I owe you more than I could ever pay. Thank you for taking care of my girls."

Jerry just stood there, stone-faced. "You would have done it for me. Besides, I'm only standing here because of you and Chief."

Mom raised his hand and cut him off before he could ask. He handed him a bundle of cash from our war chest. He told him to stay vigilant and prepared because he didn't know if he might need to call on their friendship again down the road. Jerry nodded as Mom opened his door to get in. He looked back. "He died with honor."

We headed out, confident we had not been followed or compromised. Mom turned back to face the rear. "I'm hungry, and we need a place to eat and talk. I know just the place up the road in Ocala." We knew Mark and John would be fine back at the War Wagon, so we headed for the restaurant. It was a Brazilian steak house, and none of us had ever been to one. We pulled out back, and I activated the onboard perimeter security system after everyone was out. Black Beauty had a smaller version of the War Wagon. It had an advanced security system and its own weapons package. The security system linked to our cell phones. If anyone came within four feet of the vehicle, its exterior cams would come on and display the intruders. We could alert anyone near that they were being watched through a speaker mounted in the engine compartment. We could just set off its excruciation load alarm, or it would do so automatically if anyone touched the vehicle. We went to the back door and knocked. Mom had called ahead. We were greeted by a man in a tux and a young girl holding a tray.

"Mr. Fowley, it has been far too long since you have graced my business." They shook hands.

"Alberto, you're right. It has been too long."

Alberto actually was from Brazil. Mom had met his family while on TDY (temporary duty) assignment in Sao Paulo. They also ran a restaurant that Mom and his buddies had visited often. They had asked him to visit their son's place in Ocala in the USA if he ever got the chance. While in Florida to attend a flight controls upgrade class, he had made good on his promise. He called ahead to ask for a room that offered privacy for his group. Alberto was more than happy to oblige and told him to come in the back. We were led to a large private dining room with Brazilian decor and low light. The tables were set up in a *U*, allowing better conversation.

"Will you all be having the special?"

Mom answered, "Yes."

"Good. Be sure to tell me if you lack anything." As he left, he directed the young girl to take our drink order.

After she left, Mom stood up. "Follow us." Martha and Susan led the way. We walked into the serving area where there was the largest and most delicious looking salad bar area I've ever seen. Shrimp, smoked salmon, and every fixing you could imagine for a salad. I helped Sam fill her and my plates. On one end of the room was a glassed area that separated everyone from a huge charcoal pit. Inside were multiple rotisseries with all kinds of different meats cooking. Back in the room, we all told Mom what a great feast this was.

"Oh, we are just getting started." He told the waitress to hold off on the main course till he told her as we had a meeting to conduct.

We all listened as Martha began her account of what had happened over the last week. She started, but her voice cracked. "Larry, that nice young boy that brought us here and stayed to watch over us, he's dead." The room was completely silent. After getting her composure back, she went on to explain. Apparently, they had found out where the ladies were hiding. Last week, they were having breakfast when two men rang the doorbell and claimed they were plumbers. Larry explained there was no problem, and they apologized, claiming they had a new dispatcher, and English was her second language. We watched as they got back in their truck and made a call. They waved and drove away. The three of them went back to the table to finish their meal. Ten minutes later, the door burst open, and the plumbers were back, only this time they had guns. Larry jumped up, but they shot him before he could draw his weapon. They had Martha and Susan sit on the couch while they checked the house for anyone else. "They were arrogant bastards." And they told them they were there to clean up Mr. Fowley's mess.

"What do you know of my husband?" Martha questioned.

"Just that he and his friends are no longer a problem." He got way too much pleasure from talking to the two women. "He's dead, but the upside is you'll be seeing him soon." He raised his weapon to shoot when Larry, who was laying behind them, swept his legs, cutting them from under the loudmouth. As he hit the floor on his back, Larry rolled over the top of him and took his silenced weapon from his hand. As he rolled off the other side, he shot the man that was still standing. "Clean through his ears." He and the remaining man fought over the gun, and Susan jumped on him, trying to help Larry. He got free and slapped Susan, pushing her to the floor. He drew to shoot her when Larry stuck him with a knife in the back, one he must have had in his boot. "He spun around and shot that poor boy two more times." Tears were running down both women's cheeks. "That's when I hit him with pole lamp that was next to the couch. I'm not sure if I killed him or Larry, but that son of bitch was dead." From there, Martha called Jerry, who got there in no time. He packed them up and the things they needed and took them back to his home. From there, he took them by airboat to his hidden cabin he used for hunting and private drinking binges. Mom put his arm around Martha and held her close.

Sam rolled around the table and pulled up next to Susan. "You can kick my ass if it will make you feel better." She broke down and reached to hug Sam.

"I'm so sorry about back at the cabin. I'm just so scared for me and my parents."

After a while, when everyone was somewhat composed, the door opened, and in came three men dressed as gauchos. Each one carried a short sword with a different cut of meat. They went to each of us and sliced off as much of whatever we wanted. Fifteen different meats came and went for our enjoyment. Once we were all stuffed, we ordered coffee and brandy. As we relaxed, we started to kick around our next move. It was obvious the hit crew would have been missed. I added that Mark didn't see anything disturbed in the house.

"Must have had a cleanup crew take care of the bodies and clean the area," Arch commented.

"Must have, because there was a lot of blood and broken stuff," Susan offered.

We knew that it wouldn't end there. The only positive thing was that they believed we were really all killed in Mexico. They would not stop now till they found the two women and eliminated them. So first things first, we needed to secure Mom's family. We needed to find a place for them to stay where they would be out of the reach of any more hit squads. We also needed to make them so toxic, the CIA would have no option but leave them alone. After some discussion, it was the second choice we all agreed would be the best to start with. Make the idea of killing them a very bad idea. One that could cost them the secrecy they were working so hard to protect. We needed to give it all a lot of thought and planning before we made our move.

We needed to relocate away from the area as we were sure they would be watching the house and the surrounding area. Mom called Mark and told him he needed to pull up stakes and get the hell out of Dodge. He told him to bring the War Wagon to Ocala. Sam had used her laptop to find and book us into an RV park on the outskirts. Ocala is in the middle of Florida horse country. The park we chose was an old ranch that Saudi money had bought and then sold when they lost interest. The new owners had made it into a RV park and dude ranch combination. Sam secured a site with complete hookups for the coach as well as a small rental cabin. It was their first year they were open, so getting in was easy. We wanted to set up someplace that would be very public and the last place anyone would expect us to be. Hide in plain sight. It took Mark all of forty-five minutes to fold up the War Wagon and get to Ocala. He pulled into the park and got out to register. They directed him to the site that were booked for us. He had a pass for Black Beauty and told the man in the office we would be arriving shortly.

We pushed the intercom button and were welcomed in. I pulled up between the cabin and the coach. Mark had parked so the entrance to the Wagon was facing the small porch on the cabin. He had the awning deployed and was sitting by the fireplace with Mr. Smith. They got up and came over as we were all getting out. Mom introduced him to Susan and Martha.

"This is Mark, Chief's son."

Martha threw her arms around him. "I'm so sorry, son. He was a very close friend and one of the best men I ever knew." Mom had filled her in on what happened on our way to the RV park.

Susan reached for his hand. "I only met your father a couple of times but have heard stories my whole life." Being close in age, the two would most likely find each other's company preferable to the old folks.

"Come on in. I want you to meet Mr. Smith and see the what he has built for us." The rest of us hung around outside to give them some alone time.

Mr. Smith joined us later. "I'm so glad everyone is safe. Who wants to give me a ride to the airport tomorrow morning?"

Archie was first to say he would like to take his new friend to send him back home to his family. It was dark, and the sky was full of stars, as bright as ever with no city lights to cover them. It was agreed Mom and his family would take the cabin, and the rest of us would stay in our bunks. The Fowleys headed into the cabin, and we all headed into the Wagon. Sam took her place at her station and began typing away to check in with the wizards. I brought up the security system on another monitor. I told Mom on his comm link that I was pushing out the security boundary to include the cabin. The system would monitor the area that I set for intruders or any electronic probing. I could push it over a hundred yards but didn't need anywhere near that much for our area. "Weapons" was all he replied.

"All automatic weapons systems have been shut down and double-checked," I answered.

"Rodger that." We didn't dare let the auto systems be engaged with all the civilians running around the area. The audio alarm was set to notify any of us that had it activated on their phone. Inside the War Wagon, a low-volume alarm would sound, and systems would come alive. The screens would automatically show a 360 view of the perimeter. The area of the violation would be highlighted on the main screen, and red dots would appear over the violating subjects. In each bunk was a small monitor that would show the same display so the occupant could quickly view any intruders. Any unwanted intruders could be handled in many ways from the comfort of the control center. We didn't expect any problems, so it felt good leaving the Wagon on automatic security mode. Normally we would set a watch schedule if we were unsure so someone would be monitoring the area. There wasn't much privacy to speak of in the sleeping area, so a kiss on the cheek and Sam and I were off to sleep in our own bunks.

At around 4:00 a.m., the intruder alert came online and sent the view to our screens in our bunks. It was Susan outside the cabin walking around. She was wearing a long T-shirt and seemed very restless. We all woke up with the alert, but Mark was already out of his bunk and headed to the front.

"I'll talk to her." And out the door he went. He approached her, and she jumped when he startled her.

"Sorry, I didn't mean to scare you."

She smiled and told him he was fine. She just couldn't sleep after the ups and downs of the day. She had no real idea what was going on when her mother called and told her to pack what she could because they were leaving. Mark told her he knew bits and pieces but still didn't know the whole story. He told her it was no doubt very serious if it cost the life of his father and the man that was guarding her. He explained how his father had talked about her father constantly, and he knew they were best of friends for years. From what he had been told and what he had experienced, her father was an extraordinary man who truly cared about others before himself. It was chilly, and Mark offered to get her a blanket.

"That's not necessary, but you could just hold me for a while. I need a hug right now."

In the morning, Archie had the Humvee loaded with John Smith's bags and a cup of coffee, ready for his friend to enjoy on the way to the airport. We all got our turn at goodbye and asked him to hug Mrs. Smith and Papa. We all wanted Jesus to know how much we missed him and would see him soon. As they pulled out of the site for the airport, Mom invited us all inside, including Martha and Susan. We sat in the control area and sipped fresh coffee and enjoyed Martha's cinnamon buns.

Mom started the discussion. "The pigpen boys still think we're dead. Not really an option for my family. Fool me once, fool me twice." And we all knew these guys were no fools. We needed to set up an ambush and send a message back to Langley that the price of hurting the Fowley women was too high a price to pay. If we could make them believe the two women knew absolutely nothing and to keep trying to kill them would be too costly, then maybe they'd back off. We knew that was unlikely, but we could make it so they put them on a very low priority list. The plan was simple. Sam would set up a comm link that would be untraceable, and Martha would just call Russ. It all sounded like it would work, but things never seemed to be that easy. The call was set for later that day to give Sam time to set up the link. Mom asked Susan and Martha to take a walk around the park with him.

"You want to be alone?" Six asked.

"Yes, we need to talk something out."

Six nodded and smiled after they left the Wagon. "Guess this is a good time to test out the old eye in the sky gizmo." He pulled into a workstation and brought up a program called Sky Eye. He punched in a few buttons then sat there and stared at the screen. "How come I can't get this thing to launch?"

Sam turned and hit three different buttons, and the screen now showed the top of the coach. "Rooky. You have to open the hangar door for it to take off."

He took the pistol grip joystick and plugged it in to the console. Then he increased the power slide, and the high altitude/super quiet drome responded. As it began its ascent, the War Wagon became smaller, and the RV park spread out in front of it. It had both forward and downward looking cameras for flight control and observation. He quickly located the three Fowleys as they walked down the road. He hit some more keys and then just sat back and watched. He set the altitude and laser marked the group of three people to be observed. The system then went to automatic flight control where there was no need to use the joystick. It would maintain its altitude and keep the target in full view as they walked around. If the batteries ran low, it would return on its own and land in its hangar for recharge. There was a second drone in the hangar on the roof that could deploy and relieve the first one if continuing surveillance was needed.

Mom briefly explained everything he could to the women about the past few weeks. Our adventures in Mexico and at the reservation, leading up to the reunion with them.

Susan asked, "They really threw Mark's father out of a helicopter?"

"Yes, because he was part of the rescue of these four people and what we did to keep them alive."

She started cry and held her father. "Daddy, I never knew any of this. I'm so proud of you and what you stand for. What can I do to help?"

"What can *we* do?" Mrs. Fowley stated in a matter-of-fact way. Susan kissed her father and started back to the cabin. Martha pulled Mom to her. "She's her old man's daughter." She kissed him deeply. Mom reached up and cupped one of Martha's breasts. Six almost fell out of his chair.

"*No*, damn, *no*. That's way too much. Nobody wants to see their Mom do that." He blushed as he hit the Return Home keys.

Sam looked up. "What?"

It was time. We all sat around, and Martha sat at the desk with a headset on. The phone was ringing and finally was answered by a young woman's voice.

"Assistant Director Martin's Office."

"I'd like to speak to Mr. Martin, please."

"I'm sorry. He is in a meeting. Can I take a message?"

"Tell him Martha Fowley wants to thank him for his surprise in Florida."

"Like I said, he is in a meeting."

"Listen, little girl. I guarantee you if you don't tell him right now, your job is history."

The line went immediately to hold and that annoying elevator music. Russ picked up. "Mrs. Fowley. I don't believe we have met."

"Enough bullshit," she said, and then just silence. "I don't know what your issue is with my husband, but my daughter and I have nothing to do with it." She told him how she and her daughter were just whisked away by this young Marine. "The one your people killed, but not till after he killed them."

"My people?" Russ played innocent. She went on to explain that Mom had told her if anything ever happened to him, he would be the one to blame.

"My husband spent more time away from me than with me, so if you two had beef, it's not my problem."

"It does seem to be your problem, I'm afraid," Russ said in a threatening way.

"Look, leave my daughter and I alone and I'll give you this computer doohickey he gave me. I have no idea what it is or does, but he made it clear for me to hang on to it till he got back. Your stupid men told me my husband is dead. Is that true?"

Russ hesitated. "Yes, I'm afraid it is. Killed in Mexico, I understand."

"Well, then, I don't need this damn thing. All I need is for you to leave my daughter and I alone. Anything that old bastard got himself mixed up in is not our concern."

Russ smiled at Ted sitting across from him and gave him the thumbs up. "Okay, that sounds reasonable. You give me the doohickey and I will leave you two alone. How do we get this doohickey?" Ted was laughing so hard he could barely be quiet.

Martha explained they would meet at a Wendy's burger place on 449 where there would be lots of people around. Russ agreed and said that four tomorrow worked well, and he would be sending a trusted friend to make the pickup. When they hung up, the two spooks could not stop laughing.

"Either she is too old or stupid or both to live. Ted, take a wet team with you and get that doohickey." He laughed. "Then send the Fowley women to meet Mr. Fowley."

The two women sat in a booth, watching the other people in the restaurant eating their food. Mark sat in the booth next to Mrs. Fowley and made a point of looking attentive to the other people. Sam had attached mini comms to each of them that looked like buttons on their shirts. They were dead comms that wouldn't transmit till they each pushed on them. They were dead because we were betting they would scan them for transmitters. The doohickey in question was a flash drive that was really a GPS that we could track easily from the War Wagon. The coach was parked down the road in a Publix Grocery store parking lot. Black Beauty was across the street from the Wendy's in a Sun Trust Bank parking lot. From the bank, they had a full view of the three sitting in the booth. At exactly four, a black Suburban with darkened windows pulled in and parked facing the building. Right behind it came a brown Tahoe that pulled up alongside. A man in a very expensive suit got out of the Tahoe and went in the restaurant and stood there.

He walked over to the Fowleys and asked, "Mrs. Fowley, Susan, Mr. Tough Guy?" They all nodded, and he sat down next to Susan. "You have something for me?" He smiled at Martha.

She reached in her pocket and pulled out the thumb drive. "Just one second." He pulled out this small box the size of a pack of cigarettes and set it in the center of the table. He pushed a button, and a red light came on and flashed for a few seconds. It then turned green, and he smiled. "That's perfect. Now hand it over." She handed him the drive, and he put it in his pocket and patted it. "Now if you three would be so kind as to come with me, we can complete the rest of this transaction." Mark made a half-assed reach for his Beretta in his shoulder rig. "Oh, no, tough guy." Ted let him see the .45 he had pushing into Susan's side. "Hand it over." Mark slowly pushed his gun across the table to the arrogant agent. Ted got up, shoving it in his belt. He pulled Susan with him and motioned everyone outside.

He had them get into his Tahoe where he zip-tied their hands in front of each of them. Mark started to resist, and Ted hit him with the butt of his .45. "Look, jerk, I'm certainly not alone." He pointed to the black Suburban which had rolled down its windows. Inside could be seen four or more heavily armed men in fatigues. The blood was running down Mark's head, and Susan gave him a look of regret. They pulled out, and we all followed. Mom tried to hide his concern, but we all knew he was on the edge. All three had activated their comms, and we could hear everything.

"Where are you taking us?" Susan asked.

"To an old farm we have outside town."

Sam was flying on the keys, looking for any farms listed on the road we were on, changing her search every time they turned. After twenty minutes, they were approaching a large farm that was listed for sale. Ted pulled into the long driveway and stopped at the gate.

The driver of the Suburban rolled down the passenger window, and Ted spoke. "You stay here and keep the place secure. I can handle this on my own."

The passenger looked surprised. "Are you sure, sir?"

Ted told him he was going to enjoy it and didn't need any help. Then he drove off for the barn. Mom looked concerned.

"They have split up. We did not plan for this." He knew that if we engaged the wet team, it would delay our getting to the others to rescue them. Enough delay for him to kill the women and Mark. We stopped about a quarter of a mile from the gate. Thinking fast, I told Mom and Archie along with Six to stand by behind us and wait for my signal. On my call, they were to drive as fast as they could and cut across the pasture straight for the barn.

"What about the hit team at the gate?" Six asked.

"I'll take care of them." And the process started. With Sam's help, I flew through the weapons system and set the target acquisition.

Ted had all three in the barn and was on the phone with Russ. "I have the thumb drive, and now I'm taking care of the rest. Won't be as much fun as watching that red-skin try and fly when you pushed him out."

Martha and Susan both looked at Mark, expecting he would fight or say something. He did neither. He just sat there.

"Good. Ted, call me when you're headed home. Good job." He turned and came back toward us, smiling. "I think maybe I'll make you all suffer a bit. I think this tough guy likes little miss Susan here from the way she acted when I hit him. And all mommies love their kids."

I looked at Sam. "Standby."

"So I guess I'll just shoot her first. Maybe not kill her with the first one."

"*Go, go, go!*" I screamed and punched the execute key. They took off like a rocket toward the barn, through the ditch, and straight through the field. The guys in the Suburban must have been watching, and they all started to go back to their vehicle and get in.

"Damn!" Archie exclaimed. The missile left a trail of smoke, and the guys in the Suburban could see it led to the RV. Then the explosion picked them and their vehicle up and threw it all aside in a ball of fire. Ted heard the explosion and turned to look back out the door. He could see the massive fireball where the rest of his team had been. Not willing to fail, he turned back and raised his gun. He never got to, regret having zip-tied Mark's hands in front of him instead of behind him. Mark raised his arms above his head and grabbed the handle of the knife he had in a sheath on his back behind his head. In a two-handed motion, he pulled it free and let it fly at Ted. Ted fell back against the post and just slid down it to a sitting position. Black Beauty came blasting through the door, and everyone was out and ready for a fight.

Mom ran to the women and cut their hands free, and they hugged together. Archie and Six walked over to the agent's body and looked down.

"I've never seen anything like that." Ted's eyes were wide open, and just the end of the elk bone knife protruded from his mouth. It looked like he was smoking a white cigar. Mom walked over, and Mark looked at him.

"You said I couldn't kill the man that killed my father. You did not say I couldn't kill this man that watched."

Everyone squeezed into Black Beauty, and we headed back to split up the passengers with Sam and me. We headed back to the RV resort as quickly as we dared to avoid any suspicion. Once back and parked, we went about opening up the sides and awning and hooking up the utilities. Mom and Martha were working on their second scotch, and Susan and Mark were out walking. They all needed to decompress from what had just happened. Archie was drinking a water, and the rest of us had beers.

Archie raised his bottle. "Here's to John Smith and the War Wagon. Those jerks never saw it coming."

I took a hit of my beer. "I got to admit, I never thought we would have the need for those things, but real glad we had them." We all agreed and started the fire so we could have some steaks.

The next morning, we all sat outside with our coffees. Mom came strolling over and sat on the end of the table.

"I've decided the safest place for my family is with the Smiths back in New Mexico. He is not only below everyone's radar, but the fortress could handle a full-scale assault if need be." We all agreed. He explained that he planned to take Black Beauty and drive them there. He didn't dare put them on an airplane because he was sure that Homeland had their photos by now. Mom wanted to take the time to explain everything and have some downtime with them both. He planned on being gone for about a week. The rest of us would move on to Washington and begin collecting intel on how we got close to the Chungs. The plan was set, and he was looking to head out by a thousand hours. We went about researching locations for the coach and our new headquarters. Sam found some likely locations and made inquiries online about some of them. As the Fowleys were getting ready to leave, we all hugged and kissed.

Susan came over to. Sam "I always wanted a sister. Interested in the job?"

Sam hugged her hard. "Not a job, a pleasure. And thank you as well. I never got to know my real sister."

Everyone else was waved as they started to get in the Humvee. Susan stopped and ran back to Mark, giving him a kiss that made her feelings obvious. Mom turned a bit red and coughed several times loudly. She ran to the Humvee and jumped in the back. Mom turned and pointed at Mark, shaking his finger. Then he winked and got in. As he pulled out, Mom rolled down the window.

"While you're in town, check out the sites. See all the places you sacrificed so much for."

The trip to Washington was at a leisurely pace. We took two days to make the trip. We were in no hurry and spent the time wisely. Sam spent most of her time on her mainframe terminal talking with her friends and making plans. The first line of business was driver's licenses to begin the transformation of us all. The high-resolution laser printer made short work of the new IDs, and the blank cards with the watermarks and other security features made it go smooth. Mr. Smith had supplied Sam with extra blank cards for many different states. Sam and I worked on our backstories, testing each other till we knew them front to back. Six drove most of the way while making contact with Jane from Newfoundland. He asked her to look into the charities that Mrs. Chung supported and any connection with his skills. She never questioned him and only asked if she could see him again to see if what she felt was going somewhere. We never heard what they talked about, but it took a lot of time, and he was the happiest we had seen him in a long time. Sam had told Six there was a parking lot for a National Real Estate Company down the street and across from the Dragon Enterprise building. She thought it was a waste of time, but she wanted to probe the building with her toys to see what their security looked like.

We pulled in and parked on the far end of the parking lot. The panels had been programmed to display the National Real Estate Company logo prominently around the coach and across the back. There were multiple panels around the coach that could be programed to look or say whatever we designed. We felt that no one would question this new company perk parked in the back. Just to be careful, Sam had hacked the company's e-mail and sent everyone a note saying the company's new advertising tool would be parked there for a while.

Once we pulled into the parking area, I went about the process of turning our supercharged chariot into our new home for the near future. Then I engaged the leveling system that first released all the air in the air ride suspension. Then we heard the hydraulic system lowering the leveling jacks and felt the coach lift to a perfectly level position. It was amazing how this cramped forty-eight-foot bus had become a spacious living and working area in less than two minutes. I went back to prep my sleeping area in the rear. There were six private bunk areas as Mr. Smith had called them, two on each side and two across the back. These areas had comfortable bunk beds with clothing storage under each. Inside was an entertainment system attached to the ceiling that had both TV and radio as well as CD excess. Speakers were built into the headboard to afford each user privacy and kept them from disturbing anyone sleeping. Headphones were also hanging from the side. The TV monitor had direct connection to the operations center where you could communicate with anyone anywhere in the coach. It also allowed each user to monitor the security system that gave a 360-degree view of the exterior.

I just checked my bunk and then made a stop at the bathroom/shower. To conserve room and to allow access for Sam, the bathroom stall and shower were combined. A drain in the floor collected the shower water, and everything was waterproof, including the lights and switches. Six had made many smart-ass comments about the multi-tasking it would allow. As I entered the living/work area, I noticed Archie was going through some maps and charts on this iPad. Sam was busy at her drop-down console working her magic, setting up the surveillance and monitoring systems. That ran through the dish on the roof, which had been made to look like a TV satellite dome, concealing its true purpose. The standard TV antenna for local channels had been raised and positioned in such a way that its parabolic sensors were pointed toward the targeted building. The glass windows acting as amplifiers for any conversations or noise vibrations within. We were all hungry, and Six offered to go find some food. We all agreed on Chinese, which was kind of fitting for day one of the operation.

I pulled up a stool next to Sam and watched this woman's hands fly over the keyboard as if it were attached to her directly. After a few minutes, she let out a sigh. "I knew it would not be easy, but this sucks." I rubbed her neck and let her vent. The systems we really needed to enter were hardwired and not connected to the internet or any external source. She detected a wireless system that appeared to connect to the primary system that handled most of the buildings networks. It was very good but an easily hacked program.

"I have sent a copy of some data I have collected to Oz for their opinion. I gotta bet there are hidden trip wires that would let them know if their system has been breached." She wanted her coalition of friends to make sure it was safe to hack and how to avoid detection, their specialty. She believed these guys were too big and bet to dirty, to not have the best of the very best cyber security. She was going to just monitor the traffic on the system for a few days before she developed an intrusion plan. "It's Saturday, and you guys have an interview to prep for. I want to work on my backstory a bit as well and get the backdoor program tweaked by Oz." Her plan was to load the access program on Monday during her interview, just in case she did not get hired. "Once I'm on the payroll, I can plant my data grabbers so I can collect intel on the built-in hard drive in my chair." Trying to transmit out of the building could lead to being discovered as she was sure the building was locked down on what came in or out electronically.

Six returned in a bit with bags of Chinese food and some beer and soda. We all fixed our plates and found a place to sit. Archie sat in the driver's seat that had swung around to face the rear. We made small talk and then headed to the back to get some well-needed rest. Everyone found their bunks and climbed in to watch some TV or just doze off. Sam stayed at the console and engaged the area security system. No one could get within fifty yards of our home without tripping the sonic monitor or the motion/heat sensors. She had engaged the privacy window tint on those windows not already blacked out. The windows had a gas embedded in them that turned almost mirrorlike when a certain charge was applied to them. From the outside, it made seeing inside impossible while still allowing us inside to see out. Sam rolled down the short hall and into the bathroom, shooting me a soft smile as she closed the door.

The next day began with Archie offering up his version of a Sunday morning service. We all accepted his beliefs and were somewhat comforted by the whole thing. He spoke of the years passed and the pain we had all suffered, giving thanks that we once again were together. He asked for guidance for the future and the insight to end this nightmare. The proximity alarm buzzed, and the screens came on. There was Black Beauty pulling up to the front of the coach. Mom was home. Next came a breakfast of ham and eggs, toast, and lots of coffee. Mom was still the best short order cook of the group. Sam headed to take a shower, and Six and I took off on a short run that also acted as recon of the surrounding area and buildings. As we ran, we made mental notes of buildings, their doors, whatever visible security they might have, side streets and cams that might cover the area, private and city. We also both had ear comms that allowed us to talk with each other and those back at our headquarters. I had a video feed through the logo on my head sweatband that was working perfectly. It was battery powered, and the small batteries had a short life of fifty to sixty minutes, so our run was kind of timed. This would allow us to review the tapes of our run and get the others' input. Everything looked normal, and we stayed clear of the Dragon building to keep from being seen as I had an interview there the next day.

The ground level of the dragon building was made up of a coffee shop, newspaper stand, and the offices of Dragon Security Inc. As we passed by on the opposite sides of the street, I stopped and acted like I was stretching out my legs. I had a thought I would run by everyone when we returned. The remaining part of the run was uneventful except for Six's constant ball busting about his longer strides. Once back, we grabbed some water, and Six headed to shower. I sat down next to Archie and Mom and told them about my idea.

Mom shook his head. "Man, oh, man, you certainly can come up with some beauties, I'll give you that."

We laughed as Six came out and sat down. "What's so funny, guys?"

"Oh, nothing much," Sam said over her shoulder as she continued to switch programs. "Skipper just wants you and Mom to make a hit on the dragon lady."

"Say what!" Six said, trying not to spit out his water.

"Not a real hit," I explained. "Just one that looks good enough to impress and scare her. If we time it right, it will move us up the ladder and possibly make us their first choice for protection." To get inside and have the freedom to snoop, we had to make it look like the Dragon company was under attack. Make them think they needed us for everything from security, personal and cyber. I shot Sam a smile.

"He is right," she said. "If they use me for cybersecurity, I will have access to all systems, protected and not." She was working with Oz to develop a hack that would look like someone was trying to break into their system. It would look like it has a South American hack job. If the Dragon company was involved in any drug trafficking like we suspected, it would make sense. The cartels from the south would be possible competitors and therefore want to gain access to their system. Once we had everyone on the same page, we set the start time but understood it would be fluid. Sam would monitor our comms once she established connection with their security voice system.

Last week, once we had the paperwork and background materials in place, Sam began the process of applying for our jobs at Tiger Security. Arch and I filled out the online version that Sam brought up on our screens. We used the home addresses of the apartments the three of us had rented days earlier. We knew we would need local addresses to pass any checks they did. Each of us took one-bedroom furnished apartments in different areas of the city. We looked for private owners that were renting. They were the most willing to backdate a lease one or two months if we paid cash for those months we were not there. We explained we were looking for work and wanted it to look like we had been there a while. All three landlords were more than happy to take our past months' rent and the first and last in cash. Once we submitted our applications, there was a returned e-mail that gave us appointments for interviews. Being we applied within sixty seconds of each other, the interviews were very close in time. My appointment was for Tuesday at 1300 hours. Arch's was set to be there at 1200. Our false background showed we both had experience working personal security for different companies. I had worked for an Arab Emirates security company that specialized in protecting the very wealthy. My specialties were small arms use and defensive driving and evasive driving. I had worked for them for five years before moving home to the US. Arch was the product of a German security company that specialized in corporate protection and the protection of their wealthy CEOs. He was a hand-to-hand combat expert as well as a weapons specialist. Both back histories showed several action reports that complimented us on our skills and dedication.

Sam had hacked both security companies so any inquires submitted would be rerouted to her and vanish from their system. Now it was just a matter of getting hired, which should be a no-brainer being the Tiger people were always shorthanded. Getting assigned to the Dragon building might require some work. Our thoughts were to try and get Arch assigned to Mrs. Chung. Her background check had showed she seemed to prefer Afro-American men for her personal security escorts. Archie did not like that part of the plan but agreed it would offer us the best intel.

Sam was next, and she went about getting hired like an artist worked on their paintings. First, she hacked into the Dragon company network through the basic end of the system. Nothing important or overly protected, just normal day-to-day stuff. She went through the building environmental systems, heat, air-conditioning, lights, elevators, phones, and other non-sensitive functions including alarms. She got into the human resources files and installed a virus and control program. Only the very best could find it and most likely could not remove it. Then she put in her application and waited to see how it responded. The employment software gave her an appointment at 1500 hours Monday, the same day as us, with a little help. Next, she needed to make her background look like she was some sort of walking hard drive that was rated one of the best in the world. She also downloaded her personal files. It showed she had been in a serious accident four years prior that had put her in the chair and taken the life of her husband and infant son. After that, no actual work history.

Mark's role had been picked to be at the compound that held the Chungs and their families. His Native American look and rough build and tanned skin made him a perfect selection for the grounds and maintenance crews. The crews were made up of mostly Mexican workers, so he would fit in as far as looks and manner. He was also very good-looking according to most women, and that could play well for us. Sam started looking into the landscaping company that worked at the compound. Mark's better than average knowledge of the Vietnamese language was also a card we played. Showing his military service and knowledge of electrical systems as well as networking was a background plant just to draw interest.

The maintenance company did have a website and an online application. The Thursday before, she had filled it out for Mark, while Archie took him to a rental company to get some wheels for his trip. Our new credit cards that were linked to a government agency for payment had worked without a hitch. The maintenance company called Mark on Friday afternoon to run through a phone interview. They were impressed with his background and abilities but questioned why someone with such skills would not be working for a large company. Mark explained he hated being inside every day and loved working with his hands outdoors. They asked if he objected to combining all those skills in one position. He had thought about it for a minute and said he would like that. The interviewer said they were very much interested in him. Then a pause, and the person on the other end of line asked, "Did you learn Vietnamese from your father or mother or someone else?"

Mark answered without hesitation, in Vietnamese, "My grandmother, mostly. She had fled here when the war ended."

The voice on the other end was obviously happy with the test. "Can you be at the Tiger Home on Saturday?"

"Yes" was his answer.

Back at the house, we all went to clean up for dinner. At 18:00, we all sat and dug into the meal in front of us. Sam broke the chitchat with the revelation that she had spoken with all the wizards and they were more than glad, excited actually, to help us in our quest. She said the three of them that would be involved directly were already on the hunt. One was a corporate wizard that would hunt down all the companies and subcompanies and holdings the Chungs had. The second wizard was a super hacker that enjoyed going in and out of police systems and the department of justice looking to see how he might leave breadcrumbs that might help put some bad guys away. He did mention that the name Chung did seem to stir some memory in his head, but also that it was a common name in the Asian world. The third was the history wizard who loved research and finding all the little secrets and hidden parts of people's lives, the more important the better. So far, he has caused several congressmen and even a vice president to publicly admit their indiscretions with woman or in business. They worked together yet separately to accomplish whatever the others were working on. The Scarecrow, the Tin Man, and the Lion were their nicknames. The True Wizard, the leader of this group, acted as the collector of data from them all. He was working on a very time sensitive issue but should have it resolved soon. They felt they would have some workable intel by this week. I did tell them we planned to infiltrate the den of the dragon and might need their help. We all laughed, and Six started singing "Follow the Yellow Brick Road" while Arch did his rendition of "Ding Dong the Witch Is Dead."

Monday morning the final preparations were made for the next day. Mark had been hired on the spot after a token interview and told he started on Sunday by moving into the workers quarters and getting acclimated to the job. The principals were in the compound, so he was to avoid any direct contact with them. He agreed and moved in that day. The Chungs left around seven to return to the city, so it gave Mark time to walk the compound and get familiar with the layout. It also gave him time to locate his party favors. Mom and Six visited a rundown bar that catered to veterans and settled in. They met an older vet dressed in a tattered vest with combat patches on it from Vietnam. They formed a quick bond by buying his drinks and telling war stories. He drove an old beat-up pickup that looked like it would fall off the frame from the extensive rust.

"You want to sell that old piece of crap?" Mom asked, pointing to his truck.

"Hell, yes, but it ain't worth anything, and all I get is my Social Security. And that's not much."

"We'll give you fifty grand if you do something for us."

"Who you want killed?" He smiled.

Six pulled up in a full-size Chevy pickup and parked on the street about three blocks away to avoid anyone noticing their newly purchased wheels. They both walked back to the War Wagon to begin their part of the operation. Arch and I were in lightweight suit coats that concealed our .9mms we had tucked under our arms. We had reproduced carry permits issues by the US Embassy. They would fit with our traveling as part of an out of country security detail. Just another piece to fit with our back created ground claimed. We headed out twenty minutes early for our appointments that were spaced so we did not appear at the same time or close. We had a 11:00 a.m. and 12:00 a.m. appointments so we entered at different times and sat on opposite sides of the waiting area. At exactly 10:30 a.m., Sam came rolling through the front door wearing a conservative dress to the knees and a high neck blouse that hid those favorite parts of mine. She went directly to the security desk near the elevators that serviced the upper floors of the dragon's den. The two minimum wage security men looked at each other, not knowing if she could go through the scanner or they needed to use the handheld. The one that looked like a real player walked over and put his hands on her shoulders like he was going to pat her down. His hands went down her arms and sides and brushed her breasts. He smiled briefly before she grabbed his hands and bent them backward, driving him to his knees. The ranking guard that was reading a paper in the corner threw it down and started to reach for his gun.

Sam yelled, "You can tell Mr. Johnson on the nineteenth floor that he can take his job and shove it where the sun don't shine!" She spun around to leave.

"What's going on?" he yelled as the offending guard backed away, hands up as if to say, "Who, me?"

"You get a little touchy-feely in your pat down?" He stared at the guard. "I'm so sorry, miss," he said.

"Dorothy Martin," she growled as only she can do. "I was here for an interview with Mr. Johnson in IT, *but* I won't work around people that treat women like this. If this is acceptable behavior and is apparently not the first time, I don't need this crap."

"One moment, please, Ms. Martin." He called up to Johnson's office and tried to explain but was getting an ass chewing we could hear from across the room. His face got redder as time went by till he hung up the phone. "My sincere apologies, Ms. Martin. Mr. Johnson asked me to personally accompany you to his office." He spun around and looked at the guard that got too intimate in his search. "When I get back, you are to be a bad memory that fades in time. "Be out of this building and don't ever set foot back here again." He started to reply but could see the look in the boss's eyes told it was pointless.

Archie walked by me as he headed into his interview and winked. "Bet that little bitch is a handful," he said loud enough for his escort to hear.

I smiled and just shook my head, replying, "Scares me." My turn came next. I was escorted into a small office and sat down across from this Oriental-looking guy who showed no expression. Suddenly someone from behind me had his arm around my neck in a sleeper hold. Instinct set in, and I immediately pushed back my chair and slammed him into the wall behind me. His grasp let up slightly, but enough for me to pull him down enough to drive the back of my head into his face and twist free. I drove my knuckles into his throat hard enough to take his breath but not crush his larynx. I held him by the throat, and without looking at the man at the desk, I drew my Berretta and pointed it at his head. I slowly turned my head to see my target, and he had a huge smile on his face and was clapping his hands slowly.

"You may let him go now."

He was just part of his introduction and interview process. The giant of a man grabbed his bleeding nose and gave me a look of hate as he turned and left the room. I turned back to the man behind the desk, and he motioned me to sit, which I did as I holstered my weapon.

"My name is Mr. Young, and I am the head of security for the Dragon Enterprises, here and at all our holdings worldwide."

"You interview everyone this way?" I asked as if upset.

"Not all, but when it comes to personal security, I have no tolerance for players or airheads." He explained how they employed a large number of what they call hard staff in many of the locations. But he admitted they were not what I might call the sharpest pencils in the box. They were good at their assigned tasks and had very little conscious to deal with. "Which makes them valuable but not irreplaceable." He smiled. "You bring a different level to the table, and that is just what I need. Security that can be trusted to put their charges ahead of all else." He had no place for loose cannons with guns but thinking, calculating, resourceful men. He smiled and pushed back his chair. "You got to this point by having an impeccable background and experience in protecting people in some of the most dangerous places on earth. You saved that little girl whose father was a sheik with lots of oil money." I knew it was a test as Sam made the background history about a little boy. Knowing full well that women carried a much lower price tag than men in that part of the world, I stared right at him and smiled just enough and explained how I had found the boy and rescued him, leaving his captors dead. He nodded. "Results sometimes require different tactics and levels of strength, it being the outcome that is important. It is a true man that can use his mind as well as his gun." He stood and reached for my hand. "If you would please take a seat in our special waiting area while we complete some additional cross-checks," He said he did not waste anyone's time. "You will be hired or compensated for your time before the end of day." I knew my background and history had been picked apart and scrutinized since they received my application.

As I entered the waiting room, I saw Arch sitting there, holding a bag of ice on his head. He looked up and smiled. "You should see the other guy. His nuts are still in his throat and pretty sure his arm is broke." I laughed and told him about how my interview had gone the same way. We agreed that these guys must pay real good to have thugs that were willing to get broken noses and arms just to test people. We both laughed and shook hands, introducing ourselves. There were sandwiches there and water and coffee, which we enjoyed. While waiting, we made small talk and told some war stories about our work in our past. We made sure to sit near the smoke detectors so their hidden cameras and microphones could hear and see, or so we assumed. I went to the men's room and sat down as if to make my deposit, which allowed me to remove my ear bug from my pants and inserted it while I was brushing my hair back. Once online, I rejoined Arch, and we talked about the day and other small talk. Then I mentioned my need to get laid, and Arch told me I should try the girl in the wheelchair that tore up the rent-a-cop.

I said, "Yes, maybe take a three-hour tour," in reference to the SS *Minnow*. That was the key word to start everything in motion.

In Virginia, the plan would begin. Mark was hired with the grounds crew at the Chung compound with little effort. The fact he was not Mexican and he spoke fair to good Vietnamese was a big part of it. The fact he also was an American citizen made the owners happy, as that meant they did not have to play green card shuffle.

His records and withholdings would all look great as he had a history and a Social Security number. His background showed he was Native American with no criminal record and little else. Being a vet was just icing for the owners. His duties included work up close to the house and pool. He knew when the owners were talking to him and what they were saying, which gave everyone a comfortable feeling. He had only been there a few days but had already made friends with Joe and Crystal, the Chung's children. He would take the time to throw a ball or laugh at their pool play. His ear buds had started to hum, and the music stopped. Then he received the one-word signal of "Chief is on the warpath" and then back to his rock music. He had spent the previous day and night placing the explosives around the garden and house. He did his weeding and planting chores, which acted as cover as he dropped and covered his packages. Arch had designed them, even the high-pitched sound prior to detonations, so they would appear to be motor rounds. They needed to sound like incoming rounds instead of the preplaced charges that would say it was an inside job. The show would look like a motor attack from outside the compound and was designed to do damage, to make a lot of noise but cause minimal risk to the family. Just something to scare everyone. It was hopefully going to serve multiple purposes. Get the Chungs out of DC and myself and Archie on the home team. We hoped it might help Sam show off her skills, which would be a bonus.

He walked over to the pool where the two kids were swimming. Joe and Crystal were odd names for two Vietnamese children. Perfect for integrating them into the future America they would be groomed to take advantage of. Bending down to pull some weeds, Mark acted like he was adjusting the music on his phone and set the plan in motion. The first blast leveled the guard shack at the main gate from behind the short bush alongside it. The guard that was strolling near the closed gate was knocked to the ground and would have a massive headache. He never knew how lucky he was that he was not allowed to sit in the booth when the weather was good. The next three went off almost simultaneously and blew a hole in the corner of the garage and the two outbuildings near there. Each blast was accompanied by the loud whine of an incoming motor round. Others were leaving large holes in the ground as if they were just rounds that missed their mark. The children screamed and swam for the stairs as several detonations outside the pool area set fire to a cabana and small gazebo that acted as an outside bar. Mark reached up and opened several cuts in his hairline and neck with a sharp piece of metal he had made earlier. He then dove into the water and swam to the children, holding them to his chest and trying to calm them. Crystal screamed when she saw the blood running down his face and leaving a large area of blood expanding into the pool. He told them to be strong and waited for the planned lull in the attack. When it seemed to end, he scooped up the two children and ran into the house and placed them in a downstairs interior bathroom along with the screaming nanny. They got into the tub, and he told them to be completely quiet. Then locking the door, he took up position between the door and them. He turned and stood there like a Roman warrior intent on protecting his treasure.

Arch and I could hear the commotion coming from the security offices, phones ringing and doors being opened and slammed shut. The door burst open, and Mr. Young, the head of security, came out with two assault rifles in his hands. Throwing one to each of us, he barked, "This is not a test. Follow me."

Several other guards appeared each with automatic weapons, and we formed a standard wedge at the door of the private elevator. When it opened, Mr. Chung and his sister were standing there, dressed in long trench coats. There was one very nasty looking Oriental gentleman with them that you just knew was their personal security.

"We are escorting these people to cars that will be here in minutes to take them to their home in Virginia. You new boys know the drill."

As we approached the front doors, three SUVs pulled up in front. The middle one was obviously an armored version of the other two. Just as we reached the doors, a Chevy pickup appeared and drove slowly past the front of the building. As the personal guard reached to open the door, I screamed, "Pickup at ten o'clock! Cover the packages!"

In unison, Arch and I both pushed the Chungs to the sidewalk and covered them with our bodies. Taking a kneeling firing stance, I opened up on the pickup, placing my rounds in the side or fenders. Everyone froze for just a sec until the glass began shattering all around us and covering us in a shower of pieces. The truck picked up speed, and the shooter in back kept our heads down with controlled fire.

Everyone was screaming or running to find cover when Arch looked at me. "Keep her safe or I will be back for your white ass."

Mrs. Chung looked up from under Arch with sheer terror in her eyes at first and then a calm look of thanks. He jumped up and ran out through what was left of the entrance to the sidewalk. He dove up and landed on his back on the hood of the second SUV and rolled across it and landed in the street in a kneeling position. He pulled up his rifle and let go with several shots hitting the shooter in the back. We could all see him to fall into the bed, his gun falling over the side to the street. The truck picked up speed and turned right at the corner and headed away from the scene. Arch was back up and standing next to me, looking down and offering a hand up to Mrs. Chung. The Oriental security man had grabbed Mr. Chung and pushed him into the armored SUV and covered him with his body.

"Time to leave." And Archie pulled her toward the SUVs, keeping his body in front of her. Her brother was already in the middle vehicle, the Oriental guy acting as his shield.

The security man looked back at me and gave me a nod as if to say, "Thanks for doing my job and having my back."

The first SUV had suffered terminal damage, so they were down to two. They put the Chungs in the back of the vehicle. She reached back and grabbed Archie's arm. "He goes with me." There was no arguing or hesitation as he just got in. The Chungs' personal guard had turned to the head of security and had some words. Young walked right over and told me to get in and drive the primary SUV.

He turned to walk away and spun around. "Oh, yeah, you and your buddy there are hired." He walked away.

As we started to pull from the curb, the security guard that had put me behind the wheel opened the passenger side door and pulled the dumbfounded passenger out. He had come from the rear compartment and jumped in buckling his seat belt. "Don't break ranks for anything or anybody."

I was impressed with the amount of help from the local police and state police they seemed to be able to muster in just a few minutes. With a cruiser in front and one to the rear, we had the hammer down the whole way. I liked the feel of driving at high speed again. As we headed out to meet our first escort, it required all my senses to be on high alert. Each block brought new issues, some tourists not looking all around or a taxi that thought it was his road. We made two quick turns, and we were on I-95 headed south in the third and fourth lanes traveling at light speed. We were met by four DC patrol cars, two in front and two in back. It was time for me to relax a bit and make some small talk.

"Where are we headed and what's the plan?" My passenger never looked at me or showed any emotion. The Chungs' home had been attacked. The families were there and for the most part unprotected. It appeared to have been a two-headed attack on the Dragon, the office tower, and the home complex. I told him I had friends in the Richmond SWAT and they were some of the best.

He never broke his stare. He just made the matter-of-fact statement, "No one enters the complex until we are there. You will need to exit at Ashland Virginia Exit, and it will take four minutes to reach the compound from there. Be prepared. I will direct you and take charge once I can get a feel for what has happened. We will go directly to the main house and begin our search there."

"Search?" I questioned.

"Yes. First we secure the family, children, and others. Then we look for those mindless people that have the nerve to attack our home."

* * *

Sam sat across from Mr. Johnson as he poured through her resumes for the tenth time. "I can't tell you how sorry I am for the way you were treated downstairs. Good help is a true scarce commodity here in these parts." His accent seemed to be Texan, which fit the country theme of his office. "If you fit in as well as I think you will, you'll never ride that elevator again." He explained they had private elevators for the most trusted personal on the upper three floors. "Now I see you're a widow. I won't insult you by saying I understand or know how you feel. I am a computer nerd from way back, and my social skills leave a lot of room for improvement." He told her his interest in her was only because of her background and abilities. He didn't care about handicap hiring credits or the fact she was a woman. He only cared how well her fingers worked a keyboard, and he could see she kept her nails cut for the keyboard.

Sam looked at her fingers. It was refreshing to find an honest nerd that understood they lived inside their screens. "My second language is code and may very well be my primary language."

Johnson smiled just as all hell broke loose. It was so loud, and screams could be heard inside and out of the building. He jumped up and ran to the door. "Keep this closed. I'm not sure what's going on, but it sounds like gunfire."

Such a gentleman to try and protect me, she thought. She tapped a few commands on her pad and it was done. The bug was loaded wirelessly. The pad was now purging all reference to the infection and where it entered the system. When Johnson returned, he told her there had been an attack on the Chungs downstairs in the lobby.

"Shit, there goes my new job."

Johnson shot her a disgusted look. "*No*, they're fine and have left." He told her the building was on lockdown for now. "You'll have to just get comfortable till you can leave. The interview is over." Just then, his system was sounding off all kinds of alerts. "What the hell?" he said.

"Sounds like a lot of warnings," Sam offered up as a comment. "What's going on out there?" she said, trying to sound concerned.

"I'm not sure, but this is much more of a problem."

"What's up?" Sam asked.

He was excited and told her it appeared they had been hacked. It seemed it happened about the same time the shooting started. He figured it must have come in through the wireless system they had.

"Our secure site should be safe, but this is like nothing I've ever seen. I think it's a probe, but it is acting like a pair of them." They were moving through the system at unbelievable speed.

"Can I help? As you know, I am a bit of an expert with code."

Johnson took all of three seconds to think it over. "Yes, use that workstation there on the other side of my office. The password is cowboys."

Sam stopped part way there and turned to stare at Johnson. "You wonder why you have been hacked. Amateurs," she said, shaking her head. Once the keyboard was in her hands, her fingers flew over the keys, and she kept telling Johnson to use certain codes that made him feel he was doing all the work. It took one hour before Sam told him to write a single command code and wait till she said to enter it. There were in fact two viruses running, and they needed to be shut down at the same time to stop and freeze them. When she said go, they both hit enter, and the computers flashed and went blank.

"Oh nooo!" Johnson squealed.

"Relax and wait for it," Sam said with a bit of disgust in her voice. A minute later, the system rebooted itself and came back on.

"Oh my god, how much damage do you think there is?"

"Not sure. It will take a lot of time to clean all the codes up."

"Thank you so much, Ms. Martin. You saved our system and most likely my job."

"No, it was a team effort. We never could have killed the bug without working together." That left him feeling superior. It was a probe with its own defensive code. "With some effort, you should be able to find out where the data was going. The police have some good people."

"Oh, no, the Chungs will demand we find it and clean up this mess internally. I will be honest. This is way outside my wheelhouse." He looked directly at her, "So when can you start?"

* * *

As we approached the gate, I could see the remains of the guard shack and the local contingent of police and their vehicles. Several SWAT vehicles were in place, and communication systems were being erected. We stopped at the gate, and my passenger exited and went ahead to meet with whoever was in charge. It took only minutes, and he jumped back in.

"The locals will secure the inside perimeter just as they have the outside. They are charged with securing the outside of the main house and other residences. We will secure the inside of the buildings and collect our people."

"We could use a few SWAT guys to help."

"*No*, the interior of the buildings is off-limits to all but Dragon personnel," he barked at me.

As we approached the main house on the circular drive, the second SUV placed itself between us and the perimeter to shield us from any snipers. I exited, and we hunkered down behind the side of the SUV. The head man broke us into two groups, me and two others with Mr. Chung. Arch and himself along with the dragon lady. Both the Chungs moved like well-oiled machines, each with a stainless automatic pistol. I realized these were not the spoiled kids we extracted from the warehouse all those years ago. Mrs. Chung had cut her floor-length dress off well above the knees with a knife she had hidden somewhere. Archie was careful not to let her see him enjoy the show. We moved together toward the main house and the entrance. That's where Archie's group broke off and headed to the north wing of the house. We entered the front door in combat stance and began clearing the rooms as we progressed. I turned the corner and checked several closets in the den. As I returned to the hall, I saw Mr. Chung try a locked door on the right. He motioned for us to take offensive stance around the door and whispered, "This is a full bath."

He tried the door again, and there was a scream from a woman inside. Without a second thought, he stepped back and kicked the door in. He entered, taking high cover and me the low. As we turned the corner toward the huge bathtub, there was Mark on his knees covered in blood. Mr. Chung pulled up as if to shoot him where he knelt, so I grabbed his gun and pushed it up. He was about to let loose on me verbally and most likely physically when he saw the face of a little boy. It peered around the stone tub wall from behind Mark.

"Uncle, don't hurt Thomas. He is brave and has stood guard over us and protected us from whatever is happening."

Crystal came running around the corner, jumping into her uncle's arms and crying uncontrollably. "I'm scared, Uncle."

He handed her to me and told me to get her and her brother to a safe place. Then he told one of the other men with us to get Mark/Thomas some help. He then just turned and walked out red in anger and the sole purpose of wanting someone to die. Once outside, we were behind the protection of several armored vehicles that had been brought up near the house. The paramedics were working on Mark, and the children were put inside with their nanny. I turned and returned to the main house where I met up with Archie's group and Mr. Chung's group in the living room area. The Chungs and their security men were having a conversation that looked heated.

"What's the sit rep?" I asked Arch.

"We found the brother's wife in the north wing, apparently in mid-massage mood." He chuckled. "She was wrapped in a towel hidden in a closet in the spa area. She was removed along with all the staff there. It appears we have everyone including the kids, except Mrs. Chung's husband. The staff says he was surfing the internet in his private study as was his usual activity."

After talking on her phone with the nanny and being satisfied the children were not hurt and were safe, she turned instantly red and spoke. "That spineless bastard better not be in the safe room." They finished their conversation and walked over to the bookshelf. They only spoke Vietnamese, so we could make out very little. It had been so long since we were exposed to it. Mr. Chung reached into an area of the shelf and pulled a hidden handle that allowed him to swing a section of the bookshelf aside. An oversized steel door was revealed with a keypad and thumbprint scanner.

Mr. Chung typed in a long code and then placed his thumb on the scanner. There was some faint clicking, and the door swung outward on its own. When it was fully open, there standing in the doorway was this overweight Oriental man dressed in silk pajamas with a sheepish look.

"Oh, you're here. What is happening?"

Mrs. Chung walked over and stood in front of him. "Where are my children?" she demanded, hitting him square in the chest, pushing him against the door. The color left is face, and he shuddered, telling her he did not know. Saying he thought they would come to the safe room like he had. She stood back. "So you just locked yourself inside without looking for them or protecting them?" He lowered his eyes and just nodded. Her hands flew, and she hit him three times in the chest and spun around and kicked him in the head, sending him back into the room. "*Coward!*"

She spoke quickly to the security man, and he turned and took the two other men with him inside the safe room. She turned to us, the redness leaving her face, and asked that we take her to her children. Mr. Chung left the room and we assumed went to find his wife. As we were leaving the room, we heard the sound of someone taking a severe beating but did not look back. When we reached the children, they ran to their mother, hugging her and trying to both tell their stories at the same time. Both spoke of how the man named Thomas had saved their lives and protected them. How he had jumped in the pool to get them even though he was bleeding so bad. Joe looked at his Mom and asked where their father was.

"Gone," she said with change in her tone.

"Gone where?" Crystal asked.

"He is on a business trip and will be gone a very long time." There was no emotion in her voice. The children looked puzzled and then saw Thomas sitting on the stretcher, his head bandaged. They turned and ran to him, not giving a second thought to what their father was doing. Mr. Young walked up to us, his hand out to shake ours.

"Hell of a first day, guys, don't you think? I couldn't keep up with you on the highway, but I got as fast as I could." He was there to check on things and give us a ride back to town. We turned to leave when Mrs. Chung walked up and stopped the three of us.

"I don't know where you found these two, Young, but they are the best thing you have ever done." He bowed and smiled, thanking her for her praise. "This one." She grabbed Archie's arm. "I want as my personal bodyguard from now on. He saved my life and told this one he better not let anything happen to me." She let out a soft chuckle. She looked at Arch with a look of more than just a boss looking at an employee, which I know made him uncomfortable. They would be staying in their living quarters in the city within the tower. It would take time to repair and fortify their home. Young said he had thought they would want the security of the office, so he had brought in twenty of the hard staff to beef up the already doubled in-house security. She nodded in agreement and then looked at Arch again. "Tomorrow you will begin as my protector."

He bowed his head and spoke. "It will be my honor."

Once back in the city, we all made our way to the coach at different times. Sam had lots of time before we all arrived to work on what she had found out on her first time inside the Dragon systems. Mom was taking a nap after he put a pot of stew to cook on the small two-burner stovetop. Six sat next to Sam, and they discussed what happened after their attack. After the show, they had gone about five blocks and pulled into a tow-away zone behind a dumpster near an unloading dock for an office supply distributor. Their day had started with them disabling the cameras on the receiving dock of the office supply building and the several city cameras along their route. They had taken extra care to conceal their faces by covering them with stocking-like material with painted mustaches and scars on the outside. Six had been the shooter and wore a heavy Kevlar jacket for protection. He had played dead in the back of the pickup till he reached the end of the line for the old truck. They both quickly changed clothes and threw them in the cab. Mom pulled the pin on a thermite grenade and tossed it under the front seat. The fire would be so intense the truck would melt where it was. Their faces were obscured by large brim baseball caps, and they headed down the street. They walked about two blocks to an alley where they quickly changed clothes again from clothes that were in Mom's backpack. They took care to put all the clothing back in the backpack as the local authorities could get DNA from the sweat found on the clothes. They were now in the dirty clothes bin to be washed with our other clothes.

"You boys sure made a mess in a short time," Sam said. "There was no doubt those Dragon people sure have juice with the local PD. We all were allowed to leave the building through the receiving area and were never questioned by any police." In fact, she never saw anyone but company people. They did, however, have a security person take a picture of everyone as they left and logged their names on a list. They did a reverse ID check, making sure the face and name matched the badge and that they knew their security question of the week. Johnson walked her out, so there was no issue. They were stopped by a security person that looked like a professional wrestler with a gun. He grunted as he approached them.

"Mr. Young would like to talk with you when you return tomorrow. He wants to welcome you personally to the Dragon Towers."

Johnson whistled. "Never seen that before. You must be special."

Sam smiled. "I am but wondered why the special attention."

It was close to midnight before we all got back to the house and filled up on stew and fresh bread. Sam had picked some up on her way home before heading back out to meet us. Everything had gone off as better than we could have hoped for. We had hoped to have Archie assigned to the dragon lady's security team. To have him assigned full time to her as her personal security, that was awesome luck. Mark, now known as Thomas, had secured his place at the home complex with his performance as the savior of the children. Mrs. Chung had someone bring him a huge fruit basket at the hospital and a note saying she could not express her thanks or the debt she now owed him. The person that delivered it was from the residence and informed Thomas that a small apartment was being prepared for him in the servant's complex. She also told him the children missed him.

On the way back to DC, Young told me he was putting me in as one of his personal assistants. It meant I would be traveling as part of that position. I told him travel was never an issue for me. As far as Arch, he was very quiet all the way back and still quiet as we all sat there. Young had busted him about how Mrs. Chung had taken a real shine to him and had never asked for private security before.

Once we were all together, I finally got to slap Arch on the shoulder, asking him if he was okay with this new development.

"Did you see how she looked at me at the house?"

I tried to play dumb and answered, "No, I wasn't paying attention."

"She is a beautiful woman and may have ideas about how much body I guard."

Six literally fell out of his chair to the floor, and Mom yelled from the rear, "She what?"

Sam said, "She wants to be well covered by her big black bodyguard."

We all broke into uncontrollable laughter until we could see Arch was very concerned and not amused.

"I don't know if I can do this if she has ideas other than being her bodyguard." He had not even thought about the touch of a woman or the pleasures that could be had in a very, very long time. "I'm not sure if I will be comfortable, and I don't want to blow this mission." We all became silent and just looked around at each other, not really knowing what to say. As the silence became awkward, he smiled broad and wide. "I don't remember the last time I was with a woman. I would hate to blow my cover because I don't remember what to do or I'm no good. I'm sure she has a level of expectation I may not be able to fulfill. They do say it's like riding a bike, and I was a very good bike rider." This time, he joined the roar, and we all laughed till it hurt.

Sam asked, "This mean you're rethinking your vow of chastity?"

We all headed off to our bunks except for Sam as she had a 0200 meet time with the wizards. I stopped and sat down next to her and rubbed her shoulders. "So tell me more about the wizards."

She smiled and snuggled into my arms as they circled her. I added some extra support where I could, which caused a low moan to come from her lips. She began with telling me how they all met through a hacker website that she found while surfing for fun one night. She first connected with the one known as Scarecrow in a hacker chatroom. It was just a bunch of wannabe hackers talking crap.

"For some reason, we hit it off and began talking on a regular basis in different chatrooms. One night, he asked if I was opposed to going dark and taking our connection to a place where no one could see."

She was a little put off, thinking he wanted to sext till he said, "You can bring your special chair on wheels with you."

Sam freaked as she had no idea how he could have known about her injuries, let alone that she was in a wheelchair. She was very protective of that information and had definitely not shared it with him. He calmed her down and told her that's why they needed to go away from the plain old internet and enter the place known as Oz. He sent her some code that would allow her to enter the first doorway to Oz. He told her if she found her way to Oz, then he would confirm what he already knew. There were many doors and dead ends, and it took her longer and longer to figure out the codes needed to move on.

She turned and smiled. "Ten days of some serious coding, to be exact." Once she opened the last doorway, she received a welcome to Oz message full of color and fireworks and explosions. Scarecrow welcomed her, and they talked for days. He explained how their small group of super hackers numbered four. Each had their own networks of hundreds of up-and-coming cyber people. "He told me how each of the other wizards had done their thing, and they had collected the information on me and my history. He had to admit that my life had taken some very interesting turns." There was no doubt her talents rose almost to the level of theirs. "They had talked among themselves and agreed that I just might be the Dorothy they were looking to add to their little group."

They were impressed not only with her hacking ability but the fact she was a no-nonsense woman. One that could hold her own in the real world as well as that of the cyberworld. They were very much all introverted and had little contact with the real world and next to no contact with any woman. They felt, like the movie, they needed a focal point in the group, and one that was both strong and feminine. She was flattered, of course, but it took them a good year before they felt Sam was a fit for their Dorothy. They wanted to do good things with their talents and were mortified by those that used hacking to steal and hurt people, the good people anyways. They enjoyed hurting the bad ones. They were a great team and enjoyed each other outside of a hack, though none of us them have ever met the others. She sighed and finished entering some code, which brought up a message that the wizards needed to talk. She kissed my cheek and told me it would take her an hour to get to the place where they would talk. She kissed me again on the lips. "Get some sleep, Skipper."

The next morning over coffee and donuts, we discussed what information the wizards had found. Sam said the Lion was very surprised by the deep dig that was required to get what he was looking for. On the surface, they looked like a textbook perfect company, and that's what got the Lion's attention. Too good was always a bad sign. He said he found large amounts of money being generated by the company. These obscene profits were coming from profitable but not super profitable companies throughout the Chungs' network. They owned or controlled hundreds of companies and holding companies along with other assets. The one thing he found that was imbedded within the Dragon's network of companies were nail parlors. It appeared they owned and or controlled nail parlors in almost every state in the country, in malls in small towns and cities. They were not all owned directly by Dragon Enterprise, put in one way or another end up back inside their web of control.

The Scarecrow had put together a complete history of when the Chungs first appeared in anyone's database up through today. The mother and father just kind of appeared the year after we had been blown out of the sky. That fit well into what we had guessed was the plan. The Dragon Enterprise was established and began showing large profits almost from day one. Imports of everything from rice to toys and anything you could think of from the area of Vietnam and its neighboring countries. To the eye, it would appear to be a very wealthy company that appeared to be squeaky clean. The thing that stood out was the amount of money generated by what would normally be midlevel companies and interests. That fact confirmed Lion's research as well. The parents had been killed in a horrific auto accident in Maryland, when their limo had been broadsided by a fully loaded tractor trailer. It basically drove through and over it. They were the only passengers, and they were killed instantly along with their longtime driver. The two children took control of Dragon Enterprise and never looked back. The son, Long, and daughter, Bian, were inseparable, and both lived and worked together. Bian had a son and daughter, but Long remained childless, which is odd as males always looked toward the future generations in families like this. They both had little or no digital footprint other than what was released by the company for public relations. Bian was very protective of the children, and almost no public exposure was allowed.

Tin Man had the most interesting information of the three for our first briefing. He had looked into the accident that killed the parents and found that it was pretty straightforward. He just felt it was too clean for two so important people. He also felt the fact the driver of the stolen semi was never found was very suspicious. A stolen truck and ghost driver would have made most investigators think foul play, but not in this case for some reason. Next, he said he found some pretty vague communications with, believe it or not, the CIA over the findings of the investigations. Nothing out of the ordinary for the feds to be interested when big-time businesspeople and charity donors were killed. A simple inquiry from the FBI and offer of assistance would be understandable. What didn't make sense was the CIA was copied on all findings from the investigation.

"I will need more time as getting into the CIA and not tripping some watch list or get trapped in a snare takes time and patience." They had avoided the CIA systems in the past, but the challenge had them all excited. "To be honest, an intrusion of this level will require a unanimous vote from all five." The leader, the Wizard of OZ, had always stayed away from the agency, and he was still not likely to approve.

They all said they were sure there was a lot more to find and would get at the digging, but it would take time. They were putting their best effort into it and not using any outside help yet to minimize anyone's exposure now that they knew the CIA was involved.

We all sat there and discussed the findings. It appeared that what we originally thought was true. The CIA had arranged the swap in Vietnam that day, and we were collateral damage. Now what bothered us was that we were considered a danger to anyone involved the swap. There had to be much more we didn't see or understand. Mom was direct to the point, telling us that where there is lots of money, there is always lots of room for secrets.

We chuckled and set about starting our day. Mom and Six would make stops at the apartments the three of us had rented to secure our background story if anyone checked too close. We each had cheap furnished apartments in different parts of the city. The boys would stop by them and check to see if they were under surveillance and if not go in and change some things around inside and leave dirty clothes or fast-food containers in the garbage. They would make sure the mail was picked up as Sam had put us on direct mailing lists for all kinds of advertising and such to help the cover. If it appeared the locations were being watched or checked, they would get word to us to go there after work to complete the show. We had used the addresses on our internal paperwork that we made out at the interviews and fully expected someone would check to be sure we were living there. We would stay in the apartments on occasion so the neighbors would see us and it would appear to truly be our homes.

Sam arrived at the office building early as she would need to see Mr. Young as he had asked when she had left. She rolled up to one of the three new detectors that had been installed for everyone entering the building. There was no sign of the damage from the day before as everything was repaired. Even the bullet holes that were high on the walls above anyone's heads were gone. Mr. Young was standing off to the side, overseeing the new security measures, and walked right over when he saw her.

"Ms. Martin, welcome to the Dragon Towers. Hopefully your new place of employment for many years to come." He reached out his hand, and Sam shook it with a scowl.

"I wasn't sure I would be back today after all the crap yesterday." He smiled and assured her it was an isolated incident and she was perfectly safe. It was his job to make it so. His smile remained as he told her that they were aware of her helping yesterday to stop an electronic attack. He also wanted her to know they understood it was through her efforts alone that the intrusion was found and stopped. Her skills and efforts had not gone unnoticed, and she had a bright future there. That time she did smile, saying it was good to see she was appreciated for her skills and efforts.

I walked past her as she was talking with Young and headed to the security office. He yelled for me to come over and meet someone. He introduced me as Adam Wilson and Sam as Dorothy Martin, a new computer whiz that would soon outshine everyone currently there. I told her I was happy to meet her and hoped to see her around.

She frowned and said, "Not likely," and rolled away.

Young smiled and slapped my back, telling me to give that one some space as she was a nerd with an attitude. We laughed and headed into the office area. He led me to a closed office door and pointed to the sign which had my name on it. I looked at him and smiled, then told him I was not much of an office guy. In fact, if he wanted to get his money's worth, he needed to get me out and about. He laughed and told me he was the same way and it was just a place to hang my hat and have the privacy I would need.

"Go in and get settled. Set up your computer and passwords and we will talk later. You do have a go bag?" he asked with a smirk on his face. Out of the corner of my eye, I saw Arch head into Young's office as I opened my door and headed in. Young caught up with him, and they closed the door behind them.

Arch took a seat across from Young and waited to hear what his new job would be. There was an uneasy silence when Young broke it with a belly laugh. "I don't know what you said or did or didn't say or didn't do, but you made a huge impression on the boss." She had made it clear that he was now her private security person. She expected him to be at her beck and call. Arch squirmed a little and told him he just did his job as he would have for any other client. Young smiled. "You hit the jackpot yesterday when you did your thing." Mrs. Chung was having an apartment made up for him in the main house where he would be available when needed. That gave

Archie an uncomfortable feeling. Like riding a bike. "You will be at her side at all times when she is on the move or in a public setting. She is upstairs right now and wants you to meet her in her office at ten."

Arch agreed and then asked Young if he would clear something up for him. "Why do you call her Mrs. Chung?"

Young laughed again and just asked Arch if he had met her husband when he was out at the house. Arch smiled this time and said, "Yes, just before he got a serious ass kicking."

"She is a powerful woman who would never take the name of such a man as you saw yesterday." She had kept her maiden name along with the power it stood for. We figure he must have come from good breeding stock because he was nothing more than a donor. Arch took note of the way Young had said "was nothing but a donor" and wondered if the beating had been more severe than he thought. The phone rang, and Young picked it up and lost his grin in seconds. He covered the mouthpiece and told Arch it was sensitive. "Why don't you go next door and meet my assistant? You two will cross paths often, I would think, so it is good you start out knowing each other better."

Arch nodded and stood up to leave when Young snapped his fingers to get his attention and reminded him not to be late for his ten o'clock meeting on the top floor. Arch waved over his shoulder as he walked out and closed the door behind him.

* * *

Sam rolled into Johnson's office and up to his desk. He jumped up and moved to close the door and then back to his chair. "I want you to know how much I appreciated your help yesterday in stopping that intrusion."

Sam rolled her eyes and looked straight at Johnson. "Help, my help? You know damn well you didn't have any idea what was going on, let alone how to stop it."

He turned bright red and stared at Sam. "Remember this, missy. This is my world, and you just got hired to work in it. I take the blame and the credit when it comes to this operation." Sam just threw him one of her glares of death and started to turn and leave. "Where do you think you're going?" he asked more as a demand than he should have.

Sam looked back and said, "Home." She pulled the door open to leave. Johnson jumped up and tried to block her way.

"Now let's just talk this over." His voice was now more of the begging tone. He apologized for being so harsh and agreed she had saved the day and not him. She pushed past him and headed out the door when she was confronted by Mr. Young and Mr. Chung standing just outside. Johnson immediately started to stutter as he welcomed them. Mr. Young introduced Sam to Mr. Chung as the young lady that saved the day yesterday when the system had been attacked. Mr. Chung reached for her hand and shook it, telling her how much he appreciated her efforts. He told her how he was also a novice hacker of sorts and was impressed in how she had found the multilevel attack and had dealt with it so quickly.

"We need to talk hacking over drinks someday." He then looked at Johnson and commented on how lucky they were she had been there to do his job for him and protect the company. Johnson started to say something in defense when Mr. Young, standing behind Mr. Chung, held up his hand to silence him. He looked at Sam.

"What do you think of our system and its security?"

She told him she got to see most all of it as she pried the intrusion out, and it was a good thing they kept all the real business stuff on a different server. Chung's eyebrows tilted up just a bit. He asked her how she knew there was another system, not even trying to hide the fact. She explained it was obvious this system controlled the digital controls of the building and the everyday traffic of the people working there. "A company this big would need a much more secure and sophisticated operating system with multiple layers and controlled access points."

He smiled and looked back at Young. "We have a true pro here." Then he turned and looked at Johnson, his smile gone. "You are aware that I do not tolerate any level of failure or attempt to cover up your ineffectiveness." Johnson didn't speak. He just lowered his head. "Mr. Young, escort Mr. Johnson out of the building." He then turned to Sam and asked how long it would take her to get up to speed to replace Johnson.

She turned back, rolled over behind the big desk, pulled the keyboard to her, and smiled. "I'm up to speed now."

Chung laughed out loud. "I like your style. Really like it." And he walked away. Young slipped his head in and gave her a thumbs up. She took a deep breath and began her exploration of her new system, her world.

* * *

Arch and I had a conversation in the break room and made like two guys getting to know one another and swap some war stories. So far, it appeared our plan was working. Arch got an e-mail from Mom in code that told him someone had been in his staged apartment and cleared it out of everything. I saw the text, and my hair on my neck began to stand up. Just then, Young came in and told me to go home and get my go bag and be back there in one hour.

"We're taking a short trip in and out, and you will be on my security detail." I got up to leave and shook Arch's hand, telling him it was a pleasure to meet him. He remained standing and looked at his watch, then headed off toward the corner of the security area where there was a private elevator that reached up into the Dragon's head and the private offices and living area for the Chungs.

As the elevator moved up, Arch thought it was the smoothest one he had ever ridden in. As it just started up, it stopped and returned to the ground floor, and the door opened. Two men he had learned were affectionately known as the hard staff stood there, blocking any escape. Neither spoke but just stood there. Arch felt he may have been exposed, so his options ran through his head. Which one would he would take out first? And how would he use the momentum to take out the other? He decided the bald one first because he looked to be more of a threat. The blond one looked like all brawn and no brains. He would be second, but then Young walked up with a Pad in his hands.

"Sorry, Mr. Brown, I've been on a dead run, and you have not been cleared for weapons on the top floor." The scanners in the elevator had detected a gun under his left arm and a knife of sorts in the buckle of his belt. Arch looked puzzled but offered up his .9 mmm and took his belt off without any question, handing them to one of the hard staff. As Young checked out the Pad in his hands, he said, "That's an all clear, and I'm sure you will be authorized for all weapons very soon." Young reached in and hit the one button on the wall and watched as the door closed. As it shut, Arch heard him wish him luck, and he wondered if he needed it.

Once he reached the top floor for the elevator, the doors opened, and he was shocked to see the opulence stretched out in front of him. A large receiving area was covered with oriental rugs and small tables with statues and other artifacts. The ceiling had inlayed mirrors with what he was sure was hand-carved wood. There were two doors on opposite sides of the room. The one to the right opened, and there was the Oriental man he had seen accompanying Mr. Chung the day before. He walked up and bowed then reached for Arch's hand. He spoke of his admiration for how Archie handled himself under fire and how well he had moved to protect the Chungs. What had truly impressed him was that he didn't even work for the Chungs at that time yet stepped up to protect them. He told him his name was Nguyen and motioned him to follow him through the door and into a world of more plush comforts and spotless surroundings. They took seats around a beautiful table and were soon served tea by a stunning young woman dressed in oriental robes. Nguyen explained how he had watched over the Chungs for some fifteen years, a true honor for him as he had come from a small farm near Saigon. There had never been any need for another until the events of the other day. Arch asked if they knew who had attacked them and the compound.

Nguyen just shook his head and said, "Powerful people make many enemies. Your fast actions to protect Mrs. Chung and to shoot one of the attackers is what has brought you here today." She had decided she wanted her own protection and wanted Archie to look after her and for Nguyen to protect her brother. "It seems you are her choice at this point." No signs of emotion to read in his face.

"Your background shows you are more than qualified, and yesterday showed your abilities are unmatched. I have but one rule and expect you to follow it. You will protect them with—"

Arch broke in before he could finish. "My life if. It is to be so." They felt a bond form then, and both rose as Mrs. Chung walked in. Taking Archie's hand, she squeezed it and told him she had not felt as vulnerable before such as she did yesterday. She could not begin to explain her gratitude for his actions downstairs or at her home. There were no words to express for his securing her children and returning the feeling of security to her home.

"I need the knowledge I am surrounded by strong people and can only relate to the presence of a strong man." She looked at Nguyen, and he bowed in recognition of the compliment. "Now do you think you can commit to the time and responsibility needed for my security?" she asked.

Arch nodded and told her he was committed to her safety at any cost. and for now he had nowhere else to be. She had a slight smile, and as she turned to leave, she told Nguyen, "Show Mr. Brown his office area he will be using whenever he's in the upper area of the tower."

As she walked out a side door, Arch felt a twinge of concern. The handshake had been soft, and her eyes were searching his. He was shown into a large office area with a beautiful oak desk to one side. It had plush chair and couch with a huge wide screen mounted on the wall. There were two other doors besides the one he had entered through. Nguyen pointed to the one on the right and told Archie it led directly into her private office and work area. The one on the left would put him in her private living quarters that she used when in house. She maintained a small apartment with a private bedroom for her overnight stays, which happened every few weeks but might become more often with the new threat. The children would also be staying with her.

Archie couldn't resist. "Her husband will be here as well?"

Again, Nguyen was showing no expression and just looked at Archie. "Mrs. Chung's husband is no longer around."

* * *

I returned to the security offices in less than forty-five minutes and was met by two of the notorious hard staff. "Mr. Young said you are to ride with us to the airport. We are taking a short trip to pick up some packages and a passenger." There was no other conversation as they turned and headed toward the back entrance to the building.

"A present form Mr. Young," one of the giants said, handing me a box with a bow. I opened it and found a stainless steel .9 mm Beretta with three extra clips. The tip of this beautiful weapon had green fluorescent sight points that made taking aim in the dark so much easier. I smiled as the other hard staff handed me a quick draw underarm holster from my new boss.

* * *

The door opened, and Ted entered the Director of Operations office. The director had his back to them and was in a heated conversation with someone when he finally slammed the phone down and spun around. There sat an older and well-used Russ Martin.

"These assholes can't seem to remember who funnels all that cash to their election committees. I ask only simple favors and then only occasionally." Ted walked over and sat down in the overstuffed leather chairs across from the Director. "Our asset is moving some cash around, along with a problem. They need to pass through the homeland security network in NYC tomorrow," he said. "You think a small request like that would be a quick thing to arrange." He then slammed his fist down on the table. "Just like Kevin. I send him on a simple operation, and he not only fails but gets himself and an entire wet team killed."

Ted remained silent as Russ went through the same rant as in the past. "An old lady and her kid, with God knows who, kills my friend and blows up an experienced team." Normally he would pull out all the stops to get them, but they must have friends. Powerful and resourceful friends that made taking them out a real problem. "It took every favor I had, and the agency had to cover up the explosion and the deaths. Kevin's wife thinks he died in a plane crash and the body was lost. Couldn't have some funeral director ask about the hole through his head. Do you have anything on yesterday's attack on the asset?"

Ted looked sheepish and white as he shook his head. They went on to explain that no one claimed responsibility, and terrorism seemed to be ruled out. They explained that it must be a personal attack based on the assets business plan. There was no evidence to be found. The truck had been torched only five or six blocks from the Dragon Tower. Lots of witnesses, all saw an old pickup, two men. One got shot, no descriptions. Not one credible witness or any cams saw a thing. It was apparent they were professionals, and the hit was to be made without showing who was involved or ordered it. They traced the old pickup to a retired vet, but he reported it stolen the night before. Witnesses at his watering hole collaborated it was taken from the parking lot sometime between 2:00 a.m. and 3:00 a.m.

"How the hell can this be? The freakin' CIA, and we can't find out who shot up our assets in broad daylight."

* * *

After landing in NYC, we stayed on the plane till we reached a private hangar. A large SUV was waiting for us, and we were taken to a midlevel hotel near Times Square. As we traveled to the hotel, my two new friends were as closemouthed as they were on the flight. I hadn't been to NYC in some time, and the large number of police and heavily armed SWAT teams was a real eye-opener to how things in the USA had changed. It was impressive but was in no way a deterrent to a suicide bomber that planned to die and was using his body as an instrument to that end. All the show of force was great, but no match for fanatical people that wanted to die and just take as many as they could with them. When we reached the hotel, we got out and headed to the desk. I was given my own room, and the other two headed off to their shared room. Once in my room, I went about checking for surveillance equipment just to be safe. The phone rang, and it was Young. He wanted me to meet the two bookends downstairs at four and accompany them to pick up a few packages. He made it clear they worked for me, and it was my job to keep them in line. No public displays or anything to bring attention to our little group.

"These packages are critical and should be protected at all costs." He had confidence in my ability to be a leader and think on the run. I thanked him and headed down to meet the boys. I asked where we were going, and one of my coworkers filled me in. We were headed to a restaurant supply house in Little Italy. I found it kind of funny as the Italians and the Orientals never got along in any business, let alone the dark kind. We drove past the place two times then stopped, and I got out with the bald one.

We walked directly into the office area and then into a small private area. We were met by an Italian looking man that spoke broken English with a heavy Italian accent. He just got up and led us to the back of the warehouse area. Two pallets were all alone in the middle of the storage area with an old forklift in position to move them. From the plastic wrap on the pallets, I could just make out what looked like two-gallon cans of virgin olive oil stacked three high and filling the pallet.

I whistled. "The boss must love salad." I laughed. My partner and the warehouse manager flashed me looks, telling me to shut up. I acted like I had been out of line and admonished for it. Then the other half of my party arrived, and he jumped in the forklift and headed toward the loading dock. As he approached the large door, it opened to reveal a small delivery truck which was driven into the dock area. The first pallet was loaded, and he returned to the remaining pallet and loaded it next to the first one. Nothing more was said as we walked to the back of the loading area. The truck door was closed, and the main warehouse door after the truck pulled out. We exited through a door next to the loading door and found our blond bubby behind the wheel of the truck and our SUV waiting for us. As we headed out, I asked where we were headed. The one that rode with me just grunted and asked me if this was my first collection run for the Dragon. I said it was, and he just laughed.

"We are supposed to work for you?" He shook his head. After about forty-five minutes of traffic and stop-and-go, we arrived at the airport just outside the gate that proclaimed "Customs Impound Area." We waited about ten minutes in silence, and just before I broke it with a question, a uniformed man walked up to the truck carrying our packages. He looked in at the driver and was handed an envelope. He placed it on his clipboard as if it were shipping papers. Our driver got out, the guard got in, and he drove off through a well-guarded front gate just down the fence line. Our third member of the party walked back and got in with us, and we moved out back to the hotel. Once there, we went to the bar and found a table in the back where we could talk. We discussed how sweet it was to let the Feds protect and store our packages for us. I kept the drinks coming and made nice with the two muscle men in my charge. Steaks for everyone and shots to top them off. I was able to dump my shots into the coffee I wasn't drinking while they slammed theirs back. The booze did its job, and their mouths began to flap. They had both been with the company for three years and truly enjoyed their jobs. Great money and benefits. They were laughing as they raised another shot.

I took a calculated shot and asked them, "How much money you think was on that truck?"

The blond one moved near my ear and slurred, "Millions and millions."

The other frowned and just said it was beyond our pay grade and we should think about bed as the blond put his head down on the table and passed out. I looked at the other one, and we both laughed, so I felt comfortable my little probe was not concerning to him. I asked about the next day and our return home. The remaining bald man just yawned and said Mr. Young didn't tell them. "He said to just follow your direction."

I smiled and said, "I'll tell you both when I only have to explain it." I laughed as I grabbed blondie's arm. We led him to the elevator and placed him unceremoniously in the middle of his bed. I shook the other's hand and told him to be ready and be at breakfast at 06:00.

"Make sure Sleeping Beauty is ready as well." Back in my room, I lay back on the bed and wondered when Mr. Young would let me know about the second part of our mission. I dozed off thinking of Sam and wishing we had not agreed to remain dark until we were more firmly in place.

At 5:00 a.m., the phone brought me to a sitting position. It was Mr. Young. "Did you boys enjoy the drinks and steaks?"

Without hesitation, I said, "Yes, sir, very much so. The best way to keep the lions in step is to keep them well fed and watered," I told him.

Young laughed as well. "I'm glad to see you are no worse off from the evening's activities."

I laughed and explained how I had made a cup of cold coffee about 200 proof, just in case whoever was keeping tabs on us saw anything. He laughed again, telling me it was a trick he used often, only it was his tea that became so potent. Then the conversation got serious. He explained how a trusted member of the Dragon local management team had become disloyal. He was to be escorted to the home office so he could explain in person what he had done. He gave me the address of his office in midtown and explained how important it was for us to secure him without any problems. I told him I understood, and I would not be using the two muscle heads because they stood out too much and might scare the man I was collecting. He agreed and told me he looked forward to my return.

When we arrived at the high-rise office building, I told the two of them my plan to have them remain in the SUV till I returned. Neither of them liked it but also knew better than to question someone Young had put in charge. Once in the reception area of Dragon Shipping and Imports, I asked if I could see Mr. McDonald. I was asked if he expected me, and I told her no, but I was from the main office in DC and had a private message to be hand delivered. She disappeared and came back in a few minutes and told me to have a seat. In about fifteen minutes, this gray-haired gentleman came out and reached for my hand. He had a pronounced NY accent and welcomed me to the NY office and motioned for me to follow him to his office. Once in, we closed the door and took seats.

"Now what is so important that the main office needed to send you here?"

I just smiled and handed him a piece of paper with a phone number on it. I had picked it up at the desk when we had checked out. Mr. McDonald picked up his phone and dialed the number. There was some background noise that told me it was a secure connection being established. The color left McDonald's face, and small beads of sweat appeared on his forehead. He shook his head as if the voice on the other end could see him. He reached down and put it on speaker, returning the handset to its cradle. I could hear that it was Mr. Chung's voice and could see the true fear in McDonald's face. He was explaining the fact that his customers had been seeing shortages in their deliveries. Nothing too noticeable until recently. One customer received a shipment that had been altered or was not what they had expected. Mr. McDonald was squirming but had made no defense of his actions. It seemed their very good quality product had been replaced with a much more inferior product. There was a silence, then Mr. Chung asked him if he had hit all the right areas of his treachery. Again, silence from both parties. Chung then told McDonald he was to accompany me to DC where he would give him all the details of what he had done.

"No, you'll kill me," Mr. McDonald said more as a plea than anything else.

Mr. Chung just calmly said, "Yes, in time I will." He then went on to explain that if he failed to appear in front of him in person, his family would die in front of him, starting with Angela, his sixteen-year-old daughter. Tears were forming in his eyes, and I felt more uncomfortable than I ever had. Yes, this piece of crap had ruined hundreds of lives by helping move drugs for Dragon, but no one deserved what was coming. Chung explained that he must be made an example of, as was the way it had to be to demand respect. Then I felt like I would puke. Chung asked with no level of emotion, "Which member of your family do you wish to join you in the repayment for your misdeeds?"

It was breaking this man as he sat there and contemplated the death of one of his family members because of his greed. He was told he had till he got to DC to decide, and the connection ended.

Archie was riding in the front seat of the reinforced SUV as they headed out of the underground garage at the Dragon Tower toward the Chungs' family compound. They had spent several nights at the towers, and the children remained there. Arch never saw anyone again except for the young woman that brought him his meals. Mrs. Chung was in the rear with her assistant, and they were deep in conversation as the vehicle sped along with its chase car, keeping a constant distance between them. As they pulled through the main gate at the home, it was clear the security had been beefed up considerably. There were guards with auto weapons and others with dogs on long leads. Once at the house, he jumped out and opened her door for her. As she swung her legs out, her dress parted and showed more leg than Arch had seen in some time. She took his hand and stood up, looked at him, and smiled.

"I will have you shown your new quarters by someone in just a few minutes. I hope you do not object, but everything you had at your apartment in DC has been carefully boxed and brought here for you. I want this change to be as easy and enjoyable as possible for all of us," she stated as she walked away and disappeared inside. Arch calmed some, knowing what had happened at his apartment was not a breakdown of his cover. Soon after, a young girl dressed in oriental clothes came out and offered to take Archie to his new home. His apartment was on the north side of the main house with its own outside entrance as well as a doorway that joined the common hall for the master bedroom and two children's bedrooms. It consisted of a living room area with a small kitchen with apt size refrigerator and small stove. There was a full bath with a large tub with jets as well as full walk-in shower. The bedroom was big enough for a king-size bed with dressers and closet. Archie thought his could be a great gig, and then laughed out loud. The young girl started to unpack Archie's stuff when he stopped her and told her he wanted to unpack himself. She asked if he was sure and started to leave. She turned to him and told him his meals would be prepared and delivered to him twenty-four seven upon his request. If he had any special food needs or desires, just let her know and she would make sure he was happy. She blushed and told him her name was Kim and to just call her number on the phone directory.

Later, the new in-house security manager introduced himself. He explained how the family all had panic buttons on their watches and in their rooms. They were computerized and would instantly give him the location of the party in need on his cell phone. After dinner, the family would be busy, so he would get his first walk-through of the house along with another new staff member, the children's new nanny. Arch enjoyed the roast pork and vegetables that Kim had brought him and had just finished as the security manager came knocking at his door.

"Evening," he said as he walked in at Archie's invitation. "Understand you are not under my command. If anything, I am under yours," the man stated as a matter of fact. "Please feel free to give me any direction you think is an improvement," he said. "Your private weapons locker is here." He walked over and touched an inlaid panel on the wall. It swung open, revealing multiple automatic weapons and several semiautomatic pistols and revolvers. He explained how he had stocked it with some of his favorite selections along with ammo. He would get him anything he needed or wanted if he wanted it. There was a knock at the door, and they quickly closed the locker door and yelled for them to come in. Arch had to suppress a belly laugh when the newcomer was introduced as the new nanny.

Mark stood there and reached for Arch's hand and tried to break his fingers with his grip. "This is Thomas. He is the children's nanny and earned that title by keeping the children safe and protecting them till help arrived during the attack. He is with them most of their awake time and is also on the panic notification program. Each of you will receive any notifications or important information on your cells, so stop by the com center so they can download the programs." The manager spoke to the com center through his ear wig system. He instructed them that they were doing a walk-around to make sure they stayed ahead of the family and unseen. He looked at Archie. "Your ear comms will be given to you later."

As they moved around the huge home, they noted all the access points and any possible vulnerabilities. The com center kept the family and the tour well separated. The final stop was the huge study where the safe room was located. Arch and Mark were told they would be given access if Mrs. Chung authorized it. They would be required to use their thumbprint scan along with a family member in order to open the room door. It contained a comfortable area with both food and water and could withstand the entire house burning down around it. It was completely reinforced to resist explosives. It could hold ten occupants plus the personal items the family kept inside. They were told a tour of the inside would have to wait till they were authorized. Both Arch and Mark held their thumbs to the scanner one at a time in order for both to be logged into the system. After that, they exited the main house where Mark left, and Arch was given a walkthrough of the entire grounds. The adjoining section of the main house was an identical copy of the one they had just walked through. That was the private residence of Mr. Chung and his wife and was separated by a huge wood-covered steel door in the middle of the connecting hallway. Arch was told he would most likely be given complete access to both residences, but that would be determined by Mr. Chung and Mr. Nguyen.

* * *

Sam had taken her new job to a whole new level. With program upgrades that were no big deal and moving different programs to the underutilized areas of the server, she increased efficiency by 20 percent by the middle of her second day. She could tell she was being watched because she installed a program that notified her when someone was looking at her coding. She assumed it was Mr. Chung as he saw himself as a hacker, and she was proud to show him her stuff. The thing she needed now was get her hands on the main server and programs that ran the real Dragon Enterprise. The servers were offsite, and she was almost positive they were located at the residential compound from where she could see the dataflow. There had to be a direct connection from the tower because it would be the only way to use the private system.

The name Steve Best was brought up in break room conversations about the super IT guy that worked on the tenth floor just two down from the Dragon's head. She needed to sit in his seat for just a little while so she could take a look and install the spyware she had gotten from the wizards. It was 18:30 and time for her to go and make her nightly run to her fake apartment. She would then have Mom and Six sneak her out and back to the RV. She planned to stay at the rented downstairs apartment on nights when she could work from home. It looked like this would be one of those as Mr. Chung met her at the elevator and offered her a ride home. His invitation was not going to be dismissed, so she allowed him to take her to the garage level and to his car. She declined help from the driver transferring to the rear seat. She allowed him to lift her motorized chair into the rear cargo area of the Tahoe with help of another man. She smiled to see it was a struggle for them because it still was a very hefty piece of equipment.

Mr. Chung joined her in the rear and made small talk about her new position for a short time. She took note that at no time did anyone ask for her address, which meant she had already been vetted in that area. The conversation quickly became about the changes she had made and the new efficiency it had produced. He was, as she thought, impressed and asked about why she had not been picked up by Apple or Samsung or some other major player. Sam told him she had many offers but wanted independence to try new things and make what others had done better. She enjoyed structure and wasn't one of Apple's skateboarding programmers with their T-shirts and sandals, looking to code a new operating system.

"I like challenges big and small. I like to work on the solutions and then see that they work." As they pulled up in front of Sam's apartment, Mr. Chung commented on her abilities and work ethics.

"One day, I hope we can work together on the tenth floor," he said as the driver opened her door and pushed the chair up against the car. She transferred and thanked Mr. Chung as she turned and headed to the front door where an older door man greeted her and held the door for her. She went immediately to her apartment and locked the door behind her. The alarm being turned off told her someone had been there, and it also told her there were no surveillance units transmitting or recording inside the apartment. After grabbing a soda and bag of chips, she headed to her desktop that was set up on her small desk in the dining room area. She turned it on and entered her password. She had several programed into the system. This one would open the system but tell her she had five upgrades available. That meant it had taken someone five attempts to open her computer. She then started the first upgrade, and it told her that the hard drive had been copied at 11:32 a.m. once they gained access. She smiled knowing the system and hard drive had just useless information and some coding projects she had hoped to use at Dragon once she tested them. Family photos of the ones from her backstory that she had lost in the accident were also buried in encrypted programs. Most hackers could not open those files, but she could see they had. Lots of crap that the wizards had help her load to the hard drive. Then she rolled over to a bookshelf and took a book down. She looked it over and could see it had been opened.

Wow, these guys are good, she thought. She took it back to the desk and made a small cut about one-fourth of an inch in the back on the binding. She took a short lead from her phone charger and plugged in into the slice till she felt it connect. The other end she plugged into a USB port on her desktop. She then opened the back of the tower, reached in, and unplugged the hard drive. Now it was time to make her 20:12 online meeting with the wizards and come up with a plan to get her into the system on the tenth floor. Once they were all connected and sure they were protected, the conversation began with the Scarecrow.

He took the conversation to what he had found and felt could exploit. It appeared Mr. Best was a pervert of the highest level. He enjoyed little boys and exerting his dominance over them. What concerned him was the different places he found his digital footprint. He was very good at hiding it but not as good as they were at tracking. He trolled in many game sites that the very young seemed to prefer.

Tons of photos had been downloaded to different IPs he had from sites that specialize in child porn. Mostly from outside the country, as it was easier to hide your use. He seemed to prefer the cyberworld for contact, but there were four possible real-time contacts that he spoke of with another pervert friend of his from the Netherlands.

"No details were found, so we can't link him to any reported molestations, but given time, I'm sure we can." They all agreed that they could use this to get him sidelined for a period of time so he could get into the mainframe.

It was Tin Man's turn to explain how he would go about getting this information to the right people. He told us how he had built a back door into the DC Police years ago when he was bored. He had used it several times to place information on some politician's extracurricular activities with local call girls and mistresses into the system. He bragged how they brought down several high-ranking people, both men and women. He planned to use this way in to plant some of the information they had found on Mr. Best. In order to speed it along, he would mention that Mr. Best had a pending meeting with a special needs child and then planned to relocate. He would push this directly into the cybercrimes unit and make it look like a report from a confidential informant. He would send it from a cybercafé in the downtown area remotely as soon as we all agreed. That way, the cyber unit might act on it as a high priority.

The Lion chimed in, "What do you think Mr. Chung will do when he finds out his IT guy is a pervert?"

We all agreed nobody really cared as this guy was not only a predator, but he also helped run the Dragon company that had who knows how many skeletons in their closets. It is what it is, and what will be will be.

* * *

Steve Best was, for the most part, an introvert with an IQ far above most of us. He lived in a nice yet small two-bedroom apartment with his cat, Casio, and his white python he had named Worm. He had no TV but did have two big screen monitors that were hung next to each other on the wall. In front of them, he had a large gaming table set up with all different joysticks and controllers for use with any game made. Several different keyboards were piled on top of each other on the corner of the table. He would sit in a huge overstuffed recliner that had a control pad of its own. It would massage any part of the body that needed it in multiple ways with both heat and cooling built into its cushions. The headrest could actually be pulled around his head to make the sound system even more intense. There were many Bose speakers mounted on the walls and around the room that created an unmatched surround sound environment. He lived in that special place where super gamers went to become part of another world and be with others like themselves.

Steve felt safe and indestructible in that world. At home, he could be the person he was meant to be, not just a key-punching geek that looked after the Dragon's inner world. Not just the servant that maintained all the secrets that lurked within. Here he was known as the Dragon Keeper, a carryover from his real-world self. He justified his involvement in this digital world as a way to be part of something much larger than anyone could imagine, making him more powerful than anyone else in the real world. Here he lived in the heart of the dragon and controlled it all. He knew things others could not know beyond a few key people in the company. He understood there was as much illegal parts of the Dragon as there were legal. He also knew his real life hung by the balance of his discretion. Even the life of his mother was in his hands, which added to the rush of power he always felt. That power rush was as addicting as the drugs that flowed throughout the Dragon empire. Besides, the money was great, and he was allowed to make his own hours and schedules unless there was a problem requiring his superpowers. Who cares how they made their money as long as they paid him so well? Did people die from drugs? Sure, but it was through their own weakness and not his problem.

The Chungs also paid all the expenses to keep his mother in the luxury of a very private assisted care facility. He really didn't care as she had forgotten who he was years ago. She was his responsibility though, and he took it as his one remaining debt to the real world. She had allowed him to become who he was. She never forced him to play sports or interact with the other morons. He absorbed knowledge like a sponge, and computers became his first choice for a source of knowledge and companionship. School was no more than a distraction he had learned to tolerate. His mother made him her whole life, working two jobs, to enable him to always have the most up-to-date equipment and attend classes at the local community college. He ate when he wanted, what he wanted with next to no requirements that he helped around the house. He had no recollection of his father, who had abandoned them when he was less than a year old. He had been the man of the house for as long as he could remember. He lived his online life as he saw himself. The most powerful one, with no equal, answering to no one. The Dragon Keeper.

He had designed his own game world and welcomed all challengers. Tonight, he would do battle with some new players that dared enter his realm and challenge his powers. It could take hours and might even go throughout the night. He went to the bathroom and forced himself to urinate all he could push out. Then he put on two pairs of adult diapers and then a pair of rubber pants. He returned to the living room and put down a training pad for dogs on his prized chair. He went to the refrigerator and filled his cooler with ice and as many energy drinks as he could fit. Then he sorted through his collection of chips and other snacks and placed his selections on a small table next to the chair. He surveyed his nest and smiled. Tonight he would once again teach those that tested the Dragon Keeper. It was odd to receive such a challenge by someone with almost no notice. Just an encrypted challenge posted on his personal webpage, "The Dragon Keeper." It had been placed there by the true Wizard of Oz. He had hacked into the files and downloaded the operating program of Steve's prized game where he added his touch.

Steve understood that being the best meant always being challenged and tested. It excited him beyond words. This could be a fifteen-minute waste of his time or a true battle of the best. He would soon know. He took his seat and rubbed lotion on his hands and then opened his first drink. The screens came alive with the view from the top of a huge medieval castle. He looked down as several characters entered the center of the castle courtyard. One was dressed as a knight with a lion's head and two others' heads stamped on his shield. He walked with confidence until he reached the center of the courtyard. There he drew his sword and held it in a salute to the unseen Dragon Keeper. The other challenger to his world walked through the gate, and the sight of him made Steve smile. An old man with a pointed hat and dressed in long flowing robes walked to the center, lifting his walking stick in salute. Not the first time he had been challenged by a wizard but certainly this wizard's last. There was something about this one though. He had this little black dog following him and running off to sniff at each part of the castle. He paid no attention to the dog and assumed it was there only to distract him. There was a blinding flash that caught the Dragon Keeper off guard, and he found himself in the hallways of the castle. Something was not right. The wizard had sent lightning bolts at him from his walking stick and also at the knight. The dog was gone but could be heard barking somewhere down the long passageway. Steve fought off the lightning bolts with ease, and the confrontation had begun.

They moved throughout the castle, doing battle at each turn and in in all the new rooms that appeared. The knight was no match for the Dragon Keeper. His hordes of goblin knights were keeping him busy in the dungeons in the bottom of the castle. The wizard, however, was much more of a challenge as he seemed to move about freely and often caught Steve from behind. Well into the third hour, Steve was getting punchy. That damn dog, however, was getting on his nerves. Its constant barking and running through the battle scenes was getting distracting. It seemed like the battles were at a stalemate, so Steve decided it was time for one of his dragons to join the fun. He would command it to first free him from the annoying barking and then turn to the wizard and end this game. He would take on the knight and end his quest. He freed the dragon and set him on his way to get the dog. The dog led him on a winding track throughout the castle. The dragon got close but never close enough to grab the little dog. Steve was getting so excited he never felt the first energy drink leave his body and fill his diaper. Then a large hall appeared with many doors. From three of these doors came his challengers, the knight, the wizard, and the dog. Each stood in a different door, ready to face the dragon that Steve had sent for them. The knight charged the dragon but was forced to take cover behind his shield to protect himself from the flames the dragon spewed. The dragon pinned him to the floor with his large paw and turned to the dog. His tail flipped from behind and slapped the dog against the wall. He hit hard and slowly slid down the wall, unmoving. Then he rested his tail on the dog, holding him still. The dragon smiled and looked at the wizard in hopes he would admit defeat and allow Steve to kill them all. The wizard walked up to the dragon and bowed his head.

Steve smiled, which made the dragon smile, and prepared to chew the wizard into many pieces. Being so excited to have once again been victorious, Steve did not see the wizard raise his walking stick up and slam it down hard. A blinding flash, and smoke filled the screens. Desperately, Steve tried to see through the smoke and take action against this wizard. Just then, the smoke cleared, and where the wizard had stood was a giant scarecrow with a huge sword held above his head in both hands. Before Steve could react, the scarecrow drove the sword through the top of the dragon's head and out the bottom. The dragon twitched and then fell dead. Steve was in shock and could not speak. Then he watched as the dog freed itself from the tail of the dragon and pranced over to the dragon's face. He lifted his leg and pissed all over the once proud dragon. Steve screamed in anger, but then the dog walked over, and his face filled the large screens. He barked, and his long pink tongue came out and slid across the screen as if to lick Steve's face.

It was Friday, and Sam was thinking how nice it would be for a few days of R&R as this had become an extremely boring job already. There was absolutely no way to enter the dragon's true mainframe from this generic systems, especially after the massive upgrades that had been done before and after her arrival. She was daydreaming of spending some downtime, just relaxing. It was Friday, and she wondered if the police would act over the weekend or wait till Monday. They had planted information in the DC cybercrime system to make it look like it should be a priority, or they might lose him. She chuckled to herself when she pictured that little Toto, the dog in the game, running about barking and annoying Steve. All of them had been added to the game so they could watch only. Little did he know that cyber pooch was running around opening sealed pathways to some of Steve's previous young victims. It would allow any low to midlevel hacker to enter his hidden rooms. IP addresses and dates and times of meetings were all open to the world by a mouthy little cyber dog. Directions to finding them were in the cybercrimes report that was imputed.

A phone call in the private office of Mr. Chung would make her plans for some R&R just a memory. On the other end of the line, a captain in the DC Police Department was explaining what was happening then and would be happening soon. He went on to explain that the cyber unit had received some information and was moving on it immediately. That was why there had been no time to warn him in advance. After several minutes, Chung just hung up the phone.

"Get that stupid bastard Steve Best up here!" he yelled into the intercom. "We need to make arrangements for Mr. Best's earlier retirement," he said to Nguyen without looking up.

At the same time, Steve Best was being led into Mr. Chung's office. A team of cyber investigators were breaking down his apartment door and began searching and boxing up all his computer equipment. He was pushed into a seat across the desk from the head of the Dragon.

"Steve, my boy. How long have you been a pervert?" Steve's face showed both shock and then fear at the question. "You know the police will squeeze you to give them information on me and the company." He started to speak and was cut off by the hand of Mr. Chung coming up to silence him. He was told to think really hard before answering anything further. Mr. Chung went on to describe how DC Police had found child porn downloaded to sites he controlled and owned. The police were now looking at his equipment in his home for further proof of his interest in child porn and little boys.

"They will find nothing!" Steve yelled out. He explained how his private addiction was kept on a private server under another name and could not be traced. Just then, the phone rang. It was the police, and Chung put it on speaker.

The captain explained how an anonymous tip had led them to the sites he frequented, and the backtrack was easy. The information the caller had given also told them where to look for his personal sites. They had found a game he had designed that had naked children being chased by a dragon around a castle. Steve wasn't faking his surprise or disbelief. There was even a little black dog running around being chased by some dragon. That now had the investigators looking to see if he had any connection to animal sexual deviants.

Steve just collapsed back in the chair, shaking his head. "The wizard and his dog."

Mr. Chung had a frown on his face. "I will miss you and the games we sometimes played, but you must understand I can't have the police looking into our systems."

Mr. Nguyen pushed on a nerve in Steve's neck, and he passed out, falling forward. Nguyen pulled him up and over his shoulder and carried him out of the office, closing the door as he went.

"Get me the police back," he said to the intercom. When it buzzed, he picked up and frankly told the person on the other end, "I want to report some very sad news. One of my employees has just committed suicide when he heard he was under investigation." He hesitated a second, then when he saw Steve's body fall past his window. "It just now happened," he said and hung up. He pushed the intercom again and asked the person on the other end to see if Ms. Martin was still in the building, and if so, ask her to come to his office. He leaned back, looking at Nguyen. "What do you think, my friend?" He thought then smiled. "She fits the profile we ran on her. Should be a good fit for us."

Sam set the phone down and gathered her stuff. She rolled around the desk and headed out, stopping at the corner of the desk where she patted it. "It's been fun. See ya." She headed to the elevator. She was met by Nguyen, who showed her which floor they would need to go to first to find the elevators for the top floor. He spoke very little, so she tried to make small talk about all the commotion downstairs.

"What's going on downstairs with all the sirens and people moving around?"

He just smiled and shrugged his shoulders. When they reached the top floor, she was showed straight to Mr. Chung's office. He met her at the door and shook her hand.

"I never thought we would work together so soon, but Mr. Best's unforeseen retirement has put us in a bit of a bind."

She looked at him with a questioning look. "Retirement?"

"In a manner of speaking," Mr. Chung said with a slight smile. "We have a new credit processing system going live in one week, and he was overseeing the startup." She told him he could find lots of credit card geeks to run a system like that who most likely could do it better than her. He was impressed with her honesty, but he explained there were other issues to be considered. She thought for a second and decided to go for broke.

"Are you speaking of the company's less than legal side?"

Chung sat back with a surprised look on his face. Nguyen walked over to just behind Sam's chair, where she felt his presence. "Go on," he said.

She explained that from seeing the business they displayed on the system she worked on, there was no need for all the security people, let alone being subjected to attack like the other day.

"So you think there is more to our business than what you can see?" Mr. Chung questioned. Sam smiled and told him she was far from being a dumb blond. "Your business downstairs is big and very busy, but the real money must be coming from the top floor. Dragon was too big and too flush to just be importing goods and running a bunch of nail parlors and other small businesses. After all, you own your own bank, which is listed on the NY Stock Exchange. "It seems you have done your homework, Ms. Martin," Chung said with no real clue to his thoughts.

Sam made it clear she researched anyone that she worked for or tried to hire her. "I like to know what I'm getting into before I do. I don't like surprises or secrets unless they're mine. It's all good." She explained how she had no love lost for the authorities. The man that killed her family had been released from jail five times for DWI. He then got drunk again, got in his car, and took her life away. She went on to explain that she knew her record showed she got arrested for drug sales as a teenager several times. "I'm the type that looks at the rewards rather than the deeds."

Mr. Chung smiled and told her she was right. They had done a thorough background check, and they had found all those things and some others. Sam faked a blush and told him the prostitution charges were bogus. "I was selling to both sides of that game, the girls or boys and their tricks. It was less of a hit for prostitution than for sales, being it would be my third strike."

They all laughed, and Nguyen brought over a bottle of scotch. "I need the very best and the most loyal people to work inside with us," Mr. Chung said. He spoke of his demand of total loyalty and the harsh results if you that loyalty was broken. "Steve's unplanned retirement attests to how serious we take loyalty and desecration."

Sam acknowledged that and wanted to make it clear that she was just a computer nerd with no interest in the actual workings of the Dragon. She would be glad to keep everything running smooth from behind the screens. She lived for the challenge and of course the money. Cash money was a very good motivator as well. Chung laughed. She explained that she would rather not work with a lot of other people. She knew there were times she must but wanted him to know she wasn't big on drama and petty workplace gossip. Chung acknowledged her, and they both took a long hit on the scotch. He explained he was staying for the weekend to work. If she wanted, she could come in and get herself settled in her new office and take a walk around the system. He took note she did not ask about pay or had other questions as to what she would be doing, and that made him happy. Maybe this one might last. He wondered how she would react when she found out about Steve Best's retirement. He chuckled knowing this was a woman that understood where she fit. Death would be an inconvenience to her, but not likely to slow her down. Her loyalties could be measured in dollars and fear, and he had the ability to give her all she could handle of both.

* * *

As we approached the private terminal at the airport, McDonald became uneasy. He sat next to the blond and suddenly reached for the door handle as we slowed for a turn. Unfortunately for him, this new vehicle would not allow the door to open while in motion. Before I could stop him, the huge hard staff member had him in a headlock, and his face was going white. I kept my cool and just mentioned that if he killed him or harmed him, Mr. Chung would not be happy. He immediately set him free as if McDonald's head had caught fire. Shooting me his death stare, he settled back into his seat. We drove unchallenged to the steps of the plane. I helped McDonald to steady himself as we climbed the stairs to the plane. I strapped him in next to me, and we waited for the others as they supervised the loading of the pallets of olive oil. They both checked the cargo and got in and strapped themselves in just as the plane began to move. My heart went out to McDonald, but I had to wonder if this was just another test to see if I broke character. What kind of monster would make a man pick one of his family members to be killed along with himself?

When we arrived at the private hangar in DC, we were met by a ground crew that went to work unloading the olive oil pallets and loading them into an armored car. My phone rang, and I answered it to hear Mr. Young's distinctive voice on the other end. "Nice job, son. You did good for your first assignment." He instructed me to have them take McDonald to the Rest Area. They were to keep him there till he called for him. It would be several days. He wanted him treated well and not harmed for now. He said there had been some developments in what McDonald had done that needed to be taken care of before talking with him. I was to take the rest of the day off and rest up because there was going to be some real combat headed my way. I asked my ride to take me to my apartment, and as we pulled out of the hangar, I could see McDonald being pushed into the rear of another SUV. I had no idea where or what the Rest Area was but didn't want to chance suspicion by asking. I truly wondered if anyone could be as cold as what it appeared. Once home, I swept the rooms for listening devises and changed into my sweats and headed out for a jog. My earbuds were a comm set so I could talk with the whoever might be on.

Mom chimed in with "Welcome home, Skipper."

I told him it was good to hear from a friendly voice. I could hear Six yell a hello in the background, and they explained how they were holding down the fort but getting cabin fever. I told them how my pickup had gone in the city. They both agreed it was the coldest thing they had ever heard of. It appeared something was going to happen in the very near future, and it sounded like it would be big. I asked Mom if he had any thoughts on protecting McDonald's family. There was no helping him, and besides, he had made his bed when he climbed into it with the Chungs. Mom said he would do some checking on them and get back to me in a few. I let them know I was headed for a shower and a power nap but would reconnect around 17:30.

During that time, the guys were able to find that McDonald had a wife and two children that lived in a townhouse just outside the city. Apparently, no other family except for his younger brother that worked for him in the export/import business. When we reconnected at 17:30, Mom and Six were already packed and headed to NYC with the Humvee.

As they were approaching the McDonalds' home, six gave me a rough idea of their plan. Simple but hopefully effective. "Can't kill what you can't find." Their plan was to locate McDonald's family and whisk them off to a safe place where they would be protected till things were sorted out. They had the address, and it would be a simple snatch and go, or so they hoped. I agreed it was the only way because I believed Mr. Chung was serious about killing another member of his family to show his power. I told them to keep me in the loop and I would check in whenever I could.

At 06:00, my phone rang, and there was a knock at the door at the same time. I grabbed my Beretta and cell phone in one move as I left my bed. It was Mr. Young on the phone, and he told me my ride should be at my door. I confirmed that was true and asked what was up.

He said, "You're going to Jamaica to deliver a message for the Chungs."

I asked, "What message?"

He laughed, telling, "A strong message that the Jamaicans will understand and not soon forget."

When I opened the door, there was my blond brainless buddy from the previous day. He smiled like a kid who skipped school and told me to get ready for some real fun. That bothered me because his idea of fun and mine were bound to clash. We headed back to the airport private terminal and the hangar we had just left. They were just finishing loading weapons crates into the storage area and a few in the passenger area. There was a total of ten of the hard staff and Mr. Young in line and climbing into the private jet of Dragon Enterprise. The plane had no markings except the call numbers on the tail, which had been wiped clean. We left the SUV and headed to the aircraft and climbed in.

Mr. Young waved for me to come to the front and sit with him in the larger seats. As the plane taxied to the end of the runway for takeoff, Mr. Young took the microphone that hung on the wall and started to speak. He explained that we would be headed to a private airstrip in Jamaica and would be met by a small group of Dragon people. They were already on the ground doing recon. We would split into several groups and head into the outskirts of Kingston. That was where we would deliver a very special message to those dreadlock steel drum players. They had stuck their noses into a hornet's nest, and now the sting would be unforgettable. Groups 1 and 2 would be taken to processing areas where they were to destroy everything and eliminate any resistance real or perceived. He laughed.

"I will lead a group to the head of the snake and destroy him and all that work with him or for him that are home. When we leave, we will leave this island better, free from one of the drug lords that control everything good and bad. Free of those that do not respect the true people that are in control. We will begin at 18:00 hours, or six o'clock for those that don't understand." He shot me a huge grin. For now, he told them they could fill up on food and drink, but no alcohol as he wanted no mistakes. We would all meet up again at 05:30 to meet the plane and head home. Anyone who would not make it back in time would be left to fend for the themselves and get home the best way they could.

Young and I made small talk, and he once again told me he was pleased that I brought in McDonald with no scene or issues. I told him I was doing my job the way I would have wanted it done. He smiled and downed his Coke. I decided to take a chance and ask about the threat to McDonald's family.

His smile faded. "I find it very distasteful, but it's a fate we would all suffer if we did anything against the Chungs." So I asked if he truly meant that McDonald would have to pick another member of his family to be killed. "Yes, I'm afraid so." He lowered his head and explained how it was their way. "He will need to decide when he faces the boss, or she will decide for him." I tried to not let my surprise show when he said *she*, but he caught my eyebrows moving. He explained that I hadn't been around long enough to know how the Dragon was truly run. "Mr. Chung can be ruthless, but he bows to his sister's will." He went on to explain how she was the true head of the Dragon. Cold, calculating, and with no level of compassion for anyone outside her inner circle. I wondered if she had anything to do with the jumper at the building the other day but decided I had pushed enough. Young shook his head and told me he how he had almost sent me on the job to collect McDonald's wife and kids. "I would. You would enjoy this much more."

I immediately thought of Mom and six and wondered if they would be walking into an unexpected greeting. They were both the best I knew, and I smiled thinking to myself, how I wouldn't want to be the ones they ran into. The plane began its descent, and everyone became quiet. Once on the ground, we taxied back to the end of the runway so the plane could take off again when it wanted. The crates were removed from the cargo area and opened so everyone could arm themselves with their choice of equipment. I already had my Beretta under my arm and had placed several dual clip holders on my belt. I reached down and grabbed a .44 auto mag along with a hip holster and several loaded clips. Next, I took a short-barreled version of a 12 gauge shotgun and added it to my personal collection. There were grenades in several small crates. Fragmentation and incendiary of which I took several of each and placed them on my combat vest. Most of the weapons had sound suppressors, and I had my own for my Berretta. I looked around at this small band of mercenaries and knew that this would be a long, loud, and deadly night. I knew the people we were going after were the worst of the drug lords and were responsible for thousands of deaths and destroyed lives all over the world. Young children whose lives were changed and often ended to keep their supply of money flowing. I felt no remorse in what was to come. I just hoped I could keep any innocents from getting chewed up in the fight. Soon some old pickups arrived to take the two teams into the back country. Our ride came later in the form of a well-used SUV. The SUV was painted and lettered to look like the local police vehicles with *Commandant* in bright red letters on all four sides. It was me and Mr. Young that first got in, then Blond followed while motioning for four others to get into another pickup that pulled up.

They piled in and secured a large crate I hadn't seen before. We headed out for Kingston and our target. Young began to lay out the plans for the night. The drug kingpin that had made the mistake of working with McDonald to switch the Dragon's drugs for theirs was the target tonight. The attack was planned to close 50 percent of Jamaica's drug business in one night. The other crews would destroy warehouses and other assets. Our job was to take out the headman and his lieutenants and other low-level leaders. We drove past the leader's compound twice to get a feel for the layout and position of guards. This man's power was so complete in Jamaica. His compound was protected, but it was far from the fortress you would expect. Unlike the drug lords of Mexico, he had no fear of attack as he owned the local police and his ruthless reputation protected him from any competition. In Jamaica, there were only two drug lords that ran the entire island. There were many lower level suppliers and traffickers, but no one lived in the drug world unless one of the two bosses said so. After tonight, that would leave a vacancy to be filled. There would be many long weeks of fighting and killings before someone emerged as the new number 2.

Young had a set of plans laid out on the hood of the SUV that showed the compound and surrounding streets. He had marked where he wanted two of the hard staff members to set up at the front gate after we had secured it. Their job was to stop any reinforcements from joining the fight from either direction. I thought that was a tall order for just two men, no matter how well trained. He went on to explain that we would quietly take the main entrance and then drive right up to the front door and begin our sweep of the building. We would be dressed as local police, and Young would have the colorful uniform of the commandant. The uniforms would never pass close inspection as they were just held together with Velcro strips. We could quickly resort back to our combat clothes once inside or the need arose. I questioned how with, all the video surveillance, we could secure the gate and drive in without someone seeing us and setting off an alarm. Young smiled and told us they had bought a security person that had installed a simple constant loop player into the system. It would just keep replaying videos showing the same scenes on all the monitors once we activated it. It should give us plenty of time to get inside as long as the guards monitoring them did not catch on.

"If they do." He smiled. "The operation becomes fluid." He said he would signal the other teams to attack once we had the gate secured. He wanted to avoid the people in the compound from being warned and locking down. We all understood the plan, and we prepared to go in fifteen minutes. Young told me and Blond to sweep the first floor. Then check in with him and the third member of our team on the second floor when we finished. He stood in front of us and made it clear that no one inside was to be left alive. No one. Blond and the others had huge grins on their faces, and I forced a smile to my lips. We started with Blond and me moving along the wall to get as close to the gate as we could without being detected. On Young's mark, we moved ahead as they started toward the gate in the SUV. Young started the video loop with a remote control, and we all hoped it was working. As they pulled up to the gate, three armed men blocked their way. Their guns were kept slung over their shoulders as they had police vehicles come and go all the time, so no concerns. The driver yelled something, and the guard in the gatehouse stepped out and headed for the driver's window. When the SUV driver shot him through the window, it was our cue to eliminate the other three. I shot the one on the far left once through the chest and then one to the head to avoid chance of him getting a shot off. Then the one in the middle was hit in the neck by my next round. But before I got off another kill shot, he was picked up and thrown back by a full burst of auto fire from Blond. Way too much overkill and luckily not heard by the guards inside. The word *sound suppressor* did not mean it was totally quiet and made no noise. Young had taken the third one out almost at the same time the driver had announced our arrival. We quickly grabbed the bodies and dragged them into some bushes just inside the wall and behind the guardhouse. We then listened for any sounds of alarm from within, and Young checked the monitor in the guard shack, which was now showing the last fifteen minutes worth of tape.

We beat feet to the main house, dispatching three more guards that were patrolling the grounds. Once at the main door, Young banged on the knocker and heard the dead bolts being opened. The monitor of the entrance showed me and Mr. Young in our temporary police uniforms, so the two guards had no concerns. As the door opened, we placed our pistols on the guards and stepped in, pushing them against the wall. Young asked the guard he had twice how many guards were in the house. With no answer after second time, he just fired into his head. He turned to my guard and had to calm him down so he could understand what he was saying. He spilled his guts, telling us there were ten more guards and where we could find them.

Young smiled and told him, "Thank you." He shot him between the eyes. We headed out to clear the house. Blond and I checked each room, finding one guard at the end of the hall that never saw us. As we stepped over the dead guard, we could hear crying in the next room. The hair on my neck stood up straight, and I knew it was time to make my choices. I had no regret or issue dropping these drug guns or their bosses. Like all drug lords, they lived off the suffering of innocent people and many children. As we approached the door, Blond looked at me and smiled.

"No survivors."

I grabbed his shoulder and said, "Those sound like children."

He started to turn the doorknob, and my head was spinning over my next move. No way was I going to allow any children to be collateral damage or any innocents. Just then, a guard walked around the corner about fifteen feet from us. I let my shotgun fall back on my shoulder strap and drew my .44 auto mag. As my partner turned to fire on the guard, I pulled his rifle back, and with my arm around his neck, I pulled him in front of me as a shield. He took the guards two shotgun blasts to the chest which pushed us both back. I let go of him, and as he dropped, I fired, taking the guard in the chest, thanking him for his assistance under my breath. There was no surprise now. I returned to the doorknob and slowly opened it. I kept telling whoever was inside that I would not hurt them. Once inside, I closed the door and looked around to find four women and three children on the floor, huddled behind a couch. One of the women spoke good English and explained she was the woman of the house and these were her sisters and their children.

    She looked at me and said, "You have come to kill that bastard upstairs?"

    "Yes" was all I said.

    She could see in my eyes she was right to trust me. I told her she was safe for now, but they needed to be ready to run. She told me there was a small door in the kitchen that exited into the backyard that the men used for firewood. There were no other people there that she knew of, so I directed them to follow me to the kitchen. I watched out for them in the hall as they came out and ran to the kitchen. The woman of the house stopped. "Thank you."

    I turned and walked headlong into old Blond. He was pissed and started spewing insults about me using him to hide behind. He told me, "Young will be mad that you let those people go." The armored plates in his vest had stopped the shotgun blast and had just knocked him out. He pulled a Ka-Bar knife and held it to my throat. He said he would cut my head off but knew it would be his word against mine. He planned to beat the truth out of me in front of Young. He forced me ahead of him, keeping that knife ready to cut into me. When we reached the room where the women and children had been, I slowed and stopped. It had a huge thick wood door. It was still open from when they had moved to the kitchen. I turned and looked at Blond and told him we needed to talk. He forced me against the wall and held me there with his body and told me to shut up and keep moving. He backed off and pushed me ahead. I turned again and smiled at him.

"You might need these." I held up in my fingers the safety lock pins from his grenades. When he grabbed me and slammed me against the wall, I dropped the grenade in his back pouch and pulled the pins. He looked at the pin as they flew through the air toward him. He tried to check all his grenades and pockets in a frantic attempt to fine where the pins belonged. I turned and dove into the room, rolling on the floor and slamming the door shut. I held it close with my feet on the bottom. The explosion was muted by the solid wooden door but did push me back as the door remained intact. The hinges held, allowing it to blow in. I lay there with my head ringing until Young looked in and motioned for his partner to help me get me up. He said we had to go, so if I could walk or run would help. I nodded, and we headed out to our vehicle and piled in. As we drove through the town, Young asked what had happened back there with my partner.

I thought quick and told him he had primed a grenade to throw into the room when a guard came around the corner and shot him with a shotgun. He must have dropped the grenade, and as he went down, he pushed me through the door, which saved me from the blast. Young just shook his head and said, "Didn't think that boy had it in him."

We headed back to the airport. Young was satisfied the other attacks had gone well. We sat in back in silence until he reached into a large bag he had brought from the house. He handed me a wrapped bundle of hundred-dollar bills, telling me I deserved the bonus. "Just remember, we can enjoy the spoils of our enemies but never our bosses."

* * *

As they cruised by the house on the first recon, Mom and Six saw the new van parked in front of the house. The driver's seat was filled with a large man with a blank stare on his face. They knew they were late to the party, so the plan now became fluid. Mom pulled in front of the van as if he was going to park and backed in until he hit the front bumper. As expected, the ugly large man jumped out to give Mom a real tongue-lashing if not a physical beating. Six got out down the street and walked up, keeping to the blind spot in the van's mirror. When he heard the discussion in the front of the van, he closed the distance and opened the rear door, expecting trouble but just as happy it was empty. He climbed in and waved to Mom out the front window with a big smile. That was his cue to end the discussion. He threw the driver a hundred-dollar bill and got in the Humvee and pulled out. The driver quickly grabbed the bill and laughed as he got back in behind the wheel. Once he was settled, Six dropped the garrote around his neck and pulled it tight until he passed out but did not pull through his neck to kill him. He pulled him into the back and cuffed and gagged him. Then he took the ballcap from the dash and put it on to cover his blond hair. Mom circled around and took up a position behind the van about four car lengths back. As luck would have it, he just got settled in place. Two men pushing a dark-haired woman and two young girls in their teens came down the sidewalk from the house. They hoped this would go without violence but had no plans to let these hard ass guys take the family. As they reached the van, they pulled open the side door and forced their group into the back. Six had gone into the back so as not to be seen, and he helped the women in from the dark. As the last young girl got in, he slammed the door closed, locked it, and told them to get down flat on the floor. He jumped into the driver's seat, put it in gear, and spun the tires as he pulled away. The two remaining hardmen stepped into the street screaming and drew their weapons and raised them to fire. Mom was ready for that and hit the bank of high intensity lights on the roof of the Humvee, which blinded the shooters long enough for him to ram them with the cow catcher bumper which protected the front of the Humvee. They flew some thirty feet from where they had made their stand, and Mom was able to just swerve around them and off to catch up with Six. The woman were in shock and had no idea what was going on, so Six gave them a rough rundown.

He told them they worked for her husband and were protecting them from an abduction attempt by some people that wanted to hurt him. That kept them quiet till they reached a small private airport in New Jersey. Mom had a friend that ran a small flight school and had agreed to take the three passengers to another small airport near Utica, New York. Once there, they would be met by the widow of someone Mom had served with during his early years. She would put them up in her bed-and-breakfast till it was over and safe to return home. Mom took the wife away from the kids and explained the true reason those guys had tried to abduct them. She showed little emotion and was so thankful for their help. She told them she always expected her husband's work would end him up in jail or dead. She had no idea the people he worked for were so ruthless and bloodthirsty. She promised to make no phone calls or make any contact with friends or family as Mom had told them their lives could be in danger as well if they did. They saw them off and watched as the plane grabbed air as it took off.

Mom looked at Six and said, "I've seen some coldblooded bastards in my long life, but never ones that would make a man pick one of his own family to be killed for his indiscretions."

* * *

We all got together back at the War Wagon two days later and discussed the previous day's activities and our active part in them. Mom had checked, and the McDonalds had made it to Utica and were doing fine. Young had given all of us involved in the operation in Jamaica a few extra days off. No one had heard from our two friends at the main house, but we were sure they could handle anything that came up. Sam had been given restricted access to the Dragon's private mainframe and told us it was something out of a sci-fi movie. Not only did it have hundreds of attached user systems, it was internally protected, and there was no way for her to sneak through the codes and programs without leaving a trail. She was told by Mr. Chung that they were about to begin their own credit card system that was closed to the outside world and would process their own transactions from the card swipe location to the direct billing and payment collection. Processed through their own bank and supporting the charges with their own money, it would end up just being a collection service. Their cards would require same-day drafted payment from the card holder's bank. No exceptions and immediate card cancelation upon payment failure.

Sam shook her head and said, "I can only imagine what the collection department looks like." We all agreed this huge company was true evil and dirty, but we still couldn't find that link to the CIA other than getting their parents out of Vietnam. Hopefully the boys at the main house would come up with something.

* * *

Arch rolled over and felt the naked body of his bed partner. He put an arm over her and cupped a breast. She moved to turn toward him then just kept coming and climbed on top of Arch. She sat up, the sheet falling off, exposing her exquisite body.

"I like when my bodyguard works from the inside out." She smiled and pushed off, grabbing her robe and heading to the shower. "No time to enjoy a shower together. Get cleaned up, eat, and meet me in my office in forty-five minutes." Mrs. Chung disappeared.

Arch smiled, chuckled, and said out loud to no one in particular, "Like riding a bike." He grabbed his pants and headed to his room. He would later explain how on the second week there, he was summoned to Mrs. Chung's office where he found her standing holding a sniffer of brandy. Knowing Arch didn't drink, she did not offer him one. She walked over and sat on a large oriental seat, letting her long dress fall open, exposing everything she had to work with. She told him how she found him to be everything she looked for in a man. A man with the conviction to not drink and the pure animal strength and skill to address any situation. A man that knew his place and lived to please the woman he swore to protect with his life. She knew they would work well and fit well together, and she hoped he agreed. Arch nodded then asked about her husband. Not that he cared about offending him. He just didn't want drama. She laughed and explained how that spineless coward that had abandoned her children would never be returning. Arch raised just one eyebrow, and she smiled again.

"He had an unfortunate accident. One you don't recover from." Now Arch was getting nervous. His lack of being with a woman might put an end to all this hard work. She stood, walked over to him, and kissed him deeply. Letting her dress fall to the floor, she asked him, "Do you want me?" And she reached for his crotch. She held her hand there and just smiled. "It appears you do."

Forty-five minutes later, Arch was standing in her office dressed in his new silk gray suit that had been delivered along with four others. Each had been custom tailored to fit him in a way to hide his weapon and allow free movement. He felt out of place, preferring his brown robes from before, but he felt he could get used to it. Standing in the corner, he surveyed the room, making mental notes of places he could use for protection if needed. There was a knock at the large oak door, and Mrs. Chung spoke in a low calm voice.

"Enter."

The door was opened by a young houseworker, and two men walked into the room until they stood side by side opposite Mrs. Chung. She made no effort to rise from her desk.

"Gentlemen, I'm glad you arrived so quickly after I requested it." Both men looked at each other with stone faces. "Sit." And both pulled up the chairs in front of her and looked around the room, taking particular interest in Archie standing off to Mrs. Chung's right. "Do we need a babysitter?"

The man who was definitely in charge spoke, pointing to Archie. She explained that considering recent issues, she would be more comfortable if he stayed. He was now her personal security. The need of such measures was why they were summoned there today. That took the boss by surprise, and he said, "What do you mean by that?" He looked a bit sheepish as it came out.

She sat back in the plush leather chair and smiled. She asked, "How is it possible for my office and home to be attacked in broad daylight, causing hundreds of thousands in damage? The great CIA of America never saw it coming? Or did you and just let it happen, hoping we would be taken out of your useless lives?"

Russ jumped to his feet. "How dare you accuse me of planning those attacks." His partner tapped him on his leg and nodded toward Archie. He was staring down the business end of a .44 auto mag Desert Eagle. Arch had drawn it and was pointing directly at his head. Arch saw him tense, and before the man was fully standing, the large caliber handgun was free of its holster, ready to take the threat's head clean off. Mrs. Chung laughed and just motioned for Arch to holster his weapon. The embarrassed CIA guy needed to regain control, so he looked at Arch and pointed at him, saying, "Draw down on me again, you better drop the hammer."

Arch smiled, showing those bright white teeth. "You can plan on it."

Things cooled, and everyone returned to the conversation at hand. "Do you know who attacked me?"

The sidekick opened a briefcase and took out some folders and placed them on her desk. "Here is what we have on possible players that would want you taken out. It is all about the drugs. The other stuff you're into is too complicated for anyone to recreate."

She took her time going through the folders then sat back and threw them at the two men seated before her. "This is what you cowboys call bullshit. None of these petty organizations would dare attack me. We have agreements with all of them. We let them have the sales territories they currently have if they purchase twenty-five percent of their product from us. We are not greedy, and as such we have lived in peace. They also know that I'm ruthless and often send gifts to their wives and children on their birthdays or other holidays just to show we can." She explained how she had recently sent a message to all of them. A response to a breach in their trust by a Caribbean cartel. She was obviously disgusted and spun around so she was facing away from the two. She instructed the men to leave and have better answers for her in forty-eight hours.

When Ted turned, he suggested they might not have anything in that short of time. He was answered in a way he would not soon forget. The chair that held their host spun around in a flash. Mrs.

Chung's hands moved at a speed Arch had not seen before. She reached up and took the hair comb holding up her bun and embedded it in Ted's hand, the one holding the briefcase. He screamed in pain and dropped it. "Leave it and get out of my home. I do not except failure."

Arch was never far from his employer, so all intel had to pass through Mark back to the War Wagon. That night, he made a point of having a bottle of water by the pool where Mark met him and sat down with a beer in hand. He was headed into the small town nearby for some R&R and would transmit the coded data back to the rest. Arch passed him the miniature flash drive from his watch that had recorded both audio and video of the meeting. The exchange was subtle. He just let it fall on the table when he reached for his water. Mark, in turn, placed the side of his hand on it as he took his beer. When he reached into his shirt pocket for a piece of chew, it slipped into his pocket to be retrieved later in private. Arch was convinced it was the head spook from back in the day and one of his two little buddies. Mark had the run of the place with the kids and played hide-and-seek all the time to get the layout of what was open to them. He was sure the mainframe for the in-house computer system was in the safe room. They were not allowed to play in there. And even though he had the code, he could not access the room without setting off alarms. There were desktops in all the offices and large screen ones in the two Chungs' offices. Without Sam getting into the system, there was no way to know how to gain entrance into the servers.

* * *

I reported to work like always around nine and Sam at eleven. She had no set time for check-in when Mr. Chung was out of the office. When she came in, she found an encrypted message in her e-mail from Mr. Chung. The message was short and simple for the most part: "Pack whatever you need personally for a week or more. Stay at my home." It was not an invitation in any sense of the word. She knew declining was not an option. She wondered just what this could mean, good, bad, or a combination of both. She finished checking her e-mails and pushed off any issues to the lower level IT people. Grabbing her notebook, she headed to the elevator and to her fake apartment to grab some clothes and toiletries. She wanted to clean out anything that would be out of place or make anyone think she was not what she said. It stood to reason they would sweep her apartment again, only more thorough as she would be gone for an extended time. She planted a private electronic diary where a more complete inspection would reveal. It was hidden in a false bottom in her night table. She double-checked that all other electronic items were gone as well. She had just finished when there was a knock at the door. Opening it, she was surprised to see Nguyen standing there with his usual stone face.

"Is Ms. Martin ready to leave for Mr. Chung's home?"

Sam hesitated then took the offense. "Why the hell was I not just asked or invited? I do deserve a level of respect. I'm not just some piece of meat."

Nguyen actually smiled and nodded. "I apologize for Mr. Chung. This was unavoidable and unexpected. Something that requires your special skills has become very time sensitive."

Sam faked a blush and handed Nguyen her bag, pushing past him. "Now that's better. We should get going."

* * *

My day started like many others with a quick e-mail check and coffee when my intercom buzzed with Young's secretary on the other end. I was summoned to the conference room where I found several other men. The bald-headed friend of the blond I had to eliminate a week earlier was there, seated at the far side. Two others I had not met yet were sitting opposite him. He shot me a glare that made it clear he would have preferred I had died back in Jamaica and not his friend. I gave everyone an unemotional greeting. Young walked in from the far side of the room and quickly took a seat.

"Well, boys, hope you're all healed up and rested." He did not look up. "It appears our latest cash drop has been compromised. Someone has taken the boss's money and killed the team moving it. We think it was an inside job, and the Jones brothers may have decided to go out on their own." One of the new guys spoke up, asking if we would be taking out the Jones brothers and their organization. There was a real tone of excitement in his voice. Young just raised his hand to quiet everyone and explained that we first needed to find and reacquire the cash. He went on to explain that tracking chips were embedded into several of the bundles of cash. The boss would be in the process of hunting them down. He wanted us prepped for full assault and to take up a staging area at the hangar where the company jet was on standby. Everyone got up to leave when Young asked the bald warrior and myself to remain.

After the room cleared, he explained we were his two most trusted and dependable men. This was going to be a quick reaction operation with little or no planning, so he needed us to be ready to think and act on the move. This was very serious. Five plus million serious. We both nodded in agreement and turned to go to the armory to collect what we needed to wage war. My bald friend made it clear he did not like me or trust me even though Young seemed to be blind to me. We never spoke again as we collected items for the trip and started filling the SUV for the trip to the airport. I hit the small hidden button on my watch that told Mom and Six that an immediate face-to-face needed to happen. We had preset the coffee shop in the Dragon Tower's lobby as the meeting point. I went over and asked the guys if they wanted a coffee from the shop upstairs. One asked for a regular coffee with nothing in it, and Baldy even actually asked me to grab him a Pepsi.

I entered the small coffee shop and saw Mom standing in line. He had added dark coloring to his gray hair and a fake mustache, along with a cane which he used when he walked. I got in line two behind Mom and waited till he dropped his cane. I picked it up and handed it back to him. As I handed him his cane, he dropped an ear communication device into my hand. I inserted it in my ear as I turned and acted like I was covering a sneeze. From there, I just hid my face as I gave my update. I told them there was a huge shipment of cash being brought in soon, and we needed to make plans to liberate it for our war chest and to shake up the Chungs. I had no real details, only that they needed be ready with next to no notice. They needed to take steps to protect the cash from being tracked as there were several tracking units in the bundles. This meeting took all of one minute, and I entered the men's room with my bag of drinks.

A quick relief in the one stall and a quick flush for the ear comm and I was on my way to the underground garage. As I opened the stall door, there was Rodger, the bald pain in my ass leaning up against the sink.

"I figured I would come help you so there are no delays." There was a stupid smile on his face. He didn't fool me. I knew he was checking to make sure I didn't contact anyone. We must have fooled him 'cause his gun was still holstered. As we rode down the elevator silently, I prepared a gift for him. I took the soda out and shook it as hard as I could without him seeing me. As we split up in the two SUVs, I handed everyone their drinks, and we got in to leave. As I looked back at the second vehicle, Rodger was just stepping into the front and opening his soda. I could hear the swearing and cussing as we pulled out on to the street. I saw him throw the bottle out the window and try to wipe the soda off his shirt and pants.

As the limo pulled into the courtyard of the Chung estate, Sam looked around and understood just how crime paid. A very well-dressed young man stood almost at attention as they pulled up and opened the rear door.

"Welcome, Mr. Nguyen and Ms. Martin. I hope your travels were smooth and uneventful."

Nguyen stood and walked past the young man, not even acknowledging him. He went directly to the front door and disappeared. Sam was going to ask for her chair when it suddenly appeared. The young greeter was about to offer his assistance when Sam just picked herself up and slid onto her chair. She spun and headed toward the door with the young man behind her with her bags. Just as she reached the front, the door opened, and there stood Mr. Chung with a forced smile.

"Ms. Martin, I apologize for the urgency of getting you here and the lack of the formality of an invitation. I have a very important issue that needs your special talents. If we may, let's head directly to my special control center. I will have anything you may desire brought to you."

Before she could respond, Nguyen was directing her down the long hallway while Chung went ahead. The room they entered was full of rugs and statues and other oriental collectables that Sam bet were worth a king's ransom. It was just the three of them in the room. They approached a short wall. Chung pushed a small photo aside and punched a series of numbers on the hidden keypad and then scanned his thumbprint. A loud sound of tumblers moving could be heard, and the door-size section of the wall slid out and opened on its own. As they entered, Sam took notice of the couches near the walls of the room. The doors all around she was sure held food, water, and other items needed to wait out a siege in this safe room. Very clean and everything in its place. There was room for easily ten people in this spacious area.

She must have been looking around like a kid when Chung told her, "This shows you how serious I am about my family's safety and security. Now for my special place." Chung went over to an access panel and entered another series of numbers and then held his hand up for authentication. The door slid sideways, and the cooler air rushed out to meet them. Slowly, she entered the room, not sure what to expect, but there was her dream office. Multiple screens from laptop size to ninety-inch screen on the wall above the others. Multiple keyboards lay on the work area in front of her. Some wireless and some hardwired. As she sucked all in, Chung described his inner sanctum. It was running off the power he built into the control center independent from the compound and fed from a mile away. It had more working processing power than NASA. Completely independent, it communicated through a network of satellites and was redirected all over the world to avoid any possibility of hacking. She drifted away, thinking of what her friends in Oz could do with this type of power at their fingertips. They all maintained top-of-the-line systems but could not even begin to process a small part of what went on here. "I know I sound like a proud parent, but this really is my growing child. Now let's get going on my problem."

He hit some keys, and the large screen filled with a map of the USA with a smaller map of California. He explained how he had a shipment that was being transported from California to Washington when it was intercepted and taken. Six men had been killed.

Sam asked, "What was the shipment?"

The two men looked at each other for a sec and then smiled. "What do you think it was?"

Sam thought for a second. Then in a matter-of-fact way, she said, "Money or drugs or both." The two men showed no emotion. Sam went on and explained that she was no one's fool and was sure the Chungs were much more than what showed on the surface.

"Does this bother you?" Chung asked.

"Hell no." Sam made it clear she was interested in making a good living and being able to ply her trade uncensored.

Chung laughed. "We will be good together. But do not doubt you will be dealt with severely if you turn on me or steal from me."

Sam stared at him, not blinking. "Guess Steve was stupid? This is a simple tracking program. Why do you need me?"

Chung looked embarrassed. "You'll see soon."

Sam grinned. "Okay, now, let's find that money."

The screen showed the route the cash was taking when it stopped in Elko, Nevada. And then it headed north for a short way then stopped, and the signal went dead. Sam typed several more times then turned to Chung and told him the signal was gone, but she knew he already knew that. He turned noticeably red and spoke slowly. "I'm aware of that, but can you fix it?"

"Maybe." She first told him she needed to see the marker or tracker used. Then she needed to know how many were in the shipment and how the cash was packaged. Nguyen had left and returned with a small box and handed it to Sam. She took the small tracker out and looked it over carefully. "How many in the shipment?"

Chung rubbed his head and told her four. There was one inside the money band inside, each bundle of one million.

Sam whistled. "No wonder you're upset. Four million."

Chung stormed outside, and Nguyen spoke. "Best not to play with Mr. Chung."

He stormed back in. "Can you find it or not?"

Sam smiled a huge smile and said, "Yes, I think I can."

Chung smiled, and she thought she saw Nguyen smile as well. She explained that she could hack the CIA satellite when it passed over the general area where it went dark. It stood to reason they would have a jammer for any tracking devices. They would first wait a period to see if anyone showed up to claim it. Then if not move it, most likely split it up to move it. Sam then looked at Chung and told him the big issue is the CIA hack. They were the best and might catch her, and that could be a real problem for all of them. Chung chuckled and said, "Don't worry. The CIA will not catch you. I promise."

Sam shrugged her shoulders like she wasn't sure but returned to her screen. She spent the next hour preparing her hack and download of what she wanted the satellite to look for. When she completed her work, she pushed back and looked at Chung. She explained her calculations were based on the four trackers having different IDs but a common frequency. That meant it would be a multifrequency jammer the thieves were using. Her program would task the satellite to look for any common frequencies to theirs that were being disrupted. Chung picked up his cell, made a call, and told someone to get the team in the air and wait for instructions.

Sam told the two men it was T minus sixty seconds. She turned to Chung and asked if he was sure about the number trackers. It would kill the attempt if there were more or any less. Sam liked playing with people who did not understand her powers. It actually made no difference, but it sure made Chung squirm. He suddenly blurted out, "Ten. There is ten million and ten trackers."

Sam's fingers flew over the keyboard even though it was all for show. She was actually sending a repeated copy back to the War Wagon's satellite collection program. The clock ran down, and everyone stared at the large screen, waiting as time seemed to stand still. Then a red dot appeared on the screen. "There." Sam pointed to the screen. "There in Ely, Nevada, is your ten million."

Chung tapped Sam on the back and turned to make a call. Then he stopped. "I shouldn't have lied. Trust is a hard thing to build. It won't happen again."

* * *

The pilot came back and told Young we were headed to Ely, Nevada, and would be touching down in three hours. He picked up his phone. "I want every person we have in Ely, Nevada, looking for the Jones brothers. I don't want them spooked. A hundred thousand dollars for their whereabouts and a bullet for anyone that tips them off." He hung up.

"So it is these Jones brothers we are looking for?" I asked as I had never heard of them.

"Yup, the dumb bastards. They are twins and were two of our best people. It's a shame they're dead men and don't know it yet." The shipment had originated with them in California, and they were the only ones that knew the route. "We don't supply it to them until the truck pulls out and one of them gives it to the driver personally."

"Why ground shipment? Why not just fly it?"

Young just smiled. "We have shipments going weekly or sometimes twice a week. We mix it up to keep everyone guessing. Cops we can't buy, other people in the business, any number of thieves. Always legitimate forms of transportation so it never can come back to bite us in the ass." We sat back to enjoy the rest of the flight and prep mentally for whatever was coming.

* * *

Mom and Six were going through the final layout of the operation they had planned at the airport. They would be thin on personnel, but it was worth the try. The people with the shipment would not expect any problems in their backyard DC, so that worked for them. They assumed it would be flown back after it was recovered. That meant they needed to grab the cargo between the private hangar and the tower. They figured they were all set, and the preparations were ready.

When we rolled to a stop, there woman waiting by the two SUVs and pickup parked there. As we got off, it was a good guess. She was a hooker, dressed in a miniskirt that showed the tops of her stockings and a top struggling to keep her assets in place. She spoke to Young, and he motioned for one of our crew to take her aboard and stay with her. We all got into the vehicles, Young and I taking the pickup and sending its driver with the others. He punched a name in his GPS on his phone, and we started out.

"The one brother is at the Gold Queen Motel with a couple of hookers. Our girl back there declined the offer to be there, opting to look for some gold of her own. If we take one of them, we'll get them both because they are as close as if they were connected at the ass." We pulled up, and Young walked into the office and came back out smiling. We could see the clerk counting some bills.

"He's in 112 on the ground, and he's not alone."

We formed a wedge behind Young and walked right up to the door. He didn't hesitate and just kicked it in. There were screams and the sound of two sound-suppressed shots. I entered the room, and on the floor laid one girl, and the other laid dead across the man in the bed.

"Hello, Rick. Where is Dick? And I don't mean that little thing there."

"Go to hell, Young." He started to say something else, and Young shot him in the right thigh.

"Oops, I missed the artery." He raised his gun to shoot again, and Rick pleaded.

"He's babysitting the money."

"Where?"

"At an old gas station just out of town on 50."

"How many men?"

"Four or five." He turned to one of the men and told him to stay there with Ricky and keep him alive till they got back. The gun hand went over and put pressure on the wound while another tied his hands to the headboard. The rest of us headed out and got back in our wheels.

"Next stop, the money." I was mad about the hookers but could not let it show. As we approached the old gas station, we could see some lights on in the back and a car out front. We drove by, looking to see what we could. Then we parked down the road of an old café parking lot. We walked back in pairs until we had the place surrounded. These guys were confident their jammer had concealed them and were way too lax. As we walked toward the front door, a tall surfer type walked out.

"Can I help you, Man?"

"Nope." And Young shot him.

I drew my weapon, and we slowly entered the front of the building. Like most old stations, there was an old beat-up counter with shelves behind it. An old chair that had seen way too many years. A door on the left went into the repair bays, and a large window gave us a view of inside. In the first bay was a small box truck, and next to it three men sat at a card table playing cards and drinking beer.

"I hate amateurs. I don't see Dick." I motioned toward the back where another surfer type was on the phone. "Okay, everyone on three. I want the blond surfer dude alive." On three, we all kicked our way inside. The men at the table were definitely amateurs. They died before they even touched their guns right on the table in front of them. Dick drew his gun and took a bullet in shoulder for the effort. The other team members grabbed him roughly and brought him to Young. I went to the truck and opened the back and jumped in.

Young was on the phone, and I opened the crate marked machine parts. Inside were the bundles of money and what I assumed was a jammer flashing. I came back and stood on the back. "It's here." I turned the jammer off. Young put his phone on speaker, and we could all hear Rick crying. Dick looked at Young with a knowing expression.

"I'm sorry, Rick. I never should have gotten you involved."

"It's okay, Dick." We could hear the roar of an unsilenced large caliber shot.

"It wouldn't have mattered, Dick. The Chungs would have killed him anyways." And he executed him. I knew Young and I were headed for a reckoning.

We loaded the crate on the pickup and headed back to the plane. While the others were preparing to load the crate of money, the hooker who brought us the information came down the stairs of the plane. Young smiled at her and walked over to the crate and opened it. He pulled out a bunch of bundles of cash and handed it to her.

"Let it be known the Chungs are people of their word. Mount up. I want to sleep in my own bed."

* * *

Sam sat at the keyboard, and suddenly the trackers in the shipment of cash started flashing. She yelled, "They have it! They have your money back."

Mr. Chung and Nguyen came rushing into the room, looking at the screen. They could see the money was headed to the airport. "Ms. Martin, you are truly a wonder and a valuable addition to the Dragon Enterprise. How valuable." Sam smirked. "Let's say it's time you open an offshore account. Nguyen, take Ms. Martin to her accommodations and have the staff get her anything she wishes. I will see you in the morning at whatever time pleases you."

* * *

With so little time to prepare, Mom and Six could only hope they were ready. The scanner in Black Beauty was set to the tower frequency, and they heard the Dragon corporate jet call for approach. Mom was dressed in a uniform very close to that of the guard at the gate of the small airfield.

He worked his way up to a parked maintenance truck. From there, he shot out the two security cameras that watched the gate. Hopefully no one would notice the problem that late. The guard was already on his way to check them out. When he got to Mom's window, he asked what he wanted that late at night. Mom shrugged his shoulders as Six pushed the taser against the side of the guard's neck. Catching him, Six held him till Mom got out and helped load him in the back seat. They zip-tied his legs and arms and gagged him. He was alive but out for the moment. Mom took his hat and returned to the guard shack. Six drove off to the far end of the hangars to the large salt truck with a straight plow mounted on it. It wasn't used all that much but was ready if the maintenance crews needed it. Six had hotwired it and made sure it started, which it did.

* * *

As we approached the airport, Young told everyone he was happy with our performance and we would all receive bonuses in our pay. "Take the rest of the week off, but stay in touch." He looked at me. "Any ideas what you'll do with your time off?"

I smiled. "Sleep, drink, and get laid."

He laughed as we came to a stop at the hangar. We pulled right up to the pickup and the SUV that we had left there. We got out and backed the truck to the cargo door, and they pushed the crate into the rear. Everyone got in the SUV, and my blond friend took the truck with our prize. As we approached the gate, Mom came out and went to the driver's window.

"Evening, gents. Glad you didn't have a rough landing like the last guy in a chopper." He laughed and stepped back. "Have a great night."

The SUV pulled out and started to leave when Mom stopped the pickup. He walked to the door and opened it, pulling the driver out and to the ground. He shot him with a taser, but it didn't seem to have the desired effect, so he kicked him in the head, knocking him out. Our driver was looking back for the pickup, slammed on the brakes, and yelled, "What the hell!"

He barely got it out when the snowplow hit the driver's side. It covered the entire side of the vehicle and started pushing us sideways. As it pushed us, the plow started to raise, and so did our SUV. We were on our side, and everyone was tossed in different directions.

Most of them had not buckled up as I did. Mom's warning of a pending crash had alerted me, so I prepared for whatever they had planned. Then the vehicle rolled onto its roof, and the plow just kept pushing it. We came to a bone jarring stop when the plow pushed us up against a wall of a hangar.

Six was out of his plow truck and in with Mom in a flash, and they drove off. They only went a short way and pulled under a canopy used for equipment. Six jumped out and into the back. He unhooked the top and looked inside. There was the bundle of cash and some type of electronic device. He looked it over to make sure it wasn't an explosive device and hit the switch on the side. The lights came on. He jumped down. "I'll see you at the next stop. I believe there is a jammer in the box, and it's on."

* * *

Sam was sound asleep when her door burst open and Nguyen stood there at the side of her bed. "There has been a development. Your skills are needed again."

She yawned and said, "I need coffee."

Nguyen ripped the covers off, her exposing her in the old T-shirt. "I'm sorry, Ms. Martin, but this cannot wait."

She rolled into the control center, and there at the console sat Mr. Chung. "It happened again! Someone has taken my money." He looked at Sam. "We need to find it again. Can you do the same thing you did before?"

She thought for a second. "No."

Chung flew mad. "Why not? It worked once."

She pointed to the screen. "The last ping from the tracker was at the airport here in DC." She made a few entries in the system. "The CIA is not allowed to spy on the capital for reasons that are obvious. Only the CIA satellites has the ability to scan for the frequencies that I need." Chung started pacing. Sam looked at Nguyen. "Get me some coffee, black, and I'll try another route to find them."

Mr. Chung stopped pacing and sat down next to Sam while Nguyen went to get them all coffee.

"The airport and the metro area are full of cams, from police to ATMs to private security systems. We can start at the airport and hopefully find what we want." While drinking her coffee one handed, she began her search. After a few minutes, she said, "Damn. The security cams at the hangar gate were disabled. I'll need a make, model, color of what I'm looking for."

Chung looked at Nguyen, and he picked up his phone. "A 2018 Chevy pickup, 2500, red." He went to Mr. Chung. "The team suffered no deaths. Multiple injuries and fractures only."

Chung looked very angry. "Should I look for a new head of security?"

Nguyen actually sounded reasonable. "Give me time to collect all the information before we make such drastic changes. My initial information tells me the blame was not ours."

We found the jammer was a plus, but we followed the plan. Mom took the truck to a parking garage at the airport. They chose the lowest level, which was two stories underground. Six pulled the Humvee next to the pickup. They had multiple bags similar to the old seabags squids used to use. They went about cutting the bands off the bills, thumbing through the stacks and placing the money in the bags. They moved quickly and threw the removed bands onto the truck floor. Once all the bills had been freed of their trackers, they loaded the bags into Black Beauty and left the garage.

"Well, Lovey," Six said in his best Thurston Howell voice. "Should we play monopoly with real money tonight?"

Sam had purposely started with cams she felt would not show the pickup they wanted. She had no idea how long the two would need to get clear. She got Chung into the airport security cam system, so he felt useful. He suddenly jumped up. "There, there is the damn truck." It was on an access road inside the airport road system. "Here, Ms. Martin, I got you a place to start." He pushed away, and Sam took over.

She quickly jumped from cam to cam to follow the truck.

Chung and Nguyen were talking in the corner. "Get some men and have them ready to go once we locate the money. If Young is able send him and anyone else still able to carry a gun as well." Chung was headed back to the tower to deal with something else that was developing.

Sam called them back. "It's in the parking garage. I have it going in but not leaving. They must be hiding in plain sight." Sam had seen Black Beauty go in and come out and simply deleted the seconds that showed it.

* * *

Mrs. Chung rolled over and pulled herself into Archie's arms. "Think that ass of a brother has found my money yet?"

Archie kissed her. "Does it matter?"

She smiled. "Not really. It's more the principle than the amount. I will be traveling soon for a few days. I'm afraid you will not be able to accompany me, so you will have your first days off." She reached down. "Our friend also will get a rest. I do not share, and you will never have a need for attention." She stared into Archie's eyes. "I'll let you know if I need more." She kissed him then slowly disappeared under the sheets.

* * *

I drove Young because his shoulder had been dislocated and put back in place at the hospital. His arm in a sling had not made him very sociable. We pulled into the garage and went to the bottom level. There was the pickup surrounded by twenty heavily armed men. Young got out and walked over to the man in charge.

"Well." The man looked sheepish. "Gone. Gone when we arrived. Only these were left." He pointed to the money wraps and the jammer, still flashing. Young rubbed his head.

"Clean this all up and wait for my call." He looked at me. "Go home. You have had a rough week. We all have."

After dropping him off at the tower, I dropped the car off at the company motor pool and took a cab to my apartment.

"What's up, Mom?"

He told me they had moved the furniture to a self-storage unit in case the bank tried to repossess it. "You coming home?"

"Yes, be there soon." I hung up, took a shower, and dressed. Then I called for an Uber driver. When I arrived, Six and Mom were enjoying a scotch and discussing our situation. I poured a glass and sat down.

"Well, we're cash flush." Six laughed.

"How much did you two Robin Hoods get?"

They weren't sure but figured six or seven million. We tried to put sense to the fact the CIA was so close to the Chungs that they visited their home.

"This can't just be drugs," Mom thought out loud. We knew drugs, and the money that came from them could be huge, but the CIA connection still made no sense. "We're missing something," Mom exclaimed. "The director of the CIA has a lot of clout, but from the video, it appears she runs them."

* * *

Sam kept looking for connections to the parking garage. Only three vehicles left between when the pickup went in and the recovery team arrived. The three vehicles had been scrutinized, and everyone felt they were clean. Men were assigned to watch the three owners, but Sam felt nothing would come of it. Mr. Chung came in the room.

"Ms. Martin, I must leave for a few days and want you to take some time off. I will have someone take you back to DC if you'd like. Our only shot for the money now is that we place multiple bundles of new currency in with the used. We have those serial numbers so we can have our friends watch for them." He hoped they might catch the money being used and follow it back. "I would like you to join the staff at ten to see myself and my sister off."

"Of course, sir. I'm sorry I could not have been more help."

He smiled. "You were really something last night. I'm very impressed and looking forward to a long mutually beneficial relationship." Before he left, he said, "Give Nguyen the deposit information for that offshore account."

Sam had a huge smile and gave him a thumbs up. Everyone was outside near the pool. Mark was there with the kids, who kept trying to push each other in. Sam had found a place to park and was enjoying Mark's attempts to bring order to the area. The doors to the house opened, and Mr. Chung came out, accompanied by Nguyen, and walked up to Sam.

"Lovely day, isn't it, Ms. Martin? Our ride should be here soon."

In the distance, you could see multiple vehicles patrolling the compound perimeter.

"Are those army Humvees up on the hill?" Sam pointed to what she was referring to.

Mr. Chung did not even look. He just nodded. "A little extra protection today."

The children suddenly froze and stood next to Mark, not making a sound. There was Mrs. Chung walking out with her new bodyguard. They stopped at Mark, and she allowed the children to hug her leg.

* * *

Mom could not put any answers to our questions.

What was this all about? And who else was involved. He just looked at us.

"How high up the food chain does this go?"

* * *

The children squealed. The staff pointed. They all just watched, no one saying a word. The huge helicopter flew over then returned to settle in the center of the helipad.

Mark looked at Sam and then Archie. There was the presidential seal.

"Marine One has landed."

ABOUT THE AUTHOR

D. R. Richards was born and raised in the Adirondack Mountains of New York. He worked for years in the family business and developed his strong sense of family values early in life. He enlisted in the Armed Services in the early seventies and spent most of his service time assigned to the NATO headquarters located in Mons, Belgium. It was here that he was exposed to many different branches of service as well as forming friendships with other service personnel from many different countries. His position allowed him to travel throughout most of Europe, both as duty assignments and personal interests. It was this time that allowed him to develop knowledge of many military operations (stories) by a number of different countries and personnel.

    Once he returned to the USA and processed out, he continued his thirst for both current and past events and fed his need of news, both domestic and outside the USA. Hopefully he has brought some of his real knowledge, along with some fictional additions to a book you will enjoy.

    Website: www.drrichardsauthor.com
    Email: Drrichards928@yahoo.com
    Facebook: D.R. Richards

Printed in the USA
CPSIA information can be obtained
at www.ICGtesting.com
LVHW040431020823
753949LV00007B/219